FROM SIBERIA to ST. KITTS

A Biography

by

Ira Sumner Simmonds

ACKNOWLEDGEMENTS

Sincere gratitude to my wife, family members, Christian and Laurel Mendivé, Verna Richardson, Sylvestre Wallace, Adrian Forman, Noel Bacchus, other friends and colleagues, Mrs. Katzen's son and niece, her friends and former students who shared their Katzen stories - indeed to everyone who encouraged, contributed and supported me in my efforts to write the story of this remarkable teacher.

I am especially indebted to the Kadoorie family and to Amelia Allsop and her staff at the Hong Kong Heritage Project who gave me access to a treasure trove of archived letters.

Special thanks also to Victoria O'Flaherty at the National Archives of St. Kitts, to Neil Rosenstein who has written extensively on the history of the Katzenellenbogen family and to Kirill Chashchin at the Russian Genealogy Project.

Ira Sumner Simmonds
31 Grace Court Brooklyn, NY 11201
URL: www.irasimmonds.com
Email:siberia2stkittsnevis@gmail.com

Cover design by Boryana Stambolieva

Ordering Information:
Available in print-on-demand and eBook format on Amazon.com

ISBN:

AUTHOR'S NOTE

Using the facts gleaned from my research, in some instances I've used my imagination to reenact the story of Mrs. Katzen's long trek across the globe.

With respect to the final leg of her journey, that is, the last forty years of her life which she spent in St. Kitts, her story is told almost exclusively in her own words and those of Horace Kadoorie, her friend in Hong Kong, taken verbatim from their many letters of correspondence. The letters were used sequentially with no changes made to the spelling, syntax or grammar.

In order to maintain their anonymity, the names of Mrs. Katzen's Chilean and Kittitian students were changed, as well as the names of some of her friends and family.

Contents

Dedicated to my sister Rhona, the kindest, most generous person I know

Tell me and I forget.
Teach me and I remember.
Involve me and I learn.

—BENJAMIN FRANKLIN

CHAPTER 1

Foreword

I t is an honour to have been invited by my friend Ira Simmonds to provide the Foreword for this excellent work. This book documents the life of "Une Grande Dame", our Madame Katzen, who dominated our student lives at the St. Kitts-Nevis-Anguilla Grammar School and to whom we will long pay tribute for her immeasurable contribution to our respective and collective lives. This very personal account by the author and former student of Mrs. Katzen, through painstaking research, enlightens us to so many details of Madame Katzen's life story, so little of which we knew as pupils in her French and Spanish classes.

It is truly a story for the ages as we are afforded an up close and personal revelation and witness her early life and that of her family, the trauma of wars and life in Siberia, Shanghai, China, Chile and Saint Kitts. We learn of her family life, her father a medical doctor, her mother an accomplished pianist whom we knew and loved as she accompanied us on the piano as we learned and sang our many French and Spanish songs, and her 'Aunt' who delighted our palettes with tasty morsels and that unforgettable cake, just ahead of our exams, dotted with raisins which we were informed would improve our memories!

We learn her family name, KATZENELLEBOGEN, a tongue twister which mercifully we did not know as the family had adopted the abbreviated 'KATZEN'. We marvel at Madame's early life, learning of her stint at the acclaimed Sorbonne in Paris and of her Chilean connection. We can now learn of the origin of the name of her home at New Pond Site - *Chalet La Serena*, and of her benefactors who provided the welcome financial assistance with which she ensured the well-being of some of her needy students. All of which she did without invading their privacy. We learn that she was fluent in English, French, Spanish, Russian and semi-fluent in Chinese. We learn the name of her son and of her earlier life founding a school in La Serena, Chile.

Ira Simmonds has been fortunate to have secured texts of many letters exchanged between Madame and her friends in which she recounts her life with a brutal honesty, a hallmark of her very being. Our experience of total immersion in French or Spanish served so many of us well in our later lives and gave so many of our fellow students a distinct advantage at the tertiary level.

Who would know of her earlier skill in the teaching of principles of pure and applied mathematics? From her recruitment to teach in St. Kitts from 1st January, 1961 to her passing in 2002, so many of us were favoured with her continuing concern for our well-being. Some of us can recall our journeys by French minesweeper and our six-week sojourn later at Baimbridge, Guadeloupe (me in 1968). We will forever revere the memory of Madame Katzen, the unforgettable experience of learning French and Spanish, and in my case teaching it at the Basseterre High School in 1969 with her as Head of Department.

This was an eye opener read for me. I enjoyed this narrative as it filled so many blanks and enhanced my abiding admiration for this *Chevalier de L'Ordre des Palmes Académiques*. A lifetime contribution indelibly inscribed in my memory and forever revered. We are all in Ira's debt for sharing this epic work with us.

Sir S. W. Tapley Seaton GCMG, CVO, QC, JP
Governor-General
Saint Kitts and Nevis

Bonjour classe

Mrs. Katzen's first trip abroad with her students - Puerto Rico, 1963

September 5, 1966. The first day of my third form year (10th grade), a day of promise, a day filled with the excitement and anxiety of things to come. Gangly and self-consciously awkward, clad in the school uniform's short khaki pants, white shirt, blue, yellow and red striped tie, brown shoes and socks, I was just one year closer to joining the fraternity of longpants-wearing students in the upper school (4th and 5th form, the equivalent of 11th and 12th grade).

Most important, I especially looked forward to third form because I was about to have my first taste of modern languages. An air of nervous excitement mixed with apprehension pervaded the classroom as we awaited our French teacher. In a few minutes we'll be face to face with none other than the venerable Mrs. Katzen. Somehow, in the five years since her 1961 arrival in St. Kitts she had managed to establish quite a reputation as a teacher extraordinaire. Very much aware of her stature, of her well-publicized exacting standards, I was as excited for the opportunity to learn a new language as I was anxious to see if I would pass muster.

Six months short of her fiftieth birthday when she arrived on the island, Mrs. Katzen was no spring chicken. As a matter of fact, she was downright old. Old, that is, in the manner that teenagers think of anyone over the age of forty. Unquestionably, she was the oldest member of the faculty. Now, practically ancient at fifty-five, she was about to tackle the daunting challenge of teaching French to us, a new crop of fourteen, fifteen and sixteen-year-old boys. At the very least, it would be interesting to see if she could get us to wrap our British colonial tongues (colorfully accented with colloquially-infused Afro-Caribbean inflections) around the nasal, silent consonantal idiosyncrasies of the French language.

Prior to Mrs. Katzen's arrival, to study a foreign language meant, for the most part, memorizing vocabulary, conjugating verbs in their myriad of tenses, translating passages from English to French and vice versa. Although students did all of the above quite well, their ability to communicate orally in the language was practically nonexistent. Mrs. Katzen, fluent in four languages, semifluent in two, armed with a unique teaching philosophy, special techniques, and a world of experience in foreign language instruction, immediately proceeded to revolutionize the way Spanish and French were taught on this tiny British Caribbean island of St. Kitts in the Associated States of St. Kitts Nevis and Anguilla.

As was the custom for students in schools throughout the British Empire, we stood as Mrs. Katzen entered the classroom.

Conservatively accessorized, she wore no jewelry, only a wristwatch. And white gloves! Never before had we seen a teacher wear gloves in the classroom. Notwithstanding the impractical tropical colonial British school uniform custom of wearing ties, the wearing of gloves of any kind was not exactly *de rigueur.* A bit of a puzzlement, they made her seem odd, eccentric maybe, a relic from another era. A few weeks later I was somewhat disappointed to learn that there was a rather mundane and practical reason for the gloves: protection for her delicate hands from the perils of chalk dust. Her dark hair was pulled to the top of her head and her dark brown eyes, framed by crow's feet, peered out from behind cat eye glasses. With lips painted ruby-red (a sharp contrast against her white alabaster skin) and a slightly curved forward-leaning posture, it all conspired to give her a rather matronly appearance. Uniforms were not required of teachers but Mrs. Katzen was always uniformly dressed. This was her professional garb and it never varied, not even for a day. Each day she wore a green and white plaid skirt and white shirt during the more than twenty years she spent working as a teacher, foreign language supervisor and official government interpreter of French and Spanish in St. Kitts, Nevis and Anguilla.

"*Good morning Mrs. Katzen,*" we greeted her spiritedly.

"*Bonjour classe,*" she replied.

"*Asseyez-vous, s'il vous plaît,*" she added, motioning for us to take our seats.

What a beautiful sound, I thought. It was the first time I had ever heard French spoken. Indeed, the first time anyone had ever spoken to me in a foreign language. It was easy to guess that her *Bonjour classe* and *Asseyez-vous, s'il vous plaît* were words of greeting. However, what came after, though beautiful and melodic, was totally incomprehensible as the words danced from her lips. Despite my inability to understand her, however, I knew immediately that I would enjoy her class. I was immediately engaged. We were all immediately engaged. Perhaps it was the novelty of embarking on a new language-learning journey. Maybe it was the force of Madame's personality and spirit that captivated us. I had never given any thought to language (my own or any other) and the general inherent power it possessed. After all, this is not exactly the kind of esoteric thought with which teenagers preoccupy themselves. But I knew right then, after those few French sentences, that I wanted to acquire the ability to read, write, speak and think in other languages beside English, my *langue natale*.

At five feet five inches, hers was a presence that exuded supreme confidence, one that oozed a take-no-prisoner, not-a-moment-will-be-wasted-inthis-class attitude. Whatever it was, to say that this class (that this teacher) left an indelible impression on me, on us, would be a gross understatement. It wasn't that she looked different from us, nor was it that she was a foreigner. It wasn't even that she was an old woman, or that she was white. She was different not so much in her physical attributes, but in ways that were difficult for me to describe during those teenage years.

Ten minutes into the class and I began to get an uneasy feeling. Something was amiss. It took but a moment to identify the source of my discomfort. Nary a word of English was spoken by Madame Katzen since she entered the classroom. The sound of her spoken French was exquisite. No matter that I was quite unaware of what exquisite French sounded like - it was simply pleasing to the ear. She must be French; so pleasant and mellifluous were the sounds emanating from her lips. Helped by the universal pantomimed context of greeting someone, it was easy to understand her for the first few minutes of class. Greetings dispensed with however, there was no logical reason for her to continue addressing us in French. This moment in the classroom was somewhat akin to that awkward moment experienced by many who try to acquire a second language later in life. That moment when they foolishly greet someone with a hearty "*Buon giorno*" because they want to (1) practice a newly learned expression on a real native speaker (2) impress him/her with their facility with the language. Invariably they are rendered mute by a rapid-fire assault of unfamiliar Italian words and, shamefacedly, are forced to admit that they are not at all fluent in Italian.

Now, as the minutes went by, we were at a loss and I wondered when she would switch to English. What was she saying, this strange teacher with the certain *je ne sais quoi*? I didn't have a clue. For heaven's sake, our *langue natale* is English, not French! Perhaps, as a *nouveau arrivée,* she was confused by the fact that the Grammar School is located in the distinctly French-named capital city of Basseterre. Surely, she must have thought that with villages named, *Cayon, Molineux, Dieppe* Bay, the French spoken by our 18th Century colonizers would be dormant, hidden deep in our DNA, now ready to be pried from our psyches by the constant stimulation of the spoken word. But she had lived in St. Kitts now for five years; long enough to have learned that the island's brief history of French colonization was not long enough to have any real lasting effect on our language.

Suddenly, realizing I could no longer understand her, Madame's persona was losing its luster. The more she continued to address us in French, the more I thought she was downright weird. Furtively glancing around the classroom, I sought in the faces of my classmates, reassurance that my discomfort and 'weird' characterization of the venerable Mrs. Katzen was one that was communally shared. The nuanced body language and facial expressions that greeted my surreptitious glances were quite comforting. Their facial language, devoid of words or sound, echoed my own thoughts. To wit, "What the heck is wrong with this woman? Surely she must know that this is our first French lesson!?" Someone must have forgotten to inform her that here, in the British West Indies, we spoke exclusively two non-Romance languages - English and that other popular language, known locally as Broken English. There was comfort in the knowledge that the rest of the class and I were of like minds, that we were all equally clueless. She was still speaking *en français* and did not seem at all inclined to speak English. Nor did she seem at all perturbed by the incredulous look on the faces of her students.

However, much to my surprise, little by little as the class went on the knotty fear of not ever being able to understand her, slowly, inexplicably, left my stomach and I found myself listening to Mrs. Katzen with new ears.

The next four years (1967-71) spent at the Grammar School (it later became known as Basseterre High School after the Girls High School merged with the all-boys Grammar School), studying French and Spanish with Madame Katzen were special years filled with a buffet of delights. Not simply with the regular classroom fare of *dictées*, *traductions* and *compréhension de textes*, but also filled with *la musique, la danse, le théâtre, la poésie* and *le voyage*. These years did not seem particularly special back then. Not having anything to compare it to, my teenage parochial perspective led me to believe that these language-learning experiences were normal, that this was the way all students learned a foreign language.

It quickly became clear that in Madame Katzen's language classes memorizing idiomatic expressions, learning the rules of grammar, reading, writing, etc. were just as important as learning to speak the language. She understood that one of the ultimate goals of learning a language is developing the skills necessary to communicate verbally and that, like the successful cultivation of vegetables in one's garden, second language acquisition on a proficient level is unlikely to occur if not nourished in the proper environment. Like garden vegetables thriving in well-watered, soil-rich beds, so too will language learners flourish when constantly exposed to a milieu acoustically rich in the sounds, inflections and rhythms of the target language.

Mrs. Katzen, understanding that this was a critical ingredient in second language acquisition, went to a great deal of expense and effort to ensure that her students were provided such an environment.

She was indeed a master teacher. And like all master teachers, she had a master plan. Her goal was simply to turn her students into fluent French and/or Spanish speakers. And like every teacher serious about teaching and learning, she recognized that there simply wasn't enough time during daily classes for her to attain all of her teaching goals. Consequently, after school on Mondays and Fridays all roads led to Madame Katzen's house where she presided over a weekly language club. Written in large letters on the outside front wall of her home were the words *Chalet La Serena*. Located in the New Pond Site area of Basseterre it was unlike other houses in the neighborhood in that it had two storeys. Its somewhat pretentious name added a certain cachet to this club experience *chez Madame Katzen*. Here at the *Círculo Franco-Español* we, the lucky students whom Madame deemed worthy, engaged in a variety of activities expressly designed to hone our French and Spanish speaking skills. Club rules were simple. One may discuss local, regional and international news events. Discussion of local politics, however, was most definitely not permitted. And, most importantly, on these afternoons English was verboten at *Chalet La Serena*.

Mrs. Katzen lived with her eighty-three-year-old mother Alexandra, her eighty-year-old aunt Evgenie and a menagerie of dogs and cats. The animals in this household were special. Unlike ordinary Kittitian dogs which spend most if not all of their lives outside guarding the house, the dogs of *Chalet La Serena* had the run of the house and were, like Madame and her mother, multilingual.
One of the dogs answered to the name *Chien Chien* and another, *Peleton*.

Club meetings at Le Chalet were simply delightful, filled with laughter, games, music, poetry, drama, dance and delicious food. We sang lustily in French and Spanish accompanied by Madame's mother Alexandra, a classically trained pianist. Always displaying an energy and spirit that belied her years, Alexandra played an important and instrumental part in our foreign language learning experience. As the club's de facto music director, she arranged music, prodded, coached, and rehearsed us. We learned and belted out Spanish, Latin American and French folk songs - like *Chiu Chiu, La Cucaracha, la Bella Primavera, Melodias de America, Boleras Sevillanas, La Cabana, Sur le Pont d'Avignon, Au Plaisir des Bois, Gentille Batelière, Chevaliers de la Table Ronde, La Chanson de Fortunio, La Marseillaise, Sous les Ponts de Paris*, to name a few. Alexandra participated in all things music. Whenever and wherever we performed - at school concerts, cultural events, *Chalet La Serena* - she was always there to play her part.

Evgenie also played a role in Madame's master plan to turn her students into fluent French and Spanish speakers. Her duty at the Friday club sessions was to prepare and serve sandwiches and other prandial delights. A tall somber woman, she never spoke or communicated with us as she went about her duties. In all the years I attended the club, only once do I recall ever hearing her speak - a brief exchange with Madame in a language unfamiliar to me. Seemingly incapable of smiling, Evgenie was perpetually imbued with an aura of sadness. Her face, etched with lines, seemed to bespeak an enduring pain of a long ago unspoken tragedy. With all of the wonderful goodies served at these soirées, the one thing that even today is still remembered and talked of fondly, was the deliciously moist homemade cake.

The search

I left St. Kitts in August 1971, a few months after taking my Advanced Level[1] exams. A month later I began undergraduate studies at St. Francis College, Brooklyn, New York, where I majored in Education and French and minored in Spanish. I then obtained a graduate degree in Education and another in Educational Administration at Teachers College, Columbia University, while working as an usher and head usher at Avery Fisher Hall and then as House Manager of Alice Tully Hall at Lincoln Center for the Performing Arts.

In 1984, after six years as House Manager at Alice Tully Hall, I entered the New York City Department of Education as a High School French teacher. In 2010, after seventeen years in the classroom, eight years as an assistant principal and one year as acting

---

[1] Also known as A Level – a school-leaving exam used by educational bodies in the United Kingdom.

principal, I left the employ of the New York City Department of Education.

Now that my time was my own and I was no longer preoccupied, or rather, consumed by the often physically and emotionally exhausting, yet rewarding work of educating New York City public school students, I began to reflect on my professional life experiences as an educator. Needless to say, it did not take much reflection to acknowledge the source of inspiration that led me into the classroom. Simply put, I became a teacher because of Madame Katzen. Though not conscious of it at the time, I now realize, as I think of my years in the classroom, that I tried to be the kind of teacher she was. A Madame Katzen wannabe, I tried to emulate her. I endeavored to give my students the kinds of second language acquisition experiences she gave me. If only I could, in turn, facilitate my students in the acquisition of a foreign language I would be broadening their horizons in immeasurable ways. Travel became a big part of my experience with students, frequently taking them to Quebec and France to expose them to immersion experiences in French language and culture.

My experiences with Madame Katzen in the mid 1960s did not at that time seem particularly remarkable. Madame's reputation notwithstanding, from my naïve juvenile perspective this was the way that all students learned foreign languages. Surely all British Caribbean students learning French must have had a teacher who routinely arranged to have the French Government send navy ships to their island to transport them to Port au Prince, Martinique for an immersion summer. Or perhaps the teacher might have arranged to procure a scholarship so that a student could spend six summer weeks taking University of Bordeaux courses in French Literature and Civilization at the *Lycée Général et Téchnologique de Baimbridge* in Guadeloupe. And if you, a student, are studying Spanish, your teacher most certainly would have collaborated with the U.S. Department of State, as Madame Katzen did, to have you and your fellow classmates lodge at Fort Buchanan army barracks in Puerto

Rico so that you might have an authentic Spanish language immersion experience.

Madame Katzen's tutelage has forever made me mindful of the words of Austrian-British philosopher, Ludwig Wittgenstein who said, "The limits of my language are the limits of my world."

The more I reflected on my path to becoming an educator, the more curious I became about this remarkable woman. And the more curious I became the more it dawned on me that for a teacher who has had such an impact on me and countless other Kittitian youngsters, I knew very little about her. If only she were still alive to give me answers that would satisfy my curiosity, answers that would give me valuable insights into the ingredients that went into the making of this master teacher. Madame Katzen died in 2002, eight years before my head was sufficiently uncluttered to make room for whimsical curiosities such as the mysterious life and work of a special teacher. She, her mother and aunt spent the rest of their lives in St. Kitts and are all buried in the local cemetery. To say she left an enduring legacy would be a gross understatement. A legacy so profound and far-reaching the likes of which will not soon be surpassed vis-à-vis a teacher's influence on the lives of Kittitian youngsters.

Who was she really? What fifty-year-old, well-educated, sophisticated woman pulls up stakes from parts unknown and, accompanied by her seventyseven-year-old mother and seventy-four-year-old aunt, starts life anew in a remote foreign land, a land whose culture is vastly different from anything she had ever experienced?

My curiosity soon developed into a strong desire to learn everything I could about this remarkable woman. From whence came her indomitable spirit, that all-consuming passion for teaching and learning? Who or what imbued her with the stamina, the emotional and spiritual strength, the power to transform so many lives? To be certain, there is a long list of Kittitian teachers across the generations who have profoundly impacted the lives of students.

None, however, had the kind of resources, financial or otherwise, that Madame Katzen had at her disposal to assist her students.

Where did she come from? What forces had conspired to bring her across the seas to the shores of this speck of land barely visible on a world map to this lush fertile volcanic island of sunshine and sugarcane? Was she British, or was she French? A Spanish Señora or German Frau? Such was her facility with languages that she could easily have been mistaken for a national of any of the many languages she spoke.

Needless to say, as I plied my trade during my seventeen years as a French teacher in New York City Public Schools I frequently thought of Madame Katzen. Now, twenty-eight years removed from sitting in her classroom, I wondered whether or not she remembered me. Did she know where I was or what I was doing? I left St. Kitts a few months after graduating high school and, regretfully, never kept in touch. Did she know that I followed in her footsteps, or rather, tried to follow in her footsteps? Her influence was such that it would be impossible for mere mortals like me to truly follow in her footsteps. The best one could do was to try to emulate her.

I decided it was unlikely that she would remember me. Although I was a good language student and was handsomely rewarded with all the languagelearning goodies she provided (travel, study abroad, etc.), I was far from being her most stellar of students. I made a promise to myself, however, that one day before she died I would return to St. Kitts to let her know how profoundly she had touched my life. And so, in the summer of 1998 I made that long-overdue trip to St. Kitts to visit Madame Katzen, now eighty-seven years old. It was time to thank her for her generosity of spirit and for her gift of languages.

As I turned down Edwards Street I could see *Chalet La Serena* four houses down on the left. A warm feeling swept over me as I thought of the wonderful moments spent at Madame's home. Why did Madame choose to give her house a name and why that particular name? Although it was a two-story brick house, unlike the other bungalow houses in the neighborhood, it was unlikely to conjure up images of the alpine chalets of Switzerland. But Madame would probably always be somewhat of an enigma. In many ways she was an anachronism, a woman belonging to an earlier time and place. Even the name of her house seemed to be shrouded in mystery. Why did she feel compelled to name it *Chalet La Serena*? Why the House of Serenity? Was she a refugee fleeing persecution from parts unknown who finally found peace and tranquility on this small, quiet bucolic tropical island? I could not let go of the idea that the name of her house was probably filled with the symbolisms of her past life.

I could feel my heartbeat quicken. I had not seen her since August 1971 when I left for university and suddenly the thought that she might not recall ever having me as a student filled me with anxiety. Not that I would be totally surprised; after all, we were now almost three decades removed from our days of *dictées, explications de texte* and *la poésie de Alphonse de Lamartine*. Besides, at the age of eighty-seven she might well have lost some of her faculties. I suspect however that the real source of the butterflies in my stomach had less to do with her age or the length of time since I last saw her and more to do with the realization that all former students of Madame Katzen were forever obliged to communicate with her in one of the languages of her instruction. It didn't matter if she met you in church, in the supermarket or on the street. It didn't matter if you were ten, twenty or thirty years removed from her classroom. There was no avoiding it; all former students of Madame were obliged to speak to her in French or Spanish.

As I approached the house I could see two large dogs in the yard behind the mesh wire fence. Standing in front of the latticed metal gate, butterflies all aflutter in my stomach, I screwed up enough courage to face the formidable Madame Katzen. Was my French or my Spanish up to par? The easiest thing to do of course would be to speak to Madame in English. But, *pour l'amour de dieu*, that would also be the most sacrilegious thing to do. Besides, no selfrespecting member of that special de facto fraternity of former students of Madame Katzen would have the chutzpah to address her in English.

The dogs, detecting the presence of a stranger on the other side of the fence began barking loudly as they bounded back and forth between the gate and the front porch. Warned by this raucous canine alert, Madame Katzen came to the door. She looked every bit the eighty-seven years she was - now a shrunken version of her former self, the curvature of her spine more pronounced, causing her to affect a stooped, face-to-the-ground posture.

"*¡Cállense!*" She said, ordering the dogs to be quiet.

She descended the three steps and approached the gate. Her gait was surefooted and steady, a comforting indication that she was still independently mobile. Her aunt and mother had passed away twenty and twenty-one years ago respectively and she was now alone at *Chalet La Serena* accompanied by her beloved dogs and cats.

I decided to address her in French.

"*Bonjour Madame Katzen.*" I said as she reached forward to open the gate. "*Je ne sais pas si vous vous souvenez de moi. Je m'appelle Ira Simmonds, un de vos étudiants des années soixante.*"

Her curved back and forward-leaning posture necessitated a concerted effort to turn her head sideways and upward in order to properly see my face looming two feet above hers.

Her response was as immediate as it was surprising.

"*Bien sûr, je me souviens de vous. Vous étiez tout à fait le danseur.*"

Of course I remember you. You were quite the dancer! What an odd thing to say! Me, quite the dancer! Sorry Madame, you have the wrong person, I thought. It seems after all that she really did not quite remember me. Quite the dancer? I don't think so. I had a notion to tell her that she had mistaken me for some other student, or at the very least, I should ask her to explain the "quite the dancer" reference, but immediately thought better of it. It would be oh so rude, so inappropriate to correct Madame Katzen. Anyway, what did it matter that she had the wrong student? Well, it mattered to my slightly bruised ego. Yes, I was a bit disappointed that she didn't remember me for the half decent language student I was. Surely, I was not listed among her most brilliant students but I was good enough, steady enough to be among those chosen to participate in her travel abroad language immersion programs. And for that, she ought to have remembered me.

As I followed her into the house I tried my best to hide my disappointment. Really, how could she mistake me for someone else? Here I was, a former student returning to thank her for all of her endowments, ready to let her know how much of an inspiration she was to me, only to discover I was just another face among the thousands whom she taught. But, did I really have a right to be disappointed? Why was it so important for me to be remembered? Wasn't it enough that she had given me the wherewithal to become a citizen of the world?

She offered me a seat as we entered the living room. It was a room truly frozen in time. Nothing about it had changed since the days of *El Círculo FrancoEspañol* in the 1960s. The furniture was the same and even their placement in the room had not changed. The upright piano used by her mother as accompaniment to our singing still stood upright, unmoved in the same corner, next to the entrance to the kitchen.

I brought her up to date on my post high school life abroad, complete with details of my university studies and my work experiences trying to emulate her as a French teacher in the New York City Public Schools. I could not tell for certain (there were no words of approbation) but I sensed somehow that she was pleased to hear that I had acquitted myself well. As I recounted anecdotes of my excursions taking students abroad to Québec and Paris her eyes lit up approvingly. These descriptions of my *séjours* with students seemed to have touched something deep within her psyche. Almost instantly she was transformed. The mien of stoic professionalism forever exemplified by this great lady was, for a brief moment, suddenly gone. She was transported to a different time and place and, in so doing, allowed me to see a side of her that I was heretofore not privy to. As she waxed nostalgic about her years as a student in Paris during the 1920s she was suddenly no longer the formidable, indomitable Madame Katzen.

Her eyesight was getting increasingly worse and she expressed her sadness at the thought that she would eventually lose her sight and subsequently lose the ability to do the one thing she loves most - to read. To quote her, "A life without reading is a life of the living dead."

She spoke of the wonderful times spent at the Opéra and the Théâtre du Palais-Royal. She had morphed before my very eyes into a simple, ordinary old lady reminiscing about the halcyon days of her youth. She was no longer the superhuman, intimidating larger-than-life iconic teacher but a warm, lovable lady filled with a humanity that was equally surprising to behold as it was delightful to discover. The feeling of disappointment I had moments earlier at being mistaken for someone else had evaporated, replaced by a sense that I was being honored, a sense that I was the luckiest person in the world. How fortunate to be sitting across from this extraordinary ordinary woman as she partially pulled back the curtains of her life, offering me a brief glimpse of her youthful past. Madame was always as formidable as she was mysterious, a woman who hardly, if ever, spoke about herself. Yet here I was, sitting with the venerable Madame Katzen as she offered stories of a time that was perhaps the best years of her life.

"You were quite the dancer!" As I left *Chalet La Serena* that August day in 1998 it suddenly dawned on me that she knew exactly who I was the moment she saw me. About seven years after Madame arrived in St. Kitts, she was able to convince a former ballet teacher from her school in La Serena to come to St. Kitts for the express purpose of starting a ballet school. It would appear that my performance in the Nutcracker's *March of the Toy Soldiers* made a more indelible impression on her than did my performance in her French and Spanish classes!

I was happy that I found the courage to visit Madame Katzen. I made a silent vow to return soon to engage her further, to get to know her better. Perhaps on my next visit I will gain some insights into the ingredients that went into the making of this remarkable teacher. An anomaly on this tiny island, Madame provoked a great deal of curiosity. The curious among us (who wondered about the whys and wherefores of her arrival in this unlikely of places) were either too polite or too intimidated (or both) to pose questions.

I never made it back to visit Madame Katzen. In 2007 I found out that she had passed away five years earlier. Whenever I think of that last time we met I think of the million questions I should have asked. If only the burning curiosity I now possess to learn more about her was awakened earlier when she was still alive.

Determined to learn more about Madame Katzen, in 2010 (eight years after her death) I headed back to St. Kitts to see what could be unearthed that would allow me to piece together the story of her life, the story of her unlikely journey to this tiny Eastern Caribbean island. Having spent the last forty-two years of her life on this island known as the Mother Colony of the West Indies (respectively, her mother and her aunt spent the last seventeen and fifteen years of their lives on the island) there ought to be at least a handful of Kittitians who would know something of her pre-St. Kitts life. I would seek them out and see what they knew. Perhaps they could shed some light on this mysterious stranger who landed like a tropical storm in 1961, forever changing the landscape of foreign language instruction on the island.

I found quite a few people who were willing to share their thoughts about this notable woman. Among them were many of her former students (whom I searched for and located in the four corners of the earth) as well as some old friends and colleagues of hers. If you were of a certain age and were in any way connected to the business of education, you knew Madame Katzen or you knew of her. Besides, in such a small-island community where nobody, or very few people looked like her, Madame stood out.

Although quite a few of her students returned to St. Kitts to live and work after undergraduate and graduate study abroad, the majority of her former students (myself included) did not permanently return. Whether in St. Kitts or abroad, her students can be found the world over - Canada, France, USA, Switzerland, Guyana, Barbados, Jamaica, Venezuela, UK, US Virgin Islands, Tortola, St. Maarten - living and working as linguists, teachers, lawyers, doctors, entrepreneurs, bankers, ordained ministers, politicians, to name a few.

Informed that the late Kittitian-born Sir Probyn Innis, former Governor of St. Kitts between 1975 and 1980, was Madame's close friend and lawyer (he was also her former teaching colleague at the Grammar School in the early 1960s), I went in search of Sir Probyn. What a surprise to learn from him that Madame Katzen had a son! That she had a son was not in itself surprising. The surprise came from the fact that after all these years I did not know that she had a son. How was it possible that I did not know? Was this a well-kept secret? It seems that this was always general knowledge but as a youngster there were more important things (like soccer, cricket, girls) occupying my teenage mind.

Chile

By the time I discovered that Madame Katzen had a son alive and well living in Chile, I was now totally obsessed with an ardent desire to learn everything I could about her. I wanted to know not just where she came from or what brought her to St. Kitts, I wanted to know who she was, I wanted to gain some insight into her personality - what made her laugh, what made her cry, what drove her, from whence came the patience, the energy, the passion, the endurance, the dedication she brought to this noblest of professions.

Who and what imbued her with these qualities - qualities possessed usually by only the rarest of *professeurs extraordinaires?*

Thanks to Sir Probyn Innis I was soon able to make contact with Madame Katzen's son. His name is Fyodor and he lived in Santiago, Chile. A brief exchange of email messages and, much to my delight, Fyodor was quite receptive to the idea of my paying him a visit in Chile so that I might learn more about his mother. I had a million questions and could not wait to have them answered.

Before leaving for Chile, I found an article about Madame Katzen published in St. Kitts in the 1980s in a local *Alliance Française* journal. In it Madame was interviewed by Jack Lapsey, one of her former students, now a practicing attorney in St. Kitts. One of the more interesting things divulged was that Madame was born in Czechoslovakia. Needless to say, this bit of information served to make Madame more of a mystery than she already was. At some point in my search I was prepared to discover that she was either Chilean, Spanish or French. Perhaps even German, given the teutonic flavor of the name Katzen. Of all the places of her birth imagined, Czechoslovakia was most certainly not one of them. What makes a highly educated middle-aged Czech woman, her mother and aunt choose to spend the rest of their lives on the tiny, relatively unknown Caribbean island of St. Kitts? The answer, I hoped, would be provided by Madame Katzen's son Fyodor when I visit him in Chile.

As I spoke to Madame's many friends, associates and former students a picture began to emerge about various aspects of her pre-St. Kitts life. However, the more stories I heard the fuzzier the picture became as each successive story seemed to contradict the other, making it difficult to ascertain which stories were authentic and which were not. One story I had little difficulty verifying was that Madame and her mother co-founded a school in Chile in 1946, fourteen years before her arrival in St. Kitts. A quick on-line search led me to the web page of *El Colegio Inglés Católico de La Serena*. The English Catholic School of La Serena. I was immediately struck by the school's name. This was the first of many aha! moments. La Serena, as in *Chalet La Serena*? But of course! It appears that Madame Katzen dedicated her home in St. Kitts to the memory of the Chilean City of La Serena, the place where she founded her school.

Founded in 1544, La Serena is Chile's second oldest city after Santiago, the capital. Located in northern Chile, it is the capital of the Coquimbo Region and home to the Catholic Archdiocese of La Serena. I must make it a point to visit the school in La Serena when I visit Fyodor.

I flew to Chile on July 20, 2010. It was the middle of the Chilean winter. The snow-capped peaks grew larger and larger as we descended into Merino Benitez International Airport. The proximity of the flight path to these beautiful mountains caused a few anxious moments but soon we were landing safely in Santiago de Chile, a beautiful city nestled cozily in the magnificently rugged bosom of the Andes.

I was nervous and excited in equal measure at the prospect of meeting Fyodor. Was he likewise apprehensive about meeting me, a complete stranger flying in from New York City to ask him possibly probing questions about his mother's past? When I meet him should I read from my list of prepared questions or should I just let the conversation flow naturally? Our email communication was exclusively in English, a language in which he was fluent, so there would be no need to be totally up to speed with my Spanish. I brought with me a small digital recorder to ensure that I missed nothing of our conversation. Whether or not I had brought along enough courage to ask his permission to use it was another question. It would be awful if I asked and he said no. Should I surreptitiously record our conversation? No, not a good idea. If I'm on the up and up he might be more inclined to be forthcoming and forthright.

At 9:55 am my wife Alison and I left our hotel room to wait downstairs for Fyodor who said he would pick me up at 10:00 am. I was quite surprised to see him already there waiting for us in the hotel lobby. He greeted us warmly, welcoming us to his wonderful city. We headed for his car parked outside the hotel entrance. He seemed genuinely happy to see us. He had planned to have us spend the day at his house where his lovely wife Maria was preparing lunch.

"I hope you brought a tape recorder. I'm certain you have lots of questions."

With these words my anxiety about broaching the subject of recording our conversation totally dissipated. But why was he so anxious to have me record our conversation? Perhaps he was aware that there were many versions of his mother's story and if there is a version that will be recorded for posterity it might as well be his version?

Driving through the streets of Santiago, a quite modern city, was not unlike driving through certain streets of New York City but I must confess to an odd sensation of displacement as Fyodor maneuvered his car through the traffic. Yesterday I was sweltering in the dog days of a NYC summer, today I was navigating the chilled streets of the Chilean winter. The snow-capped ranges of the Andes were constantly in view and seemed deceptively close, enveloping Santiago in a cool, comfortable majestic embrace. I could almost reach out and touch them. In less than ten minutes Fyodor was pulling into the garage of his apartment complex.

"I notice that you usually end your emails with Fyodor Dvorak K. What is the significance of the letter K?" I asked, as we left his car.

I was curious about his name from the moment we first started our email correspondence. My best guess was that in signing his name Fyodor Dvorak K he was following a Chilean convention for names, different from anything to which I was accustomed, where Dvorak must be his mother's maiden name and the K was an abbreviation of Katzen, his mother's married name?

"Yes, this is the way we write our names in Chile. Dvorak is my father's surname and the K represents my mother's maiden name, Katzenellenbogen."

"Oh, I see." I replied, struggling to make sense of what he just said. I was totally confused - perhaps more surprised than confused - to suddenly learn that Mrs. Katzen's real surname was not Katzen, but Katzenellenbogen. I wanted to ask Fyodor when and why she dropped the 'ellenbogen' from her name. The answers would go a long way towards enlightening me about this remarkable woman. Not wanting to seem too nosy, I decided not to ask. Perhaps I will ask these questions later, after we've developed more of a relationship. More confusing than surprising is the fact that in St. Kitts we all knew her as Mrs. Katzen - the title 'Mrs' indicating her marriage to a Mr. Katzen, or rather, a Mr. Katzenellenbogen. Why did she use her maiden name and not Fyodor's father's name, Dvorak? I did not have the courage to ask, hoping that with time the answer would be forthcoming. It was unusual for a married woman of her time to use her maiden name instead of her husband's. Clearly, she was not a woman of her time but one who was way ahead of her time.

As we entered Fyodor's apartment we were greeted by his lovely wife, Maria. Dark-haired and stylish she looked like she might be a descendant of the indigenous Mapuches of Chile.

In the Alliance Française journal article mentioned earlier, Madame indicated that she was born in Czechoslovakia. I was finally about to hear from her son the story of his mother's life. Her journey from Czechoslovakia to St. Kitts is bound to be a compelling one.
"My mother was born on July 8, 1911 in Nikolaevsk-na-Amur in Eastern Siberia, Russia."

"What was that? Eastern Siberia, Russia!?" I asked. My expression must have betrayed my surprise. I was about to ask why Madame would say she was born in Czechoslovakia when she was actually born in Russia, when he continued.

"Her story can be a bit confusing but it will eventually become clear. My mother was born in Nikolaevsk-na-Amur where her father, a medical doctor and her mother, a music teacher lived and worked. Yes, my mother did tell the world that she was Czech. Over the years

I've come to understand that there was a compelling reason for doing so. We emigrated to the Western Hemisphere at a time when to be Russian was the equivalent of being a Communist. My father is of Czech ancestry. My mother decided that it was easier and safer to survive in the West without being constantly regarded as a despised commie.

It was a way of protecting herself and her family."

Fyodor and Maria were simply wonderful and could not have been better hosts. After a scrumptious lunch prepared by Maria, Fyodor and I retired to his office while my wife Alison and Maria chatted in the living room. He and I discussed the politics of his beloved adopted country Chile and he told me about his forty-four-year career working for an iron-mining company, working his way up from the lowest ranks to imports-manager, eventually retiring in 2002. As we chatted he scanned numerous family pictures and immediately emailed them to me. We talked about his mother, grandmother and his great aunt, the core unit of his family who brought him to Chile in 1939 when he was but a lad of two. He said little of his father, whom he said he really never knew. His father, he was told, came to Chile with the family in 1939. For reasons still not clear to him, his father left almost immediately for parts unknown after the family's arrival in Chile. He did not know where he went or if and when he died. He might have returned to Shanghai, he said. His parents' marriage was short-lived and he was not privy to the details of its demise.

Although my visit to Chile was quite fruitful, successful beyond my wildest dreams, I returned to New York feeling somewhat empty-handed and unfulfilled. I still did not know much about who Mrs. Katzen was. The really big questions that drove my quest still went unanswered. Fyodor, thrilled at my efforts to record his mother's legacy, was quite accommodating and generous, sharing with me numerous pictures of his family. But despite the photos of his mother's childhood, college degree, honeymoon, etc., he was nevertheless handicapped in his ability to provide me with a portrait of the true essence of the woman. Or maybe he was understandably unwilling to totally confide in a complete stranger. Or maybe he was truly telling me everything he knew. Twoyears-old when he arrived in Chile, he was too young to understand much of anything, least of all the globally destructive political forces that were unleashed - forces that caused his family's displacement and that of millions of families worldwide. "I don't know. My mother never spoke to me about that." was a frequent response to many a question posed to Fyodor. Important details of her formative years were therefore not forthcoming. The pre-World War II horrors of the old country must be left behind in the old world, never to haunt the souls of the young and uninitiated whose feet are now planted firmly and safely in the New World. Not surprisingly, this seemed to have been the motto of this Russian immigrant family consisting of five adults (Mrs. Katzen, her mother Alexandra, her aunt Evgenie, her sister Raisa, Raisa's husband) and two infants (Mrs. Katzen's son Fyodor, Raisa's daughter Anastasia) as they attempted to start life anew in a strange land.

Russia

After spending the next few months looking into the possibility of travelling to Eastern Siberia to see what I could learn about her early childhood years, I decided that Nikolaevsk-na-Amur, a small town in the Russian Far East, might be too inhospitable a place for me to do research. Besides, my knowledge of Russian was limited to two words, *da* and *nyet*. I opted instead to let *Rusgenproject*, a genealogical research company based in Moscow, do the research for me.

France

I will forever cherish that wonderful 1998 visit with Madame Katzen at *Chalet La Serena*. Charmed by Madame's brief but wistful description of her time in Paris during *Les Années Folles* (as 1920s Paris came to be known), I decided that I needed to go to France to learn more about her *années parisiennes*.

After months of email correspondence with the French National Archives I was able to ascertain which of its five different centers held documents pertaining to Madame's years at the Sorbonne. Armed with the appropriate Archive Catalog Numbers, appointment dates and identification passes, I headed for Paris. I planned to spend at least a month to nose around, see what I could unearth. Hosted by the Mendivés, friends who live in the North-East city of Lille - 200 kilometers from Paris, my commute on the TGV from Lille to the *Gare du Nord* station in Paris was only an hour.

As I approached the building that houses one of the Paris branches of the French National Archives I noticed there were six policemen milling around the entrance. An unusual amount of security, I thought. Before I could present my ID and appointment documents, one of the officers told me that I could not enter because the building was closed. How could the Archives be closed? I thought. The National Archives wouldn't arrange an appointment for me to have access on a day it would be closed, would it?

"Pourquoi on est fermé?" I asked, pointing out that I had an appointment to research some documents pre-reserved for my access *aujourd'hui*. I presented my ID as well as my appointment and access documents, explaining that I travelled all the way from New York City to do this research, having made this appointment months ago. He was unimpressed with my credentialed documents - did not even deign to look at them.

"Le bâtiment est fermé parce qu'on est en grève!" Ah yes, a good old-fashioned French strike, I might add. He suggested that I telephone the Archives to make another appointment. No, he had absolutely no idea how long the strike would last. I was a victim of France's legendary propensity to strike - a propensity probably rooted in its leftist-driven insurrectional tradition dating back to the Revolution. It was now 9:00 am and I had a 6:00 pm return train ticket to Lille.

Just as I was about to feel sorry for myself, to feel that this will be a wasted day, it occurred to me that I was in Paris, the City of Lights. I decided to spend the rest of the day at the Centre Pompidou.

With a minimum of angst, I rescheduled my strike-affected research appointment for the following Wednesday. Meanwhile, I spent some time solidifying arrangements to meet Monsieur Denys Prunier, the archivist at *Lycée Lamartine*, the high school attended by Madame Katzen in 1926. Here she received her baccalauréat in 1928 before enrolling at the *L'Université de Paris-Sorbonne*. *Lycée Lamartine*, located at *21 rue du Faubourg-Poissonnière*, was named after and founded in the spirit of the 19th Century romantic poet, writer and politician Alphonse de Lamartine. Much of the philosophical perspectives and writings of this great poet and member of *L'Académie Française* would have a significant impact on shaping Madame Katzen's personality and character. All students were obliged to be engaged in community service, often ministering to many of the poor and homeless residents of Paris.

The next day I boarded the TGV and headed back to Paris. From *La Gare du Nord* I took the Metro's *Ligne 5* one stop to *Gare de l'Est* then changed to *Ligne 7*. One stop later, I descended at *Poissonnière*, four blocks from *Lycée Lamartine* where I was scheduled to meet Denys Prunier. Standing outside the school's entrance looking at the building, I guessed that the structure was at least a few hundred years old. I later discovered that the French National Department of Education acquired the building in 1891. *Lycée Lamartine* was founded at this location in 1983 as a *lycée* for girls. A landmark building, in which the panelling in one of its rooms is designated a National Heritage, it was once owned by *Pierre Beauchamps*, known for the influential part he played in the development of French baroque dance. Some of his other titles included Director of *L'Académie Royale de Danse* (1671), Principal choreographer of Molière's *Troupe du Roi* (1664-1673) and Ballet Master at *L'Académie Royale de Musique*.

Forty-year veteran of the French school system, Monsieur Prunier, sporting a bushy white beard, was awaiting me at the entrance. He gave me a tour of the building, pointing out the additions built after Madame's Katzen's departure in 1929. We then headed to the basement in search of Madame's academic record. Unsuccessful in this endeavor, he speculated that, like other academic records of that era, it might be archived off-site in the interest of space. His most valuable contribution to my visit however, was his recounting of the school's history and mission as it prepared Victorian era teenage girls for the challenges of 20th Century.

Wednesday morning. Once again I boarded the TGV at *Gare Lille-Flandres* and headed back to Paris for my rescheduled appointment at the French National Archives. As I approached the building .... Oh no! Surprise! Surprise! It was, in the words of the immortal Yogi Berra *"déjà vu all over again!"* There at the entrance stood my friends *les agents de police*. Again I was turned away.

Between the time I scheduled this latest appointment and today (a matter of a few days) the employees of the archives had ended their strike and, with other grievances to be addressed, started a new one. Crushed with the weight of two successive disappointments, I sought the solace of a nearby courtyard bench and tried to gather my thoughts and reflect on my predicament. At this rate, who knows how long it would take for this strike thing to end? Had I remembered that *la grève* is almost a daily occurrence, I would have planned to spend more than a month in France. On any given day in France you might awake to the news of farmers blocking traffic by dumping their recently reaped crops of juicy peaches onto the highway to protest newly-proposed taxation; horsebackriding protesters taking over Bastille Square against a new VAT hike; football clubs striking over proposed taxes on their franchises; parents and teachers striking in protest of the President's proposal to change the age-old tradition of no school on Wednesdays - *Enseigner le mercredi? C'est un scandale*! Perhaps I should go with the flow and chalk this one up to just another research day lost in this strike-crazy culture. I can always make another appointment. But who's to say that the *Société National des Chemins de Fer Française* (SCNF) and the Métro won't be on strike?

Forty minutes later I still sat dejectedly, trying to combat that overwhelming feeling of helplessness. To cheer myself up I thought of the many things I could do to pass the time. I could aimlessly wander around Montmartre gazing at the work of the street artists, or I could visit the large collection of Impressionists at the *Musée d'Orsay*. I could also sit in a sidewalk cafe nursing a beer, watching the world go by, all the while trying to imagine that I was Madame Katzen enjoying the sights and sounds of 1920s Paris.

Two hours later, still sitting outside the entrance to the Archives, I saw an employee flash an ID and allowed entry. I decided I would try telling my tales of woe to the next employees who came along. Perhaps one of them will have some sympathy and let me in. Let's see, what shall I say? I travelled all the way from NYC on a research mission; my time is limited; so is my budget; my dog misses me terribly might be a good one, given how much the French dote on their dogs. The third Archives employee who deigned to listen to my spiel was a matronly white-haired lady. My sob story must have engendered some empathy. She would find someone to assist me, she said, if a critical mass of scabs crossed the picket line.

Hopes raised, buoyed by the possibility of access to documents that would further enlighten me about Madame Katzen, I willed the patron saint of scabs to smile on me. And smile on me she did. A critical mass reached, at 12:15 pm my white-haired lady exited the building and came into the courtyard to get me. After registering and signing off on the Archives' rules and regulations, I was introduced to the assistant responsible for retrieving the catalogued documents placed on reserve for my use.

I deposited my jacket, camera and knapsack into a locker and was led upstairs to the main public research area on the third floor into a large brightlylit room with several rows of long tables. I was handed a clear plastic bag and a pair of white gloves. In the plastic bag went the only two items allowed in this research room, a notebook and writing utensils. Sitting at a long table awaiting the delivery of my reserved documents, I could feel my heart rate increase. This Paris branch of *Les Archives Nationales* is one of five locations housing a collective total of 252 miles of documents. Security personnel patrolled the room - ostensibly to ensure that the safety and integrity of this enormous collection of documents are not compromised. Original documents stored by the Archives date from AD 625 through today. Reason enough, I guess, to put one through the paces before allowing access. The strikes that threatened to thwart my research mission, the many levels of security to be cleared, my obsessive desire to capture the essence of a very special teacher all managed to engender a kind of adventurous excitement. I had no expectations about what I might find, nor did I care. I was totally caught up in the thrill of the hunt. Besides, whatever I discovered was certain to be more than I already knew.

The attendant arrived and placed a cardboard container of documents on the table. As I donned my white gloves, the raucous din of my pounding heart seemed to echo around the cavernous reading room. I stared at the box for a moment, transfixed. What secrets were contained within? Was it filled with the mysterious and minute details of Madame's remarkable life? Unlikely. A fantastic notion, a flight of fancy that simply took my breath away.

The box contained 8.5 x 11 index cards - registration documents of every foreign student who entered the French State System of Schools. Somewhere in this box I hoped to find information that would inform me about Madame's journey. Starting at the beginning of the K section, I began the search for Katzen or Katzenellenbogen, my heart rate increasing with the turn of each card. Racing along in excited anticipation of finding her name, without warning my search came to a screeching halt. I had arrived at the place where Madame's name ought to have been but was not. Suddenly aware of my labored breathing, I took a deep breath to compose myself. In my haste I must have accidentally skipped her name. Restarting my search, I meticulously checked every K document to make certain that Zenaida Katzen or Zenaida Katzenellenbogen was not inadvertently stuck to another document or filed out of alphabetical order. Certain that a more careful and deliberate search will bear fruit with the second pass through the Ks, the pace of my heart-beat was once again on the rise. Once again my hopes were dashed. Zenaida was nowhere to be found. There had to be an explanation for the absence of these documents. Months ago, in preparation for this research trip, I was given assurance by the French National Archives of the existence of documentary evidence of Madame's enrollment in the French State School System - evidence complete with document category, document number and document location.

Should I return the box and explain that I was given the wrong box? I examined the box's outer label. The document codes, category and location numbers matched the information I received from the National Archives months before. Perhaps Zenaida Katzen(ellenbogen's) documents were inadvertently misfiled somewhere else within the A to Z contents of this box. I had no choice. I must work my way through from A to Z examining every document.

To travel this far and not leave every stone unturned would be foolish.

The thought of having to examine every document in this box was a buzz kill, dimming somewhat the thrill of the hunt. Nevertheless, it had to be done, a task made more onerous by a bourgeoning awareness that my search might end in futility. By the time I got to the Cs, the tedium of mindlessly flipping through these documents, page by page, in the hope of finding some misplaced Ks was causing me to lose focus. To avoid the fatigue caused by this repetitive motion, I switched from sorting handfuls of documents on the table to sorting them on my lap. Less than a minute later security was tapping my shoulder, scolding me for using my lap as a table. All documents, she said, must be used in plain view of all

Archives personnel. Although I understood the need for this kind of vigilance I was nonetheless embarrassed by the insinuation that my lap-sorting behavior looked suspiciously like a document thief surreptitiously waiting for the right moment to slip artifacts into his clothing. A bit shaken by the unpleasant nature of such an implicit accusation, the thought that I might be on the verge of finding Zenaida Katzen soon washed the dreadful taste from my mouth. Undaunted, I pressed on.

Wait a second! What's this? A handful of K documents hiding among the Gs! Abetted no doubt by a careless (or inconsiderate) researcher. Four pages later, there it was - the registration document of Zenaida Katzenellenbogen! Alas, it was not filled with the minute details of her life that I dreamt of finding, not the bonanza I had hoped for but I was happy nevertheless for the opportunity to peek into her past. Having boarded a time machine, I had warped back to 1926 Gay Paree to stare at her school registration form. Yellowed with the passage of time, written in her exquisite, bold fifteen-year-old cursive reminiscent of a time when one took pride in penmanship, it informed me of the year she arrived in the City of Lights. It told me that she was lodged at 36 *rue Botzaris* (a convent directly across from *Le Parc des Buttes Chaumont* in the 19th *arrondissement*) and that, back home in China, her parents lived at 5 *rue Chapsal* in the French section of the Treaty port city of Shanghai.

I still had a few hours before my 6:00 pm train back to Lille so I decided to check out the convent where Madame lived on *rue Botzaris*. Ligne 7 took me to the Buttes Chaumont stop. Exiting the metro, I found myself on *rue Botzaris*. Walking West I searched for number 36. On the other side of the street stood the beautifully maintained Buttes Chaumont Park. An ordinary three-story brick building, number 36 did not quite resemble what I imagined a 1920s French convent would look like. As I approached I noticed two flags hanging from second floor windows, *Le Tricolore* and a flag I could not identify. The gate to the property was closed. I pushed it but it did not give. Peeking through a crack I could detect no activity within. From this eye-at-the-hole perspective the building appeared to be unoccupied. My face was still close to the fence, mind wandering, conjuring up images of Zenaida's life at this convent, wondering how strange, how interesting it must have been for a young woman of the world with a life not prescribed by a nun's vows of poverty, chastity and obedience to live in a convent. What was *la vie quotidienne* like for Zenaida behind these walls? As a child did she dream of becoming a nun? Was living here a test run to see if she'd be suited to the nun's life? So many questions, so few answers. Without warning a hand brusquely placed on my shoulder startled me out of my reverie. Jumping backwards from the fence, I was face to face with two armed security guards who seemed to have appeared out of nowhere.

"*Qu'est-ce que vous faites ici?*" asked the taller of the two men. I responded with,
"*Je cherche l'entrée du batiment.*"

He explained that the building was off limits and that I could not enter. I explained that I would like to speak to someone inside who might be able to give me a history of the building, that I'm doing research for a biography I am writing of my high school French teacher who lived at this address during her high school and college years in the 1920s. "*Elle ne vit plus ici.*"

He was having fun at my expense, explaining that she no longer lived there. But as I took a closer look at him I saw a face totally devoid (perhaps even incapable) of humor. It suddenly dawned on me that he wasn't trying to be funny, that he was indeed totally incapable of sarcasm and really wanted me to understand that Madame really no longer lived here. I ignored the voice in my head that said, 'Ira this is not going to end well. Turn on your heels and leave'. His partner, meanwhile, contributed nothing to this exchange. He simply stood there, expressionless, his unblinking bloodshot eyes fixed on me. I was somewhat unnerved but despite some uneasy seconds of silence as I looked from one to the other, I decided to forge ahead with my attempt to enter the building. I asked again if there was someone inside who might be able to inform me about the history of the building. The look on his face told me that I had already worn out my welcome. He had had enough of my questions.

"Vous voyez le drapeau en haut?"

He pointed to one of the two flags hanging from an above second floor window wanting to know if I was aware of their presence. I saw them both when I approached the building but only recognized the tricolor. Before I could respond, he answered his own query.

"C'est le drapeau Tunisien."

I froze as my heart skipped two beats. Turns out I was trying to gain access to property that now belongs to Tunisia. Yes, that North African country that allegedly initiated the events of the so-called Arab Spring. On January 4, 2011 Tunisian fruit vendor Mohamed Bouazizi committed suicide by setting himself ablaze in protest of having his wares confiscated by an inspector. Ten days later, Tunisian President Zine El Abidine Ben Ali was ousted in a coup. Recent television images of Arab Spring demonstrations and riots in Tunisia flashed before my eyes. Frightened by my predicament, my brain ordered me to beat a hasty retreat. My feet however, refused to obey. Hoping the guards could not hear my pounding heart but not wanting to exhibit any fear, I stood there looking at them both for what seemed like an eternity. How quickly things change. A moment ago I was a zealous researcher looking for fodder for the biography of the inimitable Madame Katzen. The next moment I'm a suspicious character snooping around a guarded building belonging to the Tunisian government while a revolution was unfolding in Tunisia.

Thinking perhaps that my lack of reaction to his *"C'est le drapeau Tunisien"* meant that I didn't grasp the gravity of the situation, that the full implication of his words was lost on me, the guard then pointed to the curb.

"Voyez-vous ces bouteilles cassées ? Il y avait une émeute ici."

Hearing that the broken bottles in the gutter were the result of a riot which occurred there three days ago, it suddenly dawned on me that I may be at risk, that I was persona non-grata. I turned on my heels and walked down the block away from the building - taking special care not to look back, just in case they were still watching me. A block away I parked myself on a sidewalk bench on the opposite side of the street next to Buttes Chaumont Park. From this vantage point I could still see the building but the guards were nowhere to be seen. I waited thirty minutes before pointing my camera and taking a few photos of the building. I remained seated on the bench, trying to decide on my next move. Disappointed though I was at being barred from entering *36 Rue Botzaris*, I was nevertheless titillated and amused at having my pursuit of Madame infused with a bit of international intrigue. I must make a point to learn more about the 'riot' that took place here a few days ago.

Still sitting on the bench, I noticed a poodle walking towards me in the distance, its owner, an elderly white-haired gentleman attached to the other end of its leash. Distracted by the many sidewalk canine odors that constitute the most enjoyable part of a dog's daily walk, its meandering approach was slow. Its owner, quite content to be taken on his afternoon constitutional by Fifi, had the aspect of a longtime neighborhood resident. A conversation with him might inform me about number 36. A few minutes later Fifi led him right to my bench, not to introduce us, but to sniff out the doggie messages left for her on the legs of the bench.

Greetings dispensed with, I pointed to number 36 and asked him what, if anything, he could tell me about the building prior to it becoming property of the Tunisian government. He responded with. *"C'était une fois une maison religieuse."*

As soon as I returned to Lille I went online and discovered that thousands of Tunisian illegal immigrants had recently arrived in France. About sixty of them had taken over *36 rue Botzaris* which was allegedly the headquarters of Ben Ali, Tunisia's recently deposed president. In the basement were found sensitive documents allegedly containing information on Ben Ali's enemies under surveillance in France. The French police subsequently laid siege to the building and forcibly removed the squatters. All this occurred a week before I tried to enter the building.

China

There was still a lot of research to be done if I were to ever truly know the whole story of Madame Katzen's seven thousand three-hundred-and-seventymile journey from Eastern Siberia, Russia where she was born, to St. Kitts where she spent the last forty-two years of her life. If I am to accurately record her legacy I must get to know her better. Will I ever be able to get to know her and the story of her life and work well enough to be able to capture it accurately? Well enough to do it justice? If only I could find some of her friends and colleagues who knew her well. Finding letters of correspondence, if they exist, would be even better, they would go a long way towards giving me some profound insights into the life journey of this extraordinary woman.

Perhaps there are former students with whom she became close. Using social media and my network of former schoolmates from Grammar School and Basseterre High School I set out to find as many former students of Mrs. Katzen as possible - as well as relatives, colleagues, friends and acquaintances. I was able to locate and contact over thirty Chileans whom she taught from 1946-1960 as well as over one hundred and fifty Kittitians, her students between 1961-1977. The collective thoughts shared by the many ex-alums contacted gave testament to the power of an exceptional teacher to profoundly affect the lives of her students. The admiration, love, respect expressed are simply awe-inspiring.

A big breakthrough in my quest to understand the essence of Madame Katzen came from a conversation with Danny, a former schoolmate from Grammar School. If there is one student who epitomized what it meant to be an exalum of Madame Katzen it was Danny. Mrs. Katzen, having learned that Danny's mother was a single parent struggling to raise several children, approached Danny and asked him to have his mother submit to her a list of her monthly bills. Danny's mother complied. Henceforth Madame Katzen became an important source of financial support for Danny's family. Corroborative proof, to my way of thinking, that Madame was, among other things, a woman of means, a deep-pocketed philanthropist.

However, my assumption that she was a wealthy woman was short-lived. Danny disabused me of that notion explaining that his family's benefactor was not Madame Katzen. The financial assistance she procured came from a gentleman named Horace Kadoorie. I immediately set out to find out more about Horace. Was he a friend or a member of her family? It wasn't a stretch to imagine that there must be other Kittitian youngsters who benefited from his largesse and if this was indeed the case, it would be interesting to know the extent of his philanthropic endeavors in St. Kitts. Could Horace be the key to obtaining, at the very least, some insights into Madame Katzen's epic journey from one end of the world to the other? It soon became clear that she was the conduit through which Sir Horace funneled resources to assist many a student.
As such, correspondence between the two, should they exist, would be invaluable.

A quick on-line search of Horace's name and I knew immediately that I was on to something big. Lawrence Kadoorie (1899-1993) and Horace Kadoorie (1902-1995) were famous brothers who were industrialists, hoteliers and philanthropists. Their father, Eleazar Silas Kadoorie, otherwise known as Sir Elly Kadoorie (1867-1944) was an Iraqi Jew, the patriarch of one of the wealthiest Baghdadian families. The Kadoorie family businesses are primarily in China, India, South East Asia and Australia with holdings in electric power utilities (China Light and Power Co., Ltd. - later known as the CLP Group), rubber plantations, banking, real estate and luxury hotels -

including the worldrenown chain of Peninsula Hotels. Forbes Magazine currently ranks the Kadoorie family as the 21st wealthiest family in Asia with a net worth of 9.9 billion dollars.

After the Romans destroyed the second Temple in Jerusalem two thousand years ago, Jews were dispersed to the four corners of the world. Some went north and some west to Spain, Morocco and Macedonia. Others went east and formed a large community in Mesopotamia (modern-day Iraq), and Kuwait. The Baghdad community of Jews prospered and in more recent times sent its sons abroad to America, Europe, China and India. The Kadoories, along with the Sassoons, the Sophers, the Somechs and the Gubbays were among the leading families of Baghdad. Horace's father arrived in Hong Kong, by way of Bombay (present-day Mumbai), in May 1880 where he joined the Sephardic Jewish firm of David Sassoon & Sons as a clerk. Elly was subsequently transferred to China to work in the Treaty Ports of Shanghai, Tientsin, and Ningpo. After a few years he had accumulated enough money to strike out on his own, eventually setting up companies in both Hong Kong and Shanghai.

To find out more about Madame Katzen's connection to this powerful and wealthy Iraqi/British/Hong Kong family would be a bonanza. Even better would be to get hold of letters that would give me a window into her thoughts, her fears, her musings, her motivations, if they existed. The Kadoorie brothers, Lawrence and Horace, died in the 1990s. I must write to the person or persons currently in charge of the family's holdings.

A Google search informed me that Sir Michael David Kadoorie GBS, business executive, philanthropist, son of Sir Lawrence Kadoorie, nephew of Sir Horace Kadoorie CBE, is the living heir to the Kadoorie family fortune and is considered to be the 6th wealthiest person in Hong Kong. A pillar of Hong Kong society, he was awarded the Gold Bauhinia Star (GBS) for distinguished public and voluntary services to the community.

In December 2010, I sent a letter to every business email address affiliated with CLP Holdings Ltd., an enterprise on whose Board Sir

Michael sits as Chairperson. It occurred to me that more likely than not, my emails to Sir Michael were destined to end their journey unread, relegated to the trash or the spam folder of a Hong Kong computer. I wasn't at all under any illusions that Sir Michael would get my electronic missives. After all, he was a very important and busy man preoccupied with running a multi-billion-dollar enterprise - not to mention busy using his wealth and influence to help the disenfranchised. The Kadoorie family has long had a reputation for giving a substantial part of its fortune to charitable causes. Of course there was always the chance that an email might get through the 'firewall' and make its way to Sir Michael's desk. As my mother would say, "Nothing beats a trial but a failure". Nothing ventured, nothing gained.

Imagine my surprise when in February 2012 I received an email from Susan Turner, Secretary to the Honorable Sir Michael Kadoorie, indicating that she had read my email. Sir Michael, she said, was on business abroad and not scheduled to return to Hong Kong before the first week in March. She would be happy to bring my letter to his attention the moment he returns.

A few weeks later Sir Michael replied indicating that he was aware of his uncle's philanthropic endeavors supporting Mrs. Katzen's involvement in education in St. Kitts!

Connecting with Sir Michael, heir to the Kadoorie family fortune, was indeed heady stuff. His uncle Sir Horace built a school for Jewish refugees in Shanghai before the start of Second Sino-Japanese War and Madame Katzen, according to Horace's nephew Michael, taught in this school! It must have been her very first teaching job after graduating from the Sorbonne in 1932. I'll have to do some digging. Nevertheless, having entertained flights of fancy that Sir Michael might provide more details about his uncle's relationship with Madame Katzen, I was more than a little disappointed that he did not seem to know much. All things considered however, this might be the breakthrough I needed. I promptly wrote to Susan Turner to see if she could provide me with some more leads.

Ms. Turner graciously acted on my request for information concerning the possible existence of archived material that might inform me about Sir Horace's philanthropic contributions to the education of youngsters in St. Kitts in the 1960s by referring me to ex-British Parliamentary researcher Amelia Allsop at the Hong Kong Heritage Project (HKHP). The HKHP was establish by Sir Michael Kadoorie to "acquire, collate and make available to the public, documents, photographs, film and testimony relating to the history of the Kadoorie
Family, its businesses and charitable work in Hong Kong and elsewhere."

A few emails later, I learned that the HKHP will give me access to a collection of letters exchanged between Sir Horace Kadoorie and Mrs. Katzen!

Letters exchanged between Sir Horace and Mrs. Katzen! I was beside myself with excitement. The opportunity to pore over these letters, the possibility of obtaining that often elusive in-one's-own-words perspective cherished by biographers was quite titillating. With any luck, the content of these exchanges will be equally illuminating.

In a few weeks, I was on my way to Hong Kong to visit Amelia Allsop at the Hong Kong Heritage Project. Amelia and her staff searched their archives and found hundreds of letters of correspondence between Sir Horace Kadoorie and Mrs. Katzen. I'm eternally grateful to her and her staff for having presented me copies of these letters that were chronologically sorted and neatly bound. This treasure trove of information was indeed illuminating, shedding a great deal of light on her life and work. Access to this invaluable collection of letters was unquestionably the seminal event in my 'search' for Madame Katzen. For the first time, I could hear her think. Her written words gave voice to her struggles, her successes, her fears, her concerns - all of which she shared with Sir Horace Kadoorie. For the first time in my journey of discovery, in my search to better understand the essence of this teacher nonpareil, the veil of mystery that enveloped her began to evaporate, releasing from the shadows aspects of her heretofore-elusive spirit. I was now well informed, and officially hooked, as the whole story of her fascinating journey across the globe began to unfold.

◊◊

Nikolaevsk-na-Amur

Mrs. Katzen (right) & sister

She opened her eyes and found herself in a white room lying on a strange bed. Nothing around her looked familiar. A foggy haze filled her head, inducing a semiconscious state of uncertainty. She could not tell whether she was asleep or awake. With all her might she struggled to remember where she was and how she got there. Worn out by the struggle to return to the conscious world, she was soon, once again, fast asleep. How long she was out, she could not be certain but when she next opened her eyes her brain fog had dissipated somewhat. Now conscious enough to know with some degree of certainty that she no longer rested in the arms of Morpheus, she tried to focus on the objects around her in search of clues to her whereabouts, a task made difficult by her failing eyesight. Raising herself on an elbow, she reached for the bedside table in order to get her glasses. A bolt of fiery pain in her right hip knocked her backwards. Writhing in agony, she closed her eyes and kept them tightly shut, willing the pain to disappear. When she opened her eyes half an hour later, the pain was all but gone.

Her name is Zenaida Katzenellenbogen. Her family and friends call her Zina. Lying in a hospital bed in Santiago de Chile, she was beginning to get concerned that she was losing her memory, when she realized that she was suffering the effects of the anesthesia and other after-surgery drugs. Very disconcerting, not to mention disorienting, to lose one's sense of place and time in the universe. At 90, she had lived a relatively long and healthy life. Until now her biggest health issue was her failing eyesight, a huge inconvenience for an avid and voracious reader. Being slowly robbed of her eyesight, of her ability to read was, in her own words, a fate worse than death. The pain notwithstanding, her mind was as clear as a mountain pond - lucid enough to tell the story of her life's journey from Siberia to this hospital bed, by way of China, France, Chile and St. Kitts.

It all started in Nikolaevsk-na-Amur, a small town in Eastern Siberia, Russia, a harshly beautiful and remote region of the Russian Far East. The kind of place that invariably conjures up images of brutally cold winters, political exiles, prison labor camps and leper colonies.

Situated on the left bank of the vast and mighty Amur river in the Amur River Valley, Nikolaevsk is surrounded by hills which provided some measure of shelter from the harsh winter winds but these same hills also blocked the prevailing warm winds of Spring and Summer and this in turn tended to make the already long winters even longer. Not even the primeval forest that surrounded the town protected Nikolaevsk from the permanent cold of the westerly and northwesterly winds. And, as if that wasn't enough, the easterly and northeasterly winds almost always brought humidity, rain and snow. Lots and lots of snow. Snowstorms and blizzards were commonplace, each time dumping an average of two and a half feet. Summers, on the other hand, were very short and relatively cool with an average high of 71-76 degrees Fahrenheit. This is the place Zina called home for the first eight years of her life. It may seem a truly harsh place to live but her childhood memories of Nikolaevsk-na-Amur are those of a little girl living in a beautiful world of snow and ice, a winter wonderland filled with the joys of snow angels, ice skating and sleigh rides.

Mrs. Katzen's father

It is impossible for Zina to think of ice-skating and sleigh rides without thinking of her father, the dearest, sweetest, most warm-hearted man she has ever known. She simply adored him. Growing up in the bosom of his kindness, in the shelter of his love, gave her the wherewithal to explore, to thrive, to survive, to endure. She smiled at the memory of her very first pet; a shivering kitten she found while playing in the snow. She picked it up and zipped it inside her jacket. She couldn't take it home because her mother had very strict rules about having animals in the house. Risking Alexandra's ire, she took it home anyway, found a little box and an old towel and hid it in the attic. Knowing that her father was himself a sweet and loving pussycat, she told him the story of her rescue. Not surprisingly he agreed to keep her secret, promising also to protect her from her mother's wrath when/if the upstairs illegal feline tenant is discovered.

A humble, unassuming man, her father, Mikhail Nicolaevich Katzenellenbogen would have been too embarrassed, too self-conscious at the notion of telling others about his kindness, about the depth of his compassion, his love of humanity. Unlike her father, Zina had no such qualms. Never demure about singing his praises, she took delight in telling the world about him.

The son of Chaim Leib, a Jewish Lithuanian merchant in Vilna, Lithuania, Mikhail was born on July 8, 1867. At birth he was given the name Moishe Chaim Leib (Moishe, son of Chaim Leib).

Moishe's paternal grandfather, Zvi Hirsch Simcha, was a diligent rabbinical scholar who had the good fortune to study under the two most prominent Vilna Rabbis of that era - Rabbi Abraham Abale Posweiler, head of the Rabbinical Court and Rabbi Saul Joseph Katzenellenbogen, Chief Rabbi of Vilna. A descendent of the famous rabbinical Katzenellenbogen family which includes the likes of Karl Marx and Helena Rubenstein, Rabbi Saul Katzenellenbogen traces his roots back more than 500 years to Rabbi Meir of Padua (1482-1565).

In 1804 Tsar Alexander I decreed that all Jews must adopt a surname. Rabbi Saul Katzenellenbogen was so enamored with his favorite student, Moishe's grandfather Zvi Hirsch Simcha (in Jewish nomenclature - Zvi Hirsch, son of Simcha), that he bestowed upon him the blessing of the Katzenallenbogen surname. He was henceforth known as Rabbi Zvi Hirsch Katzenellenbogen.

Zina's father, christened Moishe Chaim Leib Katzenellenbogen, was a youngster who understood that if he were to get anywhere in this world he would need to change his name. By the time he entered medical school his name was officially changed to Mikhail Nicolaevich Katzenellenbogen.

Mikhail arrived as a young doctor in Eastern Siberia, in the most remote corner of Russia in 1901. A bright and sensitive young man, at an early age he developed a keen sense of his place in the universe. He knew, somehow, that he was destined to dedicate his life to the service of others. As was the custom, he satisfied his compulsory military service by joining the Imperial Army in 1888. His military duties behind him, he returned to Vilna and began courting a Russian Orthodox noblewoman, Yana Mikhailovna Pavlovski. Shortly thereafter Mikhail converted to the Russian Orthodox religion and in 1891 the two were wedded. On February 1, 1892 their first child, Elena, was born. His love for the natural sciences in general and for medicine in particular soon led him to the Imperial Kazan University in pursuit of a medical degree. In 1897 Yana gave birth to their second child, Vera. A year later, on November 28, 1898, he received his medical degree. During his years as a medical student at Imperial Kazan University, he was sent on a year's mission to Nikolaevsk-na-Amur by The Imperial Medical Academy for Scientific Improvement. His task - to document what life was like in this most remote area of Russia and to assess the state of health services in the region. The year's experience documenting the ways of life in the region would change him forever. There was so much lacking in this area of the Russian Far East, especially in terms of health services, that he knew immediately that this would be the place for his life's work. He lobbied fervently to be given a post in the region and was overjoyed when on January 13, 1900, by order No. 17 of the Military Governor of Primorskaya Oblast, he was appointed village doctor of South-Ussuriisky District. Thirteen months later, on February 16, 1901, by order No. 55 of the same Military Governor of Primorsky oblast, he was transferred to Nikolaevsk and given the title, Town Doctor.

◊◊

Mikhail thought that it would be a hard sell convincing Yana, born to a noble Lithuanian family from the capital city of Vilna, to relocate to Siberia. It would have been a hard sell convincing *anyone* to move to Siberia, much more so a noble woman from a cosmopolitan city. Vilna was a city rich in cultural history, the arts, architecture. Indeed it was known as the European Capital of Culture. A storied city important as a center of Jewish influence, it was dubbed by Napoleon the "Jerusalem of the North" as he passed through during his disastrous invasion of Russia in 1812.

No one in his or her right mind offers to go to Siberia, no matter how noble the cause. Who goes to a place reputed to consist of nothing but exiled prisoners, cold stretches of trackless forests, criminals, man-eating tigers, Cossacks, leper colonies and frozen tundras? Zina's father, Mikhail. That's who. Of course, having spent

47

a year in the region as a medical student he knew that, like most things, Siberia's reputation was much worse that its reality. As it turned out, trying to convince his wife Yana to go East was not too difficult. She loved Mikhail dearly and believed in and supported his vision of bringing modern medicine to the Russian Far East. Besides, the thought of her and her two little girls living apart from Mikhail was unthinkable. And so, though she was in somewhat fragile health, there was something appealingly adventurous to leaving the stuffy boudoirs of Vilna to be at her husband's side in the big open country of the Eastern frontier. Besides raising the kids she would also provide Mikhail with the morale support he needed. She knew how much he looked forward to doing all he could to improve the atrocious conditions of the region's leper colonies, among other things. Perhaps some day he might even find a cure for this disfiguring disease.

The trip to Nikolaevsk-na-Amur from Vilnius was long, arduous and cold. Yana thought that with two little ones in tow, the optimum time to travel would be summer but Mikhail was due to assume his responsibilities as Nikolaevsk's town doctor in February 1901. And so, in January 1901 Mikhail, with his bride and two little girls embarked on the journey from Vilnius to Nikolaevsk by horse drawn carriage, steam boat and the TransSiberian Railway, i.e., the parts of the railway that was complete - a distance of almost 10,000 kilometers. By the time they arrived at their destination, more that a month later, Yana took ill and her health rapidly began to deteriorate. As time went by her health improved, enabling her to take a cue from her husband and she began to contribute her skills as a teacher to the well-being of this eastern territory. As late as 1915 she was teaching in a minimal school in the village of Abrazheevka, Ivanovskaya Volost. It must have been a very difficult time for Mikhail - juggling family and work, but he was a young doctor whose star was on the rise and whose priority was the hard work of improving the health conditions of the region.

By 1905, just a few years after Mikhail Nikolaevich Katzenellenbogen and his family arrived in Nikolaevsk-na-Amur, he had become a very important and influential man in the Russian Far East. By 1913 he was arguably one of the most powerful men in the region, as reflected by the list of titles and positions he held.

Nikolaevsk-na-Amur City Duma – Deputy

City Hospital – Director

Vladivostok Prison (Nikolaevsk Chapter) - Committee Member

City Sanitary Commission – Member

Nikolaevsk Charitable Committee – Secretary

Leprosarium Committee – Member

Nikolaevsk Volunteer Firefighting Society – Member

Nikolaevsk Public Assembly – Chief

Prison Charitable Committee – Director

Society to Provide the Development of Popular Entertainment & Popular Education - Board Member

Nikolaevsk is a district town of Primorskaya oblast, located 35 kilometers upstream from the mouth of the Amur river. Established in 1852 as a trading post of the Russian-American Company, it became a military post in 1856. Before the colonists arrived, the population of Nikolaevsk comprised mostly of indigenous Giljaks. After the arrival of the Japanese, Koreans and Chinese, the Giljaks' population declined dramatically - mostly from smallpox, measles, syphilis, starvation and alcoholism. In this town, winter was a time of heavy drinking, a place of horrifying drunkenness. Because of the long harsh winters, most people who worked tended to do so in the summer. The winters were so forbidding that many people sought the warm comfort provided by a bottle of vodka.

By the 1870s it was discovered that the port at Vladivostok, unlike Nikolaevsk-na-Amur, could be kept ice-free all year long and so it soon became the primary port in Siberia and the home base for the Siberian military fleet. By 1890 Nikolaevsk was at the height of its decline. However, by the end of the 1890s the town's fortunes began to increase with the discovery of gold and the establishment of salmon fisheries. On his way to Sakhalin Island in 1890 Anton Chekhov made a stop in Nikolaevsk and had difficulty finding a place to spend the night. He wrote:

Today, almost half of the dilapidated houses have been abandoned by their owners, and their dark frameless windows stare at you like the eye sockets of a skull. The inhabitants pursue a sloppy, drunken existence, generally living hand-tomouth on whatever God has provided......they make a living selling fish to Sakhalin, stealing gold, exploiting the natives, and selling deer antlers which the Chinese use to prepare a stimulant.

By 1895 the town's population had grown to 4,417 inhabitants (3, 398 males and 1, 019 females) most of whom were military troops, exiles and Kazakhs. There was a total of 328 private houses, 2 churches, a hotel, a public assembly building, a hospital, a church school and a 3-year vocational school.

By 1905 the population of Nikolaevsk was estimated to be approximately 8,000. Migration was frequent between Nikolaevsk and the neighboring district of Udsk where there was a thriving mining industry. The total population within a 265-mile radius of Nikolaevsk was thought to be about 30,000. There was no railroad or main road that connected Nikolaevsk with Habarovsk, the nearest big city. The only connection to other places was by sea and by the Amur River which could only be used during the summertime - and during the winter, when the river ice is frozen solid. On those rare occasions when the winter is relatively mild the Amur River would be navigable for six weeks in the spring and fall.

The fishing industry was always a big part of the port of Nikolaevsk. Zina could well remember the buzz of excitement generated in Nikolaevsk-na-Amur during the fishing season when the port was filled with Japanese and Chinese fishing vessels, as well as fishing boats from seemingly every nation. If she closed her eyes she could still hear the raucous calls of terns and seagulls permeating the air as they follow the fishing vessels into port, forever expecting a handout of discarded fish. For a relatively long time this was such an important strategic and productive fishing port for both salmon and open sea fishing that it is hard to believe that by the end of the 20th Century most of the fish consumed in this town was imported.

Mikhail was always quite proud of the many services, medical and otherwise, he provided for the hundreds of fishermen who frequented the port. Indeed in 1911 the Japanese Emperor, Emperor Meiji, conferred upon him the *Order of Sacred Treasure Medal, 3rd Class*. This letter that accompanied the medal speaks volumes about the good doctor's service to the town.

City of Nikolaevsk-na-Amur, City Physician
Order of the Sacred Treasure, Third Class
Awarded to Mikhail Nikolaevich Katzenellenbogen

The person above has served as a physician for the city from the year 1901. He is in charge of medical inspections for the ships of the port. Every year from June until September the number of foreign and domestic ships entering the port reaches over one hundred. Over half of those are ships from our country (Japan), carrying thousands of fishermen. During fishing season, the situation becomes particularly urgent, and for a time the harbor is congested. It always becomes a race against time (to tend to all of the ships). The doctor appreciates the situation and never wastes time performing medical inspections. His prompt handling of these affairs and his constant efforts to avoid any problems are undoubtedly a result of his goodwill, which has left a profound impression on the subjects of this country. Furthermore, the city hospital is not well-suited for the wide accommodation of patients. However, every effort is made to accept as many of our patients as possible, and this accommodation being provided is a truly great debt owed to the doctor. In addition, within the city the doctor is a prominent and highly educated man of influence, member of the city council, honorary judge in the court of public order, takes on two or three other public offices, and is an authority with the press, and because of this, if within the city council or the courts there arise any problems concerning our people, he always advocates a fair discussion, earnestly speaks his mind, and both openly and implicitly endeavors toward the protection of our people. Those and other considerate actions, for we residents, are no small matter. He is a person widely esteemed for those meritorious deeds.

Not to be outdone by the Japanese Emperor, on December 6, 1911 the Russian Tsar, Nicholas II, awarded Dr. Katzenellenbogen the *Order of Saint Stanislaus Medal, 2nd Class.*

The 1913 report below, submitted by Dr. Katzenellenbogen to the Imperial Military Medical Academy for Scientific Improvement on the status of the health conditions of the region gives a pretty good idea of the kind of challenges facing the young town doctor.

Nutrition

The food consumed in Nikolaevsk has very poor nutritional content with very little, if any, fresh vegetables available. During the winter, which was most of the year, the diet for most inhabitants of Nikolaevsk consists of frozen and pickled meat and fish. Dairy products are practically nonexistent. The hygienic and sanitary conditions of Nikolaevsk are poor.

The different races and multiethnic groups who migrated from different regions of Russia, the immigrants from Sakhalin Island, the escaped prisoners, the people sent in exile and living in fear and terror, the mentally ill from the district hospital, represent a population with more than its fair share of single, homeless, drunk, degenerate, mentally ill people.

Dominant Diseases - Sanitary Needs

Alcoholism

Alcoholism is the number one disease in Nikolaevsk. Also prevalent are tuberculosis, chronic kidney disease, chronic and acute psychological diseases. There is no precise statistics for the number of alcoholics but it is probably much higher than one suspects. Because of the combination of poor nutrition and very cold climate the consumption of alcohol is deadly, the alcohol acting as a kind of poison. In Nikolaevsk it has destroyed the lives of many single immigrant workers, teenagers and fishermen who work in the cold waters of the Fall season. There are lots of cases of chronic and aggravated kidney disease.

Tuberculosis

In my practice in Nikolaevsk from 1901-1905 I found a type of tuberculosis that seems to affect mostly exiles from Sachalin Island. It can last for as long as six months. The statistics on how many persons died of tuberculosis at this time is unknown because the hospital does not keep such records.

Eclampsia

In 20% of maternity cases women are afflicted with this life-threatening complication of pregnancy.

Mental Disease

Mostly chronic mental disease probably brought on by rampant alcoholism especially during the winter when there are lots of unemployed vagrants. The hospital is not equipped to handle these cases.

Syphilis

This disease seems to affect many people from Sachalin Island where the disease can be seen in its chronic, paralytic and tabetic forms. Typically, they receive no medical treatment as the hospital is also ill equipped to do so.

Periodontal Disease

Prevalent in the town prison, hospital, shelters, surrounding villages and in remote locations.

Leprosy

Although only four cases have been registered in Nikolaevsk, this disease is very contagious and has spread throughout the Amur River valley to Habarovsk, Udsk district Vjatsjeslav, Troetskoe, Malmugh, Orlov, Tambouku, Srednjaja, Boznesenskoe, Marienskoe, Foyorodskoe, Bolshoi-Mikailovskoe, Niza, Focinskaya, Buhta.

Most people with the disease are not registered. People panic when they think they have the disease because they do not want to be quarantined and isolated. People, like prisoners, are often misdiagnosed by police officers and remain quarantined for years. The leprosy situation in Nikolaevsk is unsatisfactory. There is a great need for more medical staff. The situation is out of control.

Infectious Diseases

(a) *There is an epidemic of measles, scarlet fever, whooping cough, especially for foreign visitors*

(b) *Occasionally people die of small pox, especially foreign visitors. But also the native population. In 1902-1903 there was a big epidemic. In 1910 a cholera epidemic took the lives of more than 200 people.*

(c) *Cholera Epidemic in 1903 and 1910. An executive committee was formed to deal with this situation. The town officials were reluctant to spend the necessary money. They refused to listen to the advice of the doctors and did very little to stop the beginning of the plague.*

(d) *Typhoid Fever is also prevalent.*

Zina's mother, Alexandra Petrovna Leontovic, was born in Valki, Ukraine on November 1, 1884, descending from a long line of Russian Orthodox priests whose family tree is deeply rooted in Siberia. As early as the 1760s, her great-great-great grandfather (Andrei Leontovic), greatgreat grandfather (Petr Leontovic) and her grandfather (Evgraf Leontovic) served as priests at the Blagoveschenskaya Church of Annunciation. Her father (Petr Leontovic) decided to break with tradition, eschewing the ministry and opted to become a veterinarian. He was said to be "a man of very progressive views". He reportedly committed suicide in 1919. It's unclear if his demise had anything to do with his breaking the family's Orthodox priest tradition or with the October 17 Revolution.

Mrs. Katzen's aunt & mother (right)

Her maternal grandmother, Zinaida Pokidailova and her maternal great grandmother also came from a family of priests. Her maternal grandfather was born in Kiev into a family of craftsmen. A church deacon and a marvelous singer, he sang regularly in the church choir. Later in life he attended the seminary and eventually became a priest. It's been said that the internationally renowned Ukrainian composer, choral conductor, priest and teacher, Mykola Dmytrovych Leontovich is also a family relative. And if this is not enough Russian Orthodox Christianity for one family, there has always been talk that the famous Archbishop Meletij Leontovic (17841840) is also a relative.

Alexandra's first husband, Valentin Nikolay Davidov was an Ukranian military doctor. Born on February 2, 1872 into Kharkov nobility, he obtained his medical degree from Kharkov University Medical School. After spending a brief period in 1897 as a member of his medical school's faculty, he moved on to serve as a uezd doctor in Sumy, a city on the Psel river in the Ukraine. Starting in 1905 he served as a military doctor in Siberia.

Zina never quite got the story of how her mother and Valentin met but it's not hard to imagine the countless opportunities there must have been for encounters between the young handsome army doctor and the beautiful precocious debutante, both born into prominent families of Kharkov society. As a youngster Alexandra had a reputation for being as rash and impetuous as she was beautiful and charming. Indeed, throughout her entire life she was a force to be reckoned with. As a little girl she showed great promise as a pianist, often playing the church organ during Sunday services. She dreamt of a life of fame as a classical pianist performing in concert halls the world over with the likes of Sergei Rachmaninov and Josef Hofmann.

However, the reality of life in the Leontovic family, a family steeped in the religious traditions of Russian Orthodox Christianity, dictated that she was more likely predestined to be the wife of a parish priest than live the life of a world-famous pianist. But Alexandra, who considered herself a modern woman, had other ideas. A teenager in 1900, she would join the ranks of the many women who were finding non-traditional ways to define themselves at the dawn of the new century. Endowed with the spirit of adventure and emboldened by her father's precedent-setting, familytradition-breaking chutzpah, in 1903 (at the age of 18) she married the 31year-old handsome army doctor, Valentin Davidov after a brief courtship. Valentin was certainly handsome but even more attractive was his promised adventure of life as an army doctor in Russia's wild, wild East. If you weren't exiled or an outcast of any kind, the Russian Far East in the early 1900s was a place for adventurers and entrepreneurs, a place where fortunes were waiting to be made in the mining of raw materials, in the harvesting of the Amur River's bounteous schools of salmon.

And so off they went to seek their fortune in Siberia. Alexandra brought some much-needed culture to the region, making a name for herself as a pianist, a music teacher in the local school and an impresario. Her presentations of and participation in concerts, musical soirées would become the cultural highlights of Nikolaevsk-na-Amur. Often these events were fundraisers for the Volunteer Firefighting Association and other such local institutions. In 1909 she gave birth to their only child whom they named Raisa. Alexandra was certain that with Valentin's education, intelligence and business acumen she had hitched her wagon to the right star. And indeed she did. By 1909 Dr. Davidov had amassed a modest fortune in the salmon fishing industry and as a pharmacist.

In 1910, he drowned in the Amur River under dubious circumstances, leaving Alexandra a wealthy widow and mother with business enterprises to run.

Nikolaevsk was a small port town where everybody knew everybody, or at the very least all the important people (doctors, lawyers, bankers, town officials, business owners) knew each other. Because they moved in the same circles, often sitting on the same Boards or Committees, Dr. Katzenellenbogen knew Dr. Davidov and his wife Alexandra who were among the most successful and powerful business owners in the region. These two doctors would eventually become business partners, establishing the only pharmacy in Nikolaevsk.

It appears that by 1910 the marriage of Dr. Katzenellenbogen and his wife Yana had been dissolved. Yana moved to a nearby town where she taught elementary school and raised their two daughters, Elena and Lyudmila. Mikhail, although quite busy with his responsibilities as hospital administrator, doctor, judge, etc, still found time for his daughters who loved him as dearly as he loved them. Not too long thereafter, Alexandra Davidov and Dr. Mikhail Katzenellenbogen were married.

The product of this union, Zenaida Katzenellenbogen, was born July 8, 1911 in Nikolaevsk-na-Amur.

Life for little Zina could only be described as privileged. She and her sister, older by two years, lacked for nothing. As she remembered it, those first years of her life spent growing up in their Nikolaevsk household with her mother Alexandra, her father Mikhail, her sister Raisa and her aunt Evgenie were simply wonderful. Her mother a classically trained pianist, the household was always filled with music. The apple of her father's eye, she dreamt of one day following in his footsteps, becoming a doctor and trying to cure the many ills that beset the world. As a child a favorite activity was creating a make-believe classroom for her dolls and teaching them everything they needed to know about life. Her aunt was not really an aunt but everyone referred to her as such. Zina cannot remember a time when Evgenie had not been a part of the family. She learned as an adult that aunt Evgenie became a permanent member of the family after Dr. Katzenellenbogen saved her life. A nurse who worked with Dr. Katzenellenbogen, for reasons unknown she supposedly drank a poisonous concoction, the good doctor finding her just in the nick of time. It is not clear what precipitated her suicide attempt.

Zina loved the smell of the salty sea air and delighted in the sight of the many ocean-going vessels that frequented the harbor. She would forever have fond memories of these early years in Nikolaevsk, a time when her life was filled with school, music lessons, playing in the snow and fairytale story books. Later in life she would be surprised, and hurt, to hear her beautiful Nikolaevsk described as a hellhole, that it was a place so far behind God's back it's inconceivable why anyone would want to go there for a visit, much less live there. As a little girl she never saw it as an unduly cold place. She never saw the seedy, ugly underbelly of life in her town - perhaps in part because she had powerful and wealthy parents who had the wherewithal to protect her from such unpleasantness. To the extent that she saw, heard of or understood the existence and extent of the rampant alcoholism, the leprosy and the contagious diseases pervasive in the region, her perspective was undoubtedly colored by her adoration of her larger-than-life father whom she thought was the most benevolent and beneficent man in the world. After all, he was a man who cured diseases, a man who fixed humanity's ills.

The Russian Revolution changed everything.

On March 15, 1917, three years after the start of the Great War and a month after the beginning of the February Revolution, Tsar Nicholas II was forced to abdicate. The Bolsheviks, who were able to galvanize mutinous soldiers and discontented workers, forced the Kerensky-led provisional government to give up power.

The handwriting was on the wall. By 1918 the accounts of atrocities perpetuated by the Bolsheviks had reached the Russian Far East. As early as 1916 Dr. Katzenellenbogen, a highly intelligent and pragmatic man had read the tea leaves and understood that the turmoil of war-torn Europe and the almost assured likelihood of a revolution in his beloved country meant that the only option for his family's survival was to flee mother Russia. To be trapped in Nikolaevsk when the Bolshevik partisans arrived in Nikolaevsk would be a death sentence.

Ishida Toramatsu, Nikolaevsk-na-Amur's Japanese Consul and a personal friend of the good doctor, would be the family's ticket out. Taramatsu had witnessed personally Dr. Katzenellenbogen's kindness towards the Japanese fishermen and submitted to Emperor Meiji a description of his good deeds. Through the Consul's recommendation, Mikhail was rewarded the Order of Sacred Treasure Medal five years earlier. In early 1919 Dr. Katzenellenbogen submitted his resignation as director of the city hospital after Toramatsu issued Japanese visas to him and his entire family. The visa document explained that Dr. Katzenellenbogen, a very important doctor/scientist, a true friend of the Japanese people, a man who has been honored by Emperor Meiji, was embarking on a scientific research trip to Japan (with his family) and that he should be afforded all of the privileges and accommodations commensurate with his position and as a man of high esteem. Taking only the family jewels and whatever liquid assets they could access, by the end of 1919 the family was in Japan. A few weeks later they were aboard a ship bound for one of the few places in the world that accommodated Russian refugees, the Chinese port city of Shanghai.

In February 1920, 4,000 Bolshevik troops laid siege to the Japanese garrison in Nikolaevsk which sheltered, among others, 450 Japanese civilians and was defended by 300 Japanese soldiers from the 2nd Infantry under the command of Major Ishikawa Masao and 350 anti-Bolshevik Russian soldiers. By then the population of Nikolaevsk had dwindled to about 1,100 inhabitants. Anticipating the worse, most of the burzhis fled fearing the wrath of the advancing Bolsheviks.

Twice the Reds sent envoys to negotiate a surrender and both times the envoys were killed by the Japanese. Major Masao agreed to surrender after the Bolshevik's third request. But this was just a ruse. The Japanese sense of honor forbade them to surrender to the enemy. A Japanese soldier's code of honor dictates that one fights and dies honorably or one commits hari kari rather than fall into the hands of the enemy. Instead of surrendering, Major Masao decided on a surprise attack. Greatly outnumbered by the Red army, the outcome was predictable. Masao was killed with all but 110 of his soldiers. Consul Ishida Toramatsu, who orchestrated safe passage to Japan for the Katzenellenbogen family two years earlier, committed suicide with his wife and two children rather than face the ire of the Bolsheviks. The leader of the Red army, infuriated by Major Ishikawa Masao's attack, slaughtered the 110 captured soldiers as well as a number of Russians and dumped their bodies in the icy waters of the

Amur river. He then had his soldiers burn the town of Nikolaevsk-naAmur to the ground.

◊◊

Shanghai

The first Opium War (1839-42), also known as the Anglo-Chinese War, was a conflict between Great Britain and China. It was precipitated when the Chinese government, wishing to stop the spread of opium among its people confiscated two and a half million pounds of opium from British ships. Typical of the great 19th century imperial powers, Great Britain, unhappy with the Chinese efforts to stem the flow of the opium trade, flexed its military muscles to settle the score. From the British imperial way of thinking, (i.e. the I-have-the-big-stickso-I-can-do-as-I-please), China did not have the right, nor the might, to protect its people from the evils of opium.

The ensuing Treaty of Nanking granted Britain indemnity and the opening of five treaty ports - Canton, Ningpo, Fuchow, Amoy and Shanghai.

The British, disappointed that the Nanking Treaty did not satisfy their expected trade goals, once again provoked a conflict with China (the Second Opium War) as a means of gaining even greater access to trade. Meanwhile, the Americans and the French, noticing the wonderful benefits of extraterritoriality and most favored nation status enjoyed by the British in China, decided that they too wanted a piece of the action. The Treaties of Wanghia (1844) and Whampoa (1844) respectively gave the Americans and the French concessions similar to those obtained by the British. By the end of the 19th century all of the major world powers had extraterritoriality rights in one or more of the Treaty Ports. These rights were the cornerstone of foreign privilege in China, giving foreigners immunity from most Chinese taxes and allowing foreign troops to be stationed in China.

In addition, they allowed the foreigners to remain subject to the laws of their own country rather than the laws of China.

Shanghai, the most prosperous of the Treaty Ports, would eventually be divided into three areas. The International Settlement controlled by the United States and Great Britain; the French Concession and the Old City of Shanghai.

In the first half of the 20th century Shanghai was considered to be the greatest city in Asia. Filled with paradoxes and contrasts, it was a city in which most of the residents were Chinese but it was not run by China. It was not a colony, despite the fact that it was run by foreigners. A haven for people who sought refuge from war, pogroms and poverty, it was referred to in equal measure as "The Whore of the East" and "The Paris of the East". The most industrialized city in China, it was known for its national and international opium smuggling, for its gambling and prostitution, for its rogues and its adventurers. It was also a center for intellectual activity and revolutionary thinkers. It was a city in which the arrogance of racial and cultural superiority of the foreigners against the Chinese was *de rigueur*, a city of which a Christian evangelist in the 1920s once said, "If God lets Shanghai endure, He owes an apology to Sodom and Gomorrah".

In 1919 when the Katzenellenbogen family boarded a ship for Japan, Zina was really too young to fully understand the nature of the destructive forces that had Russia simultaneously engaged in The Great War and a Civil War. To the extent that she might have overheard talk of the events of these troubled times, this was adult talk and meant little to her. But she intuitively understood that the approaching danger precipitated the family's need to leave Russia if they were to be safe. She took great comfort in the knowledge that her father, a man whom everyone turned to in times of need, would always keep the family safe. And although she was unhappy to leave her beloved Nikolaevsk, her sadness was mitigated somewhat by her excitement for the anticipated ocean-going adventure.

The sail to Japan South through the Tatar Strait into the Sea of Japan would leave an indelible impression on her. She immediately fell in love with the sea, with the ship, with the sound of the bow plowing through the waves, the sound of the water against the hull, the gentle rocking of the boat. There was something magical, calming, reassuring about that first boat ride. Although she did not know it at that time, for Zina, ships and the ocean would come to symbolize peace and tranquility, an escape from tyranny, from the unpleasant things in life.

Zina enjoyed the brief stay in Japan but wished it was longer. Thanks to her father's Order of the Sacred Treasure medal bestowed upon him by Emperor Meiiji, he and his family were given accommodations befitting that of honorary Japanese. Zina thought that Japan was a perfect place to start their new life but the decision to follow the path of the thousands of White Russians fleeing to Shanghai after the October 17 revolution was already made. Many of the wealthy social elite of European Russia fled to Europe while thousands from the Russian Far East fled through Vladivostok to China and settled in Tianjin, Manchuria, Harbin and Shanghai. In order to survive in Shanghai many of these émigrés, regardless of their previous social status in Russia, were forced to take jobs considered unsuitable for Europeans, jobs that were usually done by the Chinese. They were porters, construction workers, teachers, nannies, maids, dancing girls and prostitutes.

Having arrived in Shanghai, the number one priority for the Katzenellenbogens was the education of the girls. They settled in the French Concession after finding an apartment at *5 rue Chapsal*. Zina and Raisa were already bilingual, having learned French as a second language in Russia where French was the language of the Russian Imperial Court and of high society in general. The Russian Revolution had changed everything for the Katzenellenbogen family. Born a Jew, Mikhail had pretensions to Russian nobility. He had worked hard, served in the Russian Imperial Army, became a doctor, converted to the Russian Orthodox faith, served as the deputy head of the local duma in Nikolaevsk-na-Amur, was decorated by Tsar Nicholas I and honored by the Japanese Emperor. Now refugees in a strange land, the wealth, high social status and prestige enjoyed by this proud Russian man and his family were gone. In order to make their daughters citizens of the world Mikhail and Alexandra decided to enroll their girls in a British school. Before long Dr. Katzenellenbogen was seeing patients in his private practice at *21 Nanking Road* while Alexandra gave private piano lessons at home. Evgenie, now very much an integral part of the family, never again worked outside of the home. She was a live-in nanny for Zina and Raisa and took care of all things domestic.

At ages eight and ten respectively when they arrived in Shanghai, Zina and Raisa quickly adapted to English, the language of instruction in their new school. Jane, daughter of a Chinese couple, was Zina's best friend and classmate. They were inseparable, riding their bikes to school together daily, sitting together in class and frequently doing homework together. During these elementary school years growing up in cosmopolitan Shanghai Zina discovered that she had a preternatural affinity for languages. English, French and Spanish were part of the curriculum. She would be fluent in these languages by the time she graduated high school. At home Russian was the language used and she learned functional Chinese from her friend and classmate Jane. An excellent student, at the age of fifteen Zina took and passed her Senior Cambridge exams, receiving honors in French, Spanish and Mathematics.

Following in the footsteps of Mikhail who received his medical degree at the University of Paris Medical School, Zina and Raisa would soon be off to continue their studies in the City of Lights. Raisa, showing great promise as a violinist, gained acceptance to the prestigious *École Normale de Musique de Paris*. On the strength of her performance on the Senior Cambridge Exams, Zina was accepted at the Sorbonne. Because she was only fifteen and French was not her *langue natale*, she would first attend *Lycée Lamartine* so that she might gain better command of the language.

She received her baccalaureate in 1929.

◊◊

65

La vie parisienne

Lycée Lamartine, located at *121 rue du Faubourg-Poissonnière* in the 9th *arrondissement*, was named for the 19th century French poet and statesman, Alphonse de Lamartine. The French National Education Department purchased the building in 1891 and turned it into a lycée for girls in 1893. As a school, it was a great fit for Zina. It provided its charges with an environment whose ethos nurtured young ladies to be free and independent thinkers, giving them the wherewithal to be trailblazers, encouraging them to set goals that transcended those heretofore considered "appropriate" for women. An equally important aspect of the Lamartine curriculum was that it instilled altruistic values in its students. It was important that Lamartine graduates become socially responsible women. To this end students were required to spend a part of the school year participating in community volunteer projects designed to help the needy. A Baccalauréat in Science was first awarded by *Lycée Lamartine* in 1914. Jeanne Lévy, one of its first recipients and a role model for Zina, epitomized the essence of a Lamartine alumna. She later went on to become the first female professor at the Medical School of the University of Paris.

The six years (1926-1932) that Zina spent in Paris as a student were remarkable years. She arrived in the City of Lights less than a decade after the end of World War I, at the end of *La Belle Epoque*. A precocious teenager, she was poised and confident beyond her years. After five long years of distress and austerity, the post-war years ushered in an effervescent spirit in Paris and Parisians were now ready to let their hair down and party. The 1920s (at least until the 1929 Stock Market crash plunged the world into the Great Depression) came to be known as *Les Années Folles* - literally, the

Crazy Years, but more commonly referred to as the Golden Twenties. Jennifer Milligan describes this era in France as "a utopic golden age of opportunity, where everything seemed possible and fame and fortune seemed to be there for the taking." This was a decade when *La Rive Gauche*, *Montparnasse* and *Montmartre* were considered by many the artistic, cultural and intellectual centers of the universe. It was a time when the cabarets, salons, jazz clubs of these Paris *quartiers* were frequented by the likes of Ernest Hemingway, Henry Miller, F. Scott Fitzgerald, Marc Chagal, Josephine Baker, Joan Miró, Jean Arp, Jean Cocteau, Jean Paul Sartre, Gertrude Stein, Sidney Bechet, Aaron Copeland, Eric Satie, Django Reinhardt, Ezra Pound, Isadora Duncan and Pablo Picasso.

Religion was always an important part of Zina's life, thanks to her Russian Orthodox mother who made certain that she was indoctrinated in the tenets of the Christian faith. With no relatives in Paris and her daughters a long way from their home in Shanhghai, Zina's mother made arrangements for them to be lodged in a convent so that they might benefit from the structure, supervision and spiritual guidance of the Mother Superior and her community of nuns. Fifteen-year-old Zina and seventeen-year-old Raisa spent their first few years of study living in this 19th *arrondissement* religious house located at *36 rue Botzaris*, across the street from the *Parc des Buttes Chaumont*.

Zina was quite conscious of the fact that she had arrived in Gay Paree at a time when the city was buzzing with the *joie de vivre* of *Les Années Folles*. A diligent and conscientious student, she was not inclined (and really much too young) to hang out in the famous cafés and salons frequented by the musicians, artists and intellectuals who exemplified the Golden Twenties. During her high school years Zina would spend much of her free time visiting *les bouquinistes* on the *Rive Gauche*. She loved reading the antiquarian books of these secondhand booksellers. They became a huge part of her Paris life. She was a voracious reader and did not have a great deal of money to purchase books and so she befriended many of these bookstore owners along the banks of the river Seine. They would often allow her to borrow books but more often than not she would sit on the *quais* and read the works of the giants of 17th Century French Literature - Molière, Racine, Decartes and Corneille and the plays, poems and prose of her favorite 19th Century French Romantics, François Réne Chateaubriand, Alphonse de Lamartine, Théophile Gautier and Alfred de Vigny as the tourist-filled *bateaux mouches* glided up and down the Seine.

Mrs. Katzen, 1937

After she received her *Bac* from *Lycée Lamartine* and began studies at the Sorbonne, she and her sister moved to a *deux-pièce cuisine* in the *2nd arrondissement*. Now old enough to be on their own and no longer having to live under the restrictive aegis of a Mother Superior, they spent much of their free time patronizing nearby theatrical and ballet productions at *La Comédie Française* and *L'Opéra Comique*. Another favorite activity was to attend *vernissages* held by many of the art galleries in Paris. During school vacations Zina was able to help defray the costs of living and studying in Paris working as an au pair and tutor for the children of wealthy families in *Honfleur*, in *Bretagne* and on the *Cote d'Azur*.

Zina graduated from the Sorbonne in 1932, receiving teaching certificates in Science, Mathematics and Modern Languages. Her childhood dream was to follow in the footsteps of her idol Marie Curie, who in 1903 received a Ph. D. at the Sorbonne and later became her alma mater's first woman professor. Unfortunately, her dream of earning an advanced degree from the Sorbonne had to be deferred. Thanks to her parents she was given the opportunity to study in Paris but it was now time to return home and see to the well-being of her family. Her father had passed away in 1921, five years before she left for Paris, and she was anxious to return to Shanghai to use her newly minted earning power to make life easier for her mother and her aunt. Arriving in China in 1919, there was a difficult period of adjustment for her family as they tried to find ways to survive in a place where everything was markedly different from the life they left behind in Siberia. Adjustment to this new life was especially hard on Zina's father. Mikhail went from being one of the most powerful and important citizens of Nikilaevsk-na-Amur to being one of tens of thousands of stateless immigrants seeking refuge in Shanghai. Fifty-four years old when he fled Russia with his family, he was a relatively young man and was determined to make the best of his new life in China. By 1920 he had set up a general practice at 12 Nanking Road where his patients were mostly residents of the International Settlement as well as poor Chinese. He was also a man in poor health, succumbing to an unknown illness before his fiftyfifth birthday.

Return to Shanghai

In 1931 the Japanese occupied Manchuria. Six months later Manchuria was established as the Japanese puppet state of Manchukuo. In addition to this puppet state, Japan also had extraterritorial concessions in Shanghai. Looking to further increase its influence in the area, the Japanese army, as a way of justifying further military action in China, supposedly instigated an incident in January 1932. In this incident, Japanese Buddhist monks were beaten by Chinese civilians near a factory in Shanghai. One died and two were seriously injured. For the next five years there were intermittent skirmishes between Japanese and Chinese troops in and around Shanghai, preludes if you will, to the Second Sino-Japanese War of 1937.

Worried about the events in Shanghai, Zina was anxious to get back to her mother and aunt. By the time she returned home from her studies in Paris, the hostilities had subsided and life in Shanghai was almost back to normal. Her loved ones were safe but this Sino-Japanese conflict was really a harbinger of things to come. For the first time since they arrived in Shanghai seeking refuge from the Bolsheviks, there was a sense that it was only a matter of time before they might have to pull up stakes, once again, and seek refuge elsewhere. In the meantime, one had to get on with the business of life. These were difficult times. The financial resources of the Katzenellenbogens in Siberia were quite substantial. Leaving Nikolaevsk meant leaving behind a great part of the family fortune. The carefully concealed family jewels that they were able to take with them would go a long way towards fulfilling family priority number one: providing Zina and Raisa with an education. Mikhail was now deceased after a few years with a modest general practice ministering to stateless refugees. Forced by the October Revolution to leave behind the vast business fortune she inherited from her deceased first husband, Alexandra started giving private piano lessons in her Shanghai home as a means of supplementing the family income.

Her studies completed, Zina was anxious to start her career as a teacher. She would have loved to stay on in Paris pursuing a Ph. D. in Mathematics or Physics and, like her idol Marie Curie, become a professor at the Sorbonne, but the tenuous Sino-Japanese situation in Shanghai and her sense of familial duty compelled her to return home.

Ever since she was a little girl Zina had a voracious appetite for learning. Intensely curious about people, places and things, she was supported and encouraged by her doting father who always took time to answer her countless questions. Her father's dedication to a life of service to humanity made a huge impression on her, and his boundless patience and encouragement made her feel like the world was her oyster. When she grew up, she wanted to be just like him. She dreamt of becoming a Mathematician, a chemist or a physicist and thought of how wonderful it would be to further the work of two-time Nobel Laureate Marie Curie. But, at least for now, these lofty dreams had to be put on hold because her mother and her aunt needed her.

This was an era when neither a visa nor a passport was required for entry into Shanghai. It was one of the few havens for Jews fleeing the Holocaust in Europe. The exact number is not known but it has been said that before and during World War II many of the Baghdadi Sephardic Jews of Shanghai (like the Sassoons, Ezras, Abrahams, Hardoons, Kadoories) helped to save more Jews from the Nazi Holocaust than all of the Commonwealth countries combined. A European Refugee Committee was established by these wealthy Baghdadians for the express purpose of providing food, educational and social services to Jewish refugees. After completing her studies at the Sorbonne in 1932, Zina was able to get a teaching position at the Shanghai Jewish School (SJS), a school established to educate the children of Jewish refugees pouring into Shanghai. Under the guidance of its headmistress, the SJS adopted the Cambridge syllabus with the goal of preparing students for education in elite British universities. Prior to Zina's return her mother did some research and learned that the SJS had a Mathematics vacancy. It was here, on September 1, 1933 that 21-year-old Miss Zenaida Katzen started her career as an educator. Her first assignment - Sixth Form Mistress and teacher of Mathematics, a subject for which she received an A Level distinction as a student in Shanghai seven years earlier.

At twenty-one and only three years older than the sixth formers she taught, she was the youngest member of the faculty. An instant hit with her students, she immediately exhibited a poise, sophistication, instincts and *savoir faire* that belied her years. Perhaps the single most important excellent teacher attribute she exhibited, even at this very early stage of her career, was the facility with which she connected with her students, who by and large were Jewish refugees whose families fled political unrest and/or pogroms in Germany, Poland, Czechoslovakia, the Ukraine and Russia - students whose young lives had already been touched by the unimaginable horrors taking place in Europe in the years leading up to World War II. She seemed to understand at the outset, perhaps through that inherent intuitive quality possessed by great teachers, that the job of a pedagogue entailed more than simply teaching students how to read, write, add, subtract, multiply, divide and think for themselves. Like great teachers everywhere she went above and beyond the call of duty. She understood that to be an effective teacher, not only must one have the necessary knowledge and skills but, more importantly, teaching has a great deal to do with one's attitude towards one's students. She understood that good teachers make great sacrifices, working tirelessly to create challenging, nurturing environments for their charges.

Not only did she teach the principles of Pure and Applied Mathematics but, according to Isaac Shor, one of her first students at the above-mentioned SJS, "she took an interest in the personal lives of her students without invading our privacy and helped whenever and however she possibly could." In 1983, fifty years after Isaac sat in her very first class, he described the impact Miss Katzen had on his life and the life of his family.

At that period in my life, my father, my small sister and I were still under the trauma of my mother's premature death - and in a very dire financial situation. Through Miss Katzen's protekzia, her mother Mrs. Alexandra Katzen, a wellknown Shanghai piano teacher, gave me work in the form of copying music for her pupils. She paid me .50 cents per sheet. In those days one could get a plate of beef stroganoff with rice in a Chinese restaurant on Route Vallon for 20 cents, small money. After I graduated Miss Katzen sent me private pupils [so that I could] help them with their school studies. She was also instrumental in sending me to Tsingtao for my health during summer holidays of my last year in school.

The Shanghai Jewish School was a great place for a young woman to begin her teaching career. Joining the faculty in 1933, she quickly became an integral member of a community of educators who were building the foundations of a very special school. Located in a far from ordinary city in an era that could only be described as extraordinary, SJS was no ordinary school. The world was gripped in the throes of The Great Depression and throngs of refuge-seeking Europeans streamed into Shanghai, a portent of the Second World War.

Marble Hall was the name given to the Kadoorie family home in Shanghai. A large two-story palatial structure located at *64 Yan'an XI Lu*, the inside stairs, rails and balustrades were made of marble. On the first floor was a ballroom and living room which Horace's father, Elly Kadoorie, used frequently to entertain guests.

Sir Horace Kadoorie understood the important role a school can play in bringing a sense of normalcy to the lives of displaced children and their families. Over time, he and his brother Sir Lawrence

Kadoorie would dedicate a substantial portion of the Kadoorie family's wealth to philanthropic endeavors - helping Chinese farmers to improve their techniques for the cultivation of pigs, creating opportunities for women in Laos, supplying potable water in Nepal, giving sewing classes to women in Cambodia, giving small-business loans to women in Bangladesh, creating an Agricultural College in Palestine, pioneering girls' education in Iraq, to name a few.

The SJS was more than just a place to prepare students for schools in England. It was a beacon of hope for refugee children who had already experienced too much of the unpleasantness of this world at a time when it seemed that the world was going to hell in a hand basket.

Very much involved in the school, Horace frequently invited the SJS faculty and staff to his home at Marble Hall to celebrate student achievements and milestones. During these sessions Horace could not help but notice the new young teacher Miss Zenaida Katzen. She was always so full of energy and ideas about how to engage and challenge her students. It wasn't long before Horace met Miss Katzen's mother, Alexandra who would eventually become involved in the musical life of the SJS, frequently leading the student chorus on the piano and organizing student musical interludes, many such occasions taking place in the ballroom at Marble Hall.

In June of 1934, the end of her first year as a teacher, Zenaida decided that, given the continued deterioration of Sino-Japanese relations and the persistent chatter about the possibility of a European war, she would use her summer vacation to scout the possibilities of an eventual relocation of her family to the Americas. Traveling aboard the Japanese ocean liner, the *Asama Maru*, she disembarked in San Francisco on July 25, 1934 where she had made arrangements to spend a few weeks with Dr. Anton Boro-kov and his family. The Borokovs, like the Katzenellenbogens, fled Russia for Shanghai because of the October 1917 revolution. They left Shanghai for California in 1930. As Russian émigrés and fellow physicians living in Shanghai, Drs. Katzenellenbogen and Borokov had a lot in common. Both families traveled in the same social circles and the Borokov children, Oleg and Tatiana were friends and classmates of Zina and her sister.

There was another compelling purpose to Zina's California voyage to San Francisco. Ever since her return from her studies in Paris she had endured a constant stream of not too subtle suggestions from her mother about the necessity for her to be married. After all, she had passed her twenty-third birthday and fast approaching old-maid status. Unlike Alexandra, Zina did not quite feel the same sense of urgency to find a husband. There was so much to accomplish and so much of the world to see. But it would be great to see America and Alexandra would be placated, she hoped, that she was being proactive about finding a mate. She and Oleg Borokov were both fifteen when she left Shanghai for Paris. She fancied herself in love with him since elementary school and now she was about to find out if that childhood crush had endured the test of time. They tried to maintain a correspondence while she was in Paris but after he and his family left Shanghai for San Francisco in 1930, two years before she returned to Shanghai, there was very little communication between them.

Traveling to San Francisco in the summer of 1934 was an indicator that finding Zina a husband was indeed a matter of great urgency. Most people did not have the wherewithal, let alone the desire, to travel at a time when the world was in the midst of a Great Depression and there were signs of an impending European war. But Zina did. For a while it seemed that she might have to cancel her trip because of a longshoreman strike which effectively shut down docks along 2,000 miles of the U.S. Pacific coastline, including major ports in Seattle, Tacoma, Portland, San Pedro, San Diego and San Francisco. This strike, which paralyzed San Francisco for days, was marked in part by the riots of "Bloody Thursday" on July 5, 1934 leaving two dead and sixty-seven injured. Fortunately for Zina the strike ended eight days before her ship docked in San Francisco.

The trans-Pacific voyage was a complete joy. Happiness for Zina was traveling by cargo ship. She would rather have eschewed traveling aboard a luxury liner and sail the seas on a freighter. She decided on the *Asama Maru*, at that time the first Japanese passenger liner propelled by diesel engines. It was important that she got to San Francisco and back to Shanghai in time for the new school year. Considered at the time the fastest liner to cross the Pacific, the *Asama Maru* sailed regularly between Yokohama, Honolulu and San Francisco, with occasional stops in Kobe, Shanghai, Hong Kong and Los Angeles. However, with interiors modeled after some of the great palaces, hotels and manor houses of European royalty, the pleasures of sailing aboard the *Asama Maru* were not lost on her. Its passenger areas were of the finest quality with polished woods, fine dining rooms, stained glass skylights, comfortable cabins, lounges, library, hair salon and a swimming pool on deck. In her later years she would discover freighters which would become her preferred mode of travel because, in her own words, "they usually have well-stocked libraries and the handful of passengers are usually much more interesting to talk to." They afforded her opportunities to spend time on the bridge and to have meals with the captain and crew. She was happiest on the occasions when she travelled by sea.

One of the most important lessons Zina learned growing up in a household with well-to-do, well-connected parents was the importance of having well-connected friends. There was a high value placed on knowing the right people, but simply appearing to be well connected and influential would often suffice. Aboard the *Asama Maru*, she carried with her to San Francisco the Order of the Sacred Treasure, the medal which was bestowed upon her father by the Japanese Emperor in 1906 - a very important thing to have while traveling aboard a Japanese ship, if you can manage to get hold of one. In short order, whenever she displayed her father's medal, she was treated like royalty by the ship's Japanese captain and crew who would bow deferentially, scraping the deck with their foreheads. The honor bestowed on her father by the Japanese Emperor also belonged to her.

As the dockworkers strike continued and Zina got closer to her destination there was a great deal of concern about whether or not the liner would be allowed to dock. Fortunately, the strike ended eight days before the *Asama Maru* sailed into the port of San Francisco.

The Borokovs were wonderful hosts, giving Zina a taste of their beautiful adopted City by the Bay. Despite the hard times of the Depression, Zina saw all kinds of interesting and wonderful creations and transformations occurring in San Francisco. From the top of the newly built Coit Tower she could see the on-going construction of the Bay and Golden Gate bridges. She could see also Alcatraz island, where a few days earlier, on August 11, 1934 the U.S. Government opened a maximum-security prison for its most dangerous prisoners. Later that August, before Zina returned home to Shanghai, all of San Francisco was abuzz with the news of Al Capone's arrival at Alcatraz. Zina found that in many ways San Francisco was not unlike her home city of Shanghai. Both beautiful and gritty cities, one can find any and everything - opera, ballet, prostitution, opium dens, racecourses, criminals, an interesting array of architectural styles, the wealthy and the destitute. As was the case in Shanghai, almost everywhere she went in the city she saw long bread lines and many soup kitchens, hallmarks of the Depression. This was a time when there were 1.25 million Californians (one-fifth of the state's population) on public relief.

By the end of the trip Zina realized that a union with Oleg was not in the cards. So much had changed in the eight years since they last saw each other. They were the same age but she was now a worldly sophisticated woman while he seemed not to have matured much. Nagged by her mother to start looking for a husband, she realized for the first time the difficult nature of such a task, given the unrealistic romanticized example of husbandhood she internalized from having a doting, larger-than-life father.

The highlight of the steamship voyage back to Shanghai was a two-day layover in Honolulu where her exploration of the bustling, diversely populated city and a swim on beautiful Waikiki beach gave her a fleeting taste of life in the tropics.

She was happy to be back in Shanghai and anxious to get her second year of teaching underway. Her first year at SJS was quite difficult but nonetheless enjoyable. This summer afforded her, among other things, time to reflect on her first year in the classroom. Teaching was much harder than she thought it would be. Her first year taught her that it was really quite easy to be a teacher but very difficult to be a good teacher because good effective teaching entails a great deal of preparation - and to be prepared meant working many hours beyond the parameters of the regular school day. She hoped that for this her second year she would find the right balance between planning lessons, grading papers in a timely fashion, engaging in the school's extra-curricular activities and finding time to take proper care of herself. She was also under tremendous pressure from her mother to find a husband but at the moment her priority was her students. The families of most of her students were destitute, having recently fled their home country, leaving everything behind and having to start life anew in Shanghai, struggling to eke out a living. Each student had a compelling story and Zina could not rid herself of the feeling that she had an obligation not only to teach Mathematics but, where possible, to do everything in her power to help make a difference in their povertystricken lives. Whenever she could, she enlisted the assistance of established Shanghai families, including her own family, to help mitigate the difficulties experienced by her refugee students and their families. In this crazy depression-era world of Shanghai where European refugees were hard pressed to find food, Alexandra grew more and more concerned about the uncertain future of her daughters. As far as Alexandra was concerned Zina, who threw herself completely into her teaching, was not devoting enough time to the business of finding a husband. From Alexandra's way of thinking, in this harsh and unforgiving world her daughters needed husbands to take care of them.

Not quite as well-to-do as she was prior to fleeing Russia, in the fifteen years since she arrived in Shanghai Alexandra had made a name for herself as a reputable piano teacher. Piano lessons were de rigueur for the children of foreign nationals (Brits, Germans, French and Russians, Americans) living in Shanghai. From this supply of students Alexandra was able to make a decent living. Ten-year-old Pavel Dvorak, born in Suifenhe, China to Russian émigré parents of Czech heritage was one of Alexandra's piano students when Zina returned home from the Sorbonne. Pavel's mother had died a few years earlier, leaving the task of raising her two little boys to her husband, Lev Dvorak. An officer at the Shanghai Customs, Lev was one of the many parents from the International Settlement who sent their children to Alexandra for piano lessons.

In the classroom Zina was a natural. She intuitively understood her students and constantly sought ways to address their needs. She considered herself fortunate to be teaching in a school in which Sir Horace Kadoorie, who founded the Shanghai Jewish Youth Association, made himself accessible to the school's headmistress and faculty as they built an institution endowed with the ethos of addressing the varied needs of its students. It was abundantly clear to Horace that the youngest member of the faculty, Miss Zenaida Katzenellenbogen, was special. Impressed with her passion, her zeal, her dedication to her students, he would soon be supporting her on many a student enrichment project.

Meanwhile, at home Zina spoke nonstop about her work and about Horace's compassion and generosity towards her disenfranchised students. There was very little that escaped Alexandra who soon realized that it was impossible to have a conversation with Zina about her work without hearing in glowing, awe-inspiring terms about Horace's good deeds in support of the SJS and the Shanghai community at large.

Needless to say, Alexandra was pleased to see that, in teaching, Zina had found her life's work. But finding her life's work was not enough. In these uncertain times Zina needed to find a husband. If only Alexandra could get Zina to spend less time worrying about the welfare of her students and invest more time finding a man. To make matters worse a more growing concern was Zina's obvious fascination with Horace Kadoorie. In due course, she came to believe that Zina was enamored with this wealthy philanthropist. This realization was for Alexandra quite disconcerting. Indeed, Alexandra's second late husband, the good doctor Katzenellenbogen, was born a Jew and later converted to Russian Orthodox. Should she encourage her daughter to also marry a Jew, a wealthy one notwithstanding? Was Horace also enamored with Zina? Of this Alexandra could not be certain but it mattered little as it seemed highly unlikely that this wealthy high-society Sephardic Jewish family will open its arms to the daughter of a stateless Russian refugee. She would have to be more proactive about finding Zina a husband because, left to her own devices Zina seemed incapable. Perhaps incapable is not quite the right word. After all, Zina had grown up to be a stunningly beautiful, kind, compassionate woman capable of snaring any type of suitor. But if Zina was truly in love with Horace she will have to get over it because, as far as Alexandra was concerned her love will never be requited. In any case, from what she's read in the society pages, Horace did not seem to be the marrying kind. And even if he was, his powerful family was unlikely to allow him to buck tradition and marry below his social status and outside his religion. Besides, Horace was totally consumed with a preternatural dedication to his life of philanthropy. There was nothing more important to him than his philanthropic work.

Lev Dvorak, a widower raising two young boys, second in command at the Shanghai Customs, was fairly well-to-do and a man of considerable experience and influence. Fifteen years older than Zina, he may not have necessarily been a good match, but he ought to be a suitable one. For Alexandra, time was of the essence. By hook or by crook, for the good of her family, indeed for their very survival, she had to make some hard choices, not the least difficult of which was finding Zina a husband. Lev, it was decided, was as good a candidate as any. Arranging a marriage was necessary, even if all signs indicated that Zina's heart might lie elsewhere. Their lives as stateless citizens living in Shanghai were fraught with uncertainties. The Wall Street crash had just occurred, gripping the world in an economic crisis that would last a decade, anti-Japanese sentiments directed at the Japanese presence in China were becoming more and more pervasive causing an increase in violent incidents between these two nations. A mere twenty years after The Great War, the sounds of sabre rattling in Europe portended yet again the onset of another global conflict. Westerners living in Shanghai, especially the many stateless refugees who found a haven in this open port, were filled with anxiety at the very real possibility that a World War would cause them to be trapped like rats in a Shanghai barrel, leaving them at the mercy of Lord knows what. Not needing smoke signals to recognize the imminence of their demise, Alexandra knew that it was time to start planning an exit strategy. She did not know what the future held, what port of call she will next call home but as a descendant of generations of Russian Orthodox priests she was imbued with a great deal of old-fashioned faith that somewhere in this vast world there is a safe haven for her and her family. The more she thought of it the more she saw the potential for the widower Lev Dvorak, father of her piano student Pavel, as their ticket out of Shanghai.

A woman of faith, but also a practical woman who ardently subscribes to the philosophy 'fortune favors the bold', Alexandra was clearly a woman who never waited around for things to happen. She was a go-getter, a person who made things happen. This was true at the tender age of 18 when she married Valentin Davidov and persuaded him to accept a position as a military doctor in Eastern Siberia. A woman in charge then as she was later when she married her second husband, Zina's father Mikhail Katzenellenbogen, soon after the mysterious drowning of her first husband in the Amur

River. Not coincidentally, over time her hard-nosed, take-no-prisoners approach to life gained her the moniker General-in-skirts.

It took a little doing but Alexandra was able to convince Lev that as a widower with relatively young kids, there were practical benefits to marrying her daughter. Zina, though she dreamt of coming of age in a world where she would be swept off her feet by a young handsome admirer, she understood that 1934 Shanghai was a far cry from the world of her fairytale dreams. At another time, in another place, in a more peaceful world, Alexandra's choice of husband for her daughter would have been a much harder sell. Young, beautiful, intelligent, Zina was also pragmatic, grasping immediately the symbiotic nature of her mother's matchmaking. She was prepared to help Lev raise his boys. With the sounds of a worldwide conflict in the air, the ever-increasing Sino-Japanese skirmishes, the arrival of increasing numbers of stateless refugees, Shanghai's glory days were numbered. As a customs officer Lev, it was hoped, could be useful in helping the family find a way to get out of harm's way when the time comes.

Mrs. Katzen & son (right) with her sister and niece, Shanghai 1937

Zina and Lev were married in 1935. In 1937 their son Fyodor was born. Soon thereafter, pursuant to a transfer order by The Chinese Maritime Customs, Lev took his family to Canton (present day Guangzhou), an important port set up in the mid-18th century as a means for China to control trade with the West. Historically a major southern port, it was the main outlet for Chinese spices, tea, rhubarb, silk and handcrafted articles desired by western traders.

Lev welcomed the challenges of life as a customs officer in Canton with a new wife and baby boy. Zina, on the other hand, missed her mother, aunt and sister who were still in Shanghai. For a brief period she found a teaching position in Canton but as a working mother with a newborn baby, stepmother to 15-year-old Pavel and 8-year-old Leonid, she was soon feeling overwhelmed. She began to lobby for a return to Shanghai because she needed to be close to the most important people in her life. After fleeing the Bolsheviks, the Katzenellenbogens endured many hardships, the hardest of which was the loss of Mikhail. Since her father's death, and now that her sister Raisa was married with a family of her own, Zina naturally assumed the responsibility for the safety and welfare of her mother and aunt. Lev, who also had an extended family of sisters and aunts in Shanghai, understanding that Zina needed to be closer to her family, applied and received a transfer back to the Chinese Maritime Customs in Shanghai. Zina was quite eager to return to the classroom where she first began her teaching career. She missed terribly the culture of the Shanghai Jewish School - the laughter, the noise, the energy, the camaraderie, the joys, the disappointments, the challenges of teaching and learning unique to life in that school. A brief stint in the classroom in Canton, her life there as a home-maker taking care of the needs of three boys and a husband served, among other things, to heighten her desire to return to teaching. She was young and hadn't taught much before marriage and the birth of a son removed her from the classroom. The psychic rewards she received during her brief tenure as a teacher far outweighed anything she had heretofore experienced. She was anxious to be back in her element.

Upon her return to Shanghai the headmistress at the Shanghai Jewish School welcomed her back with open arms. The impact that young Zina had on her students and the culture of the school before she left for Canton was not lost on them.

Mrs. Katzen, her son & Chinese amah

For the next two years Zina flourished at the SJS as she honed her craft as a teacher. With the help of a Chinese amah to take care of her baby Fyodor, she put everything she had into her teaching, spending hours on end helping students, involving herself in every aspect of school life. It occurred to her that perhaps she ought to spend more time at home taking care of Fyodor but she quickly convinced herself that Fyodor was fine. With help from her Chinese amah, he was in good hands. Her students, many of whom were destitute, needed her more. If she had any misgivings, any pangs of guilt caused by the inordinate amount of time spent concerning herself with the educational and psychosocial needs of her charges, of being more of a mother to her students than she perhaps was to her son and stepsons, they were quickly dismissed.

Meanwhile the situation in Shanghai caused by the Sino-Japanese conflict and constant talk of a worldwide conflagration continued to become more and more untenable. Alexandra knew that if they did not leave soon, the family might be trapped in Shanghai. Hundreds of thousands of Chinese soldiers were on the move from the South and West even as Japanese ships filled with soldiers could be seen at anchor at the mouth of the *Yangtze Po River.*

It was time to leave.

Abooard the *Heiyo Maru* - Mrs. Katzen's sister, niece on lap, brother-in-law on her left

Thanks mainly to Horace Kadoorie's wealth and influence the family was able to obtain travel visas for ten family members. In August of 1938 Alexandra Katzenellenbogen, Evgenie Azarov (the aunt, a hospital nurse who worked with Mikhail in Siberia and whose life was saved by the good doctor after she allegedly attempted suicide by poison and who henceforth became a permanent member of the family), Alexandra's first daughter Raisa, Raisa's husband Konstantin and their daughter Anastasia boarded the Japanese ocean liner *Heiyo Maru* docked in the Bund and sailed to Kobe Japan. After a few days in Kobe boarding other passengers, the *Heiyo Maru* set forth on its trans-Pacific route to the Americas. After dropping off passengers in San Pedro, California it headed south to Valparaiso, Chile, the final port of call for Alexandra and her family.

Mrs. Katzen's husband

On October 23rd, 1939, a year and two months later, the rest of the family - Lev Dvorak, Zenaida Dvorak (this is the only time she officially used her married surname Dvorak), their two-year-old son Fyodor and Lev's two sons from his first wife (seventeen-year-old Pavel and ten-yearold Leonid) boarded the Japanese ocean liner, the *Hikawa Maru.*

The Hikawa Maru

The *Hikawa Maru* slowly pulled away from the dock, sliding past an assorted array of sampans and Japanese warships. Zina, anxious to get one last glimpse of the Bund, of her beloved Shanghai, quickly made her way to the stern of the vessel. For the second time in twenty years she was at sea fleeing a home she loved dearly. When the family fled Siberia she thought that Shanghai would be home for the rest of her life. At the age of 8 she lost Nikolaevsk-na-Amur and now at 28 she was losing Shanghai. What would happen to her students, to many of whom she had become quite attached? There was Issac, a hardworking conscientious thirteenyear-old lad who worked to help his father make ends meet after the untimely death of his mother.

Mrs. Katzen's Childhood classmate

There was Jane, her childhood classmate and very best friend. Would she ever see her again? Would she ever again see the secret love of her life, Horace Kadoorie? If he only knew how much she loved him. The kindest, wisest, most generous man she'd ever known. When he discovered that she was married he called her in Canton to congratulate her on her marriage. She in turn congratulated him on his marriage. "I am not married", he said. The Kadoorie wedding that she heard of was that of his brother, Lawrence. Later he sent her orchids from his garden, carefully arranged in a most exquisite Chinese wicker vase. The memory of the fragrant bouquet buckled her knees. Grasping the rail, she closed her eyes and took a deep breath.

She opened her eyes, allowed herself a slow sweeping glance of the iconic Greek revival and Neo-classic buildings hugging the crescent arc of the Bund. Would she ever return? If she does, will this beautiful "museum of international architecture", the fancy hotels, the banks, the exclusive clubs still be standing, or will the ravages of war reduce this beautiful waterfront to a pile of rubble? Though not visible, she could hear the distant drone of warplanes and the muted rumble of exploding bombs. Ahead she could see the bustling throngs (rickshaws, Chinese and Western pedestrians, motorcars, bicycles) on Nanjing Road as the *Hikawa Maru* inched its way out of the harbor. Quickly diverting her eyes from this faceless mass of humanity going about its business seemingly ignorant of any sense of pending doom, she chose instead to stare at the tower atop the Shanghai Customs House. Inexplicably, it kept moving further and further away. Eyes fixed on the tower's clock, she wondered how much time would elapse before the clock, the tower, the building, the rickshaws and the sampans disappeared forever.

Confused, hypnotized by the surrealism of it all, she could not be certain if she was leaving Shanghai or if Shanghai was leaving her. She released her grip on the rail and turned to go back to Lev and the boys. Her face was streaked with tears. But there was little time to be wistful. A whole New World beyond the vast Pacific awaited her. She must dry her eyes, steel herself for the challenges of a new country, a new continent. She adjusted her gait to accommodate the gentle roll of the ship and remembered how much she loved the ocean. And ships. And traveling the ocean on ships. She dabbed at her eyes. Quietly reciting Sea Fever, her favorite John Masefield poem, she could hear the seagulls calling out her name. What fortunes or ills the Americas held for her she did not know, but, as always, there was comfort in knowing that the mystical powers of the ocean will provide her with all the strength she needed.

.

◊◊

Chile

Port of call, Vancouver, British Columbia. Lev disembarked, taking Pavel and Leonid with him. He would drop them off at the home of his parents who had agreed to raise the boys, at least until the war was over. The *Hikawa Maru* then headed for Valparaiso where Zina and Fyodor disembarked and headed south by train to Puerto Montt, a town founded in 1853 after Chilean President Manuel Montt's government (1851 to 1861) sponsored the immigration of Germans to settle the region. Here, they were reunited with the rest of the family.

Priority number one for Zina was finding a teaching position. Prospects were dim or undesirable in Puerto Montt, so a few months later the Katzenellenbogens moved 105 kilometers North to the town of Orsono, in the northern Los Lagos Region, at the confluence of the Rahue and Damas rivers. The main center of agriculture and cattle farming in the region, Orsono's cultural heritage was shaped by German, Spanish and Huilliche influences.

A mathematician, a linguist (fluent in English, French, Spanish, Russian - semi-fluent in Chinese), Zina was a woman with skills, but the chances of finding the right teaching job in this Chilean outpost, that is, a position that would enable her to maximize the use of her skills, were slim. Why the Katzenellenbogens chose to settle in such a remote area of Chile is anybody's guess but after fleeing the October 17 revolution in Russia and, twenty years later, fleeing the battlefields of the Sino-Japanese War and the onset of a European war, it's not surprising that they would want to spend the rest of the days in a quiet bucolic setting far from the madding crowd.

Alexandra, Zina and Evgenie were now all alone. Zina's sister Raisa, who accompanied her to Paris in 1926 to pursue music studies at the Cortot Conservatory, her musician husband Konstantin and their daughter Anastasia moved south to Concepcion. Mikhail died not long after the family arrived in Shanghai. It is unclear why Lev failed to join the family in Chile after dropping off his sons in Canada. In fact, he seemed to have simply disappeared. No family member was ever able to account for his whereabouts. His wife Zina, his mother-in-law Alexandra and his son Fyodor never saw him again.

◊◊

Zina missed teaching. She was anxious to get back into the classroom. She also needed to do her part to help the family survive. The resources they possessed when they left China were fast depleting. Her mother, like she did in Shanghai, gave private piano lessons at home, but as they did not live in a metropolitan area of Chile, enough piano students to pay the bills were hard to come by. According to a family member Zina finally found a teaching position at *El Colegio Andrew Carnegie* in Santiago but soon realized that this school was a bad match for her. She shared her dissatisfaction with Alexandra, warning her that in all probability she would be looking elsewhere for another teaching position. Alexandra tried to discern what was wrong with the school but Zina did not explain. The students were like students anywhere. They were fairly well behaved and eager to learn. Except for a couple of blowhards, her colleagues by and large were quite collegial. Yet, there was a nagging sense of unease about the spirit of the school that refused to leave the pit of her stomach. Alexandra knew her daughter well and was familiar with Zina's exacting standards vis-à-vis what it means to be a teacher and what it means to 'do' school. She wondered if her daughter would ever find a teaching position in a school that lives up to her standards.

"If you are so dissatisfied with where you are, why don't you start your own school?" said Alexandra, the next time Zina complained about her school. Zina's eyes lit up. It was a brilliant idea. She wondered why she had not thought of it before. It made perfect sense for her to start her own school. Alexandra had done quite well for herself, successfully running the Siberian business interests of her deceased first husband, Valentin Davidov after he drowned in the Amur river. With Alexandra's business acumen and her own skills as an educator Zina immediately saw the possibilities. Alexandra was trained as a classical pianist and Zina envisioned a school where every child would be exposed to music, dance, art, in addition to everything else a school offers. Together with her mother they could create and grow an excellent institution of learning. The seeds planted, Alexandra and Zina became obsessed with the idea of founding a school and spent the next five years planning and searching for a location.

In 1941 the Japanese bombed Pearl Harbor. And Germany, having already conquered much of continental Europe let slip the dogs of war, opening up its Second Front by invading Russia. Having a close link with Germany, Chile initially chose to remain neutral but in 1943 it broke relations with the Axis powers and finally, in 1945, declared war on Japan just before the war ended. The scarcity of shipping and the demands of the American war industry caused shortages of consumer goods in Chile and most of the Latin American countries. Zina and Alexandra will have to wait until after the war to create their dream school.

There appears to be no record of Zina's presence in Chile from 19421945. According to a friend of the family during this time she worked with the Allies using her skills as a mathematician, linguist and cryptanalyst.

In 1946, after purportedly procuring a loan from a wealthy Chilean businessman, Zina opened a school in La Serena. Located in Northern Chile, La Serena is the capital of the Coquimbo Region and is the second oldest city after the capital, Santiago. She named her school *El Colegio Inglés Católico de La Serena*. Its ethos was to teach

English as a Second Language and to reinforce the tenets of the Catholic faith.

Now that she was safely ensconced in the New World, Zina made a conscious effort to shed all visible effects of her previous life in the East. She would tweak her persona just a little bit, not enough to totally lose her identity but enough to avoid the inevitable pointed questions concerning her ethnicity, nationality and religion. She converted to Catholicism and continued to use Katzen, the shortened form of Katzenellenbogen. Russia would no longer be her *pays natal.* For anyone who cared to know, she was born in Czechoslovakia. It would be a heavy yoke to be continuously looked at with suspicion. Better if the people of the Americas did not know that she was Russian.

The English Catholic School of La Serena, founded by Mrs. Katzen in 1946

El Colegio Inglés Católico would become her life, her *raison d'être*. At 35 she was relatively young, but in a way she had already lived several lifetimes. She had experienced a great deal of pain, grief, joy, had seen the ugliness, horror and the beauty of life. She had witnessed first-hand the destruction and misery caused by revolution and war.

And through it all she drew strength from her faith and from her 'old ladies', her endearing descriptor for her aunt and mother from whom she learned the essence of survival.

Happy to be alive, to have survived the horrors of the October 17 Russian revolution, to have escaped the atrocities of the Sino-Japanese War, grateful to have landed in a peaceful corner of the New World, she promised herself to never look backwards. El Colegio represented a new lease on life, a new beginning, an opportunity to make a difference and leave a positive mark on this mad and crazy world. At El Colegio she would teach her students how to read, write, add, subtract, multiply, think for themselves and be generous of spirit. They would thrive in an ethos that encourages esprit de corps, camaraderie, hard work, pride, duty and honor. They would learn how to be strong, how to march on and conquer their fears in the face of adversity. Together with her mother they composed a song that would embody the ethos of her school.

Shoulder to Shoulder
We march all
Proud of our School
And its name;
Happy and united in duty,
Learning and honour our aim.
March on, march on,
Just face things bravely
And march on;
Success will come to crown
Work that is rightly done.
When school days are over forever
And we have all scattered away
With kind thoughts
We 'll always remember
Old days of our work
And our play

Starting with 17 students, the English Catholic School grew and flourished under Zina's guidance and leadership. Alexandra was the purveyor of all things music and Hilda Soto, a retired primer ballerina from the Ballet Nacional de Chile who was befriended by Zina, oversaw the dance department. From its inception, every school year culminated in a celebration of music, dance and musical theater. Sports were also an integral part of the curriculum and every student was obligated to learn English.

La Serena was a perfect place for a private English Catholic School. In short order it became a huge success. Each progressive year the waiting list for parents trying to gain access for their children grew longer and longer.

Mrs. Katzen, faculty and students at El Colegio Inglés Católico

Zina worked very hard to keep the school small so that she and her faculty would be certain to properly address the needs of each individual student. But thanks to its prestige, to the fact that it was the only school in the region where English was taught as a second language and to its emphasis on discipline and a challenging curriculum, its reputation for excellence kept growing. Pressure was soon brought to bear by parents and the community at large to grow the school more quickly and more extensively than she originally intended. She resisted for quite some time, but eventually acquiesced. She would eventually become a casualty of her own success. By 1960, 14 years after it opened its doors, enrollment at the English Catholic School of La Serena had swollen to 400 students.

Establishing her school was a dream come true. She thrived on the challenges of running it but even more meaningful were the challenges of being a teacher. In truth, she became more than just a teacher. It was here in northern Chile where she created this gem of a school that she truly honed her craft and became a great teacher. As a wise person once said, anyone can be a teacher but it is difficult to be a great teacher. The basic requirement for being a teacher is to show up every day. Like great teachers however, for whom teaching is a vocation, a calling, she made incredible sacrifices, usually going way beyond the call of duty. Taking care of administrative minutiae was necessary and important but for her the joyful challenges of being an educator were found in the classroom. Prodding, cajoling, encouraging, scolding, nurturing. Witnessing the light bulbs go off provided her with the psychic rewards, the necessary sustenance she needed to maintain the insane number of hours she spent at school and at home planning, teaching, grading.

Leaving her mother, son and aunt in the south of Chile, she had come to this remote northern outpost town of La Serena in search of an opportunity to make her mark as an educator. The first year was a very lonely time for her. The rest of the family did not join her until she had scouted the area and decided that La Serena was the right place for her to establish her school. Although she liked the region and tolerated the climate, she found the town dull and did not feel like she had much in common with the Chileans. She had no friends to speak of and seemed to have made little effort to cultivate any. In truth, she worked too hard and neglected to make time for herself. She was always too busy and somewhat prone to wallowing in self-pity. Occasionally she would pause to reflect on how much she missed the intellectual life that was so much a part of her existence in Paris and Shanghai. She did have one friend in the region - British Consul, Victor Goudy whom she would consult on matters of importance. Whenever there was an earthquake, a frequent occurrence in Chile, she wondered if she and Alexandra had made the right choice of country for refuge. However, with Alexandra at her side and with the help of a good faculty they worked hard to create a good learning environment at the English Catholic School - the kind of environment to which the parents of La Serena were happy to send their kids. She was so well thought of in the region that *El Municipio de La Serena* would posthumously name a plaza in her honor.

Then, almost without warning, or perhaps because she was too busy 'doing school' to see it coming, things began to take a turn for the worse. It started when she first began hearing whispers that there was a grassroots movement afoot to take over ownership of the school.

The students at her school flourished under her leadership and guidance and in six years the school had gained a reputation for excellence. Her intent was to keep the school small but having ceded to overwhelming community pressure to expand, she suddenly found herself in the position where others thought it was now too big for her to manage on her own. Not that she didn't agree with them. Managing the financial and other managerial aspects of the school was already more than she could handle and although she pretended otherwise, she was secretly relieved that a solution might be on the horizon. In 1956 the local municipality proposed that the school be turned into an Anonymous Partnership Corporation, and recommended that the Honorary Archbishop Alfredo Cifuentes be instituted as President. In 1958, twelve years after the school opened its doors, the Ministry of Finance, through the Superintendency of Corporations approved the proposal.

Zina's father, Dr. Mikhail Katzenellenbogen, was a very important man of influence in Nikolaevsk-na-Amur and her mother, before the family fled Russia, was a successful business woman, also influential in her own right. With the creation and success of *El Colegio Inglés Católico*, Zina had quickly become a woman of note in the region.

Losing full ownership of the institution that brought her to prominence was nevertheless a blow to her pride and her psyche. Intelligent, a savvy educator, somewhat of a visionary, a great planner and organizer, the boss, the one who called all of the shots, she enjoyed being in total control of her enterprise. Understanding that the change had to be made, however, did little to mitigate her feeling of betrayal. The La Serena community did encourage her to stay on as Head Mistress and continue working her magic in the classroom but the process of how shares were to be divided was somewhat messy and would leave a permanently bad taste in her mouth.

She worked at the school for another four years before deciding to seek another position elsewhere. These were the most difficult years of her professional life. Having lost the power and prestige of full ownership of a successful school and having to regularly face people who 'conspired' against her was more than a little trying. She seriously thought about immediately resigning but having birthed the English Catholic School it was quite difficult for her to turn her back on her 'baby', even in the face of the pending 'divorce'. She swallowed her pride, because staying on gave her the opportunity to see and help usher in the transition, making certain as best she could that the ethos of the school remained intact. Besides, as the only meaningful breadwinner at home, her little old ladies depended on her.

But losing her school weighed heavily on her and took a heavy toll. She gradually became embittered, cynical, paranoid even. Feeling lonely and disappointed, she frequently became overwhelmed with bouts of nostalgia. She missed the circle of friends she had in China. She especially missed her Queen of the Orient, the nickname given to Shanghai in the 1920s and 1930s. Seven years now since the war ended and she wondered again about the fate of her childhood friend Jane and the secret love of her life, Horace. The Kadoorie family had its share of tragedy during the war, losing a great deal of its fortune. Horace's father, Sir Elly Kadoorie, was imprisoned in Cha Pei camp in Shanghai during the Japanese occupation of Eastern China after a great deal of his assets were confiscated, including Sir Elly's prized Peninsula Hotel. The occupying Japanese used it as their headquarters. In Shanghai, the triumphant Chinese Communist armies also seized Marble House, the family's mansion on Bubbling Well Road, allegedly turning it into an indoctrination center for children. She was ecstatic to learn that Horace and his brother Lawrence were alive and safe in Hong Kong. Somehow, she must get Horace's address and write to him. She remembered fondly that he was a great listener. She needed him. He would be sure to have the right words to make her feel better, to rescue her from her depths of despair - that is, if the war had not changed him. Besides, he might be able to help her find her childhood friend and classmate Jane, if she was still alive.

Horace, having witnessed the work of this 23-year-old dynamo when she was first hired to teach at the Shanghai Jewish School, did not know how she and her family had fared after they fled Shanghai in 1939. Since arriving in Chile she had made several attempts to find him but with the world in turmoil none of the many letters she wrote reached him. In 1951, twelve years after he last saw her, he was quite surprised and pleased to receive a postcard from Zina.

His letter of response began a long correspondence that saw many a missive traverse the oceans as the tycoon, philanthropist businessman in Hong Kong and his secret admirer schoolteacher in Chile caught up on their respective lives after the war.

"I have just heard from Mrs. Vera Levy that you are living in Hong Kong", wrote Zina. "I am writing this short note right away and hope that it will reach you. If it does, will you answer it? Please, just let me know how you are. I have written to you many times but have never received an answer and would be so happy to know that you are well. I am not writing any more as I don't know whether you will get this note or answer it. I do hope you are well. Till then."

In less than two weeks she had received Horace's response.

"Thank you for your card of October 24, which I was really glad to receive. It is indeed a long time since I have heard from you and I have often wondered where you are and how you are getting on. You mentioned that you have written to me many times but never received an answer. I regret to say that your letters must have gone astray, for had I received them I would naturally have answered them promptly.

Yes, I am now in Hong Kong. Conditions in Shanghai are abominable and I left just prior to the communist arrival. You will be interested to know that both schools, the Seymour Road and S.J.Y.A. (Shanghai Jewish Youth Association) are now closed due primarily to the fact that most of the children have left. There still remain about 1,700 Jews in all China, and most of them will I hope be leaving shortly. That is one of the voluntary jobs which my brother and I tackle in Hong Kong. We represent the American Jewish Joint Distribution Committee here.

What have you been doing with yourself? I think it is a safe bet that you must be teaching, for that is your life's work. I can never forget the debt of gratitude we all owe you for the assistance you gave us to help our poor children in Shanghai.

What is Chile like? It is one of the few countries I have never visited. I have just returned from a two months holiday in Australia, a wonderful country with great possibilities for anyone who is prepared to work hard.

Conditions in Hong Kong are none too bad despite the American embargo, which unfortunately has caused much unemployment. However, they now realize that Hong Kong is the show-window of democracy and if they wish to keep the people happy it is necessary to give them employment. In actual fact, very few goods manufactured here do go to China, most of them are sent to Europe, India and even America. I trust that you are well. With every good wish."

It had been 12 long years since she last saw Horace, since she, her family and thousands of other refugees fled Shanghai. Ecstatic that she had at long last reestablished contact with her idol, her secret love, the person who meant the most to her in this entire world (with the possible exception of her mother, son and aunt), in less than two weeks after receiving Horace's letter a response was in the mail bringing him up to date with news of herself and her family.

"I can't tell you how happy I was to receive a letter from you and to know that you are well and safe. It is so like you to go on working always for the welfare of other people, it does not surprise me to hear that you are still helping others to leave China and make better homes elsewhere.

We are also in your debt for the same reason.

We are now living in La Serena, where, as you have guessed, I am teaching, in a little school. It is my own school; I have started it six years ago with no support, financial or moral, from anybody - just on my own - with only seventeen pupils. At first it was quite a struggle. Nobody knew me here. La Serena is a dreadfully old-fashioned, sleepy town where everybody seems to know the maiden names of everybody else's great grandmother and their ancestry to Christopher Columbus, so it was quite a job for me to get even seventeen pupils, seeing that nobody knew where I had sprung from. However, I managed to keep afloat and by the end of the year had forty-four pupils and could have my mother and my aunt come to La Serena to come live with me. Until then it was dreadfully lonely. Now we are doing fine, I have five classes and more pupils that I can possible take, so thank God, we can relax a little and live quietly.

You say you have never visited Chile. Well I hope you may come here one day. The country in some parts is really beautiful - snow-capped mountains like in Switzerland, forests, rivers with trout in them and beautiful lakes. It could develop into a powerful country, for there are great possibilities in agriculture, mining and oil, but it will never do so because of the people. I think it would be impossible to find another nation as lazy, dirty and lacking in honor or principles as this one. Nobody seems to have the remotest idea of a sense of duty or even decency. You can't imagine the battles I have to wage with my children in the school to teach them just plain honesty, some kind of idea of their duties and even truthfulness. Still, I like it here and of course I love my work. I am happy only when I can teach, when I can give those little children some interest in study and, in many cases, the affection that they lack at home. I love children, after all they are the only human beings worth loving.

I have been writing to you so much about myself, so now please, will you tell me something about yourself? What are you doing now?

What is your work, how is life in Hong Kong and in particular how are you feeling? It is such a relief to know that nothing has happened to you during the war occupation and that you are relatively safe in Hong Kong. Has it changed much? My last memories of Hong Kong are of the lovely drives about the island. Do you still remember those lovely bougainvillea that were growing there? The sight of those flowers we have here always makes me think of Hong Kong. Please write when you have time. You can't imagine what pleasure your letter has given me."

Horace seemed to have been genuinely happy to reconnect with Zina. As a well-known philanthropist who did so much for so many stateless refugees seeking refuge in Shanghai in the 1920s and 1930s, he must have especially wondered about the fate of Zina, a star teacher at the Shanghai Jewish School, after the communists arrived and the Europeans living in Shanghai began to leave by the thousands. Although happy to finally get word that she and her family were alive and well, given his kind and generous heart and his naturally cheerful optimism, he must have been somewhat saddened, however, after reading her letter which in parts was touched with a *soupçon* of bitter sarcasm and self-pity. We will never know Horace's immediate gut reaction to the pessimism, the anger, the pain expressed in her letter but he must have been surprised to hear her describe herself as a misanthrope. This was definitely not the intelligent, kindhearted, young (twenty something) whippersnapper who taught in Shanghai and worked alongside him in helping poor children. Given his generosity of spirit and his abundance of compassion he understood that although she was still relatively young (she was now 40), she had already experienced more than a lifetime of hardship, having survived a revolution in Russia and a war in China. He responded, ignoring all negative aspects of her letter, commenting only on the positive.

"Thank you for your long and most interesting letter. Bravo to you on having, without any financial or moral aid, been able to start your own school. I can well imagine the difficulties you must have had in a new country, knowing no one and with little funds. Difficulties are given one to overcome and in conquering them one builds one's own character. You certainly are doing a wonderful job helping pupils who from the descriptions in your letter seem to need help more than most children in other countries.

I am so glad your mother and your aunt are now with you, for it must have been lonely being by yourself. It does not surprise me in the least that you love your work and are happy, for real happiness only comes from giving more than one takes from life. I can well imagine how happy the children are at school.

You asked about Hong Kong and myself. Well, Hong Kong has certainly grown. It now has a population of 2,750,000. It is a haven for refugees, both rich and poor, who flee from communist China and at the same time is the show-window of democracy. Many industrialists who managed to escape have built factories here and are doing remarkably well. Labour is also reasonably content, for conditions here are far better than what they were used to in China. Most factories, and there are over 60 different types, supply goods to all parts of the world but very little goes into China proper.

Unfortunately, it is very difficult for many of the very poor people. They have built squatters houses all over the mountainside, but as these houses are built of timber and huddled close together, we have serious fires. Last Wednesday 15,000 were rendered homeless and penniless and last night a further 50. I have suggested the opening up of more land in order that these squatters might become small farmers, but at the moment this is impossible.

You mention the beautiful bougainvillea you saw on your visit to Hong Kong. On my recent journey to Australia I brought back some 40 different types of flowers, shrubs and plants, which in due course will be planted along the country roads and hills.

We have taken a particular interest in helping the farmers who have been having a very hard time. The Kadoorie Agricultural Aid Association has been in operation for 10 months. Our main goal is to help the very poor. There are now many villages in which every family has been given free chickens or pigs by this Association. They are also given interest free loans and encouraged in every way. I am convinced that they will, with our help, be able to earn their livelihood within two and a half years. This letter is becoming overlong so I will end."

Nine years went by with little or no communication between Horace and Zina. By the time communication between the two resumed in earnest in 1960, things had gotten progressively worse for Zina in La Serena. So bad in fact, she was ready to throw in the towel.

"I was so happy to receive your letter, it was a great treat to have an answer so soon. Of course you are quite right when you say that there are few occupations as constructive as teaching. I quite agree with you - if you work in a congenial environment. However, in Chile generally, and in La Serena in particular, it is not the case. As I mentioned in my last letter, I had to engage five new teachers. I have interviewed twice that number and not one of them showed any interest to build youth up both morally and mentally. The one and only question they all asked was; 'What do you pay?' Each one tries to give as little as he can and receive as much money as possible. They don't care two pence for the children, nor do they take any pains to impart knowledge - supposing they do possess it, which is sometimes quite doubtful. One of them placed Hong Kong in Japan, another, a French teacher, was quite unable to carry on a conversation with me in that language, while a third, a Maths teacher, just shuddered when he heard me say that homework was to be given regularly and corrected personally by the teacher, and not during class hours. He had not given a single problem for homework for the last five years in the State school, deeming it a useless practice.

As for discipline, they think nothing of being an hour late, or not turning up at all without previous notice. Can you imagine the lovely time I have with a staff of 27 teachers of which just two are more or less reliable?

As for the pupils, well, I've never come across such sorry specimens. Sometimes I have the impression of working in an establishment for the mentally deficient or for youthful delinquents. Such laziness, stupidity, dishonesty and lack of interest that I have to battle against all day are hard to find. Yet those very same children are full of initiative when they try to evade study or prepare some unpleasantness. School opens next week. Everything is ready, the classrooms beautifully cleaned, desks painted and varnished, pictures on the walls, new books and toys on the shelves. A week later it will be in shambles, dirty, all the toys broken or stolen, pictures and books torn and soiled and obscene words scratched into the paint. Before you attempt to impart knowledge to these children you have to instill some sense of decency into them, for they have absolutely no idea of honor, duty, moral cleanliness or respect for anybody or anything. The parents are still worse, you can't expect any help from them. I've had this school for almost fifteen years. True, I do get results, but at what price! My day starts at 6:15 am and I go to bed at midnight. The children come to school at 8 in the morning and the older ones go home at 8 in the evening for I keep them all here to supervise their homework and to make up for the teachers' omissions. I take 15 minutes off for lunch and 15 for tea. The rest of my time is spent in teaching, supervising work and play, and talks with the children - and after dinner I do my corrections, 200 copy books a day. On Saturdays I have to interview parents and prepare my class for the week and that takes up almost all of Sunday as well. My only luxury is a walk that I take on Sunday afternoon. I get 100% pass in government exams, but it is sheer slavery. Perhaps you can understand how tired and discouraged I am sometimes. I feel as if I were battling and struggling all alone against huge waves, using all my strength and energy and knowing beforehand that I'll hardly make any headway at all. When I taught in France, in Shanghai and Canton, things were different. I loved my work, but now it often fills me with bitterness. Do you wonder that I want a change?

I know that teaching is second nature to me, it's in my blood, but I'm afraid I shan't be able to continue practicing much longer in this country.

I'm sorry that I've written perhaps too strongly and certainly too much on the subject, but it is just an answer to your statement about a change of occupation bringing me unhappiness. It is not teaching that I wish to give up, it is only teaching in Chile that I can't carry on, for it is making me terribly unhappy. I'd go to any part of the world and teach with pleasure, in a normal school, with normal children who would not look upon me as an enemy. I do not feel any pangs of conscience when I think of leaving the school, for my work is completed. The school has attained success and enjoys a splendid reputation. A competent person can run it easily. Well, enough on the subject.

Please write again soon. I always enjoy your letters and look forward to them. I have no friends here, and your little blue envelopes cheer me up greatly and remind me of the happy days spent in faraway China."

Impatient for a response and anxious to tell him of her latest plans, she dispatched another letter to Hong Kong.

"My last letter to you left over a month ago, and I think that either it went off to some other part of the world, or the man in the post office just pinched the stamps and threw the letter away, which happens quite often in South America. On the other hand, it might have reached you and you have been so bored by the outpouring of my woes, that it has gone in the waste paper basket at once or has been relegated to some bottom draw to be forgotten as quickly as possible. However, I'm writing once again; if you don't feel like answering, never mind, don't, I'll understand.

School has started a month ago and I have my hands full with all the troubles that 27 lazy incompetent teachers and 260 undisciplined and spoilt children can give me. Besides, there are all my own classes, corrections, supervision, administrating and all sorts of odds and ends so that I have been quite submerged by this tide of work and am beginning to feel the effects of it already. I have the presentiment that if I don't escape soon, it'll crush me, just like a Juggernaut.

Perhaps it was a coincidence or telepathy, or wishful thinking but last week I received the Educational Supplement of the Times from the Consulate, and in it I came across several advertisements offering work to teachers overseas. It was too late to apply for them now, as the paper was over 3 months old, but there were many useful addresses so I have written to some of them, to the Colonial Office in London, to the Director of the Teachers' Association of the Commonwealth and to a placement bureau in the United States, inquiring about teaching positions in any part of the world except Chile. I hope some interesting answer will be forthcoming, for if I could find a post anywhere, I'd leave Chile in December after completing the present school year for the *Colegio Inglés* is in perfect, smooth running order, and I would not harm anybody by leaving. Could you give me some advice as to where to apply for a job? I'm so tired of Chile in general and La Serena in particular, that I'd accept a position even on the moon if such were available.

There is another thing I want to consult you about. I would like to get in touch with an old friend of mine, a Chinese girl by the name of Jane Ying. We were schoolmates and after my settling down in Chile we kept up a regular correspondence. Then when the trouble in Shanghai started, she left her job at the Henningsen Produce Co., married a Chinese called Zeng, and sought refuge in the interior of China. She promised to let me know her whereabouts, but has not done so. Zeng being such a common name I should think it would be rather difficult to trace her. Is there any society that I could apply to?"

Horace, always the gentleman, tried tactfully to show her the value of staying in Chile and fighting her way through her difficulties.

"I can well understand your feelings, which are but natural. A perfectionist faced with the problems you have mentioned naturally feels let down, but these very problems, when overcome, build up our characters and enable us to fight with renewed strength for the betterment of the world in general."

Horace always knew that Madame Katzen would never give up teaching - but as a way of reminding her that her work was invaluable, he included in his letter the following story written by a Texas teacher.

The night before, I had attended an incredibly long (three hours long, to be exact) PTA meeting. Today nothing had gone right. My 30 first-graders seemed to squirm restlessly all-day long. The reading classes were hopelessly bogged down; in fact, they were obviously moving backward. At noon the principal called me in. I had forgotten to turn in an important report - not only forgotten it but seemingly lost it. The two playground periods were hot, windy, and gritty with Panhandle dust. The grand straw fell, I thought, when I snagged my last good nylons before school was out.

But more was to happen. As the final bell rang, Mrs. Jones burst into the room, weeping because her Mary was no longer in the top reading group. (This year Mary had had mumps, measles and chicken pox, and as her mother kept her home every time she sniffled, she had already missed 37 days.) I tried to placate Mrs. Jones, and yet retain a few shreds of good humor.

At four o'clock I yearned to go home to a relaxing tub. But today was our last grade-level meeting of the year. A distinguished out-of-town educator was to be our speaker. She talked until after five o'clock about the new era that was coming in education, and how, to be prepared for it, we must ever be professional-minded. The longer she talked, the less professional I felt. She seemed to know all my secret sins as a teacher.

When the meeting was over, I hurried to the grocery store, where the cost of bread, milk and cold cuts did little to lift my spirits. I dashed home to two teen-age sons, an eight-year-old daughter and a house that looked entirely too "lived-in." Dumping the bread and bologna on the table for the kids to eat, I snatched an apple for myself and crawled into the family car as my husband headed it toward Amarillo, some 50 miles away.

Tonight was our 'back-to-school' night. We were attending a weekly class in Amarillo, working towards the master's degrees the school board now required.

Too tired to talk, I slumped wearily in the car and began a mental review of my day. It was even worse in retrospect. That's when the idea struck me: I would stop teaching school!

There's more to life than this, I thought, and I mean to find it. I'll write a book…. I'll grow a garden…. I'll do something. But I won't teach school!

In the Amarillo class, I collapsed in my seat and did not even try to listen to the teacher. What was the use? I wouldn't be coming back.

The teacher talked on and on. Finally, the 15-minute break came. Then the friendly woman from Spearman who sat next to me leaned over and said, "I saw an admirer of yours the other day."

I sat up straight, weariness put aside. (Some long-forgotten swain still carrying the torch?) "Oh," I murmured politely, and, I hoped, not too eagerly.

I listened raptly while she continued: "I was in the bus station last week, waiting for my son, when I noticed a Mexican woman and her little girl. The mother didn't speak English, but I talked with the little girl. She told me they were on their way to Colorado to join her father. She said that she was in the second grade, and told me her teacher's name. Then she took from her pocket a worn little billfold, and pulled out a photograph. 'This is the teacher I really love,' she said. I was astonished to recognize your picture, faded and ragged and almost worn-out.

When I said I knew you and she told her mother, they beamed with joy and acted as if they wanted to kiss me, she added.

I tried to remember the Latin Americans in last year's class." "Julia? Was her name Julia?" I asked. "No? Could it have been Adelina?"

"Yes, Adelina was her name," the woman from Spearman said.

My heart swelled as I thought of Adelina. Her parents were fresh from Old Mexico. Neither could speak English, but there was an aura of happiness among them, and they were so proud of their only child. They had just left the cotton fields down near Lubbock when they brought Adelina into my classroom in late November. Wearing a clean, crisply starched, hand-medown dress too large for her, Adelina came in with her head bowed and a scared look on her face. She was so tiny, so clean and so lovable that the pupils accepted her immediately, and the frightened look gave way to a happy, beaming expression that never left her. Her cheery smile won everyone in the room.

She was a bright girl, and she was reading fluently in the junior primer when her parents took her from our school three months later. I had often wondered what happened to her.

I thanked the friendly woman from Spearman and tried to tell her what an inspiration her story was to me. My words were inadequate - it's easier to write than talk. Perhaps she will read this someday, and then she will understand what I was trying to tell her.

On the way home, I sat silently, thinking, and I made another decision: I'll not stop teaching school!

Once again my faith is renewed, and I feel inspired. I'll work out something for my reading groups. I'll try a different approach with Mrs. Jones, and I'll find that blanket-blank report before I go to bed. I may not be professionalminded with my teaching, but I'll be happy in doing the best that I can each day. No, I won't stop teaching school. No book that I could write, no flower that I might ever grow could send me love and inspiration on a dreary day.

When I am very old and no longer teach the very young, the thought of Adelina's small face as she innocently showed my picture to a stranger in a bus station will never cease to warm my heart. Stop teaching school? Why, what would I do?

"I note that after reading the Education Supplement of the Times you have written various letters enquiring about teaching posts in other parts of the world," continued Horace. I have no doubt whatsoever that they would welcome the opportunity to have such an experienced teacher as yourself, but you must remember that you may not be appointed principal of the school and might therefore be subjected to various annoyances due to things not being run in a manner to your liking.

It really boils down to being the boss and having the headaches that go with this privilege, or taking a minor position and, though not having as many responsibilities, often being frustrated through watching others do the job in a way which does not always meet with your approval.

At long last I have managed to trace your friend Jane Ying. She is delighted to hear of your whereabouts and I have no doubt she will be writing to you in the near future. You were wrong in saying that she married a Chinese called Zeng. Her family name was Zeng and she married a Mr. Ying who, I am sorry to say, died within 5 years after marriage. I understand Mrs. Ying has two sons, one in America, and she has to work very hard to support her family and herself. Her health is now much better and she has a good job with the American International Underwriters. Her address is 27A Nathan Road, Kowloon, Hong Kong."

"You are a most wonderful person! Thank you again and again for finding my Jane. She is the only friend that I have ever had, and I do not know how to thank you for tracing her. What a job you must have had, with my giving you all the wrong names! Probably you were looking all over China and then discovered her practically right on your doorstep. I received your letter yesterday, and this morning hers arrived. I can't tell you how thrilled I was to receive it. I think you are the only man I've ever met who has such a rare and beautiful faculty of bringing happiness to others.

I have received several answers to the letters I have written to the Colonial Office Overseas Appointments Bureau, and others. All very courteous, but all to the same effect, and they have left me very despondent. It seems nobody wants me - the main reason being that I am not a British subject, nor a graduate of a United Kingdom University. I am very disappointed, as I have been pinning all my hopes on getting a favourable reply from some part of the world and leaving my present hateful habitat. You are quite mistaken in thinking that I'd like to have a principal's job. On the contrary, I have not even for a moment entertained the idea of getting the position of headmistress. Far from it, that is the last position I'd like to obtain. I'd like to be just a plain school-teacher, so as to give all my time to children only, to teach them, give them the affection and understanding that they need so often, and in no case administrate a school and carry this awful load which lies like dead weight on my shoulders and hardly leaves me anytime at all for the work I love.

Well there are still two answers due, one from Australia, the other from the Leeward Islands. Perhaps I'll have better luck there. In the meantime, if you were to hear of a vacancy for a teacher somewhere, please remember me, and if you remember me, you may be quite sure that I will fulfill the most exacting expectations, for I am full of energy and with all the experience accumulated here, can cope with any educational problem successfully.

Thanking you once again for your kindness, especially in answering my letters, for I can imagine how terribly busy you must be."

Zina had also written letters to both Jane and Horace asking for their assessment of her chances for obtaining a teaching position in Hong Kong. How marvelous it would be if she could find a position there, right next to her recently found childhood friend Jane and the secret love of her life Horace. True to form, Horace obliged her and in short order sent her the information she needed to make a decision on whether or not to relocate to Hong Kong.

"As you rightly say, it is difficult for one person to give another advice of the nature you request but I will try to give you a picture of general conditions here in order to help you form your own opinion.

Passport - I feel the Immigration Authorities would probably permit you to reside in the Colony provided (a) you have a valid passport which, if necessary, would enable you to return to the country it represents, and (b) you have sufficient funds for a return passage and you will not become a burden on the community, which of course would not be the case.

Passage - Cook's inform me that Tourist Class air passage from Santiago [Chile], via Vancouver to Hong Kong would cost

US$1,013. Whereas, by steamer it would depend on the particular freighter available. There is a fixed passage once a month from Valparaiso to Los Angeles for US$565, then the journey from Los Angeles to Hong Kong could cost anywhere between US$425 and US$550. It may be worth your while to investigate the possibilities of:

(1)   seeing if you get a chartered flight to Hong Kong, or for at least part of the way here.

(2)   coming on a cargo boat. These usually have cabins for about 12 passengers and if you are a good sailor and not in too great a hurry, the trip would be more comfortable and restful and, of course, would have the advantage of permitting you to bring more baggage than by plane.

Hong Kong is a far more beautiful place than Shanghai, with a magnificent harbor, hills, beaches, etc. However, it is overcrowded and there is a continual water shortage, which means that one can only have water from the tap at certain hours during the day.

The best months are from October to January when the weather is perfect. From February to April it is very humid. May to September is hot - not as hot as in Shanghai, but the humidity ranges from 85% to 100%.

Accommodation - Flats are difficult to obtain but can be found. They cost roughly as follows: -

(a)   1-room flat with bathroom and kitchen - HK$450 per month (approx. US$80)

(b)   2-room flat with bathroom and kitchen - HK$550 per month (approx. US$90)

(c)   3-room flat with bathroom and kitchen - HK$750 per month (approx. US$120)

To this must be added 17.5% for rates or taxes payable to Government.

Income Tax is 12.5% but likely to go up shortly.

Political Situation - At the moment all seems peaceful and quiet. To my mind it will probably remain so, as long as we are useful to China, but you must bear in mind that if the Chinese wish to take Hong Kong there is nothing to prevent them from doing so and one must therefore be prepared to leave at some time or other. In this respect I feel like the Leeward Islands (though I know little about them) would be a safer place to live.

I am afraid it is not correct to say that I can influence the Education Department. However, on receipt of your letter I promptly enquired of the Director of Education, the Honorable D.J.S. Crozier, C.M.G. His reply, enclosed forthwith, is self-explanatory.

Unfortunately, I am unable to tell you what the salaries are like as these depend entirely on the position offered. I have given Mr. Crozier my personal opinion of your capabilities and, needless to say, this meant a very high recommendation. I would not suggest a position in any school except a government run institution or a few of the leading grant-in-aid schools.

I hope the above will be of assistance to you in making up your mind. You have had experience of the Communists coming into Shanghai and this is why I have stressed the political situation. Apart from all the information given above, I personally would recommend that you think very carefully before deciding to leave Chile where you have built a name for yourself. Wherever you go you will have to start from scratch all over again and whilst your teaching experience will, I am sure, hold you in good stead, it is not quite the same thing. I sincerely hope my remarks are helpful and will not confuse you further."

"It is indeed very kind of you to take such trouble to give me so much of your valuable time to answer so clearly and circumstantially. I know how dreadfully busy you are and I appreciate it greatly - my debt to you seems to be growing all the time. However now I have a much clearer idea of Hong Kong, seeing it through your eyes and not only through my dear Jane's rosy-tinted spectacles.

Thanks for the information about the passage; it is almost the same as I was given here. If I were to undertake this trip (to Hong

Kong), I'd do it only by sea, and by a twelve-passenger cargo boat at that. I have travelled so much on that type of vessel that I feel thoroughly at home on them and would not dream of traveling any other way. However, there are ever so many other things to settle before dreaming of traveling.

To begin by the end of your letter, I know your advice about thinking twice before leaving Chile is very sensible, but if you knew how utterly exhausted I am by my work here I'm sure you'll understand my desire to leave. Granted I have made a name for myself, that I am respected and esteemed by everybody - but the other side of the medal? The fifteen-odd hours of grueling work daily, the teaching, the corrections, the administration of the whole school, the continuous nervous tension, all the disappointments and disillusions, the bitterness and the responsibility? I've come to the end of my tether and I have to escape - for better or for worse. I have the impression that you think I'll miss the position of headmistress and find myself if not exactly degraded, then disappointed in doing the work of just a plain teacher. As they say in Chile - after being the lion's head I shall become the mouse's tail!

What of course is very serious, is the fact that Hong Kong now is safe, but as you say, there is no guaranty that it will continue to do so, and if it might be taken nobody knows how people such as I would fare in that case. Jane of course is different - speaking Chinese, being Chinese - a fact that would help her escape, and what would happen to me is something else again. The political situation is the first drawback, if not the only one. The second might be financial, for according to your letter and by Chilean standards, flats seem to be very expensive and probably the rest of the expenses are on the same scale. Of course, as we do not know the amount of a teacher's salary in Hong Kong, it is impossible to judge whether it is within a simple teacher's means to make a living there or not, and that brings me to your information about the education Department. It is very kind of you to consult the Honorable D. Crozier and very thoughtful of you to enclose his answer - and once again, thanks for the testimonial you have given me. I truly hope I shall be able to live up to it. I am writing to him by this same mail, giving all the particulars of my education, training and qualifications, and requesting him to let me know if there is any possibility of employment.

If I were to listen only to reason and logic, of course it is more sensible for me to accept the position in the Leeward Islands and forget about Hong Kong. Politically it is safer, being nearer Chile it is much easier to move there and come back by the time the contract ends if I don't like it. I could even assure my retreat by leaving some property here and not selling my shares of the School Company. But I know nothing at all about the Leeward Islands. It seems the headmaster is very keen on having me come over and take up duties there, even willing to wait until I windup all my affairs here in December [1960]. It sounds strange, this patience. Of course the contract is a government affair, it should be a serious position, but for all I know I might end up on a tiny mud island with a palm-leaf shack for a school and just a couple of little black children for pupils.

Anyhow, as I have to give a final answer in about 3 weeks' time, I shall wait for a reply from the Honorable D. Crozier before signing the contract and then keep my fingers crossed and hope for the best. I know it is going to be a great shock to Jane if I don't go to Hong Kong [but] after weighing all the pros and cons in your letter I think it is wiser for me to go to St. Kitts. Perhaps Jane will come and visit me and we shall spend our ripe old age in that tropical paradise. On the other hand, if it proves to be the opposite, well, then I might still try my luck in Hong Kong.

Once again, thank you for all you have done. I could have been very happy to have gone to Hong Kong and seen you - I might yet - but if God wills otherwise, well, I suppose one must just resign oneself. But please, if you ever have a free moment, will you drop me a few lines from time to time, for friendship's sake? With best wishes for your health and happiness."

Meanwhile the Honorable Douglas Crozier (head of the Department of Education in Hong Kong) responds to Horace's letter, written on behalf of Mrs. Katzen.

"I am afraid Miss Katzen's letter (returned herewith) gives too little information on her qualifications and experience to enable me to indicate with confidence how she would be employed in Hong Kong. She obviously possesses some professional qualifications, but much would depend on whether she is a university graduate or not, and on her teaching subjects. A certified teacher (non-graduate) with suitable experience might well obtain an appointment in a grant-in-aid school or in a governmentmaintained primary school for English-speaking children on a non-pensionable basis, but she might not succeed in obtaining what used to be called expatriate terms of service, that is, paid home leave, medical facilities, etc.

For appointment to the highest grade of teaching post in Government Secondary Schools, a good Honours Degree, Diploma or Certificate of Education and three years approved teaching experience are the minimum requirements. In subjects such as Music, Art and Domestic Science, equivalent qualifications are accepted.

If Miss Katzen should require further any more detailed information regarding appointments to government schools I would suggest that she write either to this Department or to the Colonial Office. Appointments to aided schools rest with the schools themselves, and enquiries might be addressed to them. If you would like me to send you a list of such schools I would gladly do so."

On May 22, 1960, Chile was hit by the most powerful earthquake ever recorded. In response to news of this devastating earthquake and ensuing tsunami, Horace wrote:

"We have been reading in the papers of the terrible earthquakes and tidal waves in Chile, and naturally my thoughts hasten to you. I do hope that you and your mother are well and that your school has not been damaged. I can well imagine how busy you must be trying to help those who have suffered in the disasters.

Two weeks ago we had a flood in the New Territories - a cloudburst that brought almost 16" of rain in a few hours. It caused some loss of life and damage. Flood relief committees have been formed to assist the villagers and, I am glad to say, things are gradually returning to normal."

"Thank you for your kind letter and sympathy in the midst of this tragedy, sorrow and turmoil. It is very comforting and soothing to know that someone was concerned about us and gave us a kind thought. Here, thank God we are well, but the catastrophe in the south is indeed horrible. Entire villages on the coast have been swept away by the tidal waves and whole towns have been destroyed by the earthquakes. Houses have collapsed burying the inhabitants under their own walls, for the first earthquake occurred at dawn, while everybody was still asleep. The plight of the survivors was really dreadful - all means of communications were severed, there was no light, no gas and no water as all the pipes and sewage canals had burst. There was no safe shelter, for violent tremors continued for days and people did not dare enter the few houses that were still standing. Many spent their nights in the streets and were absolutely drenched by the rains for it is the rainy season now in the south of Chile. Their suffering must have been awful and always coupled with fear. I don't know whether you have ever experienced earthquakes. There is nothing that I fear more, you feel so absolutely hopeless and helpless, for there is nothing you can do and you never know how the tremor will end, whether it will die down gradually or produce a cataclysm.

No help could be sent down south immediately, for there was no way of transporting things. Bridges had been destroyed, railway tracks disrupted and aerodromes damaged. The only news to be had was by wireless and it was appalling. Besides that, all day they read endless lists of dead and injured and frantic appeals for news of relatives and friends from all other parts of Chile. Yet it is really wonderful how the whole world has responded. Even my pupils wanted to help and we made up 90 bundles of warm clothing, shoes, powdered milk and other food stuff and forwarded them to Concepcion with the first jeeps that managed to get through - a drop in the ocean, but still something. We collected quite a large sum of money too and sent that down as well. Now things are much better. The tremors still continue but not so intensely and houses are being repaired. However, the people who have had this ghastly experience are still dazed, nervous and ill.

Changing the subject, I have had a letter from the Department of Education in Australia, New South Wales, to be exact, and although it did not contain an offer of a position, it did contain a promise to keep my application and consider it for future vacancy. So I'm keeping my fingers crossed and hoping that one will be forthcoming. No Answer yet from the Leeward Islands. I suppose that the letter did not get there for people at our post office did not know where to send it and I had quite an argument with them about the position of these islands. I hope you are well and are not working too hard. Thank you once again for your kindness."

"It's ages since I've heard from you", wrote Zina two months later. "I hope this is not due to ill health but simply to lack of time and pressure of work and business, and here am I taking away some more of your precious minutes, sending you another of my long and perhaps not very welcome letters. However, I'm very selfish and because the matter is very important to me I'm encroaching on your free moments to consult you, and impose again on your kindness. Unwittingly you have started all this, for it all began with your finding my friend Jane for me. As I told you, we've been very close friends ever since our pigtail school days, and now that she has reappeared we're both delighted and just dream of getting together again. I'm terribly lonely in Chile, a country in which as I've mentioned to you before, I'm not happy at all, and which I've been thinking of leaving many times. Jane is trying to convince me to move with all my goods and chattels back to China, or rather Hong Kong, assuring me that I'll get a position in any school there and making enticing rosy plans for a future together. As for the political situation, she says that she feels things will continue in status quo for quite a while and not to worry about that, adding that here in Chile we are in for greater danger from tidal waves and earthquakes. Well, she was so persuasive that I'd decided to make a trip to Hong Kong this summer, (your winter), to see for myself. I had been planning, that was before Jane appeared, to go to England this summer, and by the end of this year would have saved enough for the round trip. Having found Jane I decided at once to make the round trip to Hong Kong instead - but have been informed that the cost of such a journey is more than double the fare to England. Jane at once appeared with the solution that as I wanted to emigrate anyway, why not do it right now and therefore buy just the one-way passage to Hong Kong and never return to Chile at all. Her last letter, which I received yesterday, is very eloquent. She feels sure that I'll be able to get work and suggests asking your help, saying that one word from you to the education department in Hong Kong would be sufficient to obtain a position in any school and another to the immigration authorities would be enough to get a resident visa. This of course is perfectly true, but I do not feel I have any right to ask for it, after all you have already done to help my family leave Shanghai during the war and after all your past kindness to me. Of course it would be wonderful to see you again and be near you.

To complicate matters I have just received an offer from St. Kitts, Leeward Islands, of a 3-year contract in the Department of Education of the territory, provided I assume the duties as early as possible. So I'm faced with this problem - where do I go? I'd love to return to Hong Kong, to live near Jane, the only friend I've ever had and perhaps be of use to you - but I do not know at all whether Jane is not too sanguine and that work will be found. On the other hand,

I have a contract for three years in St. Kitts, that is if they can wait until December, when I can leave the school, but I know nothing whatever about the Leeward Islands. Of course, if I had received the offer last year, before the thought of going to Hong Kong entered my head, I'd have gone immediately, but now I don't know which is better. Of one thing I am sure, and that is that I want to leave Chile for good - not to live any more in constant fear of earthquakes, among people to whom cheating and stealing are second nature, and where try as hard as

I can I'm getting practically nowhere, since it is almost impossible to raise those children from their intellectual and moral squalor, I just feel tired, frustrated and disappointed.

I would like to know your opinion. You are wise in politics, have a much clearer view of the world situation, know Hong Kong as nobody else does and probably have heard more about the Leeward Islands than I have. What would you do in my place? Do write and tell me.

We are very busy at the school. August is the month when we work most, after that we begin revision with the ghost of the examinations looming ahead. I don't know where all of the clever children have gone to, the ones we have here are quite hopeless. Just not interested.

Fortunately, we have had no more earthquakes and the situation in the flooded area of Valdivia is also well in hand. Unluckily in the north, where we are, there have been no rain at all this winter, that means no grass and it will be a very hard time for the poor cattle. It is quite cold too, although in spite of frosty mornings roses are in bloom everywhere.

Well, Mr. Kadoorie, I'm ending off this letter and I do hope, fervently, to receive a reply from you soon. Please let me have your opinion, but do not think that if I were to follow your suggestions and not be happy about the consequences, that I would hold you responsible for it or lay the blame at your door. I'm just asking for your point of view, I know that in such matters one cannot give advice, but I have a great deal of respect for your intelligence, and I'm sure that you will find some solution that has not presented itself to me. Please excuse me for taking up so much of your time."

On August 4, the same day Zina mailed the above letter to Horace, she also sent off a letter to the Acting Personnel Officer at the Education Department in St. Kitts thanking him for his letter of July 20th and informing him that she was quite prepared to accept an appointment as teacher in the Education Department of the territory of St. Kitts-Nevis-Anguilla. She acknowledged her appreciation in advance, and requested that he send her information regarding (1) the subjects she would be required to teach (2) whether she would be a resident teacher with living quarters provided or if she would have to find a place to rent (3) the approximate budget for living in the territory and what percentage of her salary would be deducted in taxes.

"I would be grateful for this and any other information that you could let me have for as I have never visited the Leeward Islands, I have absolutely no idea of living conditions there.

As regards the date when I could resume duty, it is my wish to do so as early as possible, but I would like to point out that, as I have mentioned in my application previously, I shall be free at the end of December. As I am Headmistress of the *Colegio Inglés* I cannot leave until the school year is completed, which is a little after Christmas, seeing that Chile is in the Southern Hemisphere. I hope this date will be convenient.

Kindly let me know whether the medical certificate is to be issued by a specialist or if a general practitioner can do so. Also, please advise me when it is to be sent and if it is to be accompanied by other documents, such as recommendations, references, copies of diplomas, etc. Hoping to receive an early reply from you so as to make my plans accordingly."

Having made the decision to take the teaching position in St. Kitts, Mrs. Katzen became more and more impatient with, among other things, the length of time it took the Ministry of Education in St. Kitts to respond to her letters. She enlisted the high-profile influence of a friend, A.V. Goudie (OBE) - the British Consul in the nearby city of Coquimbo, to communicate with the St. Kitts government on her behalf.

"Dear Sir", wrote Mr. Goudie, "Mrs. Z. Katzen has shown me your letter dated the 20th July 1960, in which you advise her that, subject to her being found medically fit, it is proposed to select her for employment as Teacher Class I in the Education Department.

Mrs. Katzen asks me to do her the favour to write to you because she fears that correspondence sometimes goes astray in the mail. As an example, I may say that a letter dated the 24th May and addressed to Mrs.
Katzen by the Education Department, arrived a fortnight after the receipt of your letter dated 20th July.

Mrs. Katzen will be happy to accept the appointment which you offer her, but would like to know whether it would be possible for her to assume the post at the end of this year, when the Chilean school period finishes its labours.

I may say that I have strongly urged Mrs. Katzen to accept the post even though it may entail her leaving her present school before the end of the yearly period. She feels however that loyalty towards her school obliges her to find out whether it would be convenient for your Education Department to allow her to delay her arrival at St. Kitts until the latter part of this year. If this should not be convenient for the Education Department, she would make the necessary arrangements to leave at the earliest possible moment.

In the meantime, will you kindly send me the necessary forms to be filled in in connection with the medical examination and whatever other forms may be required.

I presume that you will grant the necessary authority for Mrs. Katzen and her mother to enter into your territory as permanent residents. This will be necessary in order to obtain the necessary passport visas.

In conclusion, I have great pleasure in stating that I have known Mrs. Katzen ever since she arrived in this country, and, as British Consul for the Province I have had frequent opportunities of observing the magnificent work she has done in connection with the English School at the neighboring city of La Serena. Not only is she a first-class teacher but she is an exceptionally brilliant organiser [sic] and she occupies an almost unequalled position in scholastic circles as well as being greatly appreciated and admired in social activities."

The acting Personnel Officer at the Ministry of Education in St. Kitts writes:

"Madam, further to my letter of the 26th August. 1960, I am directed to inform you that your obligation in your present post has been recognised [sic] and that you are now offered the appointment as from 1st January 1961.

1.   You will be attached to the St. Kitts Grammar School, and it is expected that you will be asked to teach French up to the Higher School Certificate standard (G.C.E. - A. level). It is also proposed that you introduce Spanish into the School and in this your services will be most useful.

2.   The school has a roll of 200 boys in the fifth year School Certificate range and 20 girls plus 20 boys in the Higher Certificate classes.

3.   Government does not provide quarters and teachers are expected to make their own living arrangements, though help in finding suitable accommodation would of course be given at the

outset. For one person, suitable accommodation can be found in a private home for about $120 per month more or less depending on conveniences provided. If you are accompanied by your mother then a bungalow may be rented at about $70 or less and cost of food would be about $100. On first appointment, officers from outside the Colony are eligible for an advance for the purchase of furniture not exceeding $299 payable within 3 years.

4.   Attached is the present Income Tax Schedule. An officer is assessed on his income in the preceding year so that you will pay by installment in 1962 on what you earned in 1961.

5.   The prescribed forms for medical examination are enclosed and should be completed by a qualified medical practitioner, and returned to this office by the doctor himself.

6.   I confirm that you would be permitted to enter the Colony as a permanent resident, but that a deposit of $48 would have to be made in request of your mother. This amount would be refunded when she is ready to leave this territory or at the end of two years whichever is earlier.

7.   In the meantime it would be of assistance if you would forward the original of your Birth Certificate, Examination Certificate or Diplomas and Certificate of service as well."

"Dear Sir", writes Mrs. Katzen, "Thank you for your letter of September 30 with the enclosed form for the medical examination. I have complied with your instructions immediately and have been examined by the doctor, Alonso Moreno, this morning and he will probably forward the results to you in this same mail.

I am enclosing photostats of three of my diplomas and two certificates from the Education Department to certify that I have served in La Serena as Headmistress and teacher of Mathematics and Modern Languages for the last 15 years. The school, *Colegio Inglés* has been recognized by the Chilean Government and has the same status as the Chilean schools. I must draw your attention to the fact that in all official documents, my full surname, Katzenellenbogen, appears, while I use just half of it, Katzen, for all other purposes.

As regards my birth certificate, I'm afraid I'll not be able to furnish one. The only one I had was lost when I left China, and it is quite impossible to get a copy since I was born in Nikolajevsk, a tiny village in Czechoslovakia which has been destroyed completely in the last World War. However, I have my passport and Identity Card and if required, could send you the latter.

Thank you very much for the information about the permission for my Mother and Aunt to enter the territory, it is very welcome since we need not break up our family life and continue living together as we have done for the last sixteen years. I shall arrive alone and once suitable quarters have been found, will make all necessary arrangements for their entry.

I am also grateful for the income tax schedule, however as you do not mention the salary I am to receive, I'm afraid I cannot work the tax out and would be much obliged if you could let me have this information when you write again.

I hope you will find all the Certificates and Documents satisfactory for I am very anxious to know as early as possible whether I have been definitely accepted as I have to give notice here, wind up all my school and personal affairs and book the passage, all of which takes time and I'm afraid there is not much of it left to do everything well. Therefore, I would greatly appreciate a reply at your earliest convenience."

Victor Goudie, British Consul, also responds.

"Sir, I duly received your letter of the 26th August 1960 regarding the appointment of Mrs. Z. Katzen as a Teacher Class 1 in your territory.

Mrs Katzen has now been officially informed that she has been appointed as Teacher and that the appointment will take effect as from the 1st January 1961.

I beg to inform you that Mrs. Katzen proposes to make the journey by steamer from Valparaiso to Panama, and thence by airplane to St. Kitt's [sic]. Her steamer, the "Potosi" of the Pacific Steam Navigation Company is due to arrive at Panama on the 1st January approximately, but as there may be a delay of a few days, I understand that there will be no objection on your and the school authorities' part to her arrival a few days after the date named.

I should esteem it a favour if you would send me an official communication from the Immigration Office at yours stating that Mrs. Katzen has been duly authorised [sic] to disembark at St. Kitt's in order to take up permanent residence.

According to a letter which Mrs. Katzen has received from Mr. A.T. Ribeiro, Headmaster of the Grammar School at yours, the Immigration Office requests that I send a statement to the effect that Mrs. Katzen together with her Mother and Aunt who are desirous of proceeding to St. Kitt's after she has made the necessary living arrangements, have been cleared of all 'security risks'.

On behalf of all three ladies I can give you an absolute assurance that they are completely cleared in every respect, and I should therefore like to receive the necessary authorization to grant a visa to her Mother and Aunt when they apply for the same.

In Mr. Ribeiro's letter, above mentioned, he states that non-British nationals are required to deposit £100 each to ensure that they will not be a liability on the Government.

May I be allowed to request that this stipulation be waived in the case of all three ladies? In the case of Mrs. Katzen, she of course is taking up a paid appointment and in the cases of the Mother and Aunt I can assure you that the small permanent income of the Mother is more than sufficient to maintain them without the slightest risk to the Government at St Kitts.

I am willing to give you my written guarantee on behalf of all three ladies, such guarantee being in my personal and private capacity because I'm not allowed to give an official Consular guarantee. Apart from my Consular capacity I am one of the principal maritime merchants in this port where I have resided for nearly 50 years. I am and have been for the past 22 years, President of the local Chamber of Commerce and I am Dean of the Consular Corps. I have been decorated by the Chilean Government with the Order of Merit and I have the honour of being an Officer of the British Empire (O.B.E.).

I shall be much obliged if you will be good enough to reply by return of air mail in order that I may be able to communicate the decision of your authorities regarding the fore-mentioned points.

As there is little time left before Mrs. Katzen commences her steamer journey to Panama I hope to have the pleasure of receiving your reply within 15 to 29 days."

The die was cast. La Serena and Chile were history. Mrs. Katzen would no longer have to deal with these God-awful children and their parents. Any place in the world was better. She settled for "a little mudflat island with little black boys for students."

Despite having had her fill of the lazy, difficult, amoral, foul-mouthed students however, 60 years later the sentiments expressed by an untold number of her former Chilean students suggest that her characterizations were most likely the hyperbolic chatter of a world-weary woman who had become embittered by the circumstances that caused her to lose control of *El Colegio Inglés Católico de la Serena*. They could not be more proud and grateful for the opportunity to attend the school that she created and nurtured into one of the stellar educational institutions of the region. One alum wrote:

For me, and for all of us who had the honor of being her students, Miss Katzen was a second mother, giving us all of her wisdom, her immense love and affection, making certain that each and every one of us felt special.
I can tell you that she had an immense impact on my life. From her I learned to be courageous, not to be afraid of life, to give maximum effort, to press forward in the face of adversity. She was a great example of life for all of us. I learned how to be responsible because she taught us how to be responsible and I did not ever want to disappoint her. As long as I was by her side, I was always first or second in her class.

The truth is, I cannot compare her to other teachers because Miss Katzen was much, much more than that. She was a mother who controlled, taught, educated you with love, with firmness, discipline, with incomparable humanity and nobility.

I could recount numerous stories that reflect who she was. Like how she encouraged us to be our best; giving us medals that made us shine proudly; staging end-of-year fiestas with incredible creativity and dedication; saying prayers together before the start of classes; treating us to a special lunch after our First Communion. And after we graduated from el Colegio, we would all return on the 8th of December every year for a reunion for which she would make a cake with her own hands.

During my era at el Colegio the school only went up to the 5th grade, after which we had to attend another school. Miss Katzen accompanied us to our admission exams and personally worried about where we will be placed.

On the first day of class in my new school the English teacher gave me a grade of 1 (the highest possible grade). After school, I ran back to el Colegio and told Miss Katzen. She told me not to worry, took me by the hand and led me back to my school to speak with the Head Mistress and my English teacher. From then on until I graduated high school I did work for other classes while my English teacher taught.

One day when I was seven years old I was on my way to school when a German shepherd (a giant of a dog to me at that time) grabbed my leg and threw me to the ground. Fortunately, it did not get a chance to bite me but it did leave teeth marks on my leg. Besides enjoying the chocolate that Miss Katzen gave me, I was in seventh heaven sitting beside Miss Katzen for the whole day, on her skirt, as she taught her classes.

I can only say that I was one of those persons fortunate enough to have known such an exceptional woman. She has deeply touched my life, a life that has had its share of troubles. Each time I think of her, her memory keeps me going forward once more. When she was ill in Chile my parents went to see her but I could not because my only child had passed away shortly before and I knew that even with all of the strength I had exhibited until then, I would simply collapse when I arrive at her bedside. I just could not submit her to my immense sorrow because I knew she would make it her own.

My friend, Miss Katzen, is, has been, will always be a unique and wonderful woman, the kind that one meets once in a lifetime. My love, my memories, my gratitude for her will be with me always, until the day I die.

And another:

I am currently fifty-seven years old. I entered el Colegio at the age of four and spent the next five years there. In my personal and professional life Mrs. Katzen not only made me felt capable, but she also made me feel loved and brave. I don't know how, but she managed to leave an indelible impression on me about producing work well done and always giving maximum effort. She taught me that I was quite capable and to be proud of my achievements.

Even today when I am confronted with a task (I married very young and do not have a profession) I do it with enormous responsibility. Mrs. Katzen combined love with firmness and did not tolerate laziness. As a teacher, she impacted all aspect of my life - from Mathematics to Ballet. She was even involved in the making of the costumes for the annual end-of-year festival.

She met my daughter Bernadita the last time she visited Chile and was very affectionate to her. She told me that Bernadita had large hands and would make a great pianist and insisted that I made certain that she was enrolled in piano lessons.

The truth is, I loved her dearly. When I attended el Colegio it was my responsibility to take her apron to her office. Knowing that I was somewhat of a scatterbrain she would frequently ask me what things I ought to do and what things I want to do, thus teaching me how to prioritize. Together we would make a list of the most important and essential things and a list of lesser important things that can be postponed. I still engage in that exercise today.

I recognize how fortunate I am for having her touch my life and I also realize how much I love her.

Over the years Alexandra had seen Zina grow to become, like herself, a tough, proud, strong-willed woman who knew how to fight the good fight. However, as she watched the battle unfold over ownership of *El Colegio*, over the distribution of shares, she could sense that this was one battle that her daughter would lose. She wasn't so much concerned about the effect of the loss on Zina who was as resilient as they come. More disturbing was Zina's continuous talk about leaving La Serena, not for another town in Chile - but to Australia, or Hong Kong, or South Africa, or the West Indies. The idea of relocating yet again in their advanced age (she and Evgenie were now respectively 74 and 72) was a daunting one.

And now it was decided that their next home would be St. Kitts, a tiny island in the Eastern Caribbean. She will try not to worry because Zina was once again her old self, filled with wanderlust and a desire to conquer new worlds. Wherever she leads they will follow.

Although she had reached a point of total disenchantment in the shadow of the Andes, Zina had not severed all of her ties to Chile. She would leave her mother and aunt behind until she could find a suitable residence in St. Kitts. She couldn't imagine a life without her little old ladies and hoped that it won't be too long before they could join her. It was a huge gamble signing a contract to live and work in a place sight unseen. What if she doesn't like it? What if Kittitians are unwelcoming? Would she be able to handle living and working in a place where people look and sound vastly different from her? A place where she's sure to stick out like a sore thumb? And what happens if it doesn't work out? Does she then pack up her little old ladies and start island-hopping until she finds the right place? But this was defeatist talk. For her own sake and for the sake of Alexandra and Evgenie who will hopefully join her soon, she must will herself to think only positive thoughts.

And then there was Fyodor. Try as she might she could not rid herself of the terrible feeling that she had failed him, that she would not be winning any mother-of-the-year awards. Did the tremendous sacrifices made creating a name for herself, building a school, educating the children of La Serena, come at the expense of her son? She wanted so badly for him to become a physician like her father, like the doctor her father wanted her to be. Would things have turned out differently if she had spent more time with him and less time with other people's children? If only he had listened to her, stayed in school, not get married at the age of 21. If only she had found the strength to swallow her pride, suppress her anger, attend his wedding and confer her blessings, perhaps she wouldn't be leaving Chile carrying such a heavy burden of guilt.

Perhaps I'm being too hard on myself, she thought. After all, she had taught him well, perhaps too well, and now the apple has fallen quite close to the tree. At a very early age she had taught him to be independent and strong, how to stand on his own two feet. During school holidays, while other youngsters his age were having fun he was busy working for this mining company or that mining company. And now he had grown to be an intelligent, hard-working, independent, strong-willed young man with a bright future, albeit not the one she envisioned for him. She loved him dearly and wished they had parted on more amicable terms. Perhaps by moving to St. Kitts the increased distance will make it easier to bridge the growing abyss between them.

She was happy that she had taken a well-deserved vacation earlier in the year to visit most of the other Latin-American countries, as it was unlikely that she would ever return to South America, except perhaps to take care of unfinished business in Chile.

She must now turn all thoughts to St. Kitts. And what better place to do so than aboard a Johnson Line steamship? The rise and swell of the ocean has always had the ability to invigorate her, clear her mind, lift her spirits. She must surrender herself to the mystical powers of the ocean to be purged of the gloomy pessimism and bitter cynicism that marked these last years in Chile. She had originally made plans to travel aboard the Potosi but it was delayed getting to Valparaiso and was now traveling later than planned aboard the *Kenuta*. Concerned about arriving in St. Kitts late (her three-year contract begins January 1st, 1961), she dispatched a telegram, just before boarding, to Anthony Ribeiro, Headmaster of the St.
Kitts-Nevis-Anguilla Grammar School:

Date: December 13th 1960

Leaving Chile today. Steamship Kenuta to Curaçao. Continuing K.L.M. plane. Arriving St. Kitts approximately January 5th. Merry Christmas. Katzen.

◊◊

St. Kitts

St. Kitts-Nevis-Anguilla Grammar School

St. Kitts represented a rebirth, an opportunity for Zina to once again let her star shine, an opportunity to take her high-powered teaching show on the road, an opportunity to prove that, in this her fiftieth year, she still had it, she can still transform the lives of children in a very profound way.

A few days at sea and already she felt a new spirit, a new energy coursing through her body. She had been informed that, unlike *El Colegio Inglés*, her students at the Grammar School will be mostly boys from the ages of 14-20. She had not taught children of color before and for a brief moment she wondered what difference the drastic change will have on her and her teaching. But she quickly dismissed such thoughts, a sign that she was once again imbued with that indomitable spirit that has erstwhile enabled her to conquer mountains. Her mojo had returned. After all, she has taught Jewish children and other stateless refugees in Shanghai and Canton and Latino children in Chile. There is no reason why teaching West Indian boys and girls would be any different, except of course if she arrives in St. Kitts with preconceived notions about the relative intellectual capacity of children across ethnicities and cultures. And she refused to allow herself to entertain such thoughts because to do so will only fulfill the prophecy of such thinking.

The Caribbean of the 1960s and 1970s was an era fraught with political, economic and social difficulties. It was also an era marked by a movement to democratize secondary education in St. Kitts, Nevis and Anguilla. The system of education, created more than two hundred years ago, was estab-lished by the ruling class of landed sugar estate owners almost exclusively for the education of their children for whom secondary education was a *de facto* birthright. The concept of universal secondary education did not take full effect until 1966 when the St. Kitts-Nevis-Anguilla Government passed *The Education Act*, which was essentially a declaration of war against the *Eleven Plus Examination*[2], otherwise known as the Common Entrance Exam. Its purpose, in part, was to abolish what it referred to as the "screening device for deciding who will go and who will not go" to high school in St. Kitts, Nevis and Anguilla. In short, it aimed to provide free secondary education to all children of secondary school age. By 1970 the percentage of students enrolled in secondary education had risen to
19.5%.

In 1966, five years after Mrs. Katzen's arrival at the St. Kitts-NevisAnguilla Grammar School, of the fifteen thousand eight hundred and one (15,801) children enrolled in all schools, only one

---

[2] A product of the British education system administered to some students (11-12 years old) in their last year of primary education.

thousand one hundred and twenty (1,120) children (9.6%) were enrolled in secondary schools[3].

She immediately fell in love with St. Kitts, a beautiful volcanic tropical guitar-shaped island with its dormant volcano, verdant mountains and sugarcane fields sloping gently down to the sea. Happy to put her Chilean troubles behind her, she couldn't wait to get into the classroom and begin to work her magic. She would devote all of her time to revolutionizing the teaching of foreign languages. In no time, she had a French and Spanish club up and running. After school on Mondays and Fridays all roads led to Madame Katzen's house for *El Círculo Franco Español*. In less than two years she had initiated plans for the creation of a branch of the *Alliance Française* on the island.

Horace became without question the most important person in Mrs. Katzen's life, her mother and aunt notwithstanding. For the rest of her days (St. Kitts would be the last stop on her journey), he would play an important role in both her personal and professional life, providing the resources she needed to give her students an incredible foreign language learning experience - resources which she used to feed, clothe, pay school fees and Cambridge Exam fees for the most needy among them. On a regular basis she would send Horace progress reports of all of the students chosen by her to be beneficiaries of his philanthropy. There was hardly anything that affected her life in St. Kitts that he was not apprised of. Despite a heavy teaching schedule and caring for her elderly mother and aunt, she always found time to write to Horace. Over the next forty years she provided him with running commentaries of life on the island. He learned about her work, the weather, the sugar factory - the total tons of sugar it produced annually and its importance to the local economy, her dogs and cats, her students, hurricanes, poverty,

---

[3] Halliday, Joseph J., OBE, 2000. The Struggle for Curriculum Relevance: The St. Kitts and Nevis Experience.

school and island politics, drought, her car, the health of her mother and aunt, her garden, and race relations.

As was the case at her school in Chile, Madame invested a great deal of time and energy in the progress of her students for whom she was more than just their foreign language teacher. She played a major role in helping them find jobs, counseled them in the University articulation process and, in many cases, thanks to the benevolence of Horace, providing financial assistance to their families.

1963

"I think I am about the happiest teacher in the world today. Our Cambridge School Certificate and G.C.E. results have come in this morning and every one of my French pupils has got through - and not just mere passes, there are three distinctions and the rest have credits. Among the distinctions I am very proud to inform you we have Morris Archibald. If you remember, I wrote to you that we had decided he had better take up French, for if he were lucky enough to get a scholarship next year to the University, he has to have a G.C.E. certification of a modern language. So, in Jan. 1962 we started French 'from scratch'. After a year's work, of course it was very hard work, he took the exam in Dec. 1962, on a level with students who had five years of the language, and as you see, he has scored a distinction. I consider this a great feat, and I sincerely hope that when he takes his Higher School Cert. at the end of this year he'll be just as successful. Emanuel Moses has obtained his full School Certificate also, therefore our 'godchildren' have conducted themselves praiseworthily, and you will, I am sure, feel satisfaction that the help you are giving them is bearing results."

The tradition of taking her students abroad to enrich their foreign language learning experience began in 1962, the year after she arrived in St. Kitts.

"I am sending you these snapshots taken on the trip to Martinique with my French group, in various aspects of sartorial elegance. I'm afraid the one with the students in bathing suits is a little suggestive of Tarzan and the Apes, the little blond boy in the centre being Tarzan. But really, their exterior means nothing, I find them all just as good and perhaps some even better than white boys of the same age. The one with students in uniform was taken when we were on our way to the *Préfet* to thank him officially for his kindness. I wonder if you will recognize your protégés.

Martinique 1962

Martinique 1962

I am also enclosing *The Sixthformer*, which is a sort of paper published by our sixth form, they compose it and print it themselves operating the antique printing press that somebody has donated; this accounts for the poor paper, ink and other defects, but my object in sending you the paper is that there is an article by Morris Archibald, the one named 'My First Maths Test' and signed Mathematician, and while of no means of literary value, for I find the style too ornate and artificial, it still gives you an idea of the boy's knowledge of the language, for although English is supposed to be the official language, sometimes it certainly doesn't sound like it. It seems a paradox but the Higher School candidates all passed in French, while three of them failed in English! Thereby of course they could not obtain their certificates.

I hope your period of drought is over, and that your farmers are relaxing from the strain. We have had very dry weather too and unfortunately a dreadful fire which consumed 53 acres of sugar cane. This represents a great loss and will of course have its repercussion on the economic side for the workers."

"I have just received my copy of the Reader's Digest for the month of June and was delighted to read the article about your wonderful work. I am so very happy that at least the whole world will know, realize, admire and appreciate what you have done. There are rich people in the world who give sums to charities, but none give on such a scale as you, and nobody takes a genuine interest in the people themselves, and that is your true generosity, the kind word, the smile, the encouragement, the cheerfulness, the time and personal attention that you have always given to those you help, all that is far more precious than the money itself. Thoughts of you have been with me all day - not that I need this article to remind me of you, for I think of you constantly - but today I have somehow felt your presence nearer and this has made my work easier. Especially as this afternoon your letter of June 11th. has arrived and makes me feel better on the chapter of the cheque that you have sent for the Spanish boys' trip.

I am enclosing a ticket for our fiesta, let's hope you will think of us on that day and wish us luck. We have announced the show on the radio - since last year we actually have a wireless station of our own, though it's on the air for just a few hours every day, and there is supposed to be something in the local paper tomorrow, therefore I shall post my letter to you only after the 'press release' has appeared so as to enclose it also. The boys are out on the war-path this afternoon trying to sell tickets, this is our first day after the trial exams so we have to start on our preparation for the show right away, before the results of the exams come out and dampen certain pupils' spirits. The singing and dancing are being practised [sic] with great enthusiasm, I only hope we shall have success in our enterprise, all this activity and work help take my mind off other unpleasant things, so I'll just cross my bridges when I come to them.

The water situation in Hong Kong seems to become ghastly. On the Dutch island of Curacao, it seems that fresh water is obtainable from seawater. Couldn't that be done in Hong Kong too? Our rains have suddenly stopped again, so all the plants are drooping, drying and looking pitiful."

When Horace learned that she would be taking a short leave to return to Chile for medical treatment, he promptly sent her a check.

"What shall I say? Your wonderful, warm letter has just arrived and I feel so deeply that I just can't find words to answer. What unbound kindness, infinite tact and delicacy are yours and how honored I feel that you call me your friend! You cannot imagine what consolation, what encouragement there is to know that though far away, at the other end of the world there is somebody who thinks about our welfare. How could I take this letter amiss knowing the noble spirit in which you have written it? This letter is to be treasured, to be read over and over in all difficult moments, for the knowledge that there is such an exceptional person in the world as yourself is something to sustain one's faith and help live through painful times.

With your insight and intuition you have realized at once the cause of all my worries - my Mother and Aunt. I hate to be long-winded and take up so much of your time, but I would like to write to you frankly, so that you would know how things stand.

As you surmise, I am quite far from being rich, though my salary is far better than what I could earn in Chile. Unfortunately, my post is not pensionable, but so long as I can work, we can manage. I have even been able to save to buy a tiny plot of land. My trip to Chile is paid according to the terms of the contract, therefore I shall not have the expense of the journey, both ways. Also, according to the terms of the contract I continue receiving my salary during my leave; the headmaster has promised to help me get the three months' pay in advance and I shall leave the whole of it here for my little old ladies - this should be ample for them and for Charles Archibald who is going to live with them during my absence. The expenses of my operations are of course unknown, but I am hoping to pay for them with the rent from the house I have in Chile. I have asked to have this money deposited in the bank there since I have been advised of these operations. Should this sum prove to be insufficient, for the rent is almost nominal, then I'd sell the house. I have wanted to do so for some time, unfortunately the Chilean peso has fallen so appallingly that I would not receive even a fifth of its value were I to change the proceeds into foreign currency now, as the hospital and operations are to be paid in Chilean pesos, I think that whatever I receive should be quite sufficient. So you see, I consider that financially, things are not too bad. Besides, I always think that if God gives you the gift of life, He will also give you the opportunity to earn it. And that brings me to the crux of the matter. Though, according to my doctor in Chile I have exceptional vitality and nine lives like the cat as well as their power of quick recovery, - still, an operation is a risk and one may never be sure of its outcome. Please don't get the idea that I have made up my mind that I'll not get well, I have faith that I will, but there is no harm in planning to have everything arranged. My son is on his own feet, so I don't have to worry about him; the Archibalds and Maurice, thanks to you will have finished school and should be able to fend for themselves. I still hope the former will get scholarships, as for Maurice, I think the headmaster will help him; so that leaves just my two little ladies. They are in full possession of their faculties and far more energetic about the house than many young people, though one is 78 and the other 76, but they are so old and frail that I shudder to think what would happen if they were left alone. They would of course return to Chile, selling everything here and especially the little plot of land, that should pay for their passage and leave them a little for pocket money and my son and my step-sister[4] would take care of them for the few years they'd have to live. It's the care and affection that they need though, and I don't know if they'd have enough of that.

---

[4] Mrs. Katzen referred to her half-sister, Raisa as her step-sister.

Now, please don't think me morbid; I have written all this so that you have a complete picture of the circumstances and agree that everything is financially in hand. I sincerely think it is, but I shall never forget your wonderful kindness and thoughtfulness. How I wish I had the gift of writing to express myself and thank you properly, but the more I feel, the more tongue-tied I become, so please excuse me. I can only say that you are always in my thoughts and if wishes could come true, you would have every conceivable happiness on earth, for I pray and wish it to you with all my heart. I only hope that I shall return here and that someday we shall have the joy of seeing you come for a visit, even if only for a day or two, between planes, on your way to England or back. You cannot imagine the happiness this will cause everybody here.

This letter is far too long and yet there are so many things I would like to tell you about our Fiesta and the great success we've had. I shall write to you all about it in a few days for we are repeating the whole performance, as there was not enough room in the Hall to hold all the people.
When it's all over I'll give you all the details as well as the financial report."

"Every single day of the past week I wanted to write to you, and every time something would happen to prevent me from doing it, and there is so much I want to tell you.

First of all, our concert. I'm enclosing a programme of the *Gran Fiesta y Velada*, so that you could have an idea of what I'm trying to describe. The whole thing was an immense success, all the actors in top form, the weather was very kind, (the very next day there was such a downpour that nobody could put a foot outside), the boys worked very hard to sell the tickets and advertise the show, so that, twenty minutes before the performance was to start the hall was packed and we had to turn people away. Unfortunately, the ones who came early were all young people, who paid only 50¢, but we managed to make the unprecedented sum of $360, which for a school show was a record.

The French songs were enjoyed by all, and the song and dance, the *Samba-Tarantelle* which I remembered from my far-away student days and taught the boys and girls some of the steps we used to dance at our gatherings many years ago, especially pleased the audience. The songs in English, being the popular ones that all young people sing over the world went off with great enthusiasm, and the three little girls whom my mother prepared for the piano numbers were also well applauded. The Spanish songs were performed with great brilliance, accompanied by guitars and castanets and the Chilean dance had to be repeated twice over. We had some very funny incidents preparing that, we made the costumes at my home but the principle items for boys were spurs. Unfortunately, in St. Kitts there are no horses to be had, let alone spurs; but our metal-work teacher came to our aid and fabricated some that looked quite genuine. The only snag was keeping them on, for as there was very little time, he decided to attach them to the heels of the shoes. Now he comes to school in the mornings only, the show was in the evening and the boys have just the one pair of shoes. So it was either walk all day to the jingle of spurs, or go barefoot, neither of which would be permitted at the school. However, scouting around we discovered some old tennis shoes and managed to smuggle the boys into the classrooms after assembly when all danger of their foot-gear being noticed was passed. It all added to the enjoyment of the preparations. On the evening of the repeat performance, just as one of the boys was coming on the stage somebody had the clumsiness to step on the blessed spurs and almost tore them off, there was no time to fix them, as the girls were already on the stage and the music had started, so we all held our fingers crossed while the poor lad was dancing and the spurs hanging if not by a thread, at least by just a tack. However, the things didn't fall off and he didn't trip so the dance ended with great gusto and not with the ignominious finale that I was so scared of.

Our next item was the drawing of the raffle and then came the play *The Wake*, which as you see was written and produced by the members of the French Club. It was of course in English so that the audience could understand, and I can honestly say that it was one of the funniest I'd ever seen, brilliant dialogues and the acting was superb. Probably you are thinking that I'm too enthusiastic over my boys and girls, but I really would like you to know that they have produced something really worth-while. Anyhow, the success was such that we decided to repeat the whole thing at half-price in Sandy Point, which is right on the other side of the island where the Archibalds live. It is a very poor district, mostly cane-cutters with dozens of small children who never have the chance of seeing any kind of show at all. Morris drew posters, Moses stuck them on walls and trees proclaiming the grand show, Charles rented the church hall and the piano for the great sum of $5, (afterwards they reduced the price so we paid only $3.50), and we begged one of the stores here to let us have a truck to transport all our artists the 14 miles into the country. We had to bring the school curtains, since the church hall had none and my poor mother almost fainted when she saw the piano, it must have been brought over by Nelson[5], I've never seen such a model either, it looked more like a huge wardrobe and we had to perch the players up on a crate since the keyboard was at least a yard and a few inches off the floor. In addition, eight notes didn't answer, two emitted exactly the same sound and the rest were all out of tune.

However, the success was great, even though in the middle of the show the curtains tumbled down and enveloped the band. Anyhow, after paying for the rent of the hall, the $6 for the gas for the truck and giving a tip to the driver we managed to get $138, which brought our total to $498, I gave $2 more so we deposited $500 with the Headmaster for the trip. Then the richest lady on the island, who is now in England and who heard about our efforts, directed her secretary to give us a donation of $200, so we would need just $200

---

[5] Vice-Admiral Lord Horation Nelson, who married Fanny Nisbett, the daughter of a Nevis plantation owner in 1787.

from the sum you so generously sent us to complete the total of $900 which we needed. There is quite a sizable cargo ship which charges $15 deck and we are to return by plane, $35.50; so that for the 18 boys everything was complete and I was ever so happy, for I consider that you were giving us far too much money for a holiday and it should have been spent on something more useful. And then, two days ago all our plans went awry. We received news that the cargo ship was not going to San Juan through St. Kitts, that after calling here the ship was to go south, and that she could not take us anyhow because there was no room. I am afraid I lost my temper a bit and gave the agent of the ship a piece of my mind, really, I do think it wrong first to tell us one thing and then without any reason to go back on their word. So now we shall have to go by air both ways. Two boys will not be able to go as their parents want them to go somewhere else instead, and I've been to the airline asking them for a further rebate. If we use more of the remittance that you were so kind as to send us we shall be able to travel both ways by air at the present price, but there is no harm in trying to get a cheaper rate. Our passages are reserved for August 6th, therefore please think of us on that day when with my 16 'Spaniards' I'll be setting out on our travels, when so many boys are going to get a holiday thanks to you.

We have had quite a disturbing experience on Noel's account. If you remember I wrote to you that he was living with his great-grandmother who was not quite normal. Well, I'm afraid she has lost her reason altogether for she suddenly accused Noel of stealing her things and of threatening to kill her and thereupon she simply threw him out. As you know, he never had anything to eat there, for your allowance goes for his food which a neighbor gives him, but at least he had a place in which to sleep. He was literally out in the street with no belongings whatsoever. I couldn't take him in, so I tried to find somewhere for him to stay. I thought we would be able to find some cubby-hole in the school building; however, the Headmaster helped us and has allowed Noel to use a sort of tool-shed in his own backyard, so at least the boy has a roof over his head. He has improved greatly this year, is far steadier, responsible and performs many little duties that have helped to form his character. Even if he is not a brilliant scholar I can now assure you that owing to your interest he has become a useful member of the small school community."

"I have just returned from St. Martin and have found your very kind letter of July 22nd. waiting for me. It has plunged me into the greatest confusion imaginable. The letter is kindness itself, but I was aghast and appalled at the sight of the draft enclosed. Honestly and sincerely I believe that I shall have quite enough funds to see me through; perhaps I have not expressed myself clearly enough in my letter and with your customary warm generosity you have at once sent this cheque. But, dear Mr. Kadoorie, really and truly, if all is well I am sure I shall manage. My first impulse was to send the cheque right back to you, but then I felt I might offend you, which is the last thing in the world that I'd want to do, for you are so kind-hearted and generous that I'd hate to cause you a moment's displeasure - and yet I don't want to take advantage of your noble nature and accept this money. I have been utterly miserable but at last have hit on a plan that I hope will meet with your approval, and please, don't be cross and let me carry it out.

I have placed your draft on deposit at the Royal Bank of Canada for a period of nine months, that is until May 1st 1964 when I should return to St. Kitts from Chile after all my operations and treatments. If things would go wrong and I were not to come back, then my little old ladies would be able to get this sum, for the Bank manager has arranged the deposit in such a way that this is possible. The knowledge that they would be provided for has lifted a great deal of weight off my mind, for I realize that if anything were to happen to me they would be really helpless. Now, let's hope that nothing tragic will come to pass and that in May I shall return, fit and well, to St. Kitts. That will mean that I can take up my duties at the school, continue to work and look after my mother and aunt. Therefore, on my return in May, please, will you allow me to send the deposit back to you? It would make me very happy and I hope you understand me and will permit me to do so. I am accepting your draft as a sort of loan, a trust, to be used only in case of need or emergency, (which I hope will not arise), during this time of stress. This will enable me to go off to have my operations with a tranquil mind, knowing that if the worst were to happen, then my poor little old ladies who have nobody to depend on and whom I love so dearly, would not have to worry.

You cannot imagine how happy I am to have thought of this plan - in this way, I hope you will not be offended and I shall have peace of mind.

And may I now tell you how much I value your friendship, your wonderful tact and your deep understanding? You do not know how much your thoughtfulness means to me, how I appreciate that although so far away, there is somebody to whom I may turn in my hour of need and who will understand me. God bless you."

"In an hour's time my Spanish Club and I are off to San Juan de Puerto Rico, where I hope we shall be able to make good use of the language. The boys are terribly excited. For all 16 of them it's the first time that they are boarding a plane, and only three have ever left the island of St. Kitts to go by ferry or sail boats to the neighboring islands, so it's quite an adventure for them. At the last moment two of the boys said they'd have to drop out since they could not muster the U.S. $11 needed to pay the American Army for their food, so I have taken the equivalent from your generous cheque that you sent them for the purpose and they are going, and I'm taking the balance along in case something happens - having 16 youngsters, there is always a possibility of tooth-ache, minor cuts and bruises etc; thus you are providing a good part of their fare and the keep for the boys, who are very grateful to you for giving them this opportunity of spending such a (I hope) delightful holiday.

I am enclosing a program of our Speech-Night for I am very proud of your 'god-sons', who, as you will be able to see have all obtained prizes. I am especially happy for Maurice Pinney, who, as you will notice has an extra prize for outstanding interest in the school, and who actually came up on the platform and received it, something which a year ago would have been unthinkable. There is a great change in the boy, another being whose life you have influenced greatly.

We had quite a fright with the Hurricane *Arlene*, which was heading directly for our island and Puerto Rico. I think the boys were more worried about missing the trip or postponing it than receiving damage from the storm, however it petered out so we are safe. Thank you once again for your kindness which made this trip possible, and with every good wish for your health and happiness."

"We have just returned from Puerto Rico and I have found your kind letter of July 29th. waiting for me. We have had a delightful time in San Juan and all the boys enjoyed their holiday immensely. It was a great experience for all of them, not only academically, though they did learn many new Spanish words and expressions, but for their general knowledge and outlook. It was the first time, for most of them, that they had left their little island and had no idea that there is so much to see and learn outside. They had never seen so much traffic, so many new cars, shops, schools, such different customs and had no idea that elsewhere people had other ways of living. Everything was new to them, the plane, the air-terminal in San Juan, which is a small town on its own, the lifts - and one of them got left behind in a self-operating one and kept shooting up and down until we finally managed to get him out - the beautiful beaches, factories, museums and vocational schools. What struck them was that all children in all schools could have a free lunch, and that, not as a charity but as part of the school activities. I too, find that admirable and wish we had something like that here[6].

We were very well received. When we arrived, and two hours late at that, we were met by the Commander of Fort Buchanan, a very militarylooking gentleman with so many ribbons on his uniform that

---

[6] All students went home for lunch during the lunch hour.

my boys were speechless with admiration, a delegate of the Caribbean Organization, and two members from the Department of State who welcomed us, gave each child a folder with all sorts of information on Puerto Rico, a map of the island and a present: each child was given a typical Puertorican straw hat. The Department of State had a whole programme prepared for us and took us all around town and surroundings in cars and busses, had even arranged two lectures, picnics, visits to schools and the University - in such manner that our ten days were quite full. It was most kind of them and the boys certainly appreciated it. One of the schools had a party for them, with songs and dances, and I'm afraid that some of the señoritas were very sorry to see them leave, the progress made in the language during the talks with the señoritas was amazing; I'm not sure the vocabulary learnt will be of great use in the Cambridge Exam, but certainly a high degree of fluency was attained.

As you know, we're lodged in Fort Buchanan and the military discipline was also very good for the boys. Of course, the hours were a little startling, breakfast at 5:15 in the morning, dinner at 5 in the evening and lights out at 10 p.m. Lunch was at 12 - but quite often we missed that, visiting schools, for the distances were terribly long - more than an hour's drive from the town to the Fort. San Juan is really made up of three different towns, which spread over an area almost as large as the whole of St. Kitts.

Every child has learnt something, manners and courtesy included, I was even complimented on their deportment, have all become more mature and have all put on weight. The American Army feeds better than the French Fleet! It's a far more balanced meal, with a good proportion of fresh vegetables and an unlimited supply of milk. The boys couldn't believe their eyes when they saw their first breakfast, probably thought they were still dreaming since it was so early in the morning.

On the whole I find Puerto Rico, or that part of it that I have seen, a very progressive place, there seems to be no lack of work, since there are a thousand factories, all education, primary and high school is free, there is some agriculture, chicken farming, commerce, and of course tourists and all the business that they attract. Besides these advantages for creature comforts they have something for the mind and soul - museums, art galleries, libraries, the University, a music conservatory, theaters and cinemas. However, the 'tempo' of life is too American, all bustle and hustle, a visit is pleasant, but I don't think I'd like to live there permanently.

I have great pleasure in enclosing Charles's report, I'm really proud of it! Morris's is quite good, but I'm afraid that Noel's is still disappointing. I have not been able to get a hold of him since my return two days ago, but I do want to have a long talk with him and see what is to be done when he leaves school in December. The break with his great-grandmother is a blessing, at least he lives with sane people around him, his living quarters are quite adequate, the roof does not leak and he uses your allowance for clothing and food, some of which he gets at the Headmaster's in return for little services such as driving the car and carrying out all sorts of chores and errands, it's sort of tacit give and take. The Headmaster is a very kind man, but he has a large family and can't take charge of another boy. Besides I consider that Maurice should find a job as quickly as possible after his last exam in December so as not to get accustomed to drifting and leading a precarious from hand to mouth existence. With your characteristic kindness you are ready to go on helping the boys and want me to work out some sort of budget - it is far too generous of you. Let's wait a little and see what can be done. Charles I'm almost sure will be kept on as a pupil-teacher for some time, so he does not present a very urgent problem as yet and perhaps might manage without further aid. Moses and Morris will continue as students until July, then there is the period of waiting until the results arrive from Cambridge - that is a very trying period, but it is still far off, so, again, Maurice is the only problem. I'll have a good talk with him and see what can be done.

Once again, thanks for everything you have done, not only for your godsons but for sixteen 'Spaniards' as well, as regards myself, I can only express my gratitude in prayers for your health and happiness."

"It seems ages since I have heard from you and I am getting a little concerned about it. I hope I have not offended you unwittingly and that you do not write because you are very busy or perhaps away on holiday, for I would really be miserable if somehow or other I have expressed myself in such a way that may have caused you displeasure. I also hope that your health is good and that your silence is not due to illness, the Lord forbid.

My plans for going on leave are almost complete, I am going by plane to Caracas and then will take a ship from La Guayra, the M/S *Panama*, a little 12 passenger-freighter belonging to the Johnson Line. It is supposed to leave at the end of December or on Jan 1st 1964. I have written to my surgeon in Chile, but so far have received no answer, therefore will have to write again, for my leave has been shortened to three months instead of five, and as I want to travel by sea, for rest and storing up health before and after operations, (traveling will take up two months out of the three), my medical time-table will have to be worked out thoroughly. In a way, I am glad that I shall be away for three months only, somehow it makes me more quiet on the subject of my little old ladies. I hate leaving them, they are so old and frail.

The boys send you their best regards. Morris thanks you for writing to him, but the letter has not been received yet, he is looking forward to getting it."

"We have some news about Maurice Pinney's chances of getting into the S.P.C.K[7] organization. The Anglican priest, Father Walker, has written to the organization asking them if there was any opportunity for the boy, and it seems that there might be. On Nov. 27th or 29th a representative of the organization is coming for a visit to St. Kitts and has agreed to interview Maurice. We are now keeping

---

[7] Society for Promoting Christian Knowledge - founded by Anglican priest Thomas Bray in 1698.

our fingers crossed and hoping that he will make a good impression, his whole future depends on it. As soon as the interview will be over I'll write to you to tell you about it. He is sitting for his exams quite calmly. Poor Charles loses his head at every turn, Morris is more self-controlled, and Maurice has surprisingly acquired a great deal of confidence.

At last our rainy season has started in good earnest. It is a great relief, but even so the planters seem to think that the sugar crop has suffered greatly with the long period of drought. The factory and the union have already started their talks about wages. I do hope that they will come to some arrangement soon, for the crop should start in the second part of January. Last year the talks went on for such a long time without reaching any agreement that it was already March when they finally began to reap the cane, and this created a lot of misery among the workers.

I am sure you must be very happy to welcome your brother home after his round-the-world trip. When will you take one yourself and pay a visit to St. Kitts?"

"This letter should have been written days and days ago but I was plunged into such a whirlpool or rather maelstrom of work that I have only emerged today, dazed and shaky. At last exams are over, and the term, and the reports, staff meetings and seminars are all things of the past. Now I have to attack the legion of things that I must do before going on leave, and my head literally reels at the prospect. My first step is to give you an account of the boys' funds. May I presume on your patience and outline the action I would like to take, and if you do not agree, please let me know as early as possible, for I'm leaving probably on the 27th, and would not like to do anything that you do not approve of.

Maurice Pinney has had his interview, it seems he has made a good impression but we shall know only next week what the outcome will be for the gentleman has now to report on him to the committee in London. We shall be advised of their decision next week. So I'm just keeping my fingers crossed. If accepted, he will have to pay his own passage there, once in England he will be taken care of and we do not have to worry any more. As you might remember, I have your $800 on a fixed deposit due to be withdrawn on December 21st, and a further sum of $500 on their savings account. I had intended leaving the $800 as a fund for the four boys when they leave school, reserving $200 for each one's share, and keep the $500 for Morris's and Moses's expenses until July which would take up $300 of the sum thus leaving $200 which I would like to use for outfitting Charles and getting some clothing for the others too. Charles will be accepted on the school staff as a temporary replacement - this means that he will be kept on while there is need of him, receiving a salary computed on a daily basis of $85 a month, which means that he will get his $85 a month during term but not during holidays. If he passes his Higher School Cert., his salary is increased. That can happen for March 1964 when the Cambridge results come. As he has to start teaching on Jan 3rd, but will receive his salary only at the end of the month, I thought of getting him some clothes since he can't carry on with his uniforms. Maurice, if accepted, would have at once the $200 towards his passage, (out of the $800) and some clothing from the $500. The other two, Morris and Moses, would get whatever is necessary in the way of clothes and books, and I'd keep their share of the $800, $200 each, until they'd be through school. Charles's share of the $800 would be kept for him as a start for his further education. He is going to sit all the entrance and scholarship examinations possible, and in the event of his ever being fortunate to get one, these funds will be of great help. The only thing that worries me is how to keep this money. So far, it has been placed in my name but now that I am going away for three months, during which I am to have all those operations, I'm not sure whether it is wise to go on keeping it so, after all, though not probable, there is always the possibility of my not coming out. On the other hand, as I am going to leave a letter of instructions as to what is to be done were I not to come back, I suppose I could include the instructions for the boys too. Do please write me a few lines to state your views. I'm leaving on the 27th, probably. I know I should have written before this, but perhaps I might still receive your answer. If you think that it is too late, perhaps you could write to me to Chile, Colegio Inglés, Casilla 205, La Serena, but please register, as mail goes astray very easily there, or write to me either to La Guiara, (Venezuela), Curaçao, (Netherlands Antilles) Cristobal, (Republic of Panama) Guayaquil, (Ecuador) or Lima (Peru), Writing on the envelope 'Passenger on M/S *Panama*, C/O Johnson Line.' Kindly excuse this incoherent letter, I'll write again in a few days, but want to get this off first thing to-morrow morning as I might still get your answer before I leave. With all good wishes."

"Thank you for your letter of the 9th December which I have just received. You have certainly had an extremely busy and trying time, and it is indeed good of you to have given so much thought to the allocation of the funds for the future needs of the boys when you have been so swamped with work and many problems.

I fully agree with your suggestion as to how best to utilize the money, and share your hope that the boys will continue to do well in their studies and in their future careers. They certainly owe you a great debt of gratitude for all you have done for them.

Yes, it would be as well for you to leave a letter of instructions regarding withdrawal of the funds as and when needed in the manner you have indicated. But I am sure you will face the ordeal of the operations with courage and fortitude, and do earnestly wish and feel confident that all will be well and you will be restored to full health and strength to continue the truly noble work you are doing in helping so many students receive a sound education.

This is a rush letter, as I am anxious to try to get it to you before you leave St. Kitts. As suggested, I am sending a copy to *Colegio Inglés in La Serena*, Chile, as well. My very best wishes go to you."

In an effort to make certain that Madame Katzen was not too stressed about her upcoming operations, not filled with doubts about their outcomes, Horace dispatched another letter assuring her that all will be well. Given the number of times she mentioned the possibility that she might not survive her operations, he understood that a few words of reassurance and appreciation from *him* would go a long way towards reinforcing any possible cracks to her otherwise indomitable spirit in the face of her pending surgeries.

1964

On January 1st 1964 Madame Katzen flew from St. Kitts to Caracas, Venezuela where she planned to board a ship bound for Chile. It had been almost three years to the day since she left Chile for St. Kitts in search of a new life for her, her mother and aunt. In the three short years since her arrival at the Grammar school her impact could only be described as epic. Her high-octane energy, the incredible number of hours she dedicated to her students, to her craft and to the life of the school belied the fact that, six months shy of her 50th birthday when she arrived, she was the oldest member of the faculty. It was a tough three years, made more so by an undisclosed illness that constantly sapped her energy and her constant worry over the health of her 'old ladies'. She needed to recharge her batteries. Anxious to have the surgical procedures behind her, she looked forward to getting as much rest as possible during her upcoming threemonth leave.

"I am now in Caracas waiting for my ship which is supposed to arrive in La Guaira to-morrow and leave the day after for Chile. It was dreadful leaving my poor little old ladies and I do hope nothing will happen to them while I am away. The sorrow of leaving them has for the time being blotted out every other feeling, but once again, let me tell you how very grateful I am to you, at least I know that if anything were to happen to me they will be provided for until everything is settled, and they are on their way back to Chile.

About the boys. There was still no news about Maurice's prospects, but the Anglican Priest, Father Walker, is quite confident that everything will be settled and that he will leave for England in February. I have therefore given him, out of your fund for the boys, $200, (his share of the $800 that I had on fixed deposit), this sum is in the keeping of Father Walker and will go towards his passage, and I have also given him a further sum of $50 for clothes. I have asked Maurice to let us know about his progress as soon as he hears something definite. I have bought clothes for the other three boys and have paid for Morris's school fees for the next term and also for the lunches for this same period. There now remains a sum in the bank, $200 for each boy, and a few dollars for emergencies. I hope you approve of all this.

I came to Caracas through Trinidad, taking this extra detour so as to have an interview with the French Ambassador in Port of Spain. Off and on I have been keeping in touch with him for the last year and a half, trying to convince him that he should give a scholarship to a good French pupil. Last year he promised me that he would send one of my boys to France for a year, provided we could scrape up his passage fare one way. As you may guess, I had Charles in mind, for with your $200, what he would be able to save giving lessons until Sept. 1964 and what I'd be able to give him we would get that amount. In France his tuition would be free, he would be given books, and his board and lodging would be paid for by the French Government, also his passage back to St. Kitts. The Ambassador was very polite and amiable, invited me to a dinner party and to lunch, which at once put me on my guard, and rightly so. He now says that he can't send the boy to France this year as the scholarships, only two of them destined to pupils in the West Indies, have already been given.

However, he has promised that if Charles were to take the entrance exam to the University of Barbados[8]and passed it, he would

---

[8] Cavehill Campus of the University of the West Indies (UWI).

then get him a scholarship there. I must say that I don't put much faith in his promises by now, but have written to St. Kitts, giving Charles detailed instructions about the exam and asking the Headmaster to allow him to sit the exam.

As Charles will be on the staff this term, replacing me, he will need the Headmaster's permission to take the necessary days off. It would of course be wonderful if he were to succeed, so I'm keeping my fingers crossed and hope nothing will go wrong while I am away. Again, it is all thanks to you that he may have this chance. Had you not given him those two extra years in school when he could prepare and sit for his Higher School Certificate, he would never have had this opportunity. Now it's up to him. I have no doubts at all that he will pass the exam, what I am worried about is that since I am not in St. Kitts he will not know how to go about the whole business. Nobody from St. Kitts has ever tried entering the Barbados University so as there is no precedent it will need a great deal of arranging, correspondence, information, etc., and I don't know how he will manage it all, for he is very shy and never insists when matters concern him.

I shall be very happy to leave Caracas. It reminds me too much of New York, traffic on three levels, noise and rush, political unrest and general Latin-American exaltation and exaggeration. Great stress is placed on money, it's not what is being done in the University for instance that is important, what is repeated over and over is that the building was worth 16 million dollars and that the highway from La Guaira to Caracas cost a thousand dollars a yard. The architecture is fantastic, striking, but nightmarishly so, skyscrapers everywhere of the weirdest shapes and strangest combination of colours, they think nothing of having blue, green, yellow, pink and purple, all on the same wall, in patches, zigzags and circles. It makes me think that I'm walking about in some mad producer's theatre set. Of course, it's worth seeing, but I shall be glad to escape all this and settle down on the ship. I have firmly resolved not to think of hospitals and operations, those three weeks I hope will be a complete rest, so I'm looking forward to the M/S *Panama* with great pleasure.

Will you write to me in La Serena? I shall be so happy to hear from you, it will give me courage. Today is the first day of the New Year. I have thought a great deal of you to-day and now take this opportunity to send you my sincerest wishes for your health and happiness. Once again, I thank you for all you have done, for me, for my family and for those children whom you do not know and have never seen, yet to whom you have given such chances, opportunities and happiness. May the Lord protect you, bless you and make all your paths smooth and straight giving you the inner peace, which is the greatest blessing."

"Thank you so much for your kind letters. You cannot imagine how happy I was to receive them. Your friendship is something that I value above everything else and having your letters with me is going to help me face this ordeal. I am in hospital now, all ready for the operation which is to be performed tomorrow morning, but so far, I have no fears. I hope this is a good sign. It's Tuesday tomorrow, and the Chileans say that you should not get married or start on a journey on a Tuesday. Of course, having a chunk cut out is neither of them: so I hope everything will be well.

The trip was lovely, all but the last week of it, when I suddenly had such terrible pains that I thought it was all up with me - four days of agony and I was afraid that the captain would put me ashore somewhere. However, the doctor seems to be right, I must have nine lives, like a cat, for I am full of energy again, but it took some while for me to recuperate, this accounts for my not writing earlier, I didn't want to sound miserable, and I probably would have had I written then.

Having been away for three years I am looking at Chile as a foreigner would, and I do not like the place at all. I can't imagine how I could bear it for such a long time - all the dirt, both physical and moral, the cheating, petty thieving lying and corruption. To give you an idea of the state of things, I almost had my handbag snatched, the taxis tried to overcharge and every single shopkeeper wanted to short-change me. As for the school, I was received very coldly and felt as if I had penetrated into an enemy camp. More than ever now I want to sever all connections with the *Colegio Inglés*, sell the big house and return to St. Kitts as quickly as possible. I feel so much more at home there, it's a sensation of sort of belonging to the island. All the boys and the staff and people in general are very kind to me there. I will just keep my little house for my old age here if I'll have to return to Chile again.

The nurses have just been to tell me to go to sleep. I suppose I'll have to try though I don't feel like it. I wanted to write this letter to you, nobody knows what will happen to me tomorrow, but this letter will be sent for I want you to know that my thoughts and prayers have been with you and for you the whole day, for it is thanks to you that I have been relieved of fear for my loved ones. May I take the opportunity to tell you that you are the most noble and generous man that I have ever met and that thoughts of you, your work for mankind and your kindness to everybody have given me strength and a wish to help others, and that your friendship has been the greatest treasure I have ever had."

Horace, concerned about her medical ordeal, again sent words of reassurance.

"I need hardly say that of late you have been very much in my thoughts and prayers. One must have absolute faith and trust that all will be well. Your generous remarks concerning me are characteristic of yourself. You only think of others, but what of your own achievements? Wherever you have been you have relieved suffering and brought happiness, knowledge and hope of a better life to poor children. Is there anything more worthy?

I will never forget your work in Shanghai. It was largely through your untiring voluntary efforts, much of which was done during late hours of the night, that so many children benefited. They and I owe you a debt of gratitude beyond words. I do hope you are now feeling better. Please hurry and get well, for your many students need you badly."

"It seems that my number has not been called up after all and here I am slowly coming back to life again. I'm still groggy and weak and there is quite a lot of pain, but the doctors are quite happy about my prospects. There were three surgeons and the operation lasted over two hours with continuous blood transfusions. We are now waiting for the pathological reports, however the medics think that they will be able to give me a clean bill of health. Being Chile, the operation was scheduled for the morning, and after I'd had all the preliminary injections and was quietly falling asleep, for some reason they decided to postpone it so I was taken back again and operated on in the evening. However, that was not the end of my troubles, for the day after the operation there was a general strike in the country and all the nurses and staff simply walked out and left the patients to their own devices. That's what I mean when I say that the moral values of the country are very low. Fortunately, some people volunteered to help and the army took over, which was just as well, for at least the soldiers cleaned the place up, it was sorely in need of it, nobody seemed to notice how filthy the place was. The soldiers scoured the floors and scrubbed the little kitchens and bathed the babies and fed them and prepared meals for the patients. The hospital was very quiet for no visitors were allowed, so we all had a good rest. To-day things are coming back to normal again, and as the doctors have given me permission to move about in bed, I have written a short note to my mother and now writing this to you.

You cannot imagine what consolation your letters have been to me during this period, I have been rereading them constantly and I think it is entirely due to your kindness that I was not nervous at all, knowing that my poor little old ladies would not be stranded and in want. I am hoping to leave the hospital soon and after settling some business I shall be delighted to board the M/S *Suecia*, another Johnson Line ship, on or about the 10th of March and sail for St.

Kitts. It's a poor place but it's clean and honest. And I am so happy that I shall be able to return the 'trust fund' to you as soon as I'm back. You do not know how much it has meant to me to know that it was there all this time in case of need. May the Lord bless you and have you in his keeping always for such great kindness."

"We are leaving Chilean waters sometime today and our next stop is Callao, Peru. I cannot tell you how happy I was to leave Chile, the old expression *'to shake the dust off one's feet'* is very apt. I was even tempted to throw my shoes overboard as we pulled up anchor in Valparaiso, I don't think I have ever been as miserable as during those last weeks spent in La Serena before my departure. I suppose the state of my health had a great deal to do with it, for besides losing a terrific number of pounds - a whole stone and a bit in fact - there had been so many injections and other medicines to combat the infection, that it's a wonder I am still alive. I'm afraid my energy is not back yet, but since I've come on board I have been feeling better, not so listless and indifferent to things. I love ships, and though the *Suecia* is rather skittish for we roll and pitch for no apparent reason, I am relaxing and resting and hope to be my old self again soon. Everything is so clean on board, and there is just the sea and the sky to enjoy, no people to make you bad-tempered. Please don't think that I have become a pessimist or a misanthrope, it's just a passing stage, and once I get back to work everything will be well again.

I am very happy to report that all my pupils did well in the French and Spanish on the Higher School Cert. exam. I have just had a detailed letter from the Headmaster of the school giving me all the particulars and the individual marks and it is with great pleasure that I pass the news on to you, for Charles has obtained the best mark we have had in French in this exam, in fact he has the only 'A' in the whole school. He has already sat for the entrance and scholarship examinations for the University of Jamaica [9] and also that of Barbados, and if he has reached the required standard, then the

---

[9] Mona Campus of the University of the West Indies.

French Ambassador will help him get the scholarship. Morris's marks are also good, but this time not good enough for the Leeward Island Scholarship since there is another student who has obtained better grades, but we expected that he has come back to school again to try his luck in the June examination. Meanwhile he has also sat for the scholarship exam in February for the University of Jamaica and also for the Caribbean organization. I am longing to get back and see what they have done and find some means of helping them on. I have had no news of Maurice Pinney, though I have given him a few stamped envelopes with my address on them, however he has not passed the Higher School Cert. exam and that probably accounts for his silence. I hope that the S.P.C.K. position in England has not fallen through and that he has left already for London.

I have missed St. Kitts terribly and I know that my little old ladies have been very sad without me, that is why I was so happy to be on my way back. It has been wonderful getting your very kind letters in Chile, they have helped me greatly and I do not know how to thank you for them. They have tided me over some very unpleasant moments when I was feeling extremely wretched. Will I ever have the opportunity of doing something for you some day?

I shall write to you as soon as I get back to St. Kitts. I'm leaving the *Suecia* in Curacao and shall continue to the island by plane. It is a great pity that the Johnson Line does not send ships to the West Indies. There is just one little steamer that makes the trip from Curacao to St. Kitts, but she is very erratic and the captain might go in the opposite direction if he doesn't feel like going there, he is the owner of the ship and has very strange whims sometimes."

"There is so much to tell you, and also a matter of vital importance to discuss, so please have patience with me as I'm going to encroach on a lot of your time. I am going to be selfish in this respect, but will try to be as concise as possible.

To begin with: Maurice Pinney has sailed for England. You have paid for his passage, a sugar boat consented to take him so that the W.I.$200 was just enough to pay for the journey. A passenger ship would have taken twice that amount. I do hope things will go well with him. He is to be met on arrival and will be taken to the S.P.C.K. centre where he will be trained and taken care of. This is the best thing that could have happened to him for he is turning over a completely new page, breaking away from St. Kitts where he was always feeling miserable and starting afresh. Here his past will be nobody's concern. He has lately acquired far more self-confidence so I have every hope that he will turn out well. He has promised to write to me when he gets to England, which should be in a few days' time now - the journey takes two weeks, and he has been gone for 10 days now. He promised to behave well and said that he would write to you on arrival.

Morris and Moses are starting their Higher School Cert. exams in a few days. The morale is good and both hope to get through. Morris is secretly trying to get a scholarship, it would be wonderful if he were to obtain it. The latest addition to your collection of god-sons, James Connor, is studying with all his might, I had to send him to the doctor as he was in a very bad state of health because of undernourishment and insufficient sleep. Now, after taking the doctor's prescriptions, eating better and having enough time to sleep, his health and general appearance have improved tremendously. Two more boys have benefited from your generosity, I'm sending you the letter that one of them wrote to the headmaster, and the other one was in a similar state, no shoes to come to school in and no money to pay the school fees, and as the exams were to start he would not have been allowed to sit for them, and lose the year. I hope you will approve of this.

I now come to the most important part of this letter and I really don't know how to begin. I am not quite sure that I have the right to go on taxing your generosity to such extent, and yet, you are the only hope of salvation for this case. It's about Charles Archibald again, and I'm afraid I'll have to relate the whole of this affair in detail, so please bear with me and have the patience to read all this.

A little over two years ago when the results of the School Certificate came out, as Charles's marks were the best to have ever been obtained in the territory, and as I had occasion to speak at the time with the French Ambassador in Trinidad, Monsieur Bayle, I mentioned the boy to him, he was greatly interested and asked to see some of his work. We sent him several essays, translations and other exercises and the outcome was that the Ambassador promised to try and send him to a University in France on a scholarship given by the French Government. You can now imagine how happy and excited we all were. Charles loves French and has always wanted to teach it, but of course going to France was something beyond our fondest dreams. Well, a whole year passed during which, at the Ambassador's request, we continued sending various essays, etc., to Trinidad. He would write back and say that he found them interesting and was amazed at Charles's command of the language. Then, in the second half of 1963, he stopped mentioning the French Government scholarship and finally said that he wouldn't give it to him as he had only two to give in all, and that they had to be granted to Trinidad boys. Why he made the promise in the first place, I really can't understand since he must have known that he couldn't grant the scholarship to a boy not from Trinidad. However, he asked me to see him on my way to Chile in December 1963 to discuss what could be done. When I saw him, and to do that, instead of going to Curaçao and straight to the Panama Canal and Chile, I made a great detour going through Trinidad and Venezuela, but didn't mind it since I was hoping to get the scholarship for Charles. But when I met the Ambassador, he told me that although he could not give him the scholarship to France, he would give him one to the University of the West Indies, provided he obtained University Entrance. This is an exam that Charles took last February. Of course, after the dreadful disappointment he was very downhearted but tried as hard as he could on the exam. Well, we received the results three weeks ago. Charles has obtained University entrance and had the official Offer of Entry sent to him from Jamaica. We were delighted and sent the document to the Ambassador and informed the University that he was accepting the offer - we had to do that since they wanted to know right away whether he was coming.

Imagine then our astonishment or rather shock when we received a letter from the Ambassador saying that he was very happy that Charles had obtained entrance but that he, the Ambassador, could do nothing further to help him. I really don't know how to qualify his conduct. Frankly, if you do not intend to keep a promise, why make it? You can well feel and understand what Charles has gone through and what effect all this has had on him. Having such brilliant visions and hopes all dashed to pieces. Knowing your generous nature, although I am ashamed to ask for the same person again, but could I use your funds to send him to the University of the West Indies? That is, either Jamaica or Barbados? In your last letter, you asked whether a student trained for teaching would be assured of a position in a school here. Not only would he be assured, he would be fought over. There are hardly any graduate teachers in the territory. That is why we were so happy for the Ambassador's interest. Not only would it have assured one boy's future, but he would be able to impart knowledge to generations of pupils, help them and enable them to go along the same way. But it all comes down to money again. How I hate it!

I must now give you an idea of the cost and of our currency. Although prices here are very often quoted in £, the actual money in use is the West Indian dollar. In Jamaica, they use the £, which has the same value as the English pound, though the note itself is a little different. One English, (or Jamaican) pound, is worth W.I.$4.80 when you buy, and W.I.$4.75 when you sell. Which means that the £1000 that you have so kindly entrusted to me correspond to £1000 Jamaica, but which, when I deposited it at the Royal Bank had to be exchanged into West Indian dollars, since a deposit could not be made in St. Kitts in pounds. It had to be made in W.I.$ which amounts to W.I.$4,750. There will be some interest on August 1st. at 3%. The University fees are as follows: £30 for tuition and exam fees; £8/10, guild fees and £170 for board and lodging at the University, that is, for the nine months. This comes to £208/10 for the year, besides this there is Caution money £25 that will be returned at the end of the student's stay in the University, but this does not include books, other expenses nor residence during the vacation period. Traveling between Jamaica and St. Kitts and Barbados is cheap for a boy as he can take a deck passage, it's three days but it can be done. The General degree in Education, which the Ambassador had promised was a three-year course, the first two years are at £208/10 each and the third year is £50 cheaper. But as I have mentioned, this does not include books, vacations or other items.

I really don't know what to do. On one hand, it's an awful amount of money to spend on one person. Of course, the good it would do is very great. On the other hand, you might perhaps want to spend it on some other boy. Of course once he obtains his degree Charles would be able to pay this value back little by little, for he would have an adequate salary.

Please do let me have your answer soon. If you were to sponsor him, we must send all our necessary documents and start preparing. In any case, let us know what you decide. There is nothing worse than uncertainty and this living of fluctuating from hope to despair. Perhaps you might want to send Charles up for one year, and we would try and see whether he could try and get a part-time job to help him pay for some of the cost. I really don't know what to do. The school year will be over in a few days and that means that Charles will lose his present position of pupil-teacher and as he has had no other training it'll be very difficult to find something else to do. Besides, he is a born teacher. You are the only person who can help him now to do this, but we both realize that we have absolutely no right to ask you to do it.

Please excuse me for this long letter. I hope it's clear, but I'm afraid I'm a little incoherent over the whole affair, there is nothing that hurts so much as injustice and unfairness. Had the Ambassador never mentioned his promises, things would have been easier to bear.

Forgive me again. This is a very selfish letter, but it's too long already to add to it and try to make it better. I'm afraid I'm not good at letter writing. I just can't express what I feel."

"Your wonderful, kind letter has arrived. How generous, how understanding you are and what joy you have brought to us all. If you could have seen the transformation in Charles's face as he listened to the news of his incredible good fortune! He seems to be treading on air and has gone off to write you a letter.

Now, about your enclosed remittance. What should I do with it? My letter to you must really have been quite incoherent. What I meant when I spoke to you about Charles was whether I could use the 'trust fund' for the purpose of sending him to the course. On no account did I imagine that you would send a new cheque. I did not want to touch the 'fund' until August 1st, so as not to lose the interest since the money has been deposited for a fixed period. I have paid for the sundry fees, books, Connor's weekly allowance and the shoes from the savings account that I have opened for the boys in 1961 with the cheques you have sent them previously. I still have enough there to outfit both Moses and Morris next month before they commence their duties as pupil-teachers, for happily the Headmaster has decided to take them both on; this outfitting and Connor's allowance for July will probably finish off the amount on the savings account and I planned to deposit the interest of the 'trust fund' on it so as to keep it going. Now, having received this new cheque of an equal value as the 'trust fund', the resulting sum - W.I.\$9,500 (£2,000 @ W.I.\$4.75) - is so great that the responsibility of handling such an amount makes me very uneasy. Would you like me to pay the three years of Charles's course right away? Then if anything happened to me there would be no trouble about the continuation of his studies. And what should I do with the rest of the money? There are always needy students, so some of it could be transferred to the boys' savings account and the rest could be kept on a fixed deposit, (if the interest is better, I'll find out at the bank on Monday), until needed to start another student on his career or outfit one or pay for his passage to a training school as you have done for Maurice Pinney; or would you prefer me to send some of it back to you?

I feel so terribly guilty when I think how much money you have already spent, and this new cheque is making me remorseful, I'd hate to have you think that I'm taking advantage of your kindness and that this is needless extravagance.

There need be no worry whatsoever about Charles's being able to obtain a good teaching post after he graduates. I was speaking to the Education Officer the other day and he mentioned that for many years to come every graduate will have more work offered than he can possibly cope with. The population in St. Kitts seems to consist mostly of children under 15 years of age, and schools and teachers are sadly lacking. Yet, those who leave school do not want to remain to teach in the Primary schools, as the salaries are extremely low, a primary school teacher, with a diploma from a primary teachers' training school, can never rise above roughly £500 a year, that is more or less W.I.$200 a month, but that is the maximum, they have to start at the bottom of the scale where the first salaries are somewhere in the vicinity of W.I.$100 when they have been appointed and W.I.$85 when they are still pupil teachers. Seeing that the house rents range from $60 to $100, and that the cheapest boarding houses with rather spartan conditions charge $90 a month, this gives you an idea of the inadequacy of the salary. A graduate starts at W.I.$200 a month and after going through the whole scale, ends up with $420 a month.

Unfortunately, not many young people have the means of continuing their studies at Universities, or even training colleges, of which the last do not give so many advantages. There is something radically wrong with the whole economy of St. Kitts. That is why living conditions and standards are so dreadfully poor. Our Chief Minister and the manager of the sugar factory have just gone to

England to attend a course on means and methods of helping development on the poorer islands of the Caribbean. I hope they'll learn something there and apply it with good effect here. One of the causes, so it seems to me, is that there are no small land-owners, farmers, industries or private enterprises. All the land belongs to a few rich families which have divided the island into sugar estates and who hold all of the sources of earnings. Another reason, it seems to me, is that there is so little family life, so many illegitimate children who are left to be brought up by strangers and grow up with warped minds and characters. And yet, on the whole, there are so many good qualities in these people!

I'm thinking of going to St. Martin for a few days, or perhaps a week. It is so restful there, peaceful, and in August which is right out of season, very quiet as there are no tourists. I stay in a little place, which is built on the beach itself, and I love going to sleep with the pounding of the waves as my lullaby, no radios blaring away, no people shouting or quarreling. It's a perfect rest. I'm afraid I need it, for this last term has been a bit tiring.

I'm doing something new now, you'll probably laugh when I tell you that now, at my age, I have decided to learn how to drive. I want to do that for there is a small chance of acquiring a small car through the school, and as my little old ladies have great difficulty in moving around, especially in the heat, we are all looking forward to the time when I'll be able to drive them around the island, which as I have written to you, is the most beautiful in the whole Caribbean. But I never knew there was so much to learn in this art of driving, and now I look with respect at all people who can do so. When I learned to keep the car on the road, change gears, start off, stop, and use the brakes, I thought I had mastered all there was to it. Now I see how sadly I've been mistaken. We've started reversing into things, which is a very apt expression, for that is exactly what I do and the walls, trees and posts, just haven't the sense to get out of the way when I bear down on them. There are great hazards driving in St. Kitts, for besides the usual traffic, children and dogs, the streets are also full of goats, sheep, chickens, and worst of all, ducks, which infest the little narrow streets. It's just like going along a tight-rope in a circus.

However, I enjoy it all. I'm not sure that my instructor does. He is one of my colleagues at the school and has inexhaustible patience, not to speak of bravery, for it must take a lot of courage to sit in the same car with a learner and not know what he's going to do next. Anyhow, I hope that you come to St. Kitts, I'll be able to take you around the island. I do hope that when you go on holiday you will look in on us, even if it is just for a day or two. We are only 3½ hours away from New York - you might be going to the Fair[10]? It would be so wonderful if you could pay us a visit and would see for yourself what the island is like and see the boys whom you have helped, those of them who are here."

"I'm afraid I have not made my meaning clear enough when I asked you whether it would not be acceptable to pay the three years' period of Charles's studies. Not for one moment did I have the thought of handing the amount to him, I would on no account do such a thing, in the first place precisely for the reason that you state. Some less fortunate relations and friends might start asking him for help and he wouldn't be able to refuse, and secondly, he is not used to having spare cash and might be tempted to spend some of it unwisely. What I had in mind was to pay directly to the University. I think the best plan will be to pay the University for a year and deposit the rest of the money at the bank so that it will be available only for payment to the University. As I know the manager of the Canadian Bank, I mean the Royal Bank of Canada, I'll ask him for advice. If Charles will be admitted to live in the University itself, which is very practical and far less expensive than any other arrangement, he will need just a little sum monthly for writing materials, laundry, etc., which can be remitted to him personally. As the term in the University opens on Oct. 1st, and as I considered it a good thing for him not to waste the months of July, August and September, I'm

------

10 New York World's Fair held in Flushing Meadows, Queens 1964/65.

very happy to tell you that we were able to obtain for him some temporary work in one of the Government offices - the Supply Department, whatever that may be. The salary is very small, but it will be something that he will be able to leave his mother when he goes to Jamaica, I know he will be very happy to do so, and the rest will contribute to his outfitting expenses. We have written to Jamaica to clear up this question of lodging - there is some delay because when the French Ambassador declined to give Charles the scholarship all our proceedings stopped. As soon as I get an answer from Jamaica I shall write and inform you of what is happening.

A Youth Organization in the French island of Martinique has invited two of my older members of the *Petit Cercle Français*[11] to go over to Fort de France and deliver several lectures on St. Kitts. Their passage to and from was paid and also their expenses in Martinique. I sent Charles, who has his French to think of, and another boy, Slack, who is going to Canada to study medicine in October, therefore also needs the language. They remained there a whole week, having come back to-day also, and it seems that their talks were greatly enjoyed by the audience - and I'm very proud, for it shows that they have really mastered the language if they could give their 'lectures' in it. During Charles's absence Morris replaced him at his job at the Supply Department, so everything was taken care of.

My driving is getting along. Have no fear about my going too fast, my instructor tells me that I'll probably get into trouble for going too slowly. In the meantime, every one of the ducks seems to have acquired quantities of little fluffy yellow ducklings, and they are all having a lovely time in all the puddles right in the middle of the 'duck' streets - well, at least I've learned to creep at a snail's pace."

"Thank you for your approval of the expenses for the help of the boys. I am very happy about the latter for since writing to you last, I have had to spend some more of your money to pay the fees for the Cambridge exams of three boys, £4 for each one. Pratt, your old

---

[11] French club.

friend is one, Swanston is another and George Best, a boy unknown to you, is the third. The entrance fees had to be sent to Cambridge last week and as these boys were unable to raise the sum, they would not have been allowed to sit for the exams in June, no entries or payment could be sent after Feb. 8th, and that meant that these boys would not have had a chance to get the 'O' level certificate, (used to be called the School Certificate), without which it is impossible to get work. Even the Post Office and the Police require candidates to present this certificate. Therefore, you have now given those three boys a chance of better employment when they leave school. While I am on the subject of finances, will you continue giving the same allowance to James Connor next year? The Headmaster seems to think that the boy would make a very good sixth form student and probably pupilteacher later-on, but without your monthly allowance of W.I.$20, (approx. £4-3s), he will not be able to remain in school.

This year economically speaking, will not be bright for the factory and the union of workers still cannot agree on terms of wages. The talks, bickerings and arguments have started in October, it is now mid-February and still no agreement has been reached, there seems to be no prospect of reaching one soon either. During all this time the cane is deteriorating. The cutting of cane should start in early January, for then the sugar content is greatest - only 8 tons of cane are required to produce one ton of sugar, but as the days go by the sugar content diminishes, and by July, 14 and 15 tons of sugar cane are needed to produce one ton of sugar. Therefore, the longer they wait to start reaping, the less sugar will be obtained, and as sugar is the only resource of the island, I'm afraid we shall have great misery and poverty later on.

I am very happy to tell you that we have had a visit from the French Consul-General. He is stationed in Puerto Rico but has paid a visit to all the little Caribbean islands. The Administrator [of St. Kitts] brought him to our home and I gathered my boys and girls of the French Club who entertained the guests in French so well that the Consul was very pleased with them. He said that we sang *La*

Marseillaise with as much feeling, expression and exactitude as if we were all natives of France, he complimented us all and made us a present of three subscriptions of French magazines and gave us a collection of records and books. We were all very proud, especially when he said that on no other island of the Caribbean did he find such a pleasant group of youngsters who could speak such excellent French. I hope my charges will not get swell headed and think that they don't have to study any more - with exams looming just a few months away. Our April holidays are going to be extremely short, only ten days, which will not give us much of a break when one considers that before going on holiday there are still so many odds and ends like reports, record-of-work, etc, to finish up."

"School started this morning and as soon as I arrived, your letter of August 26th was handed to me. Thank you ever so much for it, this greeting from you on the first day of term is a sort of welcome back and I consider it a good omen, besides it is so kind and I'm so happy that you approve of all the arrangements that I have carried out in regards to all money matters.

I am enclosing a receipt from the Bursar of the University of the West Indies together with the figures stating the amounts corresponding to every year. The receipt is for £700, for as I have explained to you in my previous letter, besides the Residence, Guild fees, tuition and examination fees and Caution money, I have sent £49-10s for books, gown and medical checkup which is compulsory on entry.

You will find also enclosed a snapshot of your latest 'godson', James Connor, now smiling very happily as you see - the cause of this are four new front teeth for which you have paid £3, I find this a very good bargain since it has absolutely transformed the boy, he was very self-conscious about those missing teeth, I suppose they fell out due to malnutrition. Now the allowance you give him takes care of that. He is far more alive now and of all things is developing into an outstanding cricket player. He is also making serious plans about gaining the first place in his form.

Charles will be leaving at the end of September and the University has just advised us that he will receive an air passage from St. Kitts to Jamaica as a gift from the University. Isn't that lovely? I thought only government scholarship-holders were entitled to it.

As regards Stacie Hudson, the girl pupil-teacher who is saving up to continue her music studies and Bernard Bryant and the other boy who is trying to get enough money to continue his further studies while he is carrying on with the pupil-teacher career here, they will not need help until summer 1965, and by that time the fund on fixed deposit will be renewable and some of it could be used to help them. I think if clothing and passage money were to be provided, they would be able to pursue their studies, for these young people come from 'normal' families, in the sense that they have fathers and mothers and real, though not opulent homes. This allows them to save up a good part of their salaries, which, though by no means large - about £25 a month - are distributed into three parts: family expenses, their own needs and saving towards their studies. They are both gifted and what is valuable, both want to pass on to others the knowledge that they themselves will gain.

I cannot express how grateful I am to you for your kind permission to use some of the funds to help other poor boys and girls during hard times. I know how much you are doing to help poor people in Hong Kong, and what wonderful results you are getting there, it is extremely generous of you to send help to these children here, whom you have never seen, yet to whom you have given such splendid opportunities. May the Lord repay you, we can only pray to him for your health and happiness.

I am enclosing also a little picture of my favorite beach, where for the past week I have been taking my little old ladies. It is a most beautiful place and I am so happy that I was able to let them have those few hours of pleasure. The driving is still tremulous at times, especially when I am alone in the car, but I enjoy it very much. Of course, I've had some exciting moments when I'd park in all the wrong places and had several encounters with goats, sheep and cows, also was driving in broad daylight with my lights on and was quite rattled when everyone along the road gesticulated and shouted until I found out what was wrong, but as a rule, people are very considerate, and as my instructor said, by now everyone knows on this island that I'm new at this sort of thing, and are all trying to help. I find people are far better and kinder than we generally give them credit for.

We have had quite a scare with the last hurricane, *Cleo*, and now there is a new one brewing, *Dora*. I do hope she will not strike the islands. *Cleo* came within a few miles of the French island of Guadeloupe, played havoc with the banana plantations and left 20,000 people homeless.

Thanks again for everything, you cannot imagine what joy it is to be your deputy in helping people. God bless you."

"How terrible distressing is the result of the typhoon, what dreadful damage to property and what irreparable loss of life. I can imagine how busy you are, for knowing you I can guess how hard you are working to help those people, your whole life is devoted to bringing relief, help and happiness to so many who would be absolutely wretched without your generous aid. May the Lord reward you for all you have done and are doing.

Every time a new term begins it seems to me that I have more work than the previous one. I used to have a free period every day, now I don't get any on Mondays, Wednesdays and Thursdays and the one I had on Tuesdays has also been taken away. True, I now have two on Fridays, and it is very good to have them as I have some extra work, then the writing up of a record of everything that has been done through the week, but I do wish I had some breathing-space on other days. Lessons, preparation and corrections carry me on till midnight almost every day, and now I have two clubs a week, my Spanish boys on Mondays and the French ones on Fridays. Besides the actual club meetings there is quite a bit of preparation, not the least of which is cooking, for half of these boys are always hungry, so I prepare some food for them and they get a good tea before we start on our sessions. It is wonderful to watch the progress made from week to week, it's really worth the trouble. Our School Certificate results have arrived last week. I was quite ready for the worst, seeing that my leave took up a whole term, but to my great satisfaction all my Spanish and French pupils got through. True, there were only four distinctions, the rest were credits, and two pupils have disgraced themselves by obtaining just mere passes which will not be even mentioned on the certificates, but still, I'm happy about it.

The driving is getting along very well and has come in quite handy. Last Saturday I was at the school preparing my work for the week, I usually spend both Saturday and Sunday afternoons on that, and some boys were playing football on their own. One of them slipped and injured himself, broke his arm in fact, and I was very thankful that I had the car and could rush him at once to the hospital; and would you believe it, there was no doctor on duty. I telephoned to the three doctors we have and couldn't get a single one.

Fortunately, the head-nurse took charge and knew what to do. The island is too poor to pay good salaries and thus attract competent medical staff. So if an accident occurs on a Saturday or Sunday, you have to wait till Monday for a doctor."

"I am writing to you to communicate some really wonderful news. Morris has actually won the very much coveted Leeward Island Scholarship. This has been awarded to him for his outstanding performance at the Cambridge Advanced Level Examination, which he took in July. All the sixth-formers throughout the Leewards dream of getting this chance for it means a complete course in a first-class University, no matter the length of the studies. The passage is taken care of and all tuition and living expenses provided from the moment he leaves the island till he gets back to it. The only obligation is that he is obliged to come back and work in St. Kitts for a certain period of time after his graduation. You cannot imagine how happy we all are, the Headmaster is so proud of the honour for our school that he has actually given us a day off. As for me, I can't express my joy at the news. Owing to your extraordinary generosity, Charles is getting a chance in the University, and I know how very much Morris wanted to pursue his studies. Charles of course would have helped him on his return, for he will get a good position, but that would have meant years of waiting. Morris is very reserved, but in spite of himself one can see happiness radiating from him. He is doing a very good job of his teaching at the school and is working very hard at Maths and Physics on his own as he wants to take up Nuclear Physics and Electronics at the University. How satisfied you must feel, for those boys owe so much to your kindness, without your help they would never have dreamt of getting those chances. Morris will continue this year as pupil-teacher at the school and will leave for the University in Sept. 1965.

There is also another boy, Robert Swanston, a most brilliant boy, that is, who could be at the top of his class, but he is virtually at the bottom as there is nobody to look after him at home, and for whom I occasionally get a few articles of clothing, I hope you approve, I didn't want to bother you and hope you will not consider me too extravagant. He's a very sad case, the more so as the boy is intelligent and basically good; but he has no home whatsoever and there is no one to guide him or look after him. He is now 15 or 16, that is the most difficult time of adolescence when children need so much patience, love and understanding and there is nobody to give him any. It's the whole way of life on the island that is to blame, the illegitimacy is appalling, I suppose it's the heritage of the slave times, but slavery has been over for years and years, and yet the number of children who have no families increases. Swanston lives with some sort of aunt, his father, now dead, did make some provision for him, but his legal family, I mean the father's, had the will taken to court, proved void, and as the mother has since then disappeared, the boy is destitute. Unfortunately, being left to himself, he has made bad friends, and under their influence his whole life is going downhill. I believe French and Spanish are the only subjects that he does properly. I try and speak to him whenever I can get a chance to do so, but it's such a losing game. He should of course be taken away from his present surroundings altogether, but how is that to be done? Too much financial aid is not good either, so I'm trying to give him as much attention as I can and see to his most pressing needs as to food and clothing. If those around him will begin to think that sums of money are available it will lead only to a great deal of trouble and no benefit, therefore an allowance is out of the question. I am so sorry that I have no free time, I am certain that if I could give some of those children the attention they require things would be different."

"Your very kind letter of Nov. 6th with the one enclosed for Morris, has arrived a few days ago and I must beg your forgiveness for not answering sooner. It is so thoughtful of you to send him congratulations and he is very proud of his letter from you. He has already written to several universities and we are now awaiting their replies to see where he will be able to study. There is also another little feather to add to his cap - he has just passed his driving test and has received his license this afternoon. He is a very good driver, careful and sensible - so far, and I hope he will continue being so.

I am happy to know that your health is improving. Please follow the doctor's orders and take things easy for a while. I'm looking forward to the end of term, Dec. 4th, as I'm going to take a whole week off and spend it in quiet seclusion in St. Martin. I wish I could stay there longer, but that's impossible. Besides, I dare not leave my little old ladies for a longer period. Mother was 80 last week, and though she's full of energy, there is also weakness and old age, so I can't be away for long. My own health is not too bright for I feel terribly tired. The headaches are of course due to nervous tension and a rest will do me good. We have no competent doctors in St. Kitts, and I suppose I should have a proper check up again, perhaps it's my imagination but sometimes it seems to me that I'm beginning to have the same kinds of pain again. Well, better not to think of it.

We had a visitor to the island from England, a Sir Christopher Cox[12], and I had a most pleasant surprise when I spoke to him, it seems that he was in Hong Kong some time ago and has actually met you. It was so wonderful to speak about you, and he greatly admired your giving Charles Archibald the scholarships to the universities. Charles writes regularly and it is amazing how his French is improving from letter to letter. Thank you for him."

"I have returned from St. Martin and Anguilla and find your kind letter and your lovely card waiting for me. The card is beautiful, a veritable work of art, and doubly precious, first, because it comes from you and second because it brings back so many memories of China, past happiness and the remembrance of moments the likes of which will never come again.

I spent a week in St. Martin, seven days of perfect quiet, which alas fled away, but it was sheer bliss to sleep. I must be becoming terribly lazy. I seem never to get enough sleep. But joking apart, I do realize that I should have a longer period of rest and a thorough check up again, but will have to put it off for a while. I don't dare leave my poor little old ladies for a longer period, they are getting on in years though they refuse to admit it, my aunt is hale and strong, but my mother is becoming frailer. Unfortunately, one can't phone from St. Martin to St. Kitts directly, the call has to go to Curaçao, then Trinidad, Barbados and finally St. Kitts, all around the Caribbean in fact, and by the time you do get the connection it's so bad that you can't understand a word and are left more worried than ever. All the British Caribbean islands are linked by a very efficient system, but St. Martin being half French and half Dutch, doesn't belong to it. However, they are building a new telephone and radio station so probably direct communication will soon be possible. I am hoping to have a check-up in April, when our next term ends. In St. Kitts we have several doctors, but I'm afraid they are not very

---

[12] Educational Advisor to the British Ministry of Overseas Development (1964-1970).

capable and the hospital is not equipped with modern X-ray and other apparatus. I might go either to Jamaica or to Miami, the passage costs exactly the same to either place, I'll have to go by plane to save time. I would of course prefer to travel by sea - the fare is almost the same and I love ships - but we get only a fortnight in April, and then of course there are my old ladies who refuse to let anyone stay in the house to look after them while I am away, so ten days is the maximum that I can take.

After St. Martin I went to Anguilla, which was my first visit to that island. It is famous for its beaches, and rightly so, for all of them are dazzlingly white, there is no black or dark sand, and the sea is of a transparent turquoise blue, but the island itself is almost absolutely flat, there is no electric light unless you have your own motor, and water is very scarce. As for the roads!

Two of my old pupils are natives of Anguilla and as they knew I was coming they commandeered a jeep and for almost five hours we jolted and shook and careened over cliffs, boulders, rocks and stones so that our teeth chattered and by the end of the drive I wasn't quite sure whether I still had a head on my shoulders. We reached the airstrip just a few minutes before the plane took off, I thought we'd never make it, but we all enjoyed the excitement. The pilot was very friendly and said he would have waited anyhow for me - these are very small planes, just five passengers, and on this trip there were only four of us, one being an enormous Labrador dog.

Christmas is just two days ahead, great animation everywhere, people shopping, carnivals and carol singing from house to house - and back to school in a little over a week, term begins on Jan 4th.

May the New Year bring you health, happiness and inner peace. My little old ladies join me in wishing you every good thing on this earth."

1965

"Thank you for your kind letter of Jan. 4th to which I should have replied some days ago, but as usual we are over our heads in work - not only because of the beginning of the term but also because of the midyear exams which are starting on Monday and for which we have to prepare our question papers and as I like to cut the stencils myself, it takes quite a respectable bit of time. My typing is still not very efficient, and you can't make mistakes on stencils, so I have to go slowly. On top of it all I have been given some extra duties, and one of our teachers had to go away to the neighboring island of Antigua for ten days, and I have inherited his form as well as my own for the period. However, everything seems to be under control at last, so I can take a few minutes off to write you this letter which should have been written long before as it represented a sort of 'financial statement', and I hope the items will meet with your approval.

Out of your fund I have paid the school fees for Pratt and have bought him some clothes - he has been ill and needed help. I have also purchased a shirt for Connor and a pair of pants for Swanston, who turned up to school in the most impossible garments imaginable and was sent home on that account. Now he's quite presentable again, and I must say that he is making a very good effort in French and Spanish. If only I had more time to devote to him I'm confident that he could be influenced and changed for the better, he is really intelligent, and so far, willing and helpful, to me at least. I'm afraid though that the only subjects he is getting along in are French and Spanish, it's such a shame that all members of staff are so terribly overworked and rushed that we can't spare the time to take real interest in the pupils. I'm sure things would be far different if we could know the children better, and I think that half of them need understanding, advice and affection far more than the actual teaching of Maths, Science, Literature and Languages.

There were also a few exercise books, socks and games fees that you have provided, but our greatest expenses are the weekly allowance to Connor and the help that must be sent to Charles in Jamaica. If you remember we thought he would have to be given a small monthly allowance, soap, little current expenses for repair and acquisition of clothing and books. Would it be possible to allow him £5 a month, or do you think this is too much? It's the books that are expensive, he spends very little on anything else, and as I bought him some drip-dry shirts he does all of them himself, but still there are some things that have to be laundered. His progress at the University is excellent. As there was a whole month's holiday for Christmas we decided that he'd better come home, so he travelled deck on the 'Federal Palm', three days and three nights, the round trip being £10 - but no food. The crossing was rather rough, so the food didn't matter. Fortunately, he is quite a good sailor, but for three days after his arrival he still felt unsteady on his legs. To our unpleasant surprise the university charges 3 shillings a day for the student during the holidays if he leaves the premises, and 7 shillings a day if he stays there, (without food), which I think is really wicked.

The boys' account so far stands £500-8s-5p on the savings account, and of course there is the sum on fixed deposit, so there are ample funds for your 'godsons' for at least two or three years if we go on at this rate. We might get a government scholarship for Stacie Hudson, remember the girl who wants to study music? The Chief Minister didn't want to hear of it at first, but is becoming more amenable to reason."

"The Australian Eleven cricket team, on their way from Jamaica where they played against the West Indies, to Trinidad, where they are to play the Winward Islands Eleven, have stopped in St. Kitts for a match. The whole island was in turmoil and our Government has given everybody a day off and declared this a public holiday so that all could go and watch the game - this shows you how mad everybody here is about cricket. Of course, it was a foregone conclusion that the Island Eleven would be defeated, which we were, shattered to smithereens, but some of the players did put up a good show. However, one good effect was the brief respite which enabled me to catch up on some arrears of work, so am at last able to answer your kind letter which I have received some time ago and to which I had not replied for absolute lack of time. Do, please forgive me.

We are terribly busy at the school, and in a week's time we are to have preparations for Sports Day, which event takes place on April 1st, but which takes up hours and hours of preparation. Though I'm no athlete I help to keep the records, check the entrances and keep track of candidates. However, my real work comes on the day itself for I'm in charge of the tea for seventy-odd guests: judges, the Administrator and his company, ministers and magistrates as well as all the other VIP's. This does not mean only the brewing and pouring of the tea but the making of sandwiches and baking of cakes, decoration of the hall with flowers, ferns and palms and in general am to supply all the 'little feminine touches' to the ceremony since I'm the only female of the species on the staff. After Sports day we break up, but the ensuing days are filled up with mopping up all the odds and ends, adding up of marks, percentages, record of work done, reports, staff meetings, etc., all of which take up several days of the fortnight that we are supposed to have as Easter Holiday. I'm afraid I shan't be able to take a vacation as planned, though I realize that I need one very badly. The last term though short, is very far from sweet, it's the most strenuous one since the Cambridge Exams come at the end of it. Thank you so much for approving the expenses incurred for the exam fees. And it is so generous of you to wish to continue James Connor's allowance next year. He is really a keen student of languages and makes amazing progress. Swanston has been ill, is still so, with temperature and I think flu. I am so sorry for the poor boy, it must be so terrible to feel oneself of absolutely no interest to anybody. Just hard knocks and no affection - and yet so much can be done with him by just a little kindness.

Our sugar situation is becoming steadily worse. Talks are dragging, no agreement has been reached yet, the sugar content in the cane will soon start decreasing, the cane is drying up for we are having an unusually dry spell of weather, and worse than all, several cane-fires have occurred. This is very bad as it may lead to further unrest and riots. As for the effect on the economy of the island, this is disastrous. I'm afraid there are some very hard and trying times ahead.

If things will be quiet, I'm planning to go away for a few days to Barbados, stopping in Martinique on the way. I wish I could take a few days' trip on a ship, very few ships call here, especially now that there is no sugar to export, so I'll have to go by air, which I don't enjoy as much as a sea journey."

"I can well imagine the excitement when the Australian Eleven played against St. Kitts. In Hong Kong they are also very keen on cricket. The Worcestershire team, cricket champions of England, arrived here yesterday and are having a match against our local team. Personally, I much prefer football which is far more exciting.

It seems that all the hard work of the school falls on your shoulders though I must say I do not think you would be happy if you did not take it on. I wish I could be present for your Sports Day and to enjoy the excellent tea made by you.

What a pity you will not be able to take your full Easter vacation, especially as you really must take a rest after your serious operation. I am glad, however, that at least you are going to spend a few days in Barbados. I am sorry you are not able to have a long sea voyage as you so much enjoy travelling by ship. Personally, I am the world's worse sailor.

Hong Kong is at its best. The wild azaleas, bauhinias and other blossoms are all in bloom, and shortly the lilies will start flowering. Our Experimental Farm continues to grow, and the animals and fowl are considered the finest in the Colony and much appreciated by those to whom we give them. Our latest is a chicken that netts [sic] the farmer three times more than any other bird.

I do hope your mother is better. May God bless you, and with good wish."

"Barbados is a very busy island, full of industry, factories, shops and hotels everywhere, planes and ships coming in all the time, the traffic is tremendous, true almost all streets are one-way direction but the stream of cars is continuous and goes on and on without a break. There are very many tourists and cruise ships stopping at the island almost every day. All this of course boosts up trade and therefore the island looks prosperous. Quite different from poor St. Kitts. However, I prefer the peace and quiet of our little island.

The hotel is very comfortable, built on a cement foundation that juts out into the sea, as if I were on board a ship. The beach is quite safe and very lovely, with the same soft yellow sand and transparent blue-green water as in St. Martin. It is remarkably transparent. I went out on a glass boat and it was a most thrilling experience, there is an old sunken wreck and we floated over it watching the fish swim in and out of hatches. This place is quite cheap, in spite of its many amenities, but it has a great drawback - too many people and too much noise. Of course, it was very interesting to see a new place, but as far as rest goes, nothing can be compared to St. Martin. The greatest advantage is of course the telephone, so I could ring my little old ladies and speak with them. I hope you are well; there is so little about yourself in your letters."

"I am indeed sorry to hear of the attack your mother suffered but glad she has apparently gotten completely over the effects of it. It's good that she is able to spend a lot of time in the garden, as fresh air is an excellent tonic. I fully agree with you that she should not be treated as a semi-invalid, but live a normal life without overdoing things. May she continue to be spared to you for many more happy years.

Thank you for the thoughtfulness and care of the boys in meeting their pressing needs. It is pleasing to know that they are getting on well. I had a good laugh at the Spanish saying you quoted, but feel sure that under your sound influence none of the lads will turn out to be ungrateful when they finish their schooling.

If you ever give up teaching and start a restaurant, I shall be your first customer! Well do I remember your excellent cooking from the Shanghai days, though such succulent dishes are not too good for the figure!

It is kind of you to suggest that I take a holiday shortly. That will not be possible for a while yet, as Lawrence and the family left last week for Australia and England and are not due back for a couple of months."

"I have been away for a week. St. Martin was very restful. How I wish I could spend more time there! It is the ideal place to relax and get one's energy back, however that was not possible. I also went over to Saba. If you have an atlas handy, you might be able to find that little speck of an island. It is also Dutch and is just two miles long and two miles wide, however it towers up to a great height for the whole of it is just the top of an extinct volcano. The rest of it must have sunk in the sea during the final eruption. It is a very strange and quaint island, quite isolated for it is extremely difficult to get there. The coast is all reefs and saw-toothed rocks so it is almost impossible to land from the sea, only sailing schooners and sloops make the trip and even they have to anchor far away and people and freight come ashore in little rowing boats which are usually swamped when they are half way there. The island itself being a mountain top there is no place to build an airport, however last year a tiny landing strip was built on a sort of protruding ledge of rock. It's only 1300 feet, not yards, and the only aircraft that can land there is a tiny 6-passenger Dornier Sol plane, which comes down almost vertically. After all these particulars, you can well imagine what a hair-raising experience landing on Saba was, especially as before coming down the plane circled the strip three times, once to get the feel of the wind - sometimes when there are cross winds and currents the pilot just turns back without attempting to land, the second time because some Americans on board wanted to take pictures and the third time because some goats had wandered out on the field. Every time it seemed that the wings would brush the rocks. After landing we boarded a jeep, the only method of transport, and climbed up and up all the way to Bottom, the capital, which is built, of all places, right in the old crater, fortunately extinct. I'm quite convinced that a jeep is a version of the mountain goat, for the road, like a flat spiral rose almost perpendicularly in an endless series of hairpin and 's' turns, and not long capital S either; the road clings to the mountainside, and the jeep clings to the road and the poor passengers cling to the jeep and hope for the best. Going down we had an especially magnificent view of the jagged rocks and foam way below and could imagine what would happen if the car didn't have a four-wheel drive. However, it was a thrilling experience, some parts of the island are really beautiful, especially the plants, there was a variety of orchid, a dark brown velvet with veins of almond green, growing wild everywhere.

St. Kitts is now having the short rainy season, which is merging into the hurricane period. Yesterday we had the most dreadful thunderstorm I'd seen here, thunder and lightning going off simultaneously, all our fuses were blown and my poor cats and dogs all hid under my bed."

"Last week we went guava gathering. We went into the country and it was the first time that I saw all those trees growing wild and just covered with fruit. There is so much of it that I can't understand why people have never put up a little business of canning, making jelly and jam, guava cheese and sweets. A real industry could be set up, especially if there were enough tourists coming in to buy up the produce. Having just the one sugar industry limits the island's economy. Especially as the factory and the workers can never agree on wages and the crop always starts too late and a great deal of sugar is lost because of the continual bickering.

We are starting school in a little over two weeks' time. I'm trying to get off to Nevis for a day or two before term starts to have a good sleep - I can never get enough at home. Nevis is just across the way, five minutes by plane and there is a telephone so that I can be in touch with my old ladies. They are becoming very frail and helpless

- and yet are both extremely independent and refuse to let me have somebody stay with them while I'm away.

I hope you are well and not working too hard. Once again I thank you for everything you do for those boys whom you have never seen. I hope they will be forever grateful to you for your kindness to them, I always think of you as the most generous person it has been my privilege to meet."

"What a day! School started this morning. We have about sixty new pupils, there are 8 new members on the staff, (in a total of 16), and the Headmaster has left yesterday for a week's stay in Trinidad where he is to attend a special convention. You can imagine the chaos and the confusion, especially as the man replacing the Headmaster is new himself. Still, we'll sort it all out and I'm glad classes have started. My stay in Nevis was very short indeed, for just as I was packed and ready to go there came the warning of hurricane *Betsy* and as we were in the danger area I didn't dare leave my little old ladies. Finally, I managed to get away, but it was just for two days. However, I enjoyed them greatly.

We have had quite an excitement. On my return on the 1st we received a letter from Puerto Rico for Bernard Bryant offering him a part-scholarship to the World University sponsored by the American International Institute in San Juan. It is not a complete scholarship but they are giving him an opportunity to earn the rest, as he will be assigned some work on the campus; but he had to be in San Juan on the 2nd. You can surmise the flurry and rush - getting his passport, passage, sending in his resignation as pupil-teacher, getting the money and so on. We were almost ready for the plane on the 1st, but it came in early so we missed it. Then on the 2nd it was five hours late, therefore we had ample time. Now I'm waiting for news of him for I'm a little anxious about the whole business. I have never heard of the World University, and like many other American enterprises I'm afraid it might prove if not a hoax at least not as serious as a well established institute. I am happy that he will have to do some extra work to earn the scholarship, he will appreciate it far more. I only hope that the concern is trustworthy. I have paid for his passage and given him a draft for his equipment and outfit. Things are far cheaper in San Juan and Bernard is a very serious young man who can be trusted with money, his passion is books [and] there are very good libraries in San Juan. In all, just as I mentioned to you, I have spent W.I.$500 from the fund for him. Yesterday I saw Stacie Hudson off - she was terribly scared to go, but her flight is direct and she will be met by a representative of the Trinity College of Music when she arrives. As her scholarship is quite complete I did not need to supplement it."

"I have been meaning to write to you every day of the last fortnight but have been unable to do so. It's quite late now, but I don't want to go to bed without sending you these few lines, for goodness knows when I'll have the chance of writing. We now have 370 pupils on the roll and out of them I have 140 to my share, spread in seven different forms, so the work is terrific, especially on some days when I get all seven forms and not a single free period to correct the 140 books. I wouldn't mind the work if only the new pupils were on the same level as our own pupils. As it is, I try my very best but don't seem to be gaining much headway. True, we have had only three weeks of real study, though it seems like ages.

I wanted to write to you to give you news of the boys. Bernard has had several adventures in Puerto Rico, the World University seems to be in the period of creation and organization, with no permanent premises, and as he arrived quite late in the afternoon and nobody from the organization went to meet him, he went off on his own to find the place. On arriving at the building, he found everything closed and no clue as to the whereabouts of the people in charge. San Juan is a veritable den of thieves, and Spanish-speaking ones at that, poor Bernard is excellent in French, but knew no Spanish when he left St. Kitts, (though he has acquired quite a smattering of it in the month he's lived there), therefore he was accosted by a horde of taxi-drivers and guides who all offered to take him anywhere he pleased. Fortunately, he is a sensible young man and went off to the nearest police station where the officers very obligingly hunted up a friend of mine whose address I had given Bernard at the last moment and who was able to help him. Next day he was taken by this friend of mine to the organizer of this World University, and it seems that now everything is well in hand. I only hope it will give him something worthwhile - in any case he is attending lectures and working, the last will enable him to earn his living expenses and if the World University will prove to be unsuitable, he will try to enroll in the Inter-American University which is a wellknown and serious college.

Morris has left for the University of Bangor. I was very sad to see him go, looking so small and forlorn, but he has a strong will, I'm sure he'll get through well.

Charles has returned to Jamaica, sailing on Saturday night, by the *Federal Palm* - the passage was £5 deck for three days and nights, so he should have arrived to-day. I hope his second year at the University will be as good as the first.

Matthew has at last been given a job, so now will be able to look after himself. I have given Swanston $10, (West Indian money) as a prize from you. I hope he'll be a good pupil, but the surroundings he lives in are awful. If only he could have a decent home he could grow up into a useful member of society, as it is, I have great fears for him. James Connor is getting along very well. Besides being a good pupil and an excellent cricketer, he has chosen to play for the school in football, and has already acquitted himself well in the first game of the season in a series of matches for the Island Cup.

Having given you all the news of the boys, I now wish you every happiness and hope you are well."

"I have received a letter from Morris; he has reached the University in Bangor, Wales, after a very interesting trip and is now settling down in his new environment. He finds things rather strange, but is determined to make the most of his scholarship. Bernard writes constantly - which for him is a feat. He has been studying hard and has been given the post of Editor on the University paper, this of course is his sphere, so he is very happy.

This letter is not so much to give you news of your godsons as it is to ask you for some advice for myself. I have delayed writing it for a long time as I did not wish to bother you, for I have absolutely no right to worry you with my own affairs. However, knowing your boundless kindness I am taking this liberty, for the matter is absolutely out of my scope of knowledge, but might seem simple to you. Do you know anything at all about South American finances? For this is the matter that 'stumps' me as the boys say. I'll have to go back to the beginning and I hope you will have the patience to bear with me and read this. When I left Chile, I retained part ownership of the school and besides had some property, the large house in which the school was situated and a little bungalow on the outskirts of La Serena, which is a little house but it has a large plot of land all around it and is beautifully situated. After my contract had been renewed, and when I saw that my two little old ladies liked St. Kitts and has settled here very comfortably, I thought I'd like to build a little bungalow here, for it would be cruel to disturb the two old ladies, pack them up and go off to Chile with them again; besides the Headmaster wants me to carry on here as long as I can.

Therefore, I gave up on the school in Chile and when I went on leave, I decided to sell the house in which it was situated, so as to build a bungalow here with the proceeds. Unfortunately, this was two years ago, just before the Chilean elections and it was expected that the communists would get in, nobody was interested in acquiring property. I therefore left without selling it but leaving a power of attorney to the British Consul to sell the house if he would get a chance to do so. The school board decided that they would build new premises and were not interested in buying the property though it was in a most suitable location, in the very centre, just a block and a half away from the main square. To make the long story short, the British Consul at last found a buyer and sold the house - for less than half its value."

Madame went on to say that the Chilean escudo, the currency used by the buyer, could not be converted to U.S. dollars legally, and its value was dropping steadily. There was, though, the option to convert escudo to dollars on the black market. She asked Horace for his advice.

"Why I have importuned you with this tale is this. Do you know at all what one might expect of Chilean finances in the future? Do you think that the escudo might rise again, or does it appear to you that it's a hopeless business altogether? I am absolutely at my wits end. On one hand, I may lose all of it, on the other, if I obtain the dollars on the black market, the sum that I will finally get will be sufficient at most for a chicken coop, since a cottage to be built in St. Kitts should cost something like U.S.$10,000. What is your opinion? I quite realize that what you will be able to tell me is also guesswork, but as you have so much experience in finances you certainly have a clearer understanding of what one might expect. The consul is a most honest and reliable gentleman, but unfortunately he has very little financial training, besides, he is quite old, over 76, (he's an Honorary Consul), and might not see things very clearly. Please do not think that I'm asking for your opinion just to have somebody to reproach afterwards were things to turn out disastrously. I would just like a frank opinion on the subject from someone who is competent to give one. Now if you'd rather not give any opinion at all, just say so, for I would not like to cause any inconvenience.

Our hurricane season seems to be over at last, at least according to the saying 'October - all over', so hurricane lamps, storm shutters and other items are being put away. We've had some rain, the weather is cooler and gardens are turning lush and green again. School work is getting on well too, though there seems to be no end to it. Swanston, so far is keeping up well with the class. Connor is getting along beautifully, but I see that your army of godsons will soon acquire another recruit - a very promising Vth form student, most intelligent, but as is always the case - as poor as the proverbial church mouse.”

“I know nothing about Chile and therefore am not qualified to give advice. Accordingly, I wired to some American Bankers in New York and have just received their cable reply, which reads as follows: -

‘CONCENSUS HERE CHILEAN ESCUDO FACES FURTHER SUBSTANTIAL DEPRECIATION STOP BANK RATE TODAY 3.40 PER USDOLLAR BUT WE UNDERSTAND AVAILABLE ONLY FOR MERCHANDISE TRANSACTIONS STOP WE UNDERSTAND MAYBE POSSIBILITY REMIT THROUGH BROKERS RATE TODAY 4.09 PER USDOLLAR.’

I have given much thought to your problem and regret to say I can find no palatable solution. In view of the political situation in Chile it is a pity you sold the house and land on which it stands, for property would have been a hedge against depreciation of the Escudo. To keep your money on Fixed Deposit, however good the rate may be, is not advisable as it affords no protection against further currency depreciation.

If the sum means a great deal to you, even though you would lose more by selling it on the free market to obtain US Dollars, I would suggest that you do so, and the sooner the better. On the other hand, if it does not mean a great deal then I would invest in some Chilean shares, which would be a hedge against devaluation in Chilean currency. I know nothing about the Chilean stock market, but undoubtedly you could contact some wellknown firm of brokers or your bankers and obtain their advice. I am sorry I cannot give you any advice concerning the future of Chilean finances.”

Four days later Horace received another telegram from his friends in New York and promptly forwarded it to Madame Katzen. It informed her that as far as he has gathered, one can obtain a license to remit Chilean escudos abroad through the local banks but there is no guarantee that it will be granted.

"How may I thank you for your kindness and the trouble you have taken to find out all the information about Chilean finances? I never dreamt I'd give you so much trouble and I'm quite remorseful for all the work I have given you and for the time you have spared to attend to this matter. Your first letter, dated Oct. 28th was followed by the second, both with the far-from-heartening news about the Chilean escudo. Fortunately, I had already made up my mind to face the total loss of funds therefore your letters have only confirmed my opinion of the situation. It must seem to you that it was rather foolish to sell the property, but then, not living in Chile at the present, I did not see anything else to do. The large house, the one I sold, was to remain empty since the school was moving out, it was impossible to find anybody to rent it to, whereas the upkeep of the place as well as the land and house tax are so terribly high that I just don't have the means to meet such expenses. To give you an idea, the land and house tax that I have to pay on my little house have risen from 4 escudos in 1958 to 26 escudos, then to 58 escudos, and the last semester to 120 escudos. If there is no caretaker, everything removable is removed, for Chile is full of people who carry away anything as soon as there is a chance to do so without being caught, so in no time at all the windows and doors disappear, taps and locks vanish, and even bricks and tiles get carried off mysteriously. A caretaker is very hard to get, an honest one I mean, who wouldn't just up and leave without giving you any notice, besides they demand quite a salary. I am very fortunate in having a good tenant in my little house, the one I am keeping so as to have some place to return to, it's a most comfortable little cottage, just two bed-rooms, living room and dining room combined and a kitchenette and bath, but it has a very large garden and the site of the place is lovely with a beautiful view of the sea on one side and the mountains at the back. It's on the edge of a plateau, so the view cannot be blocked. The rent which is being received by my old friend the Consul is just sufficient to pay for all the taxes and repairs, and I'm just keeping my fingers crossed hoping those people will continue living in the cottage for as long as possible.

I am writing to that friend of mine, the Consul, to sell the escudos that are there on fixed deposit, no matter the rate of exchange, for as far as I can see, if I keep on waiting there will be nothing to get at all. I'm interested in selling it for I think I have mentioned it to you before, I have acquired a little plot here, right opposite the house we have rented, and I was dreaming of building a little cottage on it. I have now discovered that there is a building firm here, who will undertake to build a house for a deposit equal to one third of the total value and the rest is spread out over quite a number of years, the payments to be made monthly. Those terms are extremely reasonable, and investing in a building here would be far safer that investing in any shares in South America, in Chile especially, where the percentage of honest business men is about 1%. The political outlook in Chile is very dark too, so even the little cottage there might be lost also - and I suppose I should start thinking of the future, at least try and get a roof over my head for my old age.

The new glasses seem to be very good, at least I am able to cope with my corrections, however the arrears of work which piled up while I wasn't quite at my best, are sky high. While in Guadeloupe I tried to arrange a little trip for my French students. Guadeloupe is very French, and although there is quite a great deal of patois spoken, pure French is heard too. The *Préfet* promised me a trip from St. Kitts to Guadeloupe on a French navy minesweeper, and a Youth Movement will let us use their premises where we can put up camp cots that the French army will let us have. Now if only I can wheedle the return trip on the minesweeper, then I'll be able to take a group for the only expenses will be for food. If all this comes to pass, may I take some of your 'godsons' along and pay for their expenses from the funds? I'd like to take James Connor who is making excellent progress in the 6th form, Eddie Walker, a Vth form boy, also a very good student but not financially solvent, and Swanston. I am worried about Swanston for I am not quite sure that he will make a success of the 6th form. He is only 16, which for St. Kitts is very young to be in the 6th form, and with the home life he leads, I am afraid of bad influence. He has an amazing gift for languages and mechanical work, I mean things like repairing electric appliances and radios. If only he could be apprenticed to some large firm I'm sure he would turn out to be a most competent worker, unfortunately there is only one such firm here and for the time being they have no opening for him. Still, I'll try again later on.

We are having something very interesting - a real agricultural exhibition and I do hope that this will give an impulse to little private concerns and benefit the island's economy. It's to take place to-morrow, I'll write to you about it after seeing it."

1966

"I have received a very kind letter from your brother letting me know that you are at last taking a holiday. I am most happy to learn that and I do hope that you have really relaxed and rested. May you start this New Year full of energy and good health.

Our holiday, alas, ends to-day and we are starting school to-morrow morning. However, this has been a really enjoyable period full of all sorts of adventures. We have had our long expected and much-longed-for trip to Guadeloupe. The minesweeper arrived at six in the morning and my fifteen boys and four girls duly embarked, although at the last moment one of the boys hurt his hand, had to be taken to the hospital for first aid and almost missed the boat. Fortunately, the Government launch had to make a trip to a steamer anchored in the bay not far from our *Croix du Sud* and our captain consented to wait a few extra minutes and the launch brought him to the minesweeper amidst the cheers of his schoolmates. We took twelve hours to reach Guadeloupe, rather Pointe-à-Pitre, for although the day was glorious, our craft being a special flat-bottomed type rolled and pitched all the way. Two of the girls were quite sea-sick, but fortunately some of the boys were in the same predicament so they weren't teased too much, though I did have to pursue two of my 'angels' who, armed with cameras, started to take pictures when the unsteady ones were quite ready to bend over the rail and feed the fishes. When we were half way there, the engine broke down, so we thought we'd have to take to the oars and row our way into Pointe-à-Pitre, but fortunately the engineers managed to repair it so we steamed into the harbor where we were met by the *Préfet* and the president of the *Maison de Jeunes* where we were to lodge. This is a wonderful organization whose aim is to help underprivileged young people - they have just completed the construction of a beautiful three-storeyed building intended for young people, where they will be able to live, cook simple meals and lead normal lives directed by responsible people who are willing to give money and especially time to help those children who lack family guidance. How I wish we had something similar in St. Kitts. It is greatly needed here.

Educationally the trip was a great success. Not only did the children speak French all the time but they made friends with boys and girls of their own age in the *Maison des Jeunes*, took part in several Fêtes, went to the *lycée* where they actually attended a few classes and understood everything, had a football game, (in which we were ignominiously defeated 3 nil) and then, because we had to do our own cooking and therefore shopping, they put all their theoretic knowledge into practice at once. However, the most valuable experience was the acquisition of friendship and a life of give and take where each child learned how to live with others and carry out duties. The girls did the marketing and the cooking, the boys carted the groceries and washed the dishes. I think we all returned richer spiritually, though poorer financially, for at the last moment the minesweeper broke down completely and we had to return by air - paying for the passage ourselves. The company was very good and gave us an exceptionally low rate; after pooling all our resources we still had to pay £1 each, so having taken four of your 'godsons', their expenses amounted to £6 each, instead of the £5 as planned. I do hope you will not consider this too extravagant. I'll administer the funds in a most sparing manner from now onwards, though beginning of term always means extra expenses. Do please write and tell me whether you consider this was too great an expenditure."

"Speaking of visits, we are all excited about the Queen's who is touring the Caribbean islands and ours is on her itinerary. Not only that, but she is actually coming to the school - for the infinitesimal space of ten minutes. And during those ten minutes she is to have the school presented to her, that is, the headmaster, two members of staff and the head boy and head girl who are to represent the rest, other schools will also form up on our grounds and then she is to plant a tree as well as listen to the school song, (composed by Bernard Bryant while he was in the sixth form) and receive a bouquet. You can imagine the activity going on. Although the visit is on Feb. 22nd, preparations are in full swing. All houses (especially the ones on the route to be taken by the Queen), are being painted, roads are mended, walls are scrubbed and grass planted and watered. The 'Clean for the Queen' programme is being carried out with a will and our school building is being also scrubbed and painted from top to bottom and inside out. I'm afraid nobody is thinking of lessons, though we have just had our trial exams to enter candidates for the G.C.E. Cambridge exams. I'm afraid my pupils this year are very far from brilliant. The only good one is Eddie Walker - 'O' level - who has become a still better pupil after the trip to Guadeloupe. David Jones - 'A' level - could be a good pupil if he had the strength, unfortunately eight years of malnutrition are now having their effect. Would you approve my giving him a small allowance towards buying some food and milk? He would be very grateful. His school fees are being paid by the St. Kitts Sugar Factory but that organization does not take any further interest in him and does not even care for whom the money is paid.

There has been a change in our administration. I'm afraid it will not be for the better. Until now we have always had an Administrator appointed from England. When I arrived, we had a most cultured and charming man, Colonel Howard[13] who spoke excellent French and took great interest in schools in general and my little French Club in particular. Unfortunately, he retired last month and we now have a native of the West Indies as Administrator. Perhaps I am wrong but I seem to sense already a certain slackness in Government offices, and there is a great deal of talk going on about a new constitution, self-government, independence, etc. I quite understand that every island should be ambitious and try to work for its own good, but I'm afraid St. Kitts isn't ready yet for self-government, there are not enough trained people to head a Government, and the result may well be absolute chaos and communism.

By the way, I have written to the consul in Chile about my funds. You were quite right, in this period the escudo has fallen still further, so I am quite resigned to the prospect of receiving $500 for my $20,000 property. The consul has just returned to Chile after a six-month trip to England and promises to exchange the funds, which has to be done privately and on the black market since no such transactions are allowed officially.

My little old ladies thank you for your good wishes for the New Year, they are quite happy here, working the garden, growing flowers and vegetables. Mother has succeeded in producing strawberries, quite a miracle in tropical St. Kitts."

"Just as you in the Caribbean are getting ready for the visit of the Queen, so we in Hong Kong are preparing for the arrival of Princess Margaret and her husband in the first week of March to open a British Week here. A large British trade group is coming and exhibitions of British goods of many kinds will be held in the huge

---

[13] Henry Anthony Camillo Howard (1913-1977), British Journalist, Military Officer, Colonial Administrator, Governor of the British Virgin Islands 1954-56, Administrator of St. Kitts-Nevis-Anguilla 1956-66.

new ocean terminal nearing completion as well as in some of the leading stores. The London Symphony Orchestra and a leading British theatrical company will be giving performances and there will be other attractions to make British week a lively success."

"This week has been very full of all sorts of activities, most varied ones. There are the usual preparations and rehearsals for the Royal Visit, and as a sort of rehearsal to that we had a visit from the entire French Fleet (composed of two mine-sweepers), who brought the French Consul, stationed usually in Puerto Rico, on an official tour of the Caribbean islands. He has just arrived from France, a most courteous and well-educated man, though not so frank as the last one. However, my French Club turned out in full force, we gave him a tremendous welcome and he enjoyed himself at the meeting, singing and playing cards with the children. The captains of the minesweepers, who accompanied him, gave the youngsters a lecture on the French Navy and all of them said that they had never before met such a pleasant and intelligent group of boys and girls. James Connor recited a poem in French - beautifully pronounced - and the consul was so touched that he thanked us *au nom de la France*, for the wonderful way in which we showed our appreciation of the French language and literature. He promised us several subscriptions of French magazines and these will be very welcome for the exam candidates. We also had two French film shows at my home, the *Alliance Française* from Trinidad has kindly loaned me four films. Our difficulty was getting a projector, the school had one, but it has been sent to Puerto Rico to be fixed, in September, and we have not had any news of it since; however, the Sugar Factory let us have the use of theirs, an old antediluvian machine, but our Swanston managed to make it work, so we had two most enjoyable evenings looking at the *Côte d'Azur* and two navy, army and aviation films.

Then there was something else. The estates that had planted cotton could not get any workers to pick it and the whole crop was going to waste, so we had a bright idea and the whole school, staff and pupils, went to help out. Of course, as regards the result, it was very negligible, but it was a gesture to help out and also to make people understand that manual labor is not something to be ashamed of, which is the current idea here. I had no idea that cotton was so terribly light! We picked and picked for four solid hours, and managed to gather just 495 lbs! That is probably the reason why they can't get the workers, they pay them 5 cents per lb! Well, our going into the fields certainly created a great stir. I hear that other schools want to follow our example and the manager of the estate says that he is very grateful. We are planning to go again, but at 6 a.m., so as to not lose another day of school, for with all those activities it does seem that teaching and studying have receded into the background."

"The Queen has come and gone. The whole island was beautifully decorated to welcome her, flags and banners flying, bunting draped everywhere, colored lights installed and arches erected along the highway all around the island. Wonderful bouquets were prepared, especially the one that was given her at the school - we wanted to have something from our own gardens and made up a basket of gerberers of every imaginary colour. It was most effective. The children behaved beautifully, sang the school song and answered questions very intelligently that the Queen asked them. The tree was planted and I was very happy that I didn't trip over when I had to make the curtsey on being presented. We were a little disappointed though for the Queen hardly ever smiled, and didn't look as friendly as we thought she'd be. Of course, she must have been tired out, every island wanted to show her everything of interest and the result everywhere was a most crammed programme with no breathing space at all.

Things were rather dismal at the garden party at Government House, for our new Administrator[14] had absolutely no idea of organizing the reception. How we missed the previous Administrator who was a real diplomat, courteous and a man of the

---

14 Sir Frederick Albert Phillips, CVO - first black Governor of St. Kitts-Nevis-Anguilla (1966-1969).

world. The present one just hovered in the background in a wrinkled white suit a size too large for him. And then to crown it all, a sudden squall of rain descended just as the Queen came out on the lawn and the band started to play the National Anthem. As nobody could move we were all drenched. Fortunately, the downpour lasted just a few minutes, and I was lucky enough to be under a banyan tree. However, that made us all laugh and relieved the tension a bit. On those tropical islands, when rain might come at any unforeseen moment, we usually hold the garden parties on the verandas, but it seems that they forgot about the possibility of rain this time.

Thank you for your approval of help being given to David Jones. I think he deserves it. There was another case, one of the fifth form boys, Ian Crosby, who lost his money for the G.C.E. Exam fees on his way to the Treasury to pay it. He was absolutely frantic for the W.I.$17 had been saved up bit by bit, there were no other funds and the fees had to be paid in that very day. I hope you will not mind my having paid them from your funds. I have also bought a good French dictionary for James Connor, he really needed one. Other expenses are the usual allowances to Charles Archibald, James Connor and David Jones.

What amazing activity goes on in Hong Kong! I read an article, rather a whole section in the Times devoted to its description. What a contrast to our part of the world. St Kitts is facing a very bleak future it seems to me. The cotton crop has been completely lost. The school went a second time to help, but nobody else did. Last week the planters made another appeal for labour, even raising the pay by 1 cent a lb., provided the amount picked would be over 25 lbs. But there has been no response. Of course, by experience I know that it takes a great deal of time to pick a lb of cotton.
And being paid 6 cts for it is not worth the trouble. Yet I don't see how they can pay more when they get 11 cts per lb themselves when they sell. Congratulations on discovering a new orchid."

"I hope you are now feeling quite fit, flu is a most treacherous illness and its after-effects undermine one's health. Therefore, please, look after yourself and don't do too much. Thanks for your sympathy about my poor *Micifuz*, I still miss her very much, she was such an understanding companion.

I am very happy that you approve of the help given to the sundry boys mentioned in my last letter, I am very reluctant about mentioning the present case, but I'm enclosing Charles's letter so that you could see that he really needs the help. Both of us realize that you have done so much for him that we shouldn't bother you again, and if I were able to come to his rescue myself I'd have done so, but unfortunately I can't. From his letter, you will see that he has to remain in Jamaica for the Easter vacation for there is no ship to return in time for the opening of next term, and if students stay at the University, they have to pay for their board and lodging, and a very high sum at that, which I find really outrageous as half of them can ill-afford the expenses. He will have to pay £18 for board and lodging and he asks for a further £6 for some books and shirts. His University fees have been paid in full, if you remember, but expenses during the vacations are not included in the total. £24 is a great deal of money and depletes the fund, but on the other hand, as he has no means of paying for his board and lodging, there seems very little else that can be done. I hope you will not consider that I'm spending the money needlessly and recklessly. So far Charles has made excellent progress and if all goes well should graduate at the end of next year - and as I have stated, the University fees have been paid by your generosity until that time. You can see by the letter that his French is now perfect, so you can have great satisfaction on that account, and you can also see that he is very reluctant to ask for help, and does it only because there is really no other way out. As I have to remit the amount before term ends, I hope you will not mind my sending him his cheque right away, without waiting for your reply. How miserable money, or rather lack of it, makes one's life, and how happy we could all be if we didn't have perpetual financial worries. Please answer quickly and tell me whether you approve or condemn the action taken. I shall wait for your reply most anxiously.

The term ends on April 1st and we are all looking forward to our two weeks' vacation. Next week we have Sports Day. For all of the past week we have been having heats and standard points, and you will have a good laugh at this; since we are so short-staffed, I was put in charge of some of the heats, pole-vaulting of all things! Not knowing anything at all about it - I was never able to jump over anything in my life, let alone pole-vault - I watched full of awe as those boys sailed over my head, since standard was 8 ft. On Sports Day they usually go up to 10 ft. 6 in, which I consider quite good since we have no games master to train the boys, they just practice by themselves and follow instructions in books. It's a wonder that no bones get broken, especially in High Jump, for last year the best athlete actually jumped all of 6 ft.

To add to our usual activities, we are now 'showing the ropes' to six American Peace Corps Volunteers. They are going to Nigeria next month, and the West Indies being the nearest point to the States where schools are run on a similar pattern, since in Nigeria students also take the G.C.E. Cambridge exams both at 'O' and 'A' level, they have been sent here to observe our methods. I think it's a very fine thing they are doing, giving two years of their lives to help the underprivileged, and I hope we have been of use to them, they are all University graduates, from American universities, but have no idea of teaching. To add to this, the American system is so different from the British, that it's quite difficult for them to adjust. I hope they will not all be sent to the same establishment in Nigeria, for that school will then run a risk of becoming an American school.

Our sugar crop is doing quite well, though the sugar content is quite low this year, but the poor cotton crop is absolutely lost. The future does not look very bright, for our new Administrator is not at all interested in his post, it seems that his wish was to manage the University in Jamaica and by his training and character he would make a far better head of a University than of the island. There is a great deal of talk of starting a tourist industry, the island of course is beautiful, but there isn't a single hotel worth staying in, and I'm afraid no tourist would return a second time or recommend the place to anybody if he is not made comfortable in the first place."

"I had a most delightful week in the little cottage on Conaree beach, but on the last day I had such a ghastly experience that am still an absolute wreck. And I don't dare mention it to anyone for fear of my poor little old ladies hearing of it, for it would have a distressing effect on them. On the last day of my holiday, on Sunday, I went for a brief visit home to see that the two of them were well and didn't need anything, then returned to the cottage, changed into a bathing suit and went for a swim. There were quite many people so I decided to go a little further away, to a cove ten minutes' walk from the cottage along the beach. There is a little shallow lagoon and I often bathe there. The coast line makes a turn, so the place is absolutely hidden. When I came out of the sea I stopped to pick up my beach bag when all of a sudden a dreadful thing happened. A man attacked me. I can't tell you how horrible it was. I was so stunned, the whole thing was so incredible, unexpected and horrid that for a moment I just couldn't do anything - then I started shouting, which was no use since the surf beyond the lagoon makes a thunderous noise as it breaks over the reefs, and then he flung me on the sand and started choking me. What his motives were, I don't know, whether it was race-hatred, rape, theft or just plain lust to kill, but in spite of all my struggles, for I realized that I was fighting for my life, he was getting the better of me and I knew that in a few moments it would all be over and he would kill me. It was chance that saved me. An old fisherman turned into the cove and my assailant fled. Had the old man not appeared I would have been murdered and the man could just throw my body into the lagoon and nobody would be the wiser. I don't know how I managed to get back to the cottage and the shock of it all is dreadful. The physical pain was awful, I must have strained every single muscle and my throat was swollen and I could hardly talk. I called my doctor and he has given me some sedatives, so that I could pull myself together and not let the poor old ladies notice anything; but the moral shock is so great that I still can't get over it. I loved this island, now I just shun everybody, nothing will ever be the same again, and it's so difficult to act as if nothing had happened. When I think of all the help you have given those boys, and suddenly it strikes me, what if they too will turn out like that man? I have no words to tell you the state I am in, why should all this have happened, and when I think of how the whole thing could have ended, I'm cold all over. I mentioned the incident only to the doctor and the headmaster. Both said: "Try to forget it, there is nothing to be done about it." True, nothing could be done, I wouldn't even recognize the man if I saw him again, but my whole outlook and all faith in human nature is shattered.

I'm sorry to have poured all this out to you, but I just couldn't help it. Telling you the whole story has somehow lightened the burden, please forgive me for bothering you with all this, but I've been so upset and there is nobody to turn to here. At first I even thought of just packing up and leaving, but what's the use? Besides I have to think of those poor little old ladies, they must never know or suspect anything, and here, at least, I can work and they can have a comfortable home. Yet, what does the future hold, if now, just a few months after the white Administrator's going, this has happened. When self-government for the island comes, there'll be no safety at all. Please write and cheer me up, I need it so much."

"Your letter of 23rd April just received has indeed shocked me and I feel for you very much. Thank God that you have come through safe and sound.

I well understand your reactions, which are but natural. Please try to push this ghastly memory away from you. You must not judge a race by the sins of one mad man. I know it is easier said than done; but you have been such a godsend to so very many young students that it would be quite wrong for you to condemn all because of one vile criminal.

May I make another suggestion? However much you like to swim in a lonely area, do not do so. It is always safer where there are other people, for one might get a cramp, or there might be a strong current, and for other reasons it is safer where one can call for help and be heard. I am glad you have not divulged anything to the old ladies, but hope that you informed the Police.

Is there anyone in St. Kitts who could teach you jiu-jitsu? It is easy to learn, gives one absolute confidence, and is a sure protection against scoundrels. I learnt it as a child, and although have forgotten much through lack of practice, I remain convinced that all girls and ladies should learn it for self-protection. Even if a man places a gun right up against one's back, he has not a chance against a person with a knowledge of jiujitsu.

Do not lose faith in humanity. I trust sincerely that time will alleviate your mental suffering."

"Thank you for your most understanding and kind letter that I received a few days ago and your second one which came to-day. I cannot express how much they have meant to me and how much courage and consolation I get from reading them over and over. I am slowly coming back to normal, though both the physical suffering and mental distress still cling to me in spite of all my efforts to completely forget the ghastly experience. I have plunged into school work so as not to have time left over for thinking, and at least don't wake up at night and live the whole desperate struggle all over again. Your suggestion for learning jiu-jitsu is excellent, though I always thought that only young people could master the art. Unfortunately, there is nobody in St. Kitts who could teach it to me, however I'll make discreet enquiries and might find someone knowing something about it. I try my very best to put all the memory away, but I'm afraid I'll have to give up spending some of my summer holiday at the cottage in Conaree, and this means so much to me. I start my day at six in the morning, and end it around midnight, and except for the few hours of corrections of homework after supper, all my working hours are spent among people - that is why I long for a few days of absolute peace and quiet, away from all noise, conversation and even sight of human beings, and Conaree was ideal for that, the cottage tiny, yet cheerful, bright and comfortable, just 10 minutes by car from home and it has a telephone, so I could always keep in instant and constant touch with the little old ladies. I'm always so uneasy about leaving them and going off to some other island, with no means of instant communication. Thank you once again for your kindness and sympathy, you cannot imagine how much you have helped me to recover and retain faith in humanity.

Another boy has been added to the long list of those helped by you - Simon Rawlings. He is a very serious, deserving lad and his circumstances were rather difficult. His father died the year I came to St. Kitts, he was driving a truck, something went wrong with the steering, the truck turned over and he was killed instantly. The mother was left with nine children to bring up, Simon, the eldest, is thirteen. It was very difficult to find work in St. Kitts so she went to St. Thomas where she was unknown and simply went into domestic service. The children all remained with the grandmother who worked on some estate and is away all day. In spite of everything they manage to live for the mother would send her salary regularly to them. Unfortunately, a few weeks ago she fell ill, fish-poisoning, and lost her job, she is almost well again now, but has not been able to get employment as yet, she has gone back to St. Thomas as soon as she was able and hopes to start earning again.

I am now carrying on a most busy correspondence with the new French Consul General through whom I'm hoping to get a bursary for a summer vacation course in Guadeloupe for Connor and Jones. There is a very good course organized by the professors from the University of Bordeaux which would help them greatly in their studies. Jones is to take his advanced level exams this year, in three weeks' time, and if he passes well, and acquires extra experience in Guadeloupe, the Headmaster might take him on as pupil-teacher in September, which would mean fixed employment for at least a year, I do hope he gets the job. May the Lord bless you and keep you and reward you for all your kindness to others."

"We heard the most distressing news over the radio about the disasters brought about by rains and landslides in Hong Kong. We all pray that you have not suffered. I know that you must be already busy helping all those unfortunate people who have lost their homes and have undergone so much misery and hardship. I do hope no more typhoons will come your way. It is so heart-rending to see such calamities brought about by the elements when one does not know what to do to help. We have just had the first hurricane of the year, *Alma*, which has done a great deal of damage to Cuba. Do, please be careful and do not take risks going to those parts that are not safe."

"Thank you for your kind letter of June 25th, which, for once I can answer right away for school has just closed and we are relatively free.

I am sorry that the farmers in the New Territories have suffered so much; I know that you have already come to their help and I am sure that everything is being done to enable them to make up for their losses and to start anew. They are indeed fortunate in having you near them.

Here, things are still the same though there is being a great deal of political activity, elections are to take place soon, self-government will be assumed after that and I only hope that life will continue to be peaceful here. I do not know if you will not consider me wise, for although I have definitely lost one house in Chile, I've decided to try and build one here. Some time ago I made enquiries and there is a contractor here, (he is at the same time a furniture dealer and the undertaker, of all things!) who will build a house for some payment down and the rest to be divided over a period of years. I sketched my own plan and showed it to him, he took it to a retired captain who is now an architect, (things are strange in St. Kitts, aren't they), and this man has made a real plan according to the sketch and Ross, the builder, has now given me an estimate. As we have received some back pay, I now have enough together with the rest of my savings, to pay him the initial down payment. However, after working out the total sum that I'd have to give him, I have decided to do things in another manner. According to him the house would cost in our W.I. currency $18,000, but, by the time I would have finished paying him I would have handed over $27,000, which really does seem a great deal too much, doesn't it? I have therefore applied for a loan to a corporation of Sugar Estates, and if it is granted, then I can have the house erected for the $18,000 cash and pay back to the sugar estate at a reasonable 8%, this I can manage if there is no change in the Education Department, for the Headmaster has asked me to renew my contract once again when the present period comes to an end. So now I am keeping my fingers crossed for two things - one, to get the loan, - two, for the political situation to remain more or less the same. My dear little old ladies are not becoming any younger, and I think it would be really cruel to disrupt their lives once again, pack them up and drag them back to Chile. They like it here, the climate seems to agree with them, and they are happy. On the other hand, with the rent that we pay monthly I could have already built half of the house during those five years, and if we are to stay for another five, it seems such a waste to have nothing to show for it at the end. Do you think I am really foolish in embarking on this project?

Tomorrow I'm moving to the cottage in Conaree. You must think me quite daft to go there again, but I will probably not venture off the veranda and keep all doors locked."

"I note that you intend building a new house. You ask if I think you are wise in embarking on this project. I personally would have waited a while in order to see what St. Kitts will be like under self-government. A country is like a child - in growing up many mistakes and rash decisions are made.

If you decide to build, go direct to the best architect, his fees will cost you no more but his knowledge will assure you of a well designed and constructed house which should not need much upkeep. An inexperienced building contractor or one who has not sufficient funds is inclined to skimp on building material, cut down on cement, etc., with the result that the upkeep can be very expensive and indeed you will have a great deal of trouble. Another thing one must remember is that a building always costs more than estimated, then one, of course, has to pay for furniture, fittings, linen, etc, for the new home.

I am so glad to hear that you have had good news from Guadeloupe and wish you all a most enjoyable time. How good of you to pay for Jones's passage. Of course I shall be delighted to pay for Connor. Should there be any other way that I may be helpful, please act at your entire discretion. I do hope you will enjoy your stay at Conaree but take reasonable precautions, do not go far from people.

Yesterday we had a severe typhoon, but fortunately it did far less damage than was expected. Two ships collided in the harbor, one went aground, a number of houses collapsed and there were the usual landslides, etc, and only one person killed by a falling tree. With every good wish."

"Ten days ago I was just getting ready to write to you for I had such good news and wanted to share it with you, and suddenly Mother became so seriously ill that for two days we thought she would never recover. Now, at last visit, the doctor thinks that she'll soon be out of the woods, and that if no complications set in, with good nursing and care she should be out of all danger in a few days' time. He thinks it was a tiny clot in a blood vessel that had caused an inflammation followed by a dreadful infection. The whole process was accompanied by excruciating pain and temperature. Since Friday her temperature has been dropping, though it's still fluctuating around 100, but the pains, mercifully have subsided. She is now quite conscious and is beginning to take an interest in things around her - though she gets cross very easily, but I consider that a good sign, it shows she's getting better and wants to have everything her own way again. I can't tell you how dreadfully worried I had been, but now, once I'll catch up on lost sleep, I hope everything will be well again. She will not tolerate a nurse, except when blood tests and injections have to be performed, and the poor little thing has needle points all over her body, there is hardly a spot left, fortunately the doctor is reducing the number of them. However, I am with her almost all of the 24 hours; now she's asleep, so at last I can write to you.

The first good news is the Consul General has actually given me the three bursaries that he had promised, therefore Jones, Connor and Morgan - another of my underprivileged students - can enjoy the full benefit of a six-week course and spend that time in wonderful conditions, having comfortable quarters, good food and receiving not only academic knowledge but acquiring all sorts of experience and general information. Two girls, who can pay their own way also went. I wanted to go for a three-week course for teachers given by those same professors from Bordeaux on contemporary literature, for here in St. Kitts there is no chance of gleaning any news of what is happening in the literary world, but will have to postpone that. There is now a very convenient air-service between St. Kitts and Guadeloupe and the round trip can be made in a few hours. This enabled me to leave Mother in the care of a nurse for a little while and take the boys and girls down to Guadeloupe myself. This was yesterday, and as soon as I get another moment I'll tell you in what wonderful surroundings I have left them. Mother hardly realized that I had gone when I was back again, the doctor had given her an injection so she slept almost through my whole absence. He had assured me that there was absolutely no danger for me to leave her for those hours, and he himself was there almost the whole time, unfortunately Mother caught a glimpse of the nurse and this made her very cross.

Now for my second piece of news. Wade Plantations have granted me the loan and I can start on the building of the house. However, here again I've come against difficulties. While I was dealing with the architect and builder by 'word of mouth', everything seemed well, but when I insisted on a proper contract, drawn up legally stating every detail of the building, the contractor seems to be reluctant to sign it. This makes me more determined than ever to have such a document for I shall certainly not embark on this project without sufficient security. To-day is election day in St. Kitts, so the contractor who was supposed to sign the contract on Saturday, which he didn't, saying that he'd do it to-day, has again put it off till tomorrow. I hope we shall be able to come to terms then. This evening we shall know what kind of Government we are to expect for the next five years. I do hope it will not have a communist trend."

"The house is getting along beautifully. The roof is on, all walls are plastered on the outside and inside, the ceiling's in place and the electricians and the plumbers have almost finished their part, therefore the architect and builder both say that in four weeks' time we would be able to move in. My little old ladies are full of plans and watch the building all day long. My French and Spanish boys have of course swarmed all over the building and are looking forward to the meetings in the large room which is intended specially for the clubs. Mercifully, hurricane *Inez* bypassed us at the last moment. I do hope that *Judith* was the last of the season and no more suffering will be inflicted on the poor islands."

"I am sure you must think me a most ungrateful creature for not writing for such a long time, but knowing your kindness of heart, I hope you will forgive me. Two weeks before end of term our Headmaster became ill and we all had to do a great deal of extra work, some of it was most amusing - nobody on the staff had enough courage to take prayers and Assembly at the beginning of his absence, so for the first time in the history of the Boys' Grammar School those duties were performed by a mere woman - me. Then we had to work out an end-of-term exam time-table, but the worst part of it all was that we had to carry out Speech Night and the performance of the School Play two days later, all without a Head. I trained the boys to receive prizes and organized the prize-giving and had to deputise for the Headmaster at the play to meet the Administrator, carry on a conversation with him during the intervals and entertain him. I have never come across a man so difficult to talk to. All of his answers were monosyllables, 'yes' and 'no', thus squelching every subject. However, apart from the girl at the piano playing the National Anthem twice, everything went well. The

Headmaster is still on sick-leave and nobody knows how long this leave will last, he is kept under sedation and the report is that his trouble is 'psychological', which does not sound very hopeful. New term starts in exactly a week's time and last term's reports have not yet been sent out since the Headmaster was unable to sign them.

All those troubles at school have been compensated by our great happiness of settling in the new house. The builder carried his contract out faithfully, not spending a single cent over the amount agreed and completed the whole building in 15 weeks. We are enjoying it immensely, it is so comfortable and the plan has turned out to be most convenient, the little old ladies not having any steps to go up or down, just one at the front porch and another at the back, everything is on the same plane for them, whereas I enjoy my second half-storey from which the view is so beautiful that I am quite content at the prospect of paying off the loan, I don't regret it at all, even if it will take me years and years to do so.

Everyone was most kind and on the day that I wanted to move, eight of my most stalwart 'French' and 'Spanish' boys appeared of their own free will and carried all the furniture across, including the piano and the crates of crockery, not breaking anything and not even scratching the new paint. All this with jokes and songs and cheerfulness, and speaking French and Spanish all the while. The metal work class in school made a lovely pair of gates for me and this gives the finishing touch to the house. The name, also in metal was presented to me by the Sugar Factory and all our neighbours came to help. The garden is beginning to look well, today I bought some Dutch Crimson Glory roses for Mother and twenty little white Cornish Cross chicks for my aunt, they are both very pleased."

1967

"How can I thank you for your kindness? You are doing so much for me already letting me help all those poor boys, and now you are sending me such a generous present. It is so embarrassing to receive so much from you and not be able to give anything in return except sincere prayers for your happiness and fervent wishes for your welfare. You cannot imagine how much all of us here appreciate everything you do, how grateful we are and in what esteem and affection we feel for you. The gift that we plan to acquire from you is something that we have always longed for but could not have. Mother especially always wanted it. It's one of those electric appliances for the kitchen which does all of your work for you, minces, mixes, liquefies, makes batter and in general does everything. As we shall use it every day we shall always remember you every day, not that we need a concrete article to remind us of you, you are always in our thoughts. So you see how very selfish I am accepting this gift?

I am enclosing some photographs of the house. The enlargement is the front view, the garden is only starting, there are just a few rose-bushes and the mauve bougainvillea, but since the picture was taken there is already great improvement, we have added more rose-bushes along the front and there are gerberers and tuberoses on the sides; the vegetable garden at the back of the house is progressing very favourably, with lettuces that are already at the edible stage, tomatoes, eggplants, sweet peppers and Chinese cabbage. Things grow here at an amazing speed. We also have an alligator pear, two mangoes, several bananas, a lime, a lemon, (bearing gigantic lemons, we planted it three years ago, when I first acquired the plot) and many papayas. There is also a soursop and a sugar apple as well as a bread-fruit tree which you can see on the outer picture with the balcony of my room.
The third picture represents the famous gates with one of the young men who helped make them.

The house is extremely comfortable, the old ladies have their room on the ground floor with no steps at all, and my domain is upstairs with a most marvelous view. I wish you could visit our island, I'd be so happy to show you everything on it and the house in the first place.

Things are still very much unsettled at school. The Headmaster is not getting any better, he did not turn up for the opening of term. He has come to school twice but has not seen any of the staff nor pupils, and the doctor seems to think that he is on the verge of a nervous break-down if not in the midst of one. I have been taking Assembly almost every day, and the pupils respond very well; one of the prefects reads a portion of the Bible, then I lead them in prayers, a hymn follows, then another prayer and then I give out all the notices, etc. The boys behave very nicely when I am there, but unfortunately they do not with the other members of staff, and little by little the discipline is deteriorating. If I had the authority, that is if I were appointed officially to take over for the Headmaster until he gets better, I am sure we would get along fairly well, but this being a boys' school, the ministry does not approve of a woman doing this job, therefore we are carrying on without a head or a responsible person to deputize for him. This grieves me very much, for no matter what good qualities the boys may have, they are still children and have to be guided.

There is one piece of good news. I have spoken with every possible person in the Ministry of Education, and I am very happy to tell you that I have at least succeeded in getting Eddie Walker transferred to a good school, the Basseterre Senior School, where he will be able to teach Spanish and have a chance of getting aid from the Government later on for further studies.

My contract is coming to an end in April, however the Government wants to renew it, which I am very happy to do, for I'd hate to move my poor little old ladies back to Chile. Nevertheless, I am not going to go on leave until June, that is, until the G.C.E. exams are over, for I'm afraid of leaving my boys without personally supervising their studies. After the G.C.E. I'm to have three months leave. I am thinking of fulfilling an old cherished dream of going to England, France and Spain, but there is just one dark spot about it, I'm so afraid of leaving the little old ladies, they are so frail and I would never have a tranquil trip thinking of all the dire things that may happen while I am away. How very interesting your work on the farm seems to be and the current warm air appears most intriguing. Is the origin of Hong Kong volcanic? How grateful your farmers must be to you for all the help you give them."

"Fortunately, we now have an appointed Acting Headmaster, a pleasant man to get along with, not very responsible but quite ready to take advice, and as the youngsters on the Staff are almost all erstwhile pupils, and as the prefects are willing to do their share, we are slowly picking up the pieces of the crumbled discipline and things are beginning to return to normal. Another week or two, and I think we will all be happy again. Unfortunately, on Feb. 9th there is a cricket match, Barbados versus the Leeward Islands, the park where the match is played is right next to the school, so it will be rather difficult to carry on classes. The Government has wisely decreed the first day of the match a public holiday, and the third is a Saturday, thus we shall have only Friday to struggle through. It is so good to see everything in order again. I hope our Headmaster will be given another month sick leave, I'm sure this will be to everybody's advantage, his own included. He is now in Barbados where he has some relatives, and as he was born on that island, it is probably the best place for him to recuperate.

What exactly is happening in China? I cannot understand it at all. It seems that there is a full-scale revolution going on, and we had no inkling that the Mao regime was being in danger of being overthrown - and yet, according to the BBC broadcasts, whole provinces were against him, and the news sounds very much like civil war. The strange thing is that Mao himself does not seem to give any discreet orders or broadcasts. I fervently hope that this state of affairs will not affect Hong Kong. We are very much concerned about you. Are things safe for you to remain there?

We are becoming fonder of our home every day, and, in spite of the wind, the garden is beginning to look lovely. True, Mother has erected a screen of white cloth around every rose-bush, rather on three sides, so as to shelter them from the wind, and the general effect is that of a flotilla of little sailing ships, but the results are certainly heartening. Yesterday we picked the first Crimson Glory rose, and it certainly lives up to its name. Very large, as if of red velvet, the soft, dark shade, and beautifully scented. The bougainvilleas are doing very well too, especially the deep purple, but the yellow and salmon-pink are starting to flower also. The pink and the red double hibiscus have also opened, and we had ten tuberoses blooming all at the same time.

We are looking forward to receiving your mixer, for St. Kitts being such a small place, they do not have such appliances in large stock, but our local Philips agent has ordered one for me. We shall enjoy it all the more when it comes and will have all this period of looking forward to its arrival. Thank you!"

"As I have mentioned to you in a post card from Nevis, I have had the great joy of having my old friend Jane Ying for a visit. We were so happy to meet again after all those years and the first few days we talked and talked so much that both of us developed laryngitis. There was so much to remember, so many things had happened since we last saw each other that we really talked the sun down. Jane has of course changed and matured - just as all of us have - but we still get along just as well as before. She was delighted with the island, I took her to every single place there was to see, and after looking into all the pro's and con's she has decided that she would very much like to retire here. This of course would be wonderful. We are both in more or less the same circumstances as far as family ties are concerned, my son has gone his way, both hers will also go theirs, and though I make myself never to think of it, there will be a time when my beloved little old ladies will leave me, and I shall really have nobody. It would be marvelous were she to settle here. Of course, we are both too independent to live in the same house, so we have been all over the island looking for a plot for where she wants to build her own home. She will be able to retire and not work anymore, unfortunately I'm not in the same category, but when I'll not be able to carry on in the school, we have thought of embarking on some little commercial venture. St. Kitts is lacking so many amenities, and if tourists are going to be enticed to the island, I was thinking of a little tea-shop - there isn't a single one here, and though it may surprise you, I am quite a good cook, or so my friends think, and I'm sure that with Jane taking on the administrative side and greeting customers with her charming smile, and my baking the cakes and making the sandwiches, we should have a successful partnership. I have quite a bit of experience with teas since I'm always in charge of such functions here, and we would have the enterprise on a small scale, so as to be able to do everything ourselves, except for the washing of the dishes, actual serving and cleaning up. What do you think of the scheme?"

"I hope you have had a successful trip as far as business is concerned, but I hope it has also been a happy and gay one, with rest and relaxation on the way. I'm only sorry that since you went out of Hong Kong you did not look in on us; also, that if you had gone a little later, in July, perhaps I would have had the great happiness of meeting with you somewhere in Europe. If all goes well I'm going on leave some time at the end of June. I still don't know when exactly for as I did not want to take the trip by air, and as I do not like passenger ships, I have booked my passage on a French banana boat of the *Compagnie Générale Transatlantique* which is supposed to leave Pointe-à-Pitre in Guadeloupe and go to Dieppe or Rouen. However, with characteristic French lack of precision I still don't know when I'm sailing, nor do I know the name of the vessel. The only black cloud is the prospect of leaving my poor little old ladies, how I hate doing that, and yet I know that I really do need a rest, a break and a complete change for the year ahead is going to be most difficult."

"What is happening in Hong Kong? I am terrible worried about the situation, afraid how it might affect you. I am hoping that you are still in Europe, but of course, sooner or later you will return. Is it safe for you to be there? Here in St. Kitts, there is still calm and peace, but nowadays one cannot vouch for the future. It seems that the Governments of all the little Caribbean islands (so-called 'states') are now beginning to see that 'freedom' is not so attractive after all. And what if England joins the Common Market and stops acquiring West Indian sugar? The colonial status was far better to my way of thinking, our little islands are too small to be entirely independent, a federation would be the only solution, but there is too much pettiness for all to agree.

It is becoming increasingly difficult to cope with the discipline problem in school. The Headmaster is beginning to realize that internal discipline is good only in theory but not in practice, so we are all very happy that there is only one month of school left. I'm taking my leave from 21st. June, but do not know yet if and when I'll set out on my travels to Europe."

With Horace traveling abroad, Lawrence responded on his brother's behalf.

"Horace and Michael are still away but expect to be back some time towards the end of next week.

I appreciate your predicament regarding the four boys you would like to send to Guadeloupe for advanced studies. In all the circumstances, I am sure Horace would be quite happy for you to use your discretion in allocating some money from the fund towards payment for their passages.

Incidentally, I read recently that there were riots (May 1967) in Guadeloupe. Even there they seem to be unable to escape the present general unrest. Truly one wonders what is going to happen to the world. The Middle East situation is perhaps the most dangerous, followed closely by Vietnam.

Here, fortunately, conditions appear to be returning to normal, but there is an undercurrent of anxiety and there is no doubt that the riots created an atmosphere of uncertainty which will do harm to the Colony's image and which may well delay or even prevent the implementation of new projects so badly needed to keep our labour employed.

If there is a lesson to be learnt, it would appear to lie in the promotion of a closer relationship between management and labour. Today it is necessary to explain to the workers the reasons which govern their employment - that wages must be limited by the ability to sell the goods they manufacture in competition with others and at a reasonable profit".

"Thank you very much for your two kind letters. It was indeed most thoughtful of you to write and I am very grateful to you. I should have thanked you before, but was terribly pressed for time, right after the play, which turned out to be a great success, we had some of our school exams, mine to be exact, for as I am going on leave in a fortnight's time I want to leave everything ship shape and no loose ends anywhere. Now we have started on our G.C.E. 'O' and 'A' levels, as doubtlessly they also have in Hong Kong.

I do hope the Middle East situation will be settled soon since at last Egypt has accepted the cease-fire, but how many tragedies have taken place, how many awful sudden deaths which represent just a senseless loss and needless sacrifice. We grieve for those poor people, and yet things being so precarious even here, we do not know when our poor little islands might meet the same fate of strife and turmoil. I hope your brother is not anywhere near the unsafe zones and that the situation in Hong Kong is under control.

I have been extremely fortunate: the French Consul General in Puerto Rico has given me a scholarship for one of the boys and our local Government has promised me two more for a course in Guadeloupe given by professors from France during the summer. I am now trying to collect some funds for yet another boy and a further sum to pay their passages to the French island. If I shall not be able to obtain the full sum required, I hope your brother will not mind if I complete it out of the fund that he has generously sent for my poor homeless boys. It is difficult to imagine in what miserable circumstances some of them live. Thank you once again and with every good wish to you, your family and your brother."

"I have just returned to Hong Kong and found your kind and welcome letters of 10th and 22nd May awaiting me.

My trip to Europe was for business purposes, but I did succeed in visiting the world-famous Koekenhoff Gardens, the Chelsea Flower Show and Wisley[15]. The flowers were all at their best and something one should never miss seeing.

I was concerned to read in the papers just prior to my return that there were riots in Guadeloupe. I do hope that all is well at St. Kitts.

Hong Kong has gone through many troubles. Communists agitators bribed thousands of young people, including many school children, to cause disturbances. They fought against the police to the accompaniment of speakers telling them to kill and at the same time requesting the police to turn against the British, but they stood fast and managed to control the rioters. The older Chinese and Europeans felt the police had done a marvelous job, and a Fund for the benefit of the police children's education was started and subscribed to largely by Chinese. This seems to have annoyed the communist leaders who lost 'face', so they are now trying to cause strikes in all industries. However, I am convinced that the situation is under control and all will be well, though, of course, confidence in the Colony has been shaken and it will take a fairly long time for us to recover.

What a pity we did not meet in Europe! I do hope that you will thoroughly enjoy your trip there. At this time of the year the weather should be excellent, and of course, there are such wonderful museums, shows, etc. to be seen.

I am delighted that you have given Karina Hudson £200. Should she require more for the third year please use your discretion and do what you think is best. You have a knack of spending the money where it is most needed.

I agree with you that it is a pity Charles did not go to France. It would have broadened his outlook.

---

[15] The Royal Horticultural Society's garden at Winsley.

Heartiest congratulations on the success of your pupils with their oral French exams. You mention that four boys have done very well indeed, and one of them will benefit by the scholarship presented by the French Consul General. It does seem hard that the other three do not have sufficient funds to go on their own to Guadeloupe. I do hope your Government will respond to your appeal. What would their passages cost? You may certainly use some of the fund to pay their passages, but how about the other expenses, i.e. tuition fees, board and lodging, etc.?

I am sorry you are having so much difficulty in coping with the discipline problem in school. Youngsters throughout the world believe they know everything and do not realize that one must pay for experience.

Please give my very best wishes to the little old ladies. I hope you are keeping well and that you will enjoy your much-earned holiday."

"It is good to know that you are back and I do hope there will be no more trouble in Hong Kong. I was most worried about the situation there and apprehensive as to how it might affect your safety.

Here too there is some unrest. It is not as bad as your cutting[16] says, but there has been some shooting and several people have been detained and others arrested. However, we living on the island seem to know less about the current events than the people abroad. Nobody knows for certain what has happened - some say the Government has staged the whole of the attack and that the police themselves fired on their own building to create an appearance of riot which they laid at once at the opposition's door thus having an excuse to arrest the leaders. Others say it was the opposition, and a third opinion states that the Anguillans are at the bottom of the whole thing.

However, for the time being, all seems quiet and my little old ladies have insisted on my going away. Everybody promised to look

---

[16] Newspaper article.

after them, yet it is with a heavy heart that I have left home. If I were
not in such desperate need of rest I would not have listened to them,
but I know that if I do not stop all work now, there are all the
probabilities of a breakdown. I am going away for two months.
James Connor will sleep at the house while I am away and I think I
have foreseen and made plans for every eventuality.

Thank you for your usual generosity. Our government has
actually given me a scholarship for one of my boys and I have begged
the general public's aid for another. With your kind blessing I am
paying the traveling expenses of three boys - £9 each, return trip. I
am so sorry that I was unable to take my leave when you were in
Europe. I cannot tell you how happy I would have been to see you.

I shall now write to you again once I'm on board the ship which
I'm to board in Guadeloupe to-morrow. Thank you for everything."

Two weeks later Madame Katzen flew to Guadeloupe and boarded
the *SS Sougueta* to begin her transatlantic vacation.

"At 4 pm we are supposed to reach Dieppe. After all, this has
been a very good voyage. I had some misgivings when I first saw this
ship, she is so small, just 2800 tons, and so low in the water that there

was no need for a gangway to go on board, just a little plank and you stepped from the wharf onto the deck. I had a very large cabin, but very Spartan, no carpets or soft arm chairs, an old-fashioned bunk (not bed) screwed to the floor, the tables also fixed to it, a very old-fashioned washstand with metal loops all about it to ensconce everything and the only two chairs had chains holding them to rings sealed to the floor. Not a very cheerful place. The stairs are extremely steep and narrow and the thresholds a foot high. I barked my shins on all of them. To bolster up our morale the captain had abandon-ship drill no sooner we were out of Guadeloupe, so we all donned our cork jackets and lined up in front of the lifeboats. There are only two of them for the whole ship, so one had better arrive early. The crew was the most ruffian-like I'd ever seen. After the exercise, the captain gave each one of us a ship biscuit - whether for good behavior or as a sample of emergency diet, I don't know. Anyhow they tasted mildewed and musty so mine went overboard as soon as nobody was looking. There were only five other passengers, two we didn't see at all as they were seasick all the time, the others were very French, crumbled bread into their coffee and soup, ate fried potatoes and lettuce with their fingers and cheese with their knives, but apart from that they were not a bad lot. The ship is surprisingly clean, neat and tidy, a very strange thing for a French ship, and a banana boat at that. She does not belong to the *Campagnie Générale Transatlantique*, she's only chartered by them. The food is really excellent, and for the first time in years I had all the sleep I wanted.

As I passed through Pointe-a-Pitre I went to the *École Normale* to make the final arrangements for the boys: Swanston, Sargeant, Jones and Perkins. The first is having the bursary given by the Consul General of France in Puerto Rico, Sargeant and Jones have the St. Kitts Government help and we manage to collect the necessary funds for Perkins after our play. I hope you do not mind. I had to take some money from the fund for their passages as they could not scrape up enough, and I have also given some help to Eddie Walker (if you remember him, my very brilliant French and Spanish student who had to stop studying and go to work). He managed to get a job in Barbados which will enable him to work and continue his studies at the college there at the same time, but he did not have enough money for his passage to Barbados, so you provided that.

As soon as we are allowed on shore in Dieppe I plan to go to Paris and thence on to Spain. On the 18th I have to be in London where I hope to receive mail, will you drop me a line if you have the time? I have booked a room at the Y.W.C.A. Central Club, Gt. Russell Street, London WC1 and although I'll be going on a tour of England and Scotland, I shall be constantly in contact with the 'Y' until the end of August.

I am hoping to enjoy my travels, but of course cannot enter into a proper holiday mood when I think of my poor little old ladies in St. Kitts. I've provided for every possible eventuality, I think, but I know that they will miss the little personal touches of care and affection without which life is always unsatisfactory and bleak.

According to the news we get, things seem to have quieted down a little in Hong Kong. I hope all is well with you. The French news broadcasts of course do not mention St. Kitts at all.

Please excuse the wobbly writing. On deck with no table or chair, the *Sougueta* does not pamper us to such an extent and the wind is quite strong."

"Thank you for your letter of July 31st, which was waiting for me at the 'Y' when I returned from my travels. I enjoyed the tour thoroughly, after Wales I went to Cornwall, visiting historical sites, King Arthur's ruined castle among others in Tintagel, then to Devon stopping for some time in Plymouth, on to Winchester and Bath, after which I returned to London. It's still very cold, but having acquired several Shetland cardigans and sweaters in Scotland, as well as a coat, rain shoes, a raincoat and an umbrella, I have stopped shivering and can take pleasure in my surroundings. People here look at me in wonder and say that this is the peak of summer. Well I can only say that I'd not like to set my foot here in winter. However, this climate seems to be wonderful for flowers and I have never seen such glorious gardens, so beautifully kept and with such a profusion of variety and colour. After a few days of intensive sight-seeing in London I have come for a little interval of rest with some friends in Bournemouth. They took me for a very interesting drive yesterday and we stopped for a few moments at the beach, where in spite of the icy wind, (and probably arctic water) people were actually bathing! My teeth started chattering at the mere sight of them.

From here I'm going back to London for more museums, theatre, ballet, opera and music, then to Grimsby to stay for a couple of days with the former Headmistress of the St. Kitts Girls' High School. I'll leave England from Hull on the 21st for Sweden so as to embark on the Johnson Line *M/S Bolivia* from Gothenburg. After the not very satisfying experience with the French Line I have decided to turn to the reliable Swedes, at least they know the names of their ships and their sailing dates. If you have time to write me a few lines I'd be very happy, your letter should be addressed to me on the *M/S Bolivia*, Johnson Line, C/O Fallenius & Lefflers A. B., Gothenburg, Sweden. (Leaving Gothenburg on Aug. 25th).

It is with great concern that I read all news pertaining to Hong Kong. It seems so disquieting. How can the inhabitants manage on such short water rations? It must create dreadful health and sanitary problems. I often think of you and pray that all is well with you. The first telephone call I had in London was from Morris Archibald, he came down from Bangor to London for the summer to look up some references in the libraries. He has already completed - with success - two years at Bangor University and has one year more to graduate. He remembers with gratitude all the help you have given him."

"Thanks for your kind letter which was handed to me as I came on board the *Bolivia* in Gothenburg. It was a most friendly welcome and made me feel even more at home on the ship. I love those Johnson Line vessels, the 12 passenger cargo ones, they are so comfortable and I have travelled on so many of them that it really feels like home. If I were rich I think I'd take up a permanent residence on one of those ships.

The stay in England was very pleasant and interesting, but marred by the cold. In Sweden it was much warmer, and now, in Norway, the most northern port of my wandering, it is so beautifully warm that at last all the ice in my bones has thawed and I am going about in sandals and a summer frock. We are spending, or rather have spent, since we're leaving in an hour's time, two days in Oslo, that's the beauty of traveling on a cargo ship, there is so much time in port. I made very good use of it and have spent the days visiting all the interesting sights, the authentic Viking boats, the polar ship *Fram*, the Norwegian Folk museum as well as the University of Vigeland Sculpture Park and ended up at the Holmenkollen ski resort. The country is beautiful with woods made of pines, birches and chestnuts, so different from our coconut palm and bright colours.

Before returning on board I bought an English newspaper and after looking at it I have been shocked to find such dreadful news about events in China and in Hong Kong. I am most concerned and worried about you. Are you safe? Do please think about yourself. Things look so threatening, perhaps you could go away for a little while? I cannot help imagining all sorts of horrors happening. Please let me know how you are faring, a letter addressed to the ship at Curaçao, Netherlands West Indies should reach me, we should be there about Sept 12th, and after the 16th I'll be back in
St. Kitts."

"I am so glad you seem to be really enjoying your holiday. What a pity it was so cold in England, but the weather in Norway and Sweden seems to have made up for it. Like you, I like the warm weather though, in Hong Kong, the humidity at times is very trying.

Hong Kong is going through a troubled period. It is suffering from a spill-over from events in China. It is extremely difficult to know what is really going on here but a good simile might be that of a political election, South American style, on a vast scale. Revolution and counter-revolution have brought about a lack of discipline, creating chaos. Children no longer respect their parents or teachers, and responsible officials cannot apply policy for fear of criticism from unruly mobs.

In spite of all my difficulties, I think that, barring accidents, Hong Kong will come out stronger than ever, since the Colony is proving its economic value to Asia generally; also, there is no doubt that its availability as a neutral base will be useful for the reconstruction of whatever stable Government may eventually emerge in Peking.

I am glad to tell you that the water situation has improved due to two typhoons having passed close to the Colony. They were indeed welcome, they did no damage but have made it possible for us to have four hours of water daily as compared with four hours every fourth day.

I trust you have been receiving good news from the old ladies and that this holiday has given you the rest you so badly needed. With every good wish."

Madame's three months of leave did do her a world of good. Well-travelled and well rested she was anxious to get back into the classroom.

"The Minister of Education has gone ahead with his idea of merging the Girls' High School and the Boys' Grammar School into one establishment which the Government pompously calls the Basseterre High School of Secondary Comprehensive Education. With no adequate preparation or planning, the schools have been joined and the result is utter chaos and confusion. We lack everything, books, rooms, furniture and teachers. After two weeks of school there is still no time table, we are working on a day-to-day basis, being told at 9 a.m. what our classes for the day are to be - since the pupils are in the same condition, they don't know which books to bring, turn up with the wrong ones, everybody is late, the teachers have no time to prepare classes, since they don't know which ones they will get, and the whole of the discipline is appalling.

It's heart-rending to watch such a wonderful first-rate school deteriorate from day to day and be powerless to do anything about it. I feel that now, something still could be done and if the Headmaster would only make a firm stand the situation could be taken in hand again, but if more time is wasted, everything will be quite lost. Our political climate is not too healthy either, and the saddest part is that somehow, skillfully and imperceptibly, racial enmity is being stirred up. When I first came to St. Kitts, there was absolutely no 'colour' distinction, now there is definite hostility brewing and often I feel worried about the future.

Charles goes back to Jamaica on Saturday. I do not think he will require further help for I expect the University scholarship provides for his living expenses. It is extremely kind of you to inquire whether he needs help, but I think, let's wait and see. Karina Hudson is also returning to Jamaica on Saturday, there is quite a number of students traveling by that boat since she goes from Trinidad to Jamaica and picks up passengers at all the islands on the way.

James Connor is teaching at the Sandy Point Secondary School, and, as far as I can see, is proving himself to be a good, reliable, junior member of staff. His French is excellent, and thanks to you, he has acquired confidence in himself. He will try in January or June to sit for the Jamaica Entrance and Scholarship Examination and I hope he will be able to win a place for himself. For the time being, I don't think he needs help. There are several pupils in rather difficult circumstances at the school, if they will not find means to pay their school fees, I shall write to you and then you will give me your instructions about them.

The news from Hong Kong is still not very encouraging. We pray and hope that you are in no danger, it is so difficult to predict what will happen, so we can only trust that the Lord will protect you."

"I was very happy to receive your letter of Nov. 1st, thank you very much for writing, I know how busy you are, and it's extremely kind of you to take time off for this.

I hope you will have an interesting trip to Ethiopia, of course we would all be overjoyed if you could make the journey via St. Kitts. You'll probably do it by air, and small though our island is, we have many airlines calling here, B.O.A.C., K.L.M., Caribair, and connections with Air France and Panam through Antigua. It would be wonderful if you could look in on St. Kitts now, while it's still a beautiful island, comparatively peaceful. I'm afraid the future looks pretty grim - to such an extent that if I were on my own and a few years younger I'd seriously think of trying to find some other spot to try my luck in. This island seemed to be the answer, I loved it and was so happy here for the last five years. Now, I don't know.

There had never been any racial problem here, however, since becoming a 'State' in association with Britain, racial feeling is being stirred up artificially, and it's so easy to sway simple people, imagined wrongs provoke violence and in the end, untold suffering. Things are not getting any better at the school, the reverse seems to be happening, the discipline is non-existent and the teachers are called to so many meetings and given so much work that has very little to do with teaching, that the academic standard is falling alarmingly. After wasting two hours almost daily at unproductive meetings, corrections have to be done at night and the result is that my eyes have started giving me continuous trouble. I shall probably have to apply for a few days' leave and go to Guadeloupe where there is a good eye specialist. All this is making me most unhappy. I love teaching and I love working with children, but I have realized that since I have returned from leave there has not been a chance to do any good at my work. Do you know of any place else where they'd need a French and Spanish teacher? Or should I really give up teaching and see if I can do better in a tea-shop that we were thinking of starting with my old friend Jane Ying?

One good thing about your trip to Ethiopia is that at least for some days you will be away from Hong Kong and its activities. Every day almost, there is some disquieting news about bombs and unrest, and I'm very much afraid that you may find yourself if not in actual danger, at least in some unpleasant situation, and we often think and pray for your safety. Jane is thinking of making a trip to Hong Kong. I think she is not very happy in the United States.

I have had a very interesting letter from Eddie Walker. He seems to be the youngest student there and they have discovered that his Spanish is so good that he has been taken into the second-year course. This is very gratifying, since it means that he'll be able to finish his studies in three years instead of four, but I am not sure that he'll be able to go on working and studying at the same time. If he were to require it, could he be given some assistance from the fund? So far, this school year, I have spent very little of it, just a few items, books, uniforms, etc. Wishing you an enjoyable trip, but please be careful, there are so many dangers everywhere now. God Bless."

"I am indeed sorry to hear that racial feeling is being stirred up and that conditions at the school are no better.

What worries me even more is that your eyes are giving you trouble - you should certainly consult the specialist at Guadeloupe. One's eyes are very precious and you should take no chance of spoiling your sight by overwork.

You asked whether you should give up teaching and start a tea shop with Jane Ying. The answer to that, of course, is *no*. There are few (indeed I know of none) teachers that are as capable as you are and it would be a sin for the children not to be able to make full use of your talent. Jane Ying will undoubtedly wish to return to Hong Kong, as living in the United States is not as pleasant as living in Hong Kong, and you would find yourself alone to run the tea shop (even I feel homesick for Hong Kong despite the troubles and the fact that my trip will only be of five weeks duration).

Bravo to Eddie Walker. Please use your discretion as to how best to assist him and any other pupil that you wish to help.

Must end or I will be late at the airport. With every good wish and apologies for this short letter."

1968

"I hope you have had a pleasant and restful trip to Ethiopia and have found everything well at home on your return. This is to wish you a happy new year, health and success in all your undertakings, peace and fulfillment of all you desire. I also hope that this year will bring you so close to St. Kitts that you'll stop and visit us, even if it's only for a day or two between planes, so that you can see this lovely island while it's still more or less peaceful, and not torn with political and racial strife.

The end of 1967 was not very happy for me. All the extra work has brought on severe eye-strain, so that finally I had to ask for two days' leave and fly to Guadeloupe to consult a specialist. Of course, he advised the impossible - a complete stop of all eye-work until I'd get the new glasses, which are quite complicated and had to be ordered from France. That was on Dec. 11th. Somehow, I was able to finish the term and now have had two weeks rest, using my eyes as little as possible - and that is so difficult, no reading, writing or sewing, typing or playing the piano. The trouble is that the new glasses have not arrived as yet, and the new term starts on Monday. The position at the school is still chaotic, we cannot work properly and the result is that all members of staff are looking around, trying to find other jobs in other islands. And this school was one of the best in the West Indies!

Because of our 'State of Emergency', we had a very quiet Christmas season, no carnival, nor dancing in the streets, even the carol singers didn't call, and this situation is going to continue for another six months - I cannot understand why, and the money it costs is terrific.

I have sent £5 to Eddie Walker from the fund to get books, he is trying very hard, is studying and working at the same time, and though his financial situation is most difficult, he is keeping his chin up and faces things with cheerfulness, common sense and humour. I do hope he will be able to carry on.

I must tell you of a wonderful surprise I received yesterday, a cable from the French Consul General stationed in Puerto Rico, (he is in charge of all the West Indies), telling me that his Government has awarded me a decoration, making me a *Chevalier de l'Ordre des Palmes Académiques*. A most unexpected honour which leaves me non-plussed, for I am not at all sure that I deserve it. My very best wishes to you, may the Lord protect you and make you happy in this year 1968."

"I'm very happy that you have had a good and restful holiday. Your letter sounds quite relaxed, and I do hope that you are not going to plunge into your work with too much energy and lose all the benefit of the brief respite. What a wonderful trip you must have had! I have never visited any of the places you mentioned, they must all be so interesting. According to news here, Ethiopia seems to be one of the very few places where there is no unrest. Mauritius is a place I'd like to see, but not at present, with all the riots going on. What a dreadful place this earth is becoming, strife and open warfare, cold war, aggression, misery, injustice and poverty everywhere. There are such beautiful, lovely spots, people could all live in peace, work and be happy, but because of human jealousy and greed, there will soon be no place left to live in quietly. Even this delightful island is experiencing hard, unsettled times.

My glasses have finally arrived, they are certainly of great help, but I have discovered that if I don't get enough sleep, I still experience discomfort, though nothing at all compared to what it was before I received them. Thank you for your offer to try and get me some glasses in Hong Kong. It is most considerate of you, and should the need arise, I shall very selfishly bother you about them. This pair, the lenses alone, were worth U.S.$60, but it's money well spent as I do get great relief from using them. The school is in a still worse mess than before since another teacher has left, therefore those who used to have two different lessons at the same time in two different buildings, now find themselves in three places simultaneously. However, I am happy to say that my prefects are doing a great job and discipline is definitely improving, though we have to use a great deal of diplomacy so as not to appear to tread on other people's toes."

"I am indeed concerned regarding your health. Flu does sap a great deal of one's strength - you should not have returned to work until you were perfectly well again. My lecture has come too late as you have already started work, but please try not to overdo it.

What a pity the discipline in school has deteriorated - the boys seem to be completely out of hand. It is also regrettable that the classrooms have not been kept in good repair. The above is to be expected in a young country that has just gained independence.

Jane Ying passed on your kind messages through Joshua Abraham - the good wishes are sincerely reciprocated. I can well imagine her being unhappy in the United States - life there is very hard.

I am glad to hear that John Stapleton and Noel Parks are working really hard. Incidentally, I did not mention to you that I had received kind letters from Noel Parks and Naomi Knight. Would you kindly thank them on my behalf?

I have told Mrs. Tebbutt (Laurence's private secretary) about the kitten you took care of. Mrs. Tebbutt is very similar to you in that respect - she collects stray cats and feeds dozens of them. They all seem to know her and congregate at the entrance of her flat every day. She really does love animals. She once mentioned to me that she knew of a lady in Hong Kong who's got a pet python who was allowed to roam the room. One thing is sure, I would never visit that flat.

At the farm, which has grown into something quite exciting and has become quite famous, we have been bothered with rats, but now dozens of cats have appeared. It seems one of them has come to an arrangement with some chickens - she sits next to them and never worries them. In exchange, the chickens allow her to eat the rats that try to steal their feed. Unfortunately, there is no arrangement between the cats and our ducks - two are missing today!"

"My sister left yesterday so at last I have a few moments to answer your kind letter which came - I'm ashamed to say - quite some time ago, but we were in such a whirl of activity that I could not do anything at all except attend to her. With the usual perverseness of things, the day she arrived it rained cats and dogs, whereas for three months on end we had the worst drought in years, therefore the hills were absolutely seared, the plants shriveled, and with a leaden sky and grey sea everything looked dismal.

All my glowing descriptions of lush green fields, golden sands, azure skies and deep blue seas appeared to be sheer inventions, therefore my sister - in the amiable way that sisters have - accused me as being just as bad a liar as ever. It never rains here for more than a few hours, however, this time of course, the bad weather lasted for three whole days. Fortunately, the remaining eleven of her stay the sun came out and when she was leaving even the hills started to look green; so my reputation has been cleared. She enjoyed her visit here, more than anything because it is still so beautifully quiet, away from the noise and bustle of large cities, and the people, though not as much as when I first came, are polite, friendly and helpful. Her departure was unfortunately marred by the plane's being two hours late and her adventures in Puerto Rico where she had to overnight were rather unpleasant. I telephoned her this morning, before she left for Jamaica where she is to take the plane to [her home in] Chile and she seems to have revived somewhat, and a few minutes ago I had a call from Jamaica to say that some of my old pupils, now in the University there, have taken charge of her, will show her around and see her safely into the plane.

This break from school has been extremely brief, just two weeks, we are back to school on Monday 22nd. This is the last term, the most strenuous one, I just hope that I'll be able to see my charges through their exams. I hate losing a single day of it, and here, from the very outset we are going to lose time, for the French Consul General is arriving on Tuesday, 23rd, with this famous *Order of Palmes Académiques*, so I'll have to scrap some of my classes since he specially wants my girls and boys to go on aboard the warship *Le Croix du Sud*, (just a mine-sweeper), and spend almost a whole day there. Well, since the officers and crew don't speak English, this will give my children a chance to exercise their French.

My kittens are growing, and so are their appetites, unfortunately they are still wild so I cannot find homes for them, perhaps they will become tamer as time goes on. When will you be moving your offices? That must be a tremendous job. Please don't overdo things and get tired out."

"I was very happy to receive your letter of April 27th and to learn that you approve of the expenses to help some of the students. You may be quite sure that I consider each case carefully before spending a single cent. Conditions on the island are steadily becoming worse, since everything has to be imported, the cost of life has risen very sharply after the devaluation of the £, and now a further rise has come into force to cover the budget deficit, and a further rise is to follow when St. Kitts joins the CARIFTA[17], a sort of common market between the Caribbean islands; it seems that some commodities were cheaper in St. Kitts, and the prices have to be raised so as to make them equal to those on the other islands. I would have thought that it would be the other way around, since a common market is supposed to create better conditions. The salaries, of course, have remained the same, therefore, as the newspapers say, 'belts have to be tightened'.

I am enclosing some cuttings about the ceremony when the French Consul General brought me the decoration. I hope you will not think me vain and conceited for sending them, some of the speeches are of course too flattering, but I think you will be

---

[17] Caribbean Free Trade Association.

interested to know that the French Consul spoke in French and his speech was rendered into English simultaneously by James Connor who had a microphone - and since he had never done that kind of work before and hadn't laid eyes on the speech previously, I think he did quite a commendable job. The boys and girls sang very well, but I must say that I was very happy when the whole thing was over. Next was far more pleasant. The Consul and the officers from the minesweeper came to a French Club meeting at my home, the atmosphere was so relaxed, family-like, that everybody had a good time, the visitors joined in all the games and songs, we had a recitation competition, and then we discovered that the Consul played the piano very well, so we had a concert, he played, and some of the boys played, and then nobody wanted to go home so the captain invited all my boys on board again, (we had been to a cocktail party there the evening before and all my charges behaved beautifully), and they were shown a French film. The day after, when the minesweeper left, they, I mean the pupils, all said that they had so much practice in speaking French that they were quite sorry they couldn't have their oral exams right away!

During the visit, I had a very interesting talk with the real Commander of the French Navy who had come from Martinique especially for the ceremony and flew back the day after, and he has promised to send the minesweeper in July so that I could take some of my boys to Martinique for a fortnight's visit. The girls are barred for lodgings will be arranged at the Fort and no girls are allowed there."

"Your letter of May 14th has just arrived. How can I thank you for your kindness, your generosity and your thoughtfulness? You cannot imagine the happiness, the help and the relief that you are giving to so many of our poor young people. If you could only see the gratitude in their eyes when they are tided over some desperate straits. Last week, Danny Douglas, the boy who was ill and whose visit to the doctor and medicines you have paid for, has had another relapse and had to stay away from school again. He is to have his

French oral exam to-morrow, and the idea that he could miss it and therefore lose the whole subject rendered him quite desperate. I decided to go and see him at his home. I wish you could have seen the conditions that the family lives in, a tiny little box of a house with rooms so small that two people can hardly squeeze in at the same time, yet everything clean polished and scrubbed.

There is no father, the mother takes on all sorts of odd jobs to keep things going, and it seems that they were not doing very well, for the boy's trouble was just absolute weakness from lack of food. That's why he can't get better, just no strength. I hope you do not mind my feeding him for a little while, until the exams are over and he can do the extra work he usually does to earn something. He is a very honest boy, so on Saturdays he helps as assistant cashier in one of the three supermarkets. This is his last year at the school, he will leave from the fifth form as he cannot afford to go on to the sixth, but hopes to take a job and go on to night school to continue his studies. That is why this 'O' level certificate is so important to him. Having it, he can count on a job paying between W.I.$90 - $100 per month, (roughly £20), without it he can expect only half. I have convinced the oral examiner, the Headmaster and the Examination Supervisor to allow Danny to have this first exam at home (since he is still in bed), so early to-morrow morning I'm to pick up the French examiner and convey him to the boy's house, while the rest of the candidates will be watched over by the Headmaster at the school, so that no communication will be possible between them. Having had some proper food for three days he is feeling stronger, so I hope he will do well and you will have helped another child.

It's the whole set up on this island that is wrong. There are so many illegitimate, unwanted, children. This is where education should really start, they should be made to realize the misery and the unhappiness that overtakes all those poor waifs. If only the youth in those islands could be taught responsibility, if there were centres and clubs for them where they could be engaged in constructive activities, and of course taught practical trades. What is the use of teaching those children Latin when what they need are mechanics, electricians, plumbers, carpenters and builders. There are about twenty different sects and religions in St. Kitts but I don't think that any of them teach real morals, and until people understand that family, industry and honesty are the only forces that will keep them together and happy, we shall continue to suffer.

Sorry to have started preaching, I didn't mean to do that. Our G.C.E. Cambridge exams are to be held at the other end of town, in the old hospital, now empty since there is a new one. I'm sorry about that, I like to see my boys and girls go in, and they like to feel that there is somebody near them who cares and wishes them well. A last word of encouragement, a pat on the back and a smile can boost morale and work wonders. I think I'll be late for school every time my children have their exams. I've told the Headmaster so, after all, I've been on time for seven years, and I think it's more important for me to see the candidates in, then appear at the school.

All your new god-children are studying well and hope to pass their exams. Thank you once again for your infinite kindness. Be assured that not a cent will be spent needlessly, I am very careful with the funds you have had the confidence to trust me with. May the Lord bless you and keep you from all ills. I pray for you always, I have never had the privilege before of knowing somebody as noble and generous as you. Thank you from us all."

"It is only to-day that at last I can answer your kind letter of May 29th received quite a while ago. We are in the midst of our examinations, but what has upset and distressed us all was a sudden heart attack that my Mother had with absolutely no warning. She was feeling quite bright and cheerful when all at once she had this seizure and we almost lost her. The doctor was out on an emergency case, so I could not get him, and even if I had found him it would have been too late if we hadn't had the necessary medicines handy. Ever since she had a coronary attack in Chile I always keep those tablets within reach for the doctors had explained that this is a spasm and if you cannot get the heart beating again within a matter of seconds it will never function again. I cannot tell what anguish and despair we went through. She is well again, thank the Lord, and is now going about her gardening and other work that she insists on doing. The doctor says to let her have her way, yet I do wish she would take things easy."

"I hope your trip to Europe was pleasant and that you have enjoyed the break. I am only sorry that every time you go travelling you always bypass St. Kitts. There are so many of us here who would be so delighted to greet you - even for a few hours between planes.

I have been doing some travelling myself since writing you last. Mother, thank the Lord, started feeling herself quite normal again, and just at that time the commander of the French Navy in Martinique decided to send a minesweeper for some of our youngsters and myself, thus, although not quite happy about leaving my little old ladies on their own, I set out with 16 boys to Fort-de-France. We spent a fortnight as guests of the French Navy, lodged at the Fort St. Louis in Martinique, and there was an extensive programme of entertainment for the boys - fishing, bathing, boating, trips on sailing ships and excursions.

En route to Martinique, aboard minesweeper *HMS Arcturus* – July 1968

The boys had a wonderful time, and this 'naval' life proved a great success for on our journey home, after all their sailor-training nobody was sea-sick, though we rolled and pitched and the propeller was more often out of the water and beating air than in the sea. We stopped at another little French island, *Marie-Galante*, a beautiful place of dazzling white sand and gold beaches and turquoise sea. When I returned I found the little old ladies in perfect health, but the Headmaster, who in my absence was supposed to have sent another group of French students to Guadeloupe to a six-week course, forgot all about them and one of my boys was left behind owing to some passport difficulty. Eight were enrolled but only seven left and when I got off the minesweeper, I found the lost sheep on the pier waiting for me to return and help. Passport offices are the most maddening institutions, I think they pick their incompetent and 'I-couldn't-careless' staff on purpose. They had been promising the document from day to day to the poor boy, and when I called there, I discovered that all his papers were still lying on the desk - after a whole month instead of having being sent to St. Lucia, the island that authorizes issue of passports. You can imagine how I felt and what I told them.

Fortunately, we were able to enlist the aid of one of the Chief Secretaries in the Ministry, and after cables and phone calls the matter was settled. However, since by that time the Guadeloupe course had already started and had been going on for a week, they did not want to accept the boy. Therefore, I set off to Guadeloupe with him and after a great deal of 'eloquence', managed to have him admitted. I think it would have had a bad psychological effect on the boy had he been left out of the course, it could have embittered him and left him with the feeling of frustration hard to overcome, especially as he is a poor boy and it was a chance of a lifetime for him, since all his expenses were to be paid out of some Canadian funds that we managed to obtain.

While in Guadeloupe I saw my own seven students, and I'm very proud to say that out of the whole number of 180 youngsters from the Caribbean islands, Central and South America who are attending the course, mine are among the best.

I don't think I'll go on the holiday that I had planned, the hurricane season is starting now, and it'll be better not to tempt fate and leave the little old ladies again. Before starting off for Guadeloupe I asked the doctor to visit mother. He found her planting flowers and vegetables and she refused to leave her gardening and be examined - she told him to go and treat the dog instead! Another man would have been offended, but this one, most good-naturedly went into the house, and once there and the dog in his arms called out through the window that he needed someone to hold him. Therefore mother had to come in after all and the doctor lost no time in examining her. Now I've got a whole lot of medicines - some for her and tablets and a syrup for the dog. It's easy to give him the tablets with meat, but have you ever tried to make a dog take a tea-spoonful of medicine? My advice is don't."

"Thank you for your kind letter of Oct. 9th. I hope your brother and his wife have arrived safely after a pleasant trip in Europe. There is nothing more wonderful than travelling, I enjoy it so much that am ready to set out to any part of the world at half an hour's notice.

I have £600 on fixed deposit and there is still W.I.$1,600 (£320) on the savings account. I have already sent a cheque for £100 to the University of the West Indies for Karina Hudson in Jamaica as per your instructions, and have sent £20 to Eddie Walker. Besides, I think it is better to let him have the other £30 later, part in January and the rest in April - £50 in one sum might tempt him to spend it too rapidly. You cannot imagine how much happiness you have given, helping those poor waifs. I do not know why there are such appalling family conditions in St. Kitts, so many poor, homeless, hungry children, illegitimate and unwanted. It is no fault of theirs that they have been brought into the world. Government really should do something about teaching its subjects to be more responsible, but conditions are such that all adults try and leave the island to find better paid jobs elsewhere - and when they go they leave several babies behind them. And who is to look after them?

School is still chaotic. To help matters we have an epidemic of dengue fever, half the staff have been down with it at one time or another, which of course means extra strain on the survivors. I have been fortunate in escaping it so far, but feel so tired and run down that I'm afraid I might catch it too. It is so difficult to battle against such odds all the time, sometimes I start wondering whether it's worth doing it. Sorry to end on such a dismal note, but I won't have time to re-write the letter."

"Life is becoming increasingly more difficult on the island, the long drought has seriously affected the sugar crop, and our government still does not seem to realize that the whole economy of the place should not depend on just sugar and nothing else. I'm afraid it will take a long time until the powers will learn how to be independent in deed, not only on paper.

School is still chaotic and next week we are to get ready for examinations, which will decide the entries for the Cambridge exams. Owing to the existing conditions when pupils have been left with no teachers for so many periods the results will be most disappointing to the children; after all, it is not their fault that they cannot pass an examination because they have not been taught properly. In all my miseries and woes there is one bright spot. One of my sixth form boys has been accepted at Fitzwilliam College in Cambridge to do International Law, and the first part of his studies is a two-year course in modern languages. He was given an examination on arrival and you can imagine our pride and joy when he was informed that owing to his high standard of knowledge and proficiency in both French and Spanish he will be allowed to complete the course in one year and not in two.

We have had a very quiet and happy day at home to-day, my Mother has had her 84th birthday. I only hope the Lord will let me have her for more years to come. I try my very best to make this time happy and comfortable for her, though I do wish I had more patience at times. Thank you once again for the Douglas family and for all your generosity to all the others.

The rains have come at last, but in spite of them the sugar prospects are not very encouraging, and this is the only source of income on St. Kitts. Therefore, the whole outlook and future of the island is becoming more and more grim. What I find very disturbing is that even here there have appeared propagandists stirring up racial trouble - something that never existed, and this, coupled with economic difficulties, may bring about unpleasant consequences. Let's hope I'm wrong and that my pessimism is just due to overwork and tiredness."

"The other day I came across this prayer and the moment I said it I thought about you; we are all asking for it, while you have already achieved it, here it is:

Lord, grant that I may not so much seek to be consoled as to console; to be understood as to understand; to be loved as to love; for it is in giving that we receive.

It has made me think of all you have done for those underprivileged boys and girls, and now, having received your generous donation to the Douglas family I do not know how to thank you. The mother came to express her gratitude, she can hardly move so I drove her back home, but she wanted to write to you especially. She said that their situation had become quite desperate and that only a miracle could have saved them, therefore she considers that all her family owe their salvation to you and they are all praying for your happiness. They are writing themselves to thank you, but neither they nor I can express the feeling of relief, joy and exquisite happiness that they, (and I) are experiencing. Our gratitude is boundless. Thank you again and again."

"Dominica is a beautiful island, almost all of it is lush tropical jungle as it rains here almost every day and the island boasts of having 365 rivers, two fresh water lakes, spectacular water falls (this is true, I went for a drive to look at them) and several hot water and sulphur springs. The drive from the airport into town takes almost two hours as the distance is 32 miles and the roads wind up and down mountains through impenetrable forests on both sides. The interior of the island has no roads, there are no maps and tourists are warned not to venture there without a competent native guide. There are plantations too - surprisingly sweet oranges, grapefruit, lemons, cocoa, coffee, nutmeg, coconuts and bananas. All of which would make you think that this is a prosperous island - but it is not; in fact it looks poorer than St. Kitts. I am afraid I have seen few towns as dirty and squalid as the capital, Roseau, although the name promises beauty, doesn't it? Of course, natural beauty is everywhere, the botanical gardens, on the outskirts of the city are breath taking, but the majority of the houses are just half-ruined shacks and the number of drunkards and mentally imbalanced people who roam the streets is unbelievable. After one visit into the town I had no wish to return to it, but I did so as not to judge by first impressions. However, I went in the company of a nun (who has been transferred here from St. Kitts) for protection.

The hotel is very quiet, it is built on the foundations of an old fort, on a cliff, so that my room and balcony are right over the sea, the view is wonderful and there is the continuous sound of the waves breaking over the rocks, I love it. The one great drawback is that there is no beach, so I have to be content with just looking at the sea. I am trying to rest, although this is rather difficult, I'm still too tired to sleep well.

Fortunately, I can telephone home every day and keep in touch with my poor little old ladies who seem to miss me as much as I miss them. Today mother said that there is a letter from you waiting for me. Thank you very much for it. It is so kind of you to take time to write to me. With every good wish to you for the New Year."

1969

"I am most happy to report that after seeing the manager of the Sugar Factory on Sunday last and talking to him personally, I have received his formal assurance that Rudy Jeffers, the sixth form boy whose father died recently in St. Thomas, will receive the scholarship, so that lad is also provided for. Now that all exam fees have been paid, I do not foresee any further large expenses from the fund which is quite respectable and will last us for a long time to come - that is, if all goes well with us on the island. I am writing this letter at home and can therefore mention something about the problematical situation at the school. As I have written to you in my last letter, we are all in a worse mess than ever at the school. I thought there was chaos formerly, now I do not know how to call the present state of things. Our Headmaster has been accused of several political offenses - which I am not quite sure had ever been committed - he has been suspended, there has been a Public Service Commission looking into the matter, meanwhile the members of the staff have split into two camps, all teaching has been stopped in protest and the children are running wild. There are posters and slogans, threats from all sides and it may mean that the government might dismiss not only the Headmaster but the staff as well.

The Anguilla situation is also worsening and coming to a climax, and this beautiful island seems to be on the verge of complete strife and collapse. I have never meddled in politics, and wouldn't dream of starting such activities now, but trying to be neutral is a very difficult and delicate matter - so far, I have been receiving blame from both sides, not at all an enviable position. I do not know at all how it will all end, and I am most concerned about it - not for myself but for my poor little old ladies who are not fit to be moved anywhere, even if I had the means of doing so. Excuse my ending on such a dismal note, I'll try to be more cheerful next time. Once again, thank you for your generous gift to the Douglas family and for all the help that the other youngsters have been receiving from you."

"Unfortunately, chaos still reigns supreme at the school. Nobody knows how long this state of affairs will continue. In the meantime, the staff is so taken up with the political issues involved, so taken with the cricket test-matches to be played here beginning to-morrow, that all thoughts of order and teaching have been given up. The noise in the classrooms is deafening, since the teachers hardly ever go there on time, if at all; two members of staff are on sick leave, another has gone to Jamaica for a week, a third prefers to rest at home and come to school when the day is half-over, the Minister of Education has gone to a meeting in Trinidad and the Permanent Secretary to Barbados. Small wonder that many pupils just disappear right after roll call and wander around town where they get into mischief. I am happy in that all my pupils have remained true to me and do not miss any of my lessons, though with bedlam all around it is rather hard to concentrate and study. My colleagues, I am afraid, all cold-shoulder and ignore me, but that does not hurt any more. I still think that my duty lies to the children, who trust me and whom I have come to teach, and to the Headmaster, who in his muddled way is honest and has always tried to look after the school's interest. The staff makes great protestations about their loyalty to him, but it seems to me that the best way to do so is to try and keep the school functioning as normally as possible, so that no further blame may be attached to him.

All this situation is extremely disturbing and nerve-racking, I am dreadfully tired out and I think my dearest wish now is to get away even for a week-end and sleep and rest. There was one lovely moment though; yesterday we had a visit from a good pianist who gave an excellent recital and for two hours I managed to forget all my troubles.

I cannot thank you enough for the conclusion of your letter, it is difficult for you to imagine what comfort your offer of assistance is to me. Not that I would ever impose on it, but it is so consoling to know that there is a friend to whom I may pour out all my troubles, who will understand and send a kind letter in return. With sincere thanks for everything."

"I am spending three days in Nevis, to which lovely island I escaped hoping to have some rest. Unfortunately, it is too close to St. Kitts, too many people know me here and very kindly come over to chat and entertain me, when the only thing I crave is sleep and rest. However, the change is doing me good, at least I do not have the usual housekeeping chores and worries, and have a few moments in which to think and try and sort out our very complicated school and island circumstances. I am afraid I am going to bore you again with my affairs, but you know, when I write the whole thing down in a letter to you, I seem to see things clearer and if you care to give your views on the situation, I'd be very grateful. Please don't imagine that I am doing all this to ask for advice with the view of having somebody to blame when things go wrong. It is not that at all, but then you might have some suggestions to make, and with your wide experience of troubled times the suggestion is bound to be valuable.

There are now two problems confronting me. One, an immediate one, the other which will arise in the near future but for which it is better to start getting ready now. Our Headmaster has been very unfairly and cruelly treated. After thirty years of service he has been dismissed with no benefits, that is, he has been turned away without a cent and with no prospect of getting any kind of work on this island. We all signed a petition to the Governor and he has appealed - of course the appeal will come to nothing since the Commission is again composed of members of the Government. The problem is that since he has appealed, the Ministry of Education says that a new Headmaster cannot be appointed until the matter is settled and this means that our new term which starts in a week's time is going to be just as chaotic as the one that has just come to an end. My problem is how to continue working without ending up with a real nervous breakdown. I dread the beginning of each day, and come home from work absolutely tired out after a senseless, frustrating and useless struggle. The discipline is finished, children come to school - not to do lessons for they do not enter the classrooms and do not study - dirty, unkempt and have become rude, impudent and aggressive.

Yet, with the G.C.E. examinations begin in five weeks' time, I do not consider that I have the moral right to give up the battle and stop teaching as almost all the other members of staff have done. Many of those children will not have another year at school, hence it is imperative that they obtain some certificate now to help them get work on leaving school. My pupils all attend my classes, but it is increasingly difficult to teach with bedlam all around, with constant noise and jeers of other 'students' through the windows when my class is in session. But the strain of carrying on against such odds is overwhelming and I'm afraid of becoming ill, and then what is to become of my poor little old ladies?

My second problem ties with the first. My contract comes to an end in Sept. 1970, and I do not know whether I should renew it or not. If not, I shall have to start looking for something now, so as to have something to turn to. Besides the muddle and chaos at the school, which I think could be put right if a suitable, honest and strong-charactered man were to take charge, there is another factor. I am very much afraid that soon we shall have the racial question coming up, and then, when there is an issue of 'colour', anything is possible, and again I am afraid for my little old ladies. Returning to Chile is about the last thing I'd like to do, the conditions of life there have become appalling, I would never be able to earn enough for our needs for there is tremendous inadequacy between salaries and expenses. Besides, since I thought we would settle permanently in St. Kitts I was advised to obtain British citizenship, for which I applied. Upon receiving it however, I have discovered that it is a citizenship of a state in association with Britain, and this will complicate matters tremendously if I wish to return to Chile. Sorry to burden you with all those problems, but as I say, it's a sort of 'thinking on paper', and if some glimmer of a solution appears to you, do please write it to me; however, on no account think that you are assuming a responsibility by doing so.

Your 'godsons' are all well. Cedric Pemberton has undergone a wonderful change for the better. I am sending the £20 to Eddie Walker in Barbados, if you remember, I split the £50 you authorized me to send him into three quotas. Please excuse this selfish letter. I know you will forgive me for it."

"I am glad you spent three days in Nevis but am sorry you did not find it much of a rest. Regarding the points raised in your letter:

Immediate Problem

Your health must take priority over everything else. For a long time you have been overworking and unless you take a real rest you run the risk of a breakdown which would be detrimental to yourself, the two 'old ladies' and to the pupils whom you wish to help.

I recommend you obtain from your doctor a letter addressed to the School Authorities stating that you have been overworking and to prevent a breakdown, you must take at least two to three weeks holiday. Preferably a boat trip, which would give you the best rest.

G.C.E. Examinations

After a few weeks rest you will come back refreshed and able to do much more good to your pupils than if you were to continue teaching them now. It will also give time for things to settle down.

Your Contract

Before making any decision as to whether you should renew your contract, take your holiday. I personally think if conditions are worse, and I believe they will improve, you will wish to renew the contract for the following reasons: -

a)   You have a home in St. Kitts.

b)   The 'old ladies' also enjoy it there.

c)   You have gained the respect of the adults and pupils alike for the out-standing examination results attained by your pupils.

d)	If you were to go elsewhere it would be starting anew. It is a 'feather in you cap' that your pupils have remained loyal to you and continue to study conscientiously.

<u>Changes in the political situation</u>

Why look for trouble which may never arise? The Government of any country that has just gained its liberty often makes mistakes while growing up and, therefore, one must think a little as to the future but I recommend you do not do this until you return from your holiday.

<u>Citizenship</u>

Although your British citizenship is limited, nonetheless it allows you to go to Commonwealth and other countries. I am sorry though that it would hamper matters should you wish to return to Chile.

I, naturally, hope and believe all will happen for the best, but please remember that you have good friends who wish to stand by you in times of need."

"It's so good of you to write as you did, and I am indeed grateful, it is so heartening to know that I can always count on your friendship to help me sort things out.

I quite agree that health constitutes a priority problem, unfortunately a sea-trip, much as I would have profited from it, was impossible, the G.C.E. orals are only two weeks away now, besides even a fortnight's trip on a cargo ship is too expensive and would upset my 'balance of payments', however I compromised and for the last three days of the Easter vacation rented the little bungalow on Conaree beach and spent them quietly, lying in the sun and bathing. This has given me some energy and to add to the good state of things our old Headmaster, the one who was in charge of the school when I first arrived here and who is now Permanent Secretary in the Ministry of Education has come back to the school temporarily to rule it until the G.C.E. exams will be over. Although he is having a very difficult time, since almost the whole Staff resents his presence and creates unpleasant situations, at least there is now some sort of order, bells are rung on time, the students are back in decent uniforms, stay in classrooms, there is silence in the corridors during lesson-periods, and although unwillingly, most of the teachers go to their forms - so there are no disturbances caused by children running wild as last term. Of course, this semblance of order is only external, I am afraid the harm done is very deep and it will be difficult for the pupils to revert to normal studies and regain their sense of duty. Still we have to be thankful for this temporary respite. At least I can work in peace and the boys and girls will have some chance of passing their exams.

As for the future, of course I understand all the difficulties that would arise were I to leave St. Kitts. Had it not been for racial animosity that is being artificially and constantly stirred up, I would not even dream of wishing to change. What I have to be ready for is the possibility of the Government not wishing to renew my contract even if I want to do so when my present one expires in September 1970. That is why I think I'll make discreet inquiries about possibilities of jobs elsewhere, hoping that the need for such an eventuality will never arise. I know how difficult, almost impossible it would be to 'start anew' without any contacts in some strange place, especially with my little old ladies in tow. I'm afraid they would not be able to stand a cold climate, and besides, the upheaval might prove too much for them. They are not getting any younger and there are endless little ills and ailments that crop up when they are settled in their comfortable home here. As you say, why look for trouble which may never arise. I hope it never will. It's just my newly-acquired pessimistic outlook on things that makes me so despondent. I think it must be because all my friends have already left St. Kitts or are leaving in the near future, and although all my time is taken up with school work, still one does need a few friends to discuss things and have some quiet conversation from time to time. When the summer holidays start I'll have to have a change of scenery and atmosphere, as a therapeutical measure."

"I am sorry you did not take a sea trip as I feel it would have done you much good. Three days on Conaree beach is a pleasant change but not a holiday. However, I sincerely hope that you will make amends by taking a really good vacation during the summer.

I am glad the old Headmaster has returned to the school and has brought some sort of order. I agree with you that the harm done is deep but it is not insurmountable. In Hong Kong, and indeed in many other countries, the stupid behavior of children encouraged by still more stupid teachers who have an imaginary grievance has also done much harm. Youth today only think of themselves, this is encouraged not only by teachers but by tradesmen who stand to benefit enormously by catering to the wants of the new younger generation.

Regarding the situation in September 1970, you are right in making discreet inquiries about possibilities of jobs elsewhere. Many changes can take place between now and then and I cannot help feeling that anyone in their right senses would ever terminate the contract of a star teacher whose pupils never fail in their exams. Although it is better to work for the school, you can give consideration to setting up classes of your own.

I am sorry to hear that you are undergoing a severe dry spell. We have, fortunately, been having good weather, but early this morning there was a terrific thunderstorm, with continuous lightning and thunder which lasted some hours. It was most spectacular and made one realise what nonentities we are. With every good wish to you and the old ladies."

"As you notice I am in Montserrat where the Education Department has sent me to examine the Cambridge G.C.E. candidates in Spanish. The exam is over, all marks entered, the report drawn up and I can now relax for an hour or two until it is time to leave for the airport. The view here is magnificent, the hotel is beautifully situated on a cliff with a terrace overlooking the Caribbean, sparkling blue this morning after last night's rain and the mountains on the other side are brilliantly green so that Montserrat to-day really lives up to its name of emerald isle.

It was good to have this break and get out - if only for 48 hours - of St. Kitts. The situation there is still very tense and unpleasant. The Government has been spending public funds quite recklessly, the cost of living is steadily rising, the salaries remain the same, a new tax has come into being, therefore there is general discontent. This as usual results in finding some scape goat, in the present instance - the white race. Anguilla does not want to return to the St. Kitts administration[18] and our government is much put out - not only for loss of face, but also because now funds intended for Anguilla from Britain will be sent there directly, thus there will be no chance for appropriating a portion for unspecified uses here. Our Minister of Education has now decided to merge the Senior School of some 700 children with our establishment without planning for extra classrooms, furniture and most important, additional Staff or Headmaster. The merger is to take place in September therefore we can look to another chaotic school year. In the meantime, our dismissed Headmaster has found a good post in Puerto Rico and is leaving at the end of the week. Several other members of staff are pulling out too. I have had a few replies to my letters - judging by them I had better try and get my contract renewed in St. Kitts, only young people (22-35 years) are welcome in the teaching profession. Again, the risk of moving my poor little old ladies seems very great, the upheaval would tax their strength and mental endurance too much. I have also met with little success in my search for a comfortable cargo ship for a short journey in the Caribbean this summer. Either they are too expensive or they will not take a lone woman. There is only one possibility that I have discovered, a trip from Trinidad to Surinam, but I shall have to join the ship in Trinidad and also, she belongs to a - to me - unknown line, the *Alcoa Steamship* and I have been told that the vessels do not belong to the

---

[18] In 1971 an "interim agreement" was worked out with Great Britain whereby Anguilla was allowed to secede from the Associated States of the St. Kitts-Nevis-Anguilla. Anguilla would eventually be formally disassociated from St. Kitts and Nevis in December 1980.

company, are only chartered and sail under the Liberian flag. Not being anxious to fall into a den of thieves, cutthroats and pirates, I have written to the main office in New York for further details before buying my ticket.

I have some good news to close the letter - all my candidates have successfully passed their oral exams, at 'O' and 'A' levels, both in Spanish and in French. Of course, the real test will come in the written exam, but those results have bolstered our morale - both the children's and mine."

"I am very happy to learn that you might visit the West Indies someday. I shall have to make my accounts of the islands more glowing to tempt you, the Bahamas and Bermuda are too crowded, here we still can find beautiful spots with no people, so that one can enjoy the loveliness and quiet of nature. On week days Conaree is wonderful, there is nobody there and I drive there every afternoon for a few minutes of peace. I have also found there an abandoned dog, a most friendly and affectionate creature. I do not know how people can be so cruel and callous as to go away and leave their pets to starve. It is obvious that she belonged to somebody, she is not a wild dog, and most intelligent. I wish I could bring her home, but she is too big and besides my cats wouldn't like it, neither does my dog who snarls at *Chien-Chien* as I call this one. I take food to her every day and she waits for me faithfully at the same place on the beach. The first times she tried to follow me home, which was dreadful and terribly pathetic, but now that she knows I'll come back the next day she remains there, standing all forlorn and sad, watching me drive away. The welcome when I drive up is usually frantic, she even jumps in and out of the car through the window, to my aunt's terror.

We are in a worst state than ever at the school and are all longing for this term to end. The written G.C.E. exams will be over at the end of this week. I am afraid my students have not done very well, at least my own have, but then some ten others have been foisted on me just two months before the exam, and although I have managed to get them through the oral it will be a miracle if they pass the written, especially in French which was very stiff this year. Well, we shall have to wait till September to know the final results, in the meantime it is no use worrying."

Island politics, school politics, her tough teaching schedule, ministering to her little old ladies, made the semester one of the most difficult since her arrival in St. Kitts. Once again, she sought peace and quiet on the high seas, this time aboard cargo ship *SS Discover*.

"I am the sole passenger on a 9,000-ton bulk-ore ship en route to Surinam. This is the queerest ship I have ever travelled on, no masts, no derricks, no canvas covered hatches. The whole vessel is flat, long and narrow and the space from bow to stern is used for carrying bauxite and it is only on the stern that a strange structure houses the crew, officers, captain and passengers, on several decks rising high up. The accommodation is wonderful, being the only passenger I have been placed in the owner's suite, feel quite like a princess. Unfortunately, the trip is very short, I joined the ship in Trinidad and am getting off in Paramaribo. There, I'll stay a day or two and will then take the next Alcoa ship up the river, through the jungle to Moengo where bauxite is loaded. Then by the same ship - or either the *Pathfinder* or the *Wanderer* - I'm returning to Trinidad and then taking the plane home.

I will be in Paramaribo for 7 or 8 days. Since those ships have to navigate down rivers and negotiate sand banks, they are absolutely flat-bottomed and of course owing to that the rolling is terrific, as soon as we left Trinidad everything began to slide off the tables, during the night I was almost rolled out of bed several times and had to place my belongings on the floor - the lowest shelf, as the captain calls it - to prevent crashes and breakage. The ship is chartered by the Alcoa Co., flies the Liberian flag, was built in Scotland and has a Norwegian crew. Yesterday, it rained all day and the outlook was quite miserable. We had sunshine to-day, so things are quite different and I'll be sorry to leave the ship when she docks in Paramaribo to-night.

I am not sure it was wise of me to undertake this trip, for short as it is and the cheapest I could find, it is still quite expensive, however I am quelling my conscience saying to it that I need a break; a change of surroundings was really imperative as I need to pick up some energy and have a rest. September is to bring so many troubles that I'll need a great deal of strength to survive. A new Headmaster has been chosen from among our present members of staff. A young man - that I can only welcome - but unfortunately he does not believe in discipline or order, is very slack in his dress and work, and worst of all, is the president of the local Black Power movement. The last seems so senseless, St. Kitts is a predominantly black community, the Governor and all ministers are black, so I do not see the reason for having such a party here. Against whom is the movement to be directed?

The French Consul General has made me a present: a bursary for one of my boys to go to Guadeloupe for six weeks. The *Alliance Française* promised to send me some money for another boy to attend this course, but their cheque has been delayed. There was no time to consult you so I hope you will not mind my having given this sum to the boy from the Fund. Probably on my return I will find the cheque waiting for me and will at once deposit it into the Fund's account. The course has started on the 15th and they do not allow late arrivals. I do hope you approve."

"What an unearthly time to start writing a letter! A good thing that you will not have to read it at such an hour. Time and tide wait for no man, and the *M/V Pathfinder* is waiting anchored beyond the outer sand bar at the entrance of the Suriname river, until the water rises high enough to come in. I was told to be ready at 1:30 a.m. and since then, the agent of the Alcoa line kindly rings me every twenty minutes with the glad tidings that we shall have to wait a little longer. The *Pathfinder* is not stopping in Paramaribo, the agent is taking me along the river on the company launch and there I'm supposed to perform some acrobatics and climb aboard. Fortunately, it is dark so I shan't see the water streaming away below and get dizzy.

Paramaribo is quite a large city with some very wide streets with palms on either side of the road. There are some good shops and you can buy anything, although the prices are rather high. The bicycle traffic is very heavy but most sensibly there are roads divided into parallel lanes: pedestrians - bicycles - cars - bicycles - pedestrians. The people are very friendly and though they are representatives of five different races - Chinese, Javanese, Hindus, Negroes and Dutchmen, English is spoken by almost everybody and is understood by all. There is no problem about getting around and obtaining whatever one wants."

Four days later Madame Katzen wrote:

"We are on our way to Trinidad after a wonderful trip through the jungle. We went up and down the Surinam River, the Commewijne and the Cottica rivers, the last in places was so narrow that sometimes the branches of the trees would brush the decks. The *Pathfinder* is even quainter than the *Discoverer*, being built in Scotland, she was later taken to Japan where they remodeled her. They cut her in two and inserted a new middle - just like a sandwich - and then tacked on the stern and the bow. I was anxious about our arriving all in one piece after the trip across the ocean, but it seems we have made it. This addition of length has made the ship longer than the rivers are wide, so you can imagine the excitement every time we came to a sharp turn in the Cottica, and I think there must have been a hairpin bend every mile. We were officially escorted by a tug and unofficially by bushnegroes in canoes who would turn out in swarms to welcome us. The canoes were very swift and made out of hollowed trunks, but alas, civilization has reached here and several canoes were incongruously equipped with outboard motors. The jungle was fascinating, dense trees interwoven with creepers came right down into the river and we would occasionally get glimpses of brightly-coloured birds.

The rivers are muddy, just like the *Whangpoo*, but at sunset the colours were marvelous, the water becoming golden with pearly tints and the jungle a dark emerald, more mysterious than ever. Coming out of the river into the sea we seemed to be creeping along the bottom of the river owing to our load of 11,000 tons of bauxite, but now, in the open sea we are rolling about even merrier than on the *Disvoverer*. I'm clutching the desk with my left hand so as not to land on the floor. I'm enclosing a picture of the ship taken as she is gliding along the Cottica. This has been a most enjoyable trip and I'm very happy I made it. We are to reach Trinidad sometime this evening. We are going very slow as our propeller was damaged by a log in the river."

"I found your letter of July 15th on my return from my travels. What wonderful work you are doing, factories in Bangkok and Singapore, a trans-harbour tunnel - how many people must bless you for the opportunities that you are giving them, jobs for the workmen and all advantages to the future users of the tunnel, without mentioning the products of the factory, though what the name 'Tai Ping' means, I haven't any idea.

Chien-Chien, the dog at Conaree was absolutely wild with joy when I came back. While I was away I had arranged for her to be fed by some people who are building a house on the beach, and now I have rented the little bungalow here and she is with me day and night, for a week. I have been trying to find a home for her, but nobody wants to give her one, so I suppose I'll have to continue my drives every afternoon to feed her, all very good while there is no school, but once classes start it'll be rather difficult. Still, she's so affectionate and so full of life that I can't abandon her just like that.

My little old ladies are well, but after even a short absence I can see how much frailer Mother is becoming. I would do anything in the world to keep her well and fit and to let her have everything she wants.

I have just sent you, by surface mail, a copy of the School Year Book for 1967-1968 which has just been finished. It is the work of our Headmaster, the one who has been so unfairly treated. He started this book in 1967, to have it issued in 1968, but because of all the trouble its publication has been delayed. As he is now in Puerto Rico, that is where the book has been printed. It will give you an idea of what the school was like before the new Education Policy started. Almost all the activities have gone by the board and the children are no longer tidy and neat as they look in the pictures. You will find several of your 'godchildren' there, although the book being for 1967-1968, most of them were in the 4th form then and their photographs are not there. However, you will find Danny Douglas, Naomi Knight and John Stapleton. In the Undergraduate Staff, you will find among the pupil teachers, Emanuel Moses, one of the first boys to be helped by you and David Jones, whom you have helped with studies in Guadeloupe. In the group of 4th formers who have attempted the 'O' level exams is Lance Brown, who having finished the 5th form, and who was able to take 'O' level London thanks to you. Only the shell of the school is left, the spirit is gone, but at least you will get an idea of what it looked like. I do not know why the Headmaster decided to dedicate the book to me, this was a surprise, I found this out when he sent me a copy.

I'm afraid I don't deserve any of the flattering things he has put in.

In a few days' time I'll be back at home permanently, we have been advised that staff meetings are to start soon, so no more wandering about the islands. Still, I've had a good rest and am ready for work."

"I am home again, not planning to move any more until the next vacation. I rounded up my holiday by going to Nevis where I spent a few days with the only friends I have left in this State. They used to live in St. Kitts but have now retired in Nevis. It used to be a large sugar plantation but is now in ruins, they have made the old house habitable, their sister and invalid brother live in it, they themselves live in a little cottage that they have built and I was lodged in the old sugar mill - a conical tower with 3ft thick stone walls, made me feel like a princess in a mediaeval castle. The view from it was breathtaking, since it was a former wind-mill it's half way up a mountain, on a sort of plateau with the lush, green valley stretching out below, thickly wooded hills beyond and the Atlantic glistening on one side and the Caribbean on the other. I had a very good rest - first the Surinam trip with a stopover in Barbados, then the ten days on Conaree, and finally the three days in Nevis. So I now feel ready to face the staff meetings and discussions.

Congratulations on the brand new little girl, may she have a life full of health and happiness and take after her kind, noble and generous granduncle.

The *Alliance Française* sent the promised cheque, but unfortunately they made a mistake in the name, I have sent it back to have it corrected and then will deposit the amount in the Fund, thus paying back what I had borrowed from it to pay Kevin Perkins's course in Guadeloupe. May I continue to assist Eddie Walker when he returns to Barbados next month? The economy of the island is not too flourishing so I do not know what kind of positions they'll be able to find. Almost all the young people are trying to leave the island and find employment elsewhere. The island's only industry is sugar, of which it seems there is a surplus in the world, so our Government, quite rightly is trying to devise some other means of income.

However, I am not sure that they are going about it the right way.

There is great talk of Tourism as an industry, but so far very little has been done to attract visitors, and meanwhile, on hopes of this rosy future, the sugar industry has declined alarmingly, which means a bleak future. I don't know anything about economies, but it seems to me that before scrapping a well-established industry one should have an equally or better organized one to take its place. For my part I would rather favour chickenfarming. My little old ladies, in spite of their age, are making quite a success of their few chickens. Vegetable produce is not a very certain enterprise for quite often there is water-rationing and in this heat one day without water means the end of lettuce, cabbages, tomatoes, etc., which with an adequate supply do very well. I hope your experimental farm is recovering from typhoon *Viola's* devastation, it is heartrending to see the damage caused by those storms. *Camille* has passed us by, but the havoc caused in the States by her is frightful."

"Being far away I can probably see the situation clearer than you, who are so close to it. To me, the fact the school has 'settled down' is a great achievement after the turmoil you have recently been through. It is unfortunate that a number of experienced and trained teachers have left but, even if only a few of the new teachers will accept your guidance, they will be able to show what they can do and will gain 'face'. This will encourage the others to make a strong effort to improve their teaching.

Youngsters today never listen to their elders for they think they know everything, until something goes wrong and it is just this, the knocks they receive, that builds up their character, gives them the experience needed and the desire to forge ahead.

It is hard on the older members of the staff just as it is hard for parents to see that their efforts to help youngsters to avoid the hurdles are not appreciated, but as we in our days had to go through the stumbling blocks, the present generation has to follow suit.

The fact that you are the only white member on the staff would, in the beginning, make the young teachers resentful, but as they grow up they will find that you are the one who can make things easier for them and your popularity will grow and you will receive the respect you deserve.

I am sorry you have had such a tough time with your mother, but am delighted to hear that she is making good progress. Please give her my very best wishes. You must now try and take more rest so that you keep well.

When next writing to Eddie Walker kindly give him my best wishes and please finance him to the extent you see fit. It is very wrong that he should go without his meals through lack of funds.

I am a true believer that true happiness comes from kindness to others. I know that your goodness to *Chien Chien* not only brings her happiness but brings it to you as well, and what is far more important, it gives you relaxation and a change of mind from the many daily problems you have to cope with. Take care of yourself. With every good wish."

"This letter should have been written many days ago, but I just didn't have the heart to do so. Mother is still unwell, she has been ill for the whole month and we still don't know what is wrong with her. The doctor comes in every day, sometimes even twice a day, she has had so many injections that there isn't a single spot on her poor body that doesn't hurt from them and she is losing weight alarmingly. Fortunately, she is not in pain from the illness itself - if we only knew the source of it. There is an infection that is definitely localized in the gall-bladder, but what is the source of it, where it stems from is still a mystery. Her temperature is subnormal for two days, then on the third it soars up to 103. On top of it all she has developed jaundice and has to be on a very strict diet. As it is, she has no appetite, and now has to give up all the little tidbits with which I used to tempt her before. I am terribly afraid that her heart will not be able to bear this strain brought about by such sharp changes in the temperature.

My only bright spots for the present are the daily trips to Conaree to feed poor *Chien Chien* who seems to have learned how to tell the time by the clock as she is always ready waiting for me when I turn into the side road near which she must have her abode. If you could only see the happiness on that dog's face - and yet there are people who say that animals have no feelings! My other visits are twice weekly to the hospital. One of my 3rd form pupils has been very badly hurt in a car accident and it seems that he will have to remain in the hospital for at least four months. The boy is so keen on learning Spanish that I go and give him two lessons per week, on the two days when I have a free period which is the first lesson in the morning, so I go to the hospital at 8:30 and get back in time for the second lesson of the day. The lad is making very good progress, as a matter of fact he is keeping up with the rest of the class, and his face lights up when he sees me. It was rather difficult to get permission to enter the hospital at such an hour, but now after a whole month, all the patients and nurses are accustomed to see me come so I proceed unchallenged past the porters and matrons."

"It is so heartening to know that though miles and miles away, there is somebody on whose sympathy I can count. Thank the Lord, for the last fortnight my mother has been feeling much better, her temperature did go up yesterday, but just three points (not degrees) above normal and I'm hoping it's just a temporary and isolated happening and will not repeat itself. She would never go to a hospital - first of all she would be terribly unhappy there all alone, and secondly, though we have a very modern building, as in everything else here, there is very little more. The nurses are willing, but very few are really trained and qualified, besides they are understaffed and there is no resident doctor - as a matter of fact half the time there is no doctor at all on the premises, and unfortunately, so many people have ended their days there that few are willing to go in. I hope we shall never have to take her there.

I am very happy to know that your nephew has already returned and that you are expecting your brother back on the next day. Does that mean that you will now be taking a holiday too? Any chance of your passing near enough to us to make a stop, even a short one, in St. Kitts? It would be so wonderful for all your 'godsons' to meet you, and we would all be delighted to show you around. I must say though, that during the past week this has not been a happy place to live in and I'm afraid there is worse to come. An apprentice has been suspended from the Factory, that is the Sugar Factory, our only industry, and this fact has been at once seized as a pretext for disturbances, a strike, the manager and his family have been insulted, although he was not even on the island when the apprentice was sent home for the day, and last night the main office of the factory was set on fire and almost completely destroyed. The whole affair has been pounced upon by politicians, black-power supporters and of course, inevitably, the racial aspect is being given full prominence. You can imagine that now our position has become even more uncomfortable than it had been.

My very bright spot is the little boy at the hospital, he is making remarkable progress in Spanish. Not only is he keeping up with the class but he is ahead of some of the best pupils. I wish his leg would heal as quickly, but not much is being done about it. He has been here for almost two months now and the nurses will not, or cannot tell me anything about the progress made. He can move around in bed, but he is not allowed to move the leg which has two casts - one on the foot and half-way up the calf, the other from below the knee and some way up the thigh."

"Greetings to you from St. Martin, I have come here for the week end, to relax and to sleep. I wish I could stay here longer, it is so quiet here; the island is lovely and since nobody knows me here I am sure of a complete rest. Just last month telephone connections between St. Kitts and St. Martin have been established, so on arrival I rang home and could speak to my mother and now I am quite ready to enjoy two full days - if my conscience will let me do so, for although this is the cheapest place on the island I still feel a little guilty when I think of the expense.

The Dutch side has developed greatly during these four years since I've been here last, hotels have gone up and the American tourists have completely spoilt the place - therefore I am staying on the French side which has not changed at all, there wasn't a soul on the beach and everybody in the guest house - servants, management and visitors - still display oldfashioned politeness and courtesy, there is no noise, no blaring, shrieking radios, so my poor jagged nerves will have a chance to heal. The bathing is not good - too many rocks, the Dutch side has the beautiful sandy beaches, but I went for a walk and spent a very pleasant hour watching fishes, crabs and sea snails in little pools among the rocks."

"What blessed relief to get your letter! Not hearing from you and having most disquieting dreams about you I was becoming more and more worried. Do, please take care of yourself, your health is precious, the office can wait; don't go back until you are 100% fit again. My sincerest wishes for a speedy and complete recovery go to you, and I pray for you and hope that you are now feeling strong again and are up and about. Why don't you take a real holiday and leave your work for a while? There is nothing like a leisurely, sea trip to regain one's health and zest for life. Please think about yourself a little.

Poor Christopher Coker, the little boy who had a broken leg and to whom I used to give lessons in Spanish in the hospital is now home, but full of grief. His mother who was also badly hurt in the same accident, and who was also getting well, needed a minor operation on her foot - and died under anesthesia. To escape being killed in the accident, to suffer and get almost well, and then to die on the operation table, just because there is no competent staff in the hospital. And do you know that the father, the one who was responsible for the accident has again crashed another car last week! This is his third accident within a year. I just can't understand it.

My mother, thank the Lord, is continuing in more or less good health. I take as much care of her as possible and she's quite annoyed with me sometimes, but she gets carried away working in the garden and wouldn't stop for hours, not realizing she is tired - and then of course the reaction sets in. Still, so long as she is happy I don't mind her grumbling at me, let her be bad-tempered but alive.

We have had our first staff meeting this morning. It looks as if this term is destined to be even more trying than the last, for me at least, for the Headmaster says he can't fit my time-table and that I will have to give one or two lessons every day after school. This is most unsatisfactory for it makes a very long and strenuous day both for the children and for me. Another teacher, a University graduate has just sent in her resignation, she finds the conditions too frustrating to work in. This means that we shall have another untrained, unskilled, inexperienced and callow youth to take up such an important post. The attitude of our islanders is also changing, so much stress is laid on Black Power!

My stay in St. Martin was delightful - too short of course, but that couldn't be helped. When Jane and I win the lottery or the sweepstakes, there are no lotteries or sweepstakes in St. Kitts so Jane buys tickets for the Hong Kong ones, we'll go on a proper holiday. As things stand, I'll have to be content with an occasional week-end, one appreciates the pleasure all the more, but of course such a brief respite does not give enough strength to store for the coming term. However, I was able to spend the last three days at the cottage in Conaree - this was wonderful. *Chien-Chien* stayed with me and with such a bodyguard I felt very well protected. She was really 'frantically' happy, I think not only because she had good food but because she felt she 'belonged', she loves to be spoken to, sits and listens and seems to understand everything. I had a picture taken with her, if it comes out I'll send you a copy so that you'll see what a lovely dog *Chien-Chien* is."

"Mother is ill again, for three days her temperature was again fluctuating between subnormal and 103°, the doctor is again here morning, noon and night, and it's only to-day that at last she is beginning to take an interest in things and that for a whole day her temperature has remained a constant 99°. As far as I can see the doctor is just as puzzled about the origin of the disease as I am. We only know that there is something wrong with the gall bladder or the bile ducts for she is quite yellow again, but what causes the jaundice he doesn't seem to know. If she were younger he would operate, see what is wrong and remove the diseased parts. As it is, at her age, no operation is possible. And she is getting steadily weaker, is losing more and more weight and looks absolutely ghastly. I'm so afraid that her heart will not be able to cope and will give out. The whole of this last week has really been harrowing. The worry, the fear for her very life, the helplessness are really becoming too hard to bear. And with all this, to have to leave the house at 8 a.m. and to return only after five, and never to know what I'll find. I rush home at every playtime, and of course there is the 40 min. lunch period, but for the rest of the time it's just torture."

"The sugary crop has at last started, just to-day. Everybody's spirit has risen, and although it should have begun in early January, still, experienced people say that there is a good prospect of reaping and producing 46,000 tons of sugar, which to our sugar-workers seems like a great promise of prosperity. The season, unfortunately, is very dry, and this it seems is not to the advantage of the industry.

You mention feeling quite exhausted prior to your very short holiday. I do hope you are now feeling better and I think it would be quite a good thing for you to follow some of the most reasonable advice you are giving me: don't overwork. Easier said than done, isn't it? Still, try and follow your recommendations."

"How can I thank you for your wonderful generosity? Your cheque for the fund has just arrived. To-morrow morning I shall place half the amount on fixed deposit and the other half on the savings account so as to have funds available whenever needed. There was still a good balance there, but with school coming to the end of this academic year in June, some of your charges might need help. You cannot imagine the relief and happiness you are bringing to so many. And it is not only the immediate help, given now, when it is so urgently needed, that is so valuable. I am hoping that your kindness will have a lasting effect, for since those boys and girls are receiving this aid from you now, when they are at the most impressionable age, perhaps it will change their outlook in the future too, cure them of bitterness and make them realize the evil and the futility of youth's present attitude of selfishness, full of hatred and racial prejudice. I am hoping that they will always remember the help you have given them, not knowing them, never having seen them and yet providing so many of them with a chance to make something out of their lives. The most striking case is that of your first 'godson', Charles Archibald, whom you have seen through the sixth forms in the school and through three years in the University of the West Indies. On terminating his B.A., thanks entirely to your help, he was granted a scholarship for further studies by the University, and has now won a special award and will be sent to Switzerland for research and studies in International Relations. Seven years ago, the boy was wretched and almost starving, in such poor financial circumstances that he would have had to leave school without obtaining even the necessary 'O' levels to get a post as office boy. Whereas now, thanks to you, he has a brilliant future before him, a diplomatic career in which I hope he will be able to work for his people, for he at least, is grateful, fully understands the benefits that he has received from you, and realize that violence, hatred and Black Power will not achieve happiness and peace in the world.

I am most delighted to report that my mother's temperature has been normal for almost four weeks, the yellow tinge has disappeared from her skin and she is beginning to look a little like her old self. I hope and pray that this means that she is fully recovered. Of course, the illness has left her irritable and capricious, but I'm so happy that she is alive that I'm quite willing to bear all her tantrums and outbursts, though sometimes I'm really rushed off my feet trying to satisfy all her whims. She is back in her garden again and is really enjoying being among her plants. I also have the great pleasure of having a friend from Chile staying with us, a young woman who used to teach ballet in my school in La Serena and who has decided to try her luck here. She used to live with us in Chile and is just like one of the family, and although this might sound selfish, I'm hoping thanks to her to be able to go away for a few days in the summer if everything is well with mother, for I know that she will look after my poor little old ladies for me. I have not had a proper holiday - when I wouldn't have to worry about things at home - for a very long time, and I know I need it badly. My problem now is lack of sleep. There seems to be so much to do that I can never finish everything, even though I go to bed around midnight and am up before six. If I could only have a ten-minute nap during the day I'd feel quite well, unfortunately I can't do that. However, on Wednesdays and Thursdays I have a free period and just put my head on my table in the staff-room and sleep for a few minutes - in spite of the noise. To-day being Thursday I've had my ten-minute 'shut-eye' and am feeling quite lively. Term ends in exactly one month, then I'll sleep the clock 'round.

As usual I have carried on all about myself, not even asking about your health, and you don't mention it in your letter either. I do hope you are well. Thank you once again for your inestimable kindness."

"I hope you have had a pleasant trip to Japan and that you have thoroughly enjoyed Expo '70. We have read very much about it and there were some beautiful pictures at our local air-line, trying to entice our inhabitants to make the journey; but even though they are giving a special price, still I don't think they will get any passengers. Besides, half the people in St. Kitts wouldn't know where Japan is.

I am writing to you from Conaree, my Mother has been feeling a little better this week, so I have paid a flying visit to some friends of mine who live in Nevis. I don't know whether I have mentioned in my last letters that a very good friend of mine, a Chilean girl who used to teach ballet in my school in La Serena, has come to St. Kitts to try her luck here. Well, she went with me to Nevis where she gave us a performance, dancing extracts from the Nutcracker Suite, the Sleeping Beauty and the Swan Lake. She danced at sunset, on the lawn with the tropical flowers and palms as a backdrop. The light was wonderful, better than any on stage, everything seemed so ethereal and fairy-like. We all enjoyed it greatly and it made me forget all my troubles and worries for a few moments.

Mother's temperature has now become my barometer. When it is normal, it is fair weather and everything is well, but those days are so few and far between, and when her temperature goes up, the barometer falls and we are engulfed in a sort of dismal fog through which I just can't see my way. I'm afraid the doctor is stumped too, we can't get to the real reason, why should those bile channels get obstructed.

Mother, of course, thinks the worst and is quite sure that she has a malignant growth pressing on them, but I hope that she is wrong, for I've never known that to be accompanied by fever. Whatever it is, I thank the Lord that she feels no pain, that would have been unbearable.

The Nutcracker's *March of the toy soldiers*

Conaree is beautiful now, the colours are marvelous, the sea a sparkling, greenish blue, with the deeper blue and indigo in the distance. I have rented the bungalow for a few days, since the tourist season is over the owner is letting me have it for half price, much to the delight of *ChienChien* who moved in with us right away - only to present us with a new family this morning! SEVEN of them! What are we to do? Just imagine finding homes for all of them!"

"School is all upset, no more discipline, no order or respect. I'm keeping a very tight hold on my French and Spanish students, and because of that I'm afraid I'm not too popular with the rest of the staff nor with many of the students. I must say though, that generally my boys and girls try to work and respond. Their oral exams, French and Spanish 'O' and 'A' levels are next week, I think they have a reasonable chance in this part of the examination, but in the written section, as there is so much English and as their English is appalling, I'm afraid some of them will fail the foreign languages because they do not know English, which is supposed to be their own tongue.

To add to all our problems, we had some torrential rains - absolutely unusual at this time of year. The roads were all flooded and broken up, mud, sand, boulders and all sorts of debris came hurtling down the mountains and into the town, transforming streets into rivers and many parts of the island were cut off. After the storm passed, bulldozers, tractors and other equipment were brought in to clear the streets. Fortunately, no lives were lost, but we are in a state of devastation, and worst of all there is no water. The mains have become choked with silt, some have burst, and the result is that our section of the town has no water at all - therefore, over and above the rest of my work I now drive every day to the sugar factory and fill bottles, canteens and pails, and water is heavy to cart. When I had the house built I so wanted to add a cistern, for when there is a heavy rain we get bucketsful of water in a few minutes, but was unable to build one. Last year I installed a 400-gallon tank, but as that has to be filled from the main, it is of no use, besides, since the foundations wouldn't be able to stand it, I had to have it put up on a special support, and because of the menace of hurricanes it is not placed high enough to supply water to my 'apartment'. So life is far from rosy. Still, I try to keep cheerful, and if it weren't for mother's illness,

I would have been able to take it all in my stride. My Chilean friend, Señorita Hilda Soto is a good companion and helps me enormously. I'm so happy she'll be here on the 24th. I have to go to Montserrat and Nevis to examine 'O' and 'A' level candidates in French and Spanish, and she'll stay home and hold the fort."

"On May 30th we had our *Soirée*, I am enclosing a programme. All my boys worked very hard, we had to make new 'flats' for the stage out of all sorts of odds and ends, one of my chief helpers, Robert Swanston, a future electronics engineer wired the whole place for lights and sounds, others turned carpenters and the third lot became painters. We all enjoyed the work and the 'sets' looked very professionally finished. Especially Blue Beard's tower. The whole performance was a great success, nobody forgot anything, all the costumes and props fitted and even the wigs stayed on during the great duel of Bluebeard and the soldiers. Financially we did quite well, though of course we have not enough money to send all the five boys that I want to send. Each scholarship is of U.S. $140, I now have enough for two boys and the French Consul General has promised to look after one boy, my 'business manager', who was in charge of all financial matters, 18-year old Winston Hicks, who was also chief painter and almost broke his neck falling off the ladder, but seems not to have suffered any after-effects. However, there are two more boys left, so once our exams are over I'm going to start begging and wheedling aid. Our own Government has flatly refused to grant a scholarship, which is really a shame. Those boys speak excellent French, three of them will probably join the Staff of the school in September as pupil-teachers, so this is really an investment. A six-week course given by bona-fide University professors from France, in a French atmosphere, is the best preparation those youngsters would ever get for the job. And yet the Ministry of Education does not seem to understand this.

Ms. Soto and Mrs. Katzen

I have just had a letter from the Ministry informing me that the Government wishes to renew my contract for another period of three years. I am happy about that, for although the working conditions are quite difficult, and the pay most inadequate, at least I will not have to pull up roots and disrupt the lives of my poor little old ladies. However, if I accept the contract, I must take 84 days leave, to be spent abroad, and I don't see how I can leave my poor little old mother here; even with Señorita Hilda Soto's willingness to look after her. I would have to go in September. Just can't think about it now."

"First of all, the Douglas family. I have given Mrs. Douglas the final remainder of their funds and they are now quite able to continue on their own. I hope they will be grateful to you always, as for me, I do not know how to express my thanks for your kindness.

Now for the Guadeloupe students. Out of the five I have been able to secure funds and scholarships for four. Since you have been so generous as to say that I could use some of the fund if necessary, may I send the fifth boy? He is a very good student, is now to enter the VI A having successfully passed his VI B internal exams. Besides being a good student his is also honest, hard-working and well-mannered. He will be most grateful, and in my opinion he deserves to go.

The doctor has just received some new tablets and for the past two weeks my mother's temperature has been normal. You can imagine what a relief that has been, coming just at the time when the school exams were due. She has started to take an interest in things again, actually came out into the garden and into the kitchen, and even went for a drive or two.

The atmosphere in the house has changed radically, we walk about normally, not on tip-toe, talk, and even joke and laugh. I was even beginning to think of my leave and of a trip on a cargo ship to recuperate and get back some of my much-needed sleep when suddenly another problem has arisen, quite out of the blue, and to which I have to find a solution, fast.

I am hesitating about writing about it to you, yet the burden is so heavy that I'm yielding to the temptation of pouring out my troubles. Perhaps, too, if I put it all down on paper some way out may present itself.

I think I have mentioned in my last letter that the Government of St. Kitts has offered to renew my contract for a further period of three years. I was very happy about that for I would not like any change at this time, my little old ladies are far too weak and fragile to move and the upheaval might be too much for my mother. However yesterday, with no previous warning I was informed that there would be a change in the terms of the contract and this fills me with dismay.

My current take-home monthly pay-cheque (after all deductions) is £78. Out of this £40 go towards household expenses: food, electricity, telephone, water rates and upkeep - soap and cleaners etc., repairs and replacement of old utensils - £14 pay for the food I give my French and Spanish Club children and this leaves me £24 for all the rest: clothing, running of the car, unforeseen expenses and a few very small charities. Out of these three sections I have to save as much as possible to pay three insurance policies, (house, furniture and car), and put something by for doctor's fees, medicines and emergencies.

The cost of living on the island has been rising steadily while salaries have remained the same, however I have been able to manage and I think I'd still be able to get along if it were not for the house.

When I arrived in St. Kitts the housing situation was very difficult. It is even worse now. An unfurnished house can be had only from £20 upwards monthly, these are very scarce, usually £25 and even £30 are charged. It seemed such a waste to pay £20 a month for rent and get nothing in return that I started thinking of building. To this end I sold one of the two houses I had in Chile - very disastrously for I didn't get anything worth mentioning for it - but as at that time the O.S.A.S. (Overseas Aid Scheme) came into being, I decided to get a loan and build, since I'd have the O.S.A.S. monthly inducement allowance to pay it back with. This allowance was £42-16-10d a month. Therefore, I borrowed the money, £3000, added the £1000 I had saved and built the house. That was three and a half years ago, and since the scheme was to be in operation until 1976 and since the Government had promised that my contract would include it, everything seemed perfect.

Now, all of a sudden, the Ministry has informed me that this allowance would cease as of Sept 1st. You can imagine my consternation! I have been faithfully paying in the money to Wade Plantations and for the three years they have received £1,360 from me. Unfortunately, as the interest is quite high I still owe them about £2,200 - and I really do not see how I shall be able to keep up the monthly payments after September.

Since mother's illness I have cut down on all expenses, have stopped all entertaining, reduced life to its simplest form, have even cancelled all subscriptions to newspapers and magazines. We don't keep a servant and make no new clothes. So I don't know what else I can curtail. I could give up the French and Spanish Club sandwiches, but I know that the meal represents perhaps the only good one that some of the children get that day. It is no use selling the small house I have left in Chile - it would go for very little and besides I wouldn't be able to get that money out of the country anyhow. Also, supposing I'd have to go back to Chile - the Lord forbid - at least I'd have a place to live in. I have no jewelry and the doctor and the chemist have already taken the last of my savings.

I do not want to consider selling the house, I would not get its full value, for the roof has never been painted, the baths and kitchen only partially tiled and the land is not properly enclosed. And if I sell it for the £2200 that I owe Wade Plantations, we'd have to find some place to live in, and that again means £20-£25 a month for rent which I wouldn't have. Besides, if I cannot get another contract I could start French and Spanish classes or a little school at home - if I have a home. I could perhaps give up my leave, then my passage money could go towards paying some of the loan - but my passage allowance is just £200 and I don't know whether the Government would be willing to let me have it for any other purpose besides travelling. Then I realize that I need this leave, my eye-sight has deteriorated so much, what with lack of sleep and corrections at night that I have to get medical attention before it is too late, and I can't get it here.

Some time ago I was offered another post as headmistress of the Sugar Factory School - but the salary was even smaller and there is no inducement allowance either. So, no matter which way I turn I can't see a way out. Does any solution occur to you?

I have written to the Permanent Secretary of Education begging to have this decision reconsidered, but I'm afraid there is not much hope of that. If I can get a good rest and feel strong again I'll take on some classes at the Evening Institute. I have refused to do so until now because it involves more teaching and corrections at night and I'm usually too exhausted to give proper lessons after a whole day's work - still, as a last resort I suppose I'll have to try.

I'm sorry to have recounted all my woes to you, but I do feel a bit better now that I have shared my troubles with somebody, and perhaps you might think of something that escapes me.

Now I'm wondering whether I should send this letter to you after all, you might think that I'm begging you for monetary help and I would not like you to have that idea. I have written all this because I have no friend with whom to discuss the situation and I do need sympathy and moral support, for with mother's illness, the unpleasant conditions of work at the school, my utter exhaustion and now this blow from the Ministry, I really think that I'm coming to the end of my resistance. Do write soon and give me a word of comfort."

"I am in London for a few days before going on to the Continent. First and foremost, may I say how happy I am that your Mother is better. I hope she will be perfectly well again soon.

Regarding your problem, you did quite right and I am honoured that you share your troubles with me. I fully concur with your point of view that you must not give up your job despite the disgraceful way the Government of St. Kitts has behaved. No-one has done as much as you have for the youth of that island and the appreciation of everyone was shown when they honoured you recently. For the Ministry of Education to suddenly stop giving you a housing allowance is really disgraceful.

In order to relieve your anxiety, I immediately send you a telegram as per copy attached, and instructed Hong Kong to remit to you immediately, Three Thousand Pounds, which I hope you will accept as a gift from me. May I suggest that you pay off the mortgage on your house, and make all necessary repairs to it. Please also see a good eye specialist and take a welldeserved holiday, for it is essential that you keep good health.

I am so thankful to you for all you are doing for our various protégés. It is indeed great news to hear that the Douglas family are now able to make both ends meet. By all means pay the necessary funds for the fifth Guadeloupe student. I hope he does well.

I leave for a 12-day holiday on the continent on Tuesday visiting Vienna, the Dolomites, Venice and Milan. From there I proceed to America and I hope to be able to visit the National Parks on the West Coast of the U.S.A. and also the Canadian Rockies before returning to Hong Kong. With every good wish to you and the old ladies."

"I wonder where you are now, it is so strange to write without knowing your address, sort of sending the letter into space - I'll post it to Honk Kong and hope that it reaches you soon.

How can I thank you for all you are doing? I came home on Friday from Nevis after two days' absence and found your cable, which left me completely dazed, this was followed an hour later by another from Hong Kong and last night I received your letter from London.

I do not know how to set about answering you. My first impulse was to cable your Hong Kong office and countermand your instructions - and then I felt it would be discourteous, churlish even, to respond in such a manner to your noble, generous action. There is absolutely no reason for you to make such a munificent gift and I do not think I have the right to accept it.

It is true that as from September I shall not be able to keep up the payments and Wade Plantations will not think twice about turning us out. The Ministry has not as yet replied to my appeal asking them to reconsider their decision, and the longer they take, the less probability there is of the continuation of this housing allowance.

I am sorely tempted to accept your help - the thought of my poor little helpless old ladies haunts me all the time. However, may I consider it not as a permanent gift but as a temporary loan which I may refund bit by bit? I know this sounds ridiculous, even impudent, like planning to refill an empty reservoir with an eye-dropper - and yet it will make me feel not so ashamed and mercenary, as if I have taken advantage of your kind, generous heart. To-morrow, Monday, I shall go to Wade Plantations and find out exactly how my debt with them stands, and then, as you suggest, I'd pay it off, have the necessary repairs done to the house, and whatever is left over, may I return to you? After that, supposing a miracle happened and my monthly housing allowance were to continue when I return from leave, if I go at all, I would remit it at once to you. Then my conscience will not torture me so cruelly. If there is no more housing allowance, then I'd remit whatever would be left over from my salary - this of course would vary every time and would be just a drop in the ocean compared to what you are sending, and it will probably take years and years to complete what in your kindness of heart you are remitting now. Will you allow me to do this? Please say yes.

I shall write again as soon as I have all the figures from Wade Plantations, but I want to send this letter off first thing to-morrow morning, a delay may make you think me ungrateful. Oh, it is so difficult to express what I want to say, words are so meaningless.

Just a few words about life here: the boys have gone to Guadeloupe for their six-week course. I have written up all my records of work, filled in reports and have put all my school affairs in order, after which, taking advantage of Mother's state of health I went to spend two days in Nevis. Some people I know there sometimes let me use their home. It's miles away from everything, no traffic, no noise, no telephone. A wonderful place to sleep and rest for a day or two.

Mother has completed a month with no temperature. Yesterday, all of a sudden it went up to 101.4, but it is normal again to-day, so I'm hoping it was just the excitement of my coming back. She knows nothing of course of this whole matter of housing allowance, contract, etc. I'm afraid she wouldn't be able to stand all the worry.

Once again, may the Lord bless you, I have no words to thank you, anything I can write would not give you an idea of the gratitude and happiness that you have brought to me. I hope your holiday is peaceful and enjoyable, may you rest and relax."

"How I wish I knew how to thank you for all you are doing! You have given hope, help, a new life to so many youngsters and their families here, and now you have literally saved me, for I must acknowledge that I was really in despair, at my wits' end, not knowing what to do and going absolutely insane with worry. Wade Plantations would have felt no compunction about turning us out, and my heart was breaking as I looked at my poor little frail old ladies, not knowing what to do, how to break the awful news and what steps to take. The Ministry, by the way, simply ignored my appeal, I'm to call at the Personnel Officer at Establishments, next week, to see what can be done. I was told this after writing last week again. You have changed all that, even if it takes years and years to repay the funds to you in little bits, I have the security that my little old ladies will not be deprived of their home and can live in it in peace. God bless you!

I do not want to bother you with all business matters while you are on holiday, when you return to Hong Kong I shall send you a detailed statement with the Bank's exchange slips, Wade Plantations receipt and the contractor's estimate.

Where are you now? London, Europe or are you on your way to Canada? Wherever it is, I hope you are relaxing and having a restful vacation. You certainly deserve it and travelling is so pleasant. How are you touring Europe, driving yourself? I find that is the only way to enjoy and see everything. I wonder if you remember Morris Archibald? He was one of your first 'godsons', and later won a scholarship for a three-year course in a University in Wales. During his holidays he worked his way to France and then hitch-hiked all around Europe - and walked and cycled, he said he really enjoyed it.

St. Kitts is going through an anxious period. Owing to several circumstances, weather included, the sugar crop which promised to be exceptional, has proved a great disappointment. Usually at this time of the year 30,000 tons of sugar have been elaborated, this year only 17,000 have been produced and the political climate is very unsettled. It's all a question of wanting to run before you know how to walk, probably all 'new' countries are going through like stages. Dreams won't run a State. Common sense is far more vital. Projects are all good but you have to carry them out."

"This letter is to welcome you back home. I hope you have had an enjoyable and restful holiday, my prayers and thoughts have been with you constantly and not a day goes by that I do not think of you and wonder at your kindness and generosity. I still can't believe that we are really out of the nightmare, I often wake up with a start in the middle of the night, fear just clutching at me, and then I remember that you have rescued us and that the Wade Plantations have been paid and that we are in no danger of being turned out. You cannot imagine the harrowing days and nights I have been through and I do not know how I shall ever be able to thank you for what you have done for us.

Wade Plantations have received their due and I have their receipt to forward to you when I know that you are in Hong Kong. The contractor has already put up the wall dividing our house plot from the neighbours on the left - a good solid wall, so now our flowers and other plants, fruits and vegetables as well as my pets are all safe from their sheep, dogs and children. The neighbours on the right are very friendly and helpful, we are on excellent terms so the wire fence that we have now fixed up is quite sufficient to separate our respective gardens. The roof has been painted - the contractor says just in time; it could not have stood up much longer without starting to rust and rot. Two tanks have been put up, one linked to the main water supply to insure having water when the reservoir is closed, this happens every day from 8 a.m. to 6 p.m. and again from 8 p.m. to 6 a.m. and with an invalid in the home it was most difficult, I'd fill every pail, bucket and pan available every time water was to be turned off and the time and effort needed were great and so needless. The other tank is to store rain water, this will be finished next week as there is spouting to be fixed on to the eaves. After this the kitchen and baths are to be tiled and then I shall be able to send you a complete statement of cost and expenses, as well as return any balance if such will be left. A word of thanks and gratitude to you goes with every item added.

My mother's health, thank the Lord, is fair. A fortnight ago the doctor said I could go ahead and book my passage to Chile, and then suddenly she had some trouble with her heart and the doctor said 'hold everything and don't commit yourself'. Now she has rallied again and he says that he does not see any reason why I should not make the trip. On one hand, I'm terribly afraid to leave my poor little old ladies, although my Chilean friend, the ballet-dancer is going to look after them, she is reliable, honest and just like a member of the family. On the other hand, I realize that I'm in no state to embark on a new contract without having a complete rest - and that is possible only if I leave the home circle for a little while. I know this sounds selfish, but if I remain at home without a break the constant worry and lack of sleep will finish me. If only I knew I'd find her alive and in the same state as now on my return, I would not hesitate. Such a pity we cannot know what's in store for us, if only for a month or two! The poor people who were drowned in the *Christena*[19] didn't think that they'd die such an awful death, just as they were setting out on a pleasure jaunt! We cannot foretell the future, I'll still have to keep my fingers crossed and hope for the best. That is if I really go.

Sorry to have ended on a pessimistic note again, I didn't mean to. Please write when you have a moment to spare, I know this will be difficult since you are just back, so I'll be patient and wait."

Once again, the peace and calm of an ocean voyage beckoned. Bound for Chile aboard the *Seattle*, Madame Katzen was once again in her element.

"A fire on board, a stowaway, 12% of the crew missing the boat and getting left behind in La Guaira (Venezuela), the Captain's cabin broken into and the ship's nylon cables stolen from the deck as we were at anchor waiting for a berth in Buenaventura (Columbia) - all this to add more spice to a delightful voyage. The fire started - of all places - in the fire alarm system, all the batteries were ruined and since the ship cannot sail if the fire alarm circuit is out of order, we were held up for two days while equipment was flown to us from

---

[19] The Christena, the daily ferry between St. Kitts and Nevis, sank on August 1, 1970. There were 233 casualties.

some other country, since Venezuela, where the fire happened didn't have anything suitable.

I was very happy for the delay, every extra day spent on board is regarded by me as a bonus. When I settled in my cabin I went to sleep and slept and slept until I just couldn't sleep any more. The trip has been lovely, very peaceful and relaxing - barring the few exciting incidents mentioned above - unfortunately I have not been able to enjoy it fully for there are still no letters from home, and I have reached almost the end of the journey, disembarking in Valparaiso next week. At one time, I became so anxious that I sent a cable to my little old crocks. They cabled back that all was well and that they had already posted eight letters. This has relieved my anxiety somewhat but there has been no further news since, so where those eight letters are, goodness knows.

There are only three other passengers on this 9,000-ton ship, all very pleasant people, but even if they weren't, there is so much room that nobody can even get into anybody else's way. The captain is an old friend, I had already made a trip previously with him. The weather was wonderful at first, but ever since we approached the equator, a week ago, it has turned 'bitterly' cold - 62° - with rain squalls, sharp, strong winds and rough seas. As we have already discharged almost all our cargo, the ship is very light and we roll and pitch and dive all the time. I was almost tossed out of bed last night, and in Matarani (Peru), our last port of call, when we had to pick up the pilot, the poor man couldn't climb on board for more than ten minutes, we were swaying up and down, and his boat was bobbing erratically and was almost smashed against the ship's side.

I have had enough time to think and reflect about everything, your innate kindness and your generosity. I cannot tell you how much I value your friendship, it is impossible ever to repay you for all you have done. The financial repayment will start as soon as I return to St. Kitts, as for your kindness and friendship - I can only pray the good Lord to protect you always and let you experience as much happiness as you have given to others."

"Thank you so much for your two letters, one received at my sister's home and the other yesterday here in Valparaiso. I was most happy to hear that you are back home, in good health for your letter sounds relaxed and contented. I can quite realize how you are with the progress of the farm. I think there is nothing so fascinating as watching the earth produce and I always marvel at the beautiful vegetables and flowers produced from a handful of seeds in our little garden, I can imagine your proud feelings when you see your crops of fruit, especially when they have grown on land considered valueless. Mother always says that every plant responds to love and care never mind the poor quality of the soil.

With my usual knack of getting into trouble I just managed to slip out of Santiago before the state of emergency had been declared. As you may have heard the results of the presidential elections were not decisive, Allende getting 31,000 votes more than Alessandri, which means that the Congress will have to decide which one of the two will rule definitely. The Congress is to meet to-morrow and the whole country is in turmoil, demonstrations, meetings and now bombs everywhere and shooting. Yesterday the army Chief of Staff, General Schneider was attacked and shot, he is still unconscious, in spite of two operations, that is the reason for the state of emergency, all gatherings are banned and all vehicles leaving the capital are stopped and searched. Many people have been arrested and there is an atmosphere of panic. All last month people have been leaving the country in thousands, all trains and planes are booked up till the end of November, and even the *Rio de Janeiro*, which carries only 8 passengers is full. She has sailed into the harbour this afternoon, but will come alongside only to-morrow as there is no available berth. Valparaiso is an important port, and it has just four berths, quite incredible. The ship will load and unload for two or three days and usually passengers are allowed on board just two hours before sailing, however the captain has allowed me to move in early to-morrow, as soon as the vessel docks; this is most considerate of him and has made me very happy. First, I'll be out of this political crisis, in peace on board the ship and secondly, I'll have the pleasure of exploring the boat at leisure. I love ships, had I been a man I probably would have been a sailor, being a mere woman I can only be a passenger!"

"Here I am back in St. Kitts. The lovely halcyon days of *dolce farniente* on board ships are over and I have already plunged into a maelstrom of activity, having been away for over two months you can imagine the piles and mounds of work to be cleared up and things put to rights.

Everything at home is perfect. To my greatest joy I found my little old ladies in excellent health, thanks to the Lord and to our good doctor. Mother is actually pottering about her garden again, waging war on weeds and ants and producing an abundant crop of beets and lettuce with several promising beds of all sorts of vegetables in progressive stages of growth as well. The pets gave me a great welcome, even *Minette* my dowager cat condescended to purr and rub against my legs, *Peloton*, the dog, barked and jumped and raced around in spite of his fat and almost choked with asthma as a result, the seven strays turned out in full force in the evening and *Chien-Chien* went absolutely wild, recognized the car a great distance away, streaked to meet me and jumped into it through the window.

Among all the letters waiting for me - since none had been forwarded during my absence - I found one from you dated 10th September and I was most distressed by its second part. Dear Mr. Kadoorie, whatever is the matter with your right hand? You have never mentioned anything at all about it and I am very deeply concerned to learn that you have trouble with it, and what is most disturbing, that you had been given an inaccurate report of its state. It must have been extremely worrying to face the prospect predicted those two years ago and I am happy that the specialist that you have now consulted is of a different opinion. All my thoughts and prayers for your health go to you. The Lord cannot permit you to suffer, you have done so much good around you, have helped so many, changed the course of so many lives bringing hope and plenty where there was misery and despair, that it would be cruel and unfair to have sadness shadowing your own life. Please keep me informed about your health, even though I cannot help, I will think of you and pray."

"Thank you for your registered letter of Dec 15th with all the enclosures. I'm filing them all away if required for further reference, for now, owing to your great generosity, I can have all deeds and documents relating to the house transferred to my name - hitherto because of the mortgage it was almost all in the name of Wade Plantations. The attorney is working on the transfer, but as for everything in St. Kitts, one has to wait for ages before anything is done. Can you imagine that although I have reported for work on Dec. 9th my contract has not yet been drawn up and I am in absolute ignorance as to terms and salary. The only thing that I have been told is that the duration of this new contract would be of only two years and not three as my previous ones have been.

The kitchen and baths are lovely to behold. I obtained some green tiles in Puerto Rico to complete my bath and was fortunate to find the blue ones for my old ladies here. As for the kitchen, I was lucky to hear of a lot of tiles sold at half price because of a fire in the ware-house where they had been kept and was allowed to pick out myself what I wanted. The mason was an extraordinary workman who didn't waste a single moment, he would come at 7:30 in the morning and leave after 6 in the evening, so I gave him breakfast, lunch and dinner every day and he made a lovely job. I have painted the doors myself with paint left over from the roof and the only thing missing now is to pave the veranda area, 14' by 7', but I have decided to wait until the contractor would have some 'flags' or quarry tiles left over from some other building and which will then be cheaper. I first thought of cementing it, but owing to sudden squalls of rain the contractor says there will be spots and the surface will be pitted. Therefore, it is better to wait. I can still not make up my budget since I do not know what my salary will be. When that is known I'll be able to start the repayments.

The last part of your letter has made me ever so happy and has given me something to look forward to and to enjoy thinking about. I mean the holiday you might take to visit the Caribbean Islands and South America. Never mind South America, but please, please come to the Caribbean. There is a daily flight from New York right to St. Kitts, unfortunately it's not direct, you have to change planes in Puerto Rico, but it is not a tiring journey, by jet from New York to San Juan de Puerto Rico and then by prop-jet to St. Kitts. You can also fly via Antigua, changing planes there. We would be overjoyed to see you. First, you'd meet many of your 'godchildren', although almost all of them are now away, studying in Universities or working - you have helped so many of them over all these years, but the ones you are helping now will be on hand to welcome you. Then you will look at the house and see for yourself everything that has been done to it, and thirdly, you'll relax and enjoy the beauty of this island, it will be such a wonderful rest for you and happiness for us. Please let me know in advance so that I can arrange a substitute at the school and devote all my time to you - that is if you will be willing to accept me as a guide. Please come and do not disappoint us all. With every good wish to you and yours for the New Year. May your hand become quite whole again."

1971

"At long last I am back in Hong Kong, having undergone a rather serious operation in the United States. I am glad to say that all is well and that I am now feeling much healthier and stronger than before. With the exception of having to go slow for another month or two I am perfectly recovered.

On my return here, I was met at the airport by the family and a large gathering of friends. The reception I received from the staff, bus drivers and farmers has done much to make me forget the past.

When I was away I understand you wrote a number of letters to my brother for which many thanks. As yet I have not had time to read them but will do so as soon as possible. I also understand that you sent me a Get-Well card. It was most considerate of you.

In due course I will be answering your letters more thoroughly, in the meantime please accept my sincere thanks for your kindness and consideration."

Later that day Horace writes:

"Since writing this morning I now find that I have time to acknowledge your letters of February 28th, March 1st, 7th addressed to me, and also your kind letter to my brother of March 23rd. I also have to acknowledge the letters from Larry Woods and Inez Butler. I am delighted that you are helping them and have decided to continue your assistance to the other boys who are studying in Barbados. Please help whoever needs it most.

Indeed, you were right about the Post Office strike in Britain. It is absurd that letters from St. Kitts have to go to England before coming here. I so much appreciate your thinking of me and can assure you I am most grateful.

Congratulations on receiving a communication from the Ministry offering you a new contract with an increase. I hope that by now you have received the money. Failing which I trust you have written to them again.

You mentioned in your letter of March 7th that you are anxious to pay back, as soon as possible, the amount forwarded to you. Please do not hurry over this, but if you insist I would suggest you open a savings account in your own name, crediting whatever sum you wish to pay to this account; I think it will be easier and cheaper for you than remitting the sum to me each time."

"Our school year has at last drawn to its bitter and painful end, we had our last staff meeting this morning, I have signed all my reports, turned in my record of work, given detailed comments on each one of the 102 students whom I teach, composed and typed the over-all report as head of Modern Languages department giving

all particulars, handed in the new syllabus and am presumably free
to relax.

It is raining cats and dogs, but the whole wall facing the sea
consists of windows, and though I had to close them, I can see the
ocean with the waves breaking over the reef's white surf contrasting
with the grey water and I can hear the roar of the breakers. Even in
somber colours it's beautiful. *Chienne-chienne* has of course moved in
with me and is lying contentedly at my feet, gorged with a huge
lunch. I'm afraid another litter of little *chiennes-chiennes* and *chiens* is on
its way, quite imminent; more homes to be found!

My only 'fly in the ointment', is that last week my mother had a
fall - in the garden - and has injured her knee quite seriously. She
has to rest a great deal, the doctor says she should stay in bed for at
least a week. She stayed there for three days but declares that she's
getting up to-morrow.

Because of this predicament I spend most of the day at home and
come to Conaree in the afternoon, when she is all settled for the
night. Then early next morning I drive home again. Still, even a few
hours are so restful that I feel strength and energy returning with
every breath of ocean-filled air I take. The great advantage is that
there is a telephone here, so I keep in touch with home, and the
doctor who comes to look at mother constantly, gives me his bulletin
after each visit.

Dear Mr. Kadoorie, please don't be cross with me, but before
receiving your letter, and as soon as I actually received my new salary,
(paid from December 1970), I made arrangements with my bank to
send you monthly, not a drop in the bucket, but rather a drop in the
ocean, to embark on the repayment of my debt - which no money in
the world can ever repay, you do not know what peace and happiness
you have brought us by your kind gesture. Please don't be annoyed,
but do allow me for the duration of this contract, that is until
December 1972, to go on with this microscopic remittance. This is

probably the last time the Government renews my contract[20], and who knows if I shall be able to keep up payments after that, do let me have the satisfaction at least of trying to return a mite, while I have a chance of doing it.

I was planning to go away for a week to some other island for a complete rest - either St. Martin or Barbados, but it all depends on my mother, if she'll be quite well, I'll go, if she's better but not 100% fit, I might go for a long week-end to Nevis, it's only a five minutes flight away and there's a phone connection. The drawback is I know too many people there, so it won't be a rest. And if I do go, I have to return by mid-August, then we are in our hurricane season and I prefer to be home. School starts in September, we have to report for duty on Sept. 1st. The Ministry wanted us to give extra classes all through August, but I declined. If I don't get a rest now I won't be fit to face another strenuous school year."

Madame writes from Barbados:

"The doctor said that the 'health situation' at home was such that it was quite permissible for me to leave my poor little old ladies for a few days and to get some rest, away from the familiar atmosphere. After three days, I feel a completely different being, to-morrow I'm taking the plane home. This has been a complete rest and total relaxation. Here, away from home, there is nothing for me to do but just relax and lie in the sun, enjoying the music of the surf. In St. Kitts, I spend half the day at home, whereas here there are absolutely no duties nor responsibility and I telephone home every evening and speak with mother. The great attraction for me here is a lovely sailing ship that the hotel maintains for its guests, and I spend almost the whole day on her, I'm enclosing a picture of her, she is a yawl and has been built for people to live on her. The hotel uses her only for sailing and has completely neglected the living quarters. The cabins

---

[20] Ten years since she arrived in St. Kitts, Madame Katzen is now 60 years old.

- two of them - are closed up, dirty and full of rubbish, nobody ever uses them. Aren't people incomprehensible? They have such a wonderful possession and they do not enjoy it! The 'captain' and the deck hand live ashore - and come on board only if somebody wants to go for a sail. Do you like sailing? The silent way in which a sailing ship moves is a miracle, no noise of engines, just the wind and the lapping of the water!

I have to report for work on Sept 1st. - just a fortnight and two days from now. This school year promises to be even worse than the last. The government has declared that no money is to be spent on books - the children have to buy their own. Where, goodness knows, since there are no proper bookshops in St. Kitts. The school used to order them from England, but will not now.

I hope your health is still improving steadily and that you are almost 100% fit now. However please listen to your doctors and do not overwork. As my old ladies say, *work is not a wolf, it will not run away*."

"It seems ages since I have heard from you. I go to the Post Office every day hoping to find a letter from you in the mail, but so far there has been nothing and I am beginning to be most uneasy about you. Are you well? Perhaps you do not write because you are too busy - but then the doctors have all advised that you do not work too hard, and I'm sure you would listen to them. Do, please send me some news, even a few lines from your secretary would be welcome; as it is, we are still quite worried.

I have had a great sorrow, losing a most dear and faithful friend. My poor *Chienne-Chienne* is no more. She began feeling ill and looked all swollen, so I enticed her into the car and took her to the vet. After one look at her he said that she seemed seriously ill, and when he had examined her he diagnosed cancer. I asked him to operate and do everything possible to save her, but when he opened her he found her absolutely riddled with the disease, so I asked him to give her another injection while she was still under the anesthetic so that she would never wake up. I suppose, in theory, it was the best thing to do, but it was horrible all the same. I could not bear to go to Conaree for a whole month, just forced myself to go there to-day. She was so affectionate and even when the vet was giving her the injection before the operation, she nestled up to me, put her head on my shoulder and gave me her paw to hold. So many criminals, evil and cruel people go on living and cause suffering elsewhere, while this creature, so good and gentle had to lose the precious gift of life."

"Since you are making a trip to Australia your health must be improving, I only hope you will not over-exert yourself and get tired. I suppose it is unreasonable of me, but then, when I get no news from the few people I really care for and esteem, all sorts of dire thoughts come into my mind, so please forgive me.

Here everything is gathering momentum downhill. One teacher has been away for a week with fish poisoning, another has been away for two weeks, I really don't know what for since he drives to school every day to bring two of his fellow-teachers and then simply drives home again. One form had just 12 periods of teaching last week, out of the 35, so with all those children running wild it is most difficult to teach, I must say though that my French and Spanish students are always on time and are doing their best to study. If not it would be sheer frustration.

My only relaxation is a drive to Conaree where I stay for ten minutes every afternoon and listen to the surf and enjoy the view and the air. Even that is tinged with sadness, for I miss *Chienne-Chienne* who would come bounding to me as soon as she'd hear the car.

Last week I was dreadfully tired, and sitting there started to think about the future. May I share my thoughts with you? Your advice is the most valuable I could get, and if you think my plan daft, just say so frankly. I don't know whether I have written to you that my present contract is going to come to an end in December 1972, and there are not many chances that it will be renewed. The Government might of course take me on a month-to-month basis after that, but that would go on for a year or two and then I'd be faced with the same problem of getting another job and less chances of obtaining same, time and age not being on my side. Suddenly I had a brain-wave. Conaree beach is miles long, there are now fifteen cottages and houses on it and there is a village close by - and not a single shop of any kind. Do you think it would be a good idea to set one up? I'm sure one doesn't need much training to run one, my little old ladies had one in Chile years ago and managed quite well. I started at once to make enquiries about a small plot, all the sites are parallel, a front on the ocean and the other side on the road. I am looking for a narrow one, so that I'd build a little shack - and when I say shack I really mean something very small - facing the ocean for us and a one room general store facing the road. I'd pay for the plot with the gratuity I'm supposed to receive at the termination of the contract, would then mortgage our house, rather yours, since you have paid for it, and would build with the mortgage money.

Then we'd move to Conaree and rent our present home, there is such a shortage of houses in St. Kitts, I think it would be very easy to rent it. That would pay for the interest. The little old ladies would attend to the shop in the mornings as I will take on a part time job in some school or other for our living expenses until the shop would start bringing some profit. The whole snag is to find a suitable plot. There is a beautiful one, but it's huge 136.85 feet of ocean frontage, whereas just the 36 feet would be ample. However, the owner will not divide it. Another is just right, but there is a house on it already, therefore it is very expensive. There is a perfect little one - 35 ft. by 50ft., but the owner is in England, so I'm writing to him to find out whether he'd sell. Do write and tell me what you think of my idea. I have a little over a year to sort it out, but will have to find something. If I could only sell my little house in Chile that would help, for I'll never be able to return to Chile, having acquired British Nationality now the Chilean Govt. does not want me back. Excuse the selfish letter."

Cottage at Conaree beach

"I am indeed sorry that things are going from bad to worse at the school. However, I am glad that your students are doing well.

Regarding your problems, my first feelings are that your whole life has been devoted to teaching and that you have made a great success of it. All your pupils have done well and, therefore, to give it up in order to run a shop - a new trade - does not strike me as being wise. Early in 1972, I would enquire as to the possibility of your contract being renewed for a reasonable period.

Give consideration to the possibility of running a school of your own for a number of pupils or, failing this, to coach students on a part time basis, and have the rest of the time off for whatever you wish. It is true that as one becomes older there is less chance of obtaining a job, but it is equally true that the experience you have gained in all these years has made you a 'super teacher' and you could utilize some of your spare time coaching students.

Regarding the shop at Conaree Beach, if there are 15 cottages and a village close by, a shop is needed irrespective of who runs it. It is a specialized trade and, in order to gain clients, it must look attractive. Provided you run it yourself it should do well, but there is always the possibility of it not being a success. You are right about making enquiries about the narrow plot. I would also obtain particulars concerning the beautiful one of 136.85 ft. of ocean frontage. Note:

even if you were only to build a small shop on this site, you have the land for future development and provided it is cheap, the chances are it will go up in value. How does the third site - the one that is just right but there is a house on it already - compare pricewise? What would be the cost of the perfect little one 35.50 ft. - the owner of which is in England?

When you have got all the particulars concerning the above and an estimate of the cost of building, you will be in a better position to judge which is more attractive and which you can afford.

It is important that the site is accessible to all the houses and the village and that it would also be good from an investment point of view, i.e. that it will go up in value by, say, at least 18% per annum. Against this, one must consider the possibility of St. Kitts not thriving due to political or other reasons, in which case houses might become empty and your prospects of doing well by having a shop may not be a good idea.

It may be possible to sell your present house and, with the proceeds and the gratuity you will receive, buy a new site and put up a small house on it with a good size shop at the back facing the road. In view of there being a shortage of houses in St. Kitts, land would probably go up provided the political situation is good.

I am sorry I am not able to answer your questions more specifically but until I know the above, it is difficult to give more advice."

"It is so kind of you to write and give me your views and I'm exceedingly grateful. I'm afraid I'm going to be very selfish and shall continue to write to you on the subject, not having any body with whom to talk things over here, it's a great help to state all the particulars to you, and please let me have your frank opinion on all aspects of the matter. I am starting this letter to-day but will have to go on to-morrow and the day after as I'm waiting for several details on Conaree lands and more information on building costs, all this will come in the second part of the letter, I can only hope you will have the patience to read it all.

Conaree beach

First of all, about the teaching problem. As you say, my whole life has been devoted to teaching, and that is about the only thing that I know how to do properly. I certainly do not intend to give up teaching so long as I am able to do so. Unfortunately, the Government is not of the same opinion and there was a great deal of talk before I was granted my present contract, which, by the way, was arranged for two years only and not for three as my previous ones were. The chances of getting another contract are even slighter now, and if I do get one, I'll be faced with the same problem in a year's or two years' time, with the difference that I'll be another year or two older and will have spent more energy and strength as our teaching conditions and general discipline are deteriorating so rapidly that it takes a tremendous effort to do one's work. I know that I'll be able to get a part-time position after that, but the salaries are very low for that kind of service and there is no pay during holidays - only working days are considered. As for coaching, there is a great demand for that only during the month before the examinations, and as for all private lessons, the pay is small and irregular, in some cases it never materializes. If there is another source of income, part-time teaching and coaching will be a most welcome supplement, but as sole source, I'm afraid will not be adequate. That is why, having a whole year ahead, (or perhaps even more), I want to make plans to have something to fall back on, or rather to start or continue. If I wait until there is a very scant chance of earning anything by teaching, it will be too late to start something else from scratch. Hence the idea of setting up a very simple shop in a place where there is no other. I would never dream of opening one in town with all the competition, nor would I embark on anything elaborate, no perishable goods, just tinned stuff, toilet articles, stationery, etc. I would run it myself concurrently with a part-time job, and could have my little old ladies - who by the way are very good at figures and have had some shop-keeping experience in Chile - look after it while I'm in town. Now if I could sell my house and land in Chile, I could buy a plot at Conaree and build a small shack without having to mortgage the present house, then, even if the shop were not a swift success, the rent I could get from *Chalet La Serena*, plus a part-time salary would be ample to live on.

Now about the Conaree lands. (1) The narrow plot. It has to be separated from a large one and the owner has decided not to do it. So that's out. (2) The large one of 136.85 ft of ocean frontage is beautiful, level, and is a perfect rectangle in shape - 340 ft deep. The owner does not want to divide it and wants to sell the entire piece - at W.I.$20,000 that is U.S.$10,000, so that's out. Besides, it's too huge, there is something like an acre and a half. (3) The third site with a very well-built but small house on a 20 ft ocean frontage plot is being sold for £5,000, it is the furthest down the beach and rather isolated. (4) The fourth plot, whose owner is in England, is absolutely perfect. The frontage, on the ocean, is more than I thought, 48 ft, and the depth is long enough to put up a house to live in and a building for a shop facing the road. It is situated on the beach road and almost in front of it, on the other side of the road, there is a foot-path that leads to the village. The main water-supply line passes along the edge of the plot and there is an electric post right on the corner. From all views, including the investment aspect, this is the best plot. As there is no harm in inquiring, I have asked the lawyer who is in charge of the land, to contact the owner and find out whether the plot is really for sale and its price. I have spoken with the original owner of all those lands. He sold them all about ten years ago at 12 cents, (W.I. currency) a square foot. The market value of this same land at present is between 45 and 50 cts. a square foot.

If it were possible for me to acquire this plot I would not build a proper house on it right away. So long as I have a teaching job, and so long as my little old ladies can work in their beloved garden, we would continue living in *Chalet La Serena*. But I would erect a sort of dwelling, a one-room shack with a bath and kitchenette as a sort of refuge for myself. Then I'd not need to leave the island for any holidays which would save a great deal, and could spend some time there on week-ends and even after school to get relief from the ever-continuous noise at school and in the neighbourhood. Even my daily 10-minute visit to Conaree revives me, and you cannot imagine how I need the break.

During this period of a year or more, I hope, I'd gradually prepare for building and moving. The kind of structure I have in mind, just one room with two little cubby-holes screened off in it, with no ceiling, no tiles, nor paint, nor floor, just cement, but built of concrete comes to about $12 per square foot. That I could borrow from the bank giving the land itself as security, for after much thought I have decided never to mortgage the house we live in now. Your house. As soon as the lawyer lets me know all details about the plot, I'll write to you. The trouble is that I have heard that two other persons are interested in acquiring it.

Our term is coming to an end, but before it is finished we have Speech Night and a Fair to get over, without counting the examinations, reports, records of work etc. I don't think I've ever felt so tired in my life! The stress under which we work is really appalling, but then, is there any peace anywhere in the world? I dread opening a newspaper or turning on the radio. The only heartening thing is that my little old ladies are both well and happy.

My, what a lengthy epistle! Please excuse me for being so loquacious."

"You will probably think me rather unwise, if not downright foolish - but I have bought the plot at Conaree. Call it fate, or subconscious influence, or what will you, the facts are that several things happened simultaneously and made me feel that I should take the chance. If you remember, I mentioned that there were two other people interested in acquiring the plot. One was the original owner who had sold that very same piece to the present owner at 12 cts. per sq. ft. He wanted to purchase it back offering double the price he had received for it some twelve years ago, but the present owner wanted more, 40 cts. per sq. ft. The second man finally changed his mind and decided to buy another piece, on the other side of the island, facing the Caribbean - Conaree is on the Atlantic. So it was my turn to decide. By some strange coincidence the British Consul in Chile who looks after my little house in La Serena was somehow able to get to me the amount that he had received for its rent for this last eighteen months - a veritable 'tour de force', so I found myself with a thousand U.S. dollars. Of course, by all rights I should have remitted the money at once to you to pay off some more of my debt, and I am sure I would have done that had this opportunity not turned up of buying the Conaree land. The temptation proved too strong, I added to that sum all I had saved for my Christmas holiday, a trip to St. Martin, cashed the last of my traveler's cheques remaining from last year's trip to Chile, and paid it all to the lawyer who is in charge of the sale. I still owe quite a bit but he is willing to wait until December of next year when I get the gratuity on the termination of the present contract - and, this is quite an unbelievable miracle, he says I'll not have to pay any interest. I can have immediate possession of the land and will receive a formal agreement of the sale and its conditions from the firm of the lawyers as soon as it is registered at the Notary's office.

I'm writing this to you in a great hurry, but next week, when school closes, I shall write in full detail and make a sketch of the plot and its surroundings so that you'd have an idea of what I have acquired. I'm only afraid that you will judge me not quite honest, in truth I should have sent the money received from Chile to you; but then, I don't think I've ever wanted anything so much as this bit of land on the beach. There are so many possibilities for the future because of it. I hope you will understand and forgive me when I'll write you all about it next week.

I'm ending this off now. It's very late, just past midnight and I have to be up at 5:30 a.m., but I wanted to give you this news right away."

"Congratulations on having bought the plot at Conaree. I am still not quite clear which site you purchased, the large one of 146.85 ft or the one whose owner is in England and which you considered the perfect site. However, I am delighted you have been able to purchase one of them and I hope you will be very happy with same.

It is indeed a lucky omen that the British Consul in Chile sent you the amount he received for rent. The lawyer who is in charge of the sale seems to have been very kind.

Of course, I do not judge you badly and any wise person would have done the same. May I suggest that instead of reimbursing me the money you regularly send, you use it towards the purchase of the new site. Please remember that if there is any way that I can be of help financially or otherwise do not hesitate to let me know."

1972

"I'm most happy to know that you feel I have done wisely in acquiring this bit of land. It really is beautifully situated and you cannot imagine the peace and rest I experience when I get there and stay even if it is only for ten minutes or so. When the shack will be up then I plan to take all my corrections and preparation of lessons to it immediately after school every day, I'll be able to do my work there much better and at the same time relax and rest by the mere fact of being able to work in quiet. You do not know how terribly tired I get, utterly worn out and weary from the incessant noise and disorder at school and in the neighbourhood when I get home. This shack will be my refuge now and our home for the future, the site being very suitable for a shop.

The second part of your letter disturbs me greatly. Dear Mr. Kadoorie, your suggestion is most generous and I feel tempted to accept it, although I know it would be terribly selfish and wrong to do so. £1,000 is a great deal of money, and goodness knows how and when I'd finish paying it back. At £10 a month means one hundred months and that is 8 years! While my present contract lasts, well and good, but what happens after December? If it is renewed, I can continue, but if not there will have to be an interval until the shop gets going. I'm hoping for a part-time job, that of course will not bring in as much and to be able to rent *Chalet La Serena* I'll have to build on two rooms to the shack to transfer the little old ladies over there, so 8 years might stretch into 10, if not 12! Besides, I owe you so much already. I really don't know what to do. I have not yet signed the necessary papers at the bank for the contractor will not be able to start building until next week and I have my W.I.$1,000 to pay him when he starts. We are just emerging from the New Year Carnival in St. Kitts, a most strange time to hold such an event, but the whole of the island went absolutely crazy, steel bands from morning to night and all through the night again, for a whole week, with people masquerading and dancing in the streets. Not a single workman was available and now they are all sleeping it off. I did not want to take the money from the bank too early since the interest will have to start from the day I accept it, and I don't want to pay the interest if I'm not using the money. Then again, the Conaree plot will have to be placed as guaranty, and that of course I'm reluctant to do. At first, I was inclined to refuse your generous offer, now, I think I'll stifle the pangs of conscience and will say thank you, if you wish to lend it to me, I accept most gratefully. You see, since writing to you last, my mother has had to have a little operation, a very minor one, removal of a toe-nail and she is perfectly well again. However, such emergencies are followed by doctor's bills.

There is one matter though that I'd like to suggest. Instead of depositing the £10 monthly on the children's account, may I join them to the £25 that is sent to you, so that the monthly remittance will be £35? I have quite a substantial sum on the children's account, not having as yet touched the last sum of U.S.$2,000 that you were so kind as to send for them, so this is enough to last them for quite a while since I take everything into consideration before spending anything. There will be several boys and girls who I will help to pay their Cambridge G.C.E. examination fees, but there is more than enough money to last for a year or two. And it will make me feel better if it is forwarded to you. I know I am taking advantage of your kindness and shouldn't accept, but am not strong enough to withstand the temptation. The Lord bless you."

"Thank you for your 'welcome home' letter of 28th March. Actually, I have been back for about a fortnight but, as you can imagine, have been extremely busy catching up with what has taken place during my absence.

My trip to Australia and South Africa was partly business and partly pleasure. In South and East Africa it was more pleasure than business. I have come to the conclusion that I am not meant to be eaten by lions for on one occasion when the land rover broke down in the bush and I was unable to communicate with the camp as the radio was also broken, I had to walk three-quarters of a mile in lion territory. Fortunately, I did not encounter any of them that day, but at the same place and hour the next evening I was met by eleven hungry lions which made me realise how lucky I am to be in one piece.

I had an interesting time in Kenya where I visited a number of game parks, including Samburu, Treetops, Keehorak and the Nairobi Game Park. Each and every one seemed more exciting than the previous. On my last day, just before my return, I saw three lions followed by five cheetahs darting in front of the car to kill an impala.

I am sorry to hear that you are overworking - it does not pay. Please think of your own health and take matters more normally. I am delighted to hear that the beach cottage will be completed next week and hope you will be very happy in it. With kindest regards to you and the old ladies."

"I can well imagine how very busy you must be now, and I only hope that you will not work too hard and lose all the benefit of the pleasure and relaxation of your holiday, even if it were only partly a vacation and mostly business.

I have had a short break from school, we had almost two weeks of holidays, unfortunately my poor little Mother had a relapse of her old trouble - obstruction of the bile channel - and all through the first week she had a temperature, gnawing pains and then her skin became a bright saffron yellow, however the doctor has managed to pull her through again, the colour became first a brilliant lemon, then faded to an orange-ripe pumpkin and now is almost normal again. That is how she describes her complexion herself, and so long as we can joke about it, all is well. The last two days she has been almost her old self again, so I could turn my energies to the Beach Cottage, now called grandiloquently *Vientomarsol*, meaning a combination of wind, sea and sun, in Spanish. The building is finished, that is, the contractor has done all that he was going to do, and now I have taken over and am using the last three days of our holidays to make it comfortable and attractive. I've painted the inside, the large room in 'pink whisper', which is really a very beautiful, soft shade of pink, and the two small cubby-holes of kitchen and bath in a cool, clear, ice-green. At once the rooms seem to have gained in size. I started the window frames to-day, they are in Spanish brown, and am hoping to paint the floors to-morrow, also in the same colour - Spanish brown. Our metalwork master and his senior class have made me four lovely Spanish-looking grills for the windows, I have painted them black so they have acquired a wrought-iron appearance and make the house look quite distinguished. Besides adding to the beauty, they are very secure, so that my 'castle' has become an impregnable fortress. I am now very busy making curtains and have repainted and covered over two old deck-chairs and a small day-bed which I had bought when I arrived in St. Kitts, eleven years ago. They now seem quite new and the house is sufficiently furnished to live in. I have borrowed a writing table from the school and have carted over a load of books and other school equipment; now when classes start on Monday I hope to take all my corrections and lessons to *Vientomarsol* and do all my work there in peace. I have enclosed the site, just ordinary barbed wire and a wooden gate, but now I feel secure and at home in the place. In the summer I plan to start a 'side line' to the so far inexistent shop. There is one other thing that I can do besides teaching, and that is cooking. So I have tried my hand at making sweets - fudge, toffees and creams and have produced a whole collection of them which was very favourably received, not only by the family but also by friends and members of Staff. As there is no money to be invested either in equipment or in premises, I shall not lose anything by trying, and if sweets will sell, then I can organize the business. What is your opinion on the matter? I can do all the cooking peacefully in *Vientomarsol* and one of the local supermarkets might allow me to display my wares, they usually charge a 10% commission in such cases. I shall write to you more about the project, it seems to me worth trying since there are no risks.

I hope the bank is sending monthly the 'drop in the ocean' which with great optimism might repay the building. Until then, the house is yours and I hope you will visit it one day."

"I am writing this to you from *Vientomarsol,* and how I wish you could see it and enjoy the peace and beauty of the place. As soon as the outside is presentable I'm going to take pictures of it to send you. Alas, it's the time that I lack. I come here for an hour and I get more corrections and preparation done than in double that time at school. A neighbour, the one who owns the chicken farm down the road, has made me a regal present: three dozen dwarf coconut palms, but they had to be planted right away. I brought down the odd-job man of the neighbourhood and he dug the pits, we filled them with earth and manure - the 'land' on my plot being sheer sand - and planted the whole lot in three rows of twelve each, to make an 'avenue'. If just half of them survive I'll be happy, but the amount of water they need in order to take hold is terrific. I come every afternoon with a couple of buckets and run up and down to water them - thirty-six plants, two and a half buckets for each one. I can assure you it's very good exercise! The water tap is at the house, I couldn't put it near the gate as then every passer-by would open it, and the hose is too short, so the only way is pails of water. I enjoy it immensely."

"I apologize for not answering sooner but I was so sad that I just didn't have the heart or courage to do anything. My poor dog, *Peleton*, whom I have had for eleven years died and we were all terribly downcast. He was just like a member of the family, knew all our habits, we all loved him, and in spite of his tiny size, he was just as big as the cat, he was extremely intelligent. You will probably think me a sentimental old fool, but we all mourned for him, and every time I come home from school I can't help looking at the spot where he always waited for me. Mother misses him dreadfully too, he was her constant companion, following her around the garden and accompanying her all the time when I was out. He was very old, of course, for that breed Lilliput terrier, and we all knew that he would go soon, still, when it happened, it was a deep shock. The only consolation is that he had a very happy life."

"Now, to make you smile. I have made my first 'sale' of sweets! I laugh at the word sale, for the lot consisted of two small boxes and two larger ones, but I have received an order for four of each for to-morrow, and have actually received money for the ones sold - the tremendous sum of three dollars. I have spoken to the owner of a small but greatly patronized store, asking whether I could display some homemade sweets for sale. The owner very kindly consented and the sweets were sold right away. I'm amused, yet pleased, for this sale shows that sweets can be sold, since it wasn't a case of buying them just to please me. I don't know who bought them, and those who bought them didn't know who made them, so it was a bona fide sale, not a favour. Once this week is over I'll have time to think, devise plans for the future and make sweets. If you remember, my contract ends in December, I have to consult in September whether the St. Kitts Government wishes to prolong it. If it does, well and good. If not, I'll have to look for a part-time job and start either the shop - which requires lots of planning and effort, and since I have no experience, will take a long time to get going, or develop the sweets factory which is far better since there is hardly any expense to incur in installation, no help needed in the actual work which can be done at any time of day, (or night) at home, at my own convenience, and is something that I know how to do. What is your opinion?

We are now anxiously watching the weather - not only our hurricanes but your typhoons as well. I dread listening to the radio when they start giving the news of all those calamities.

Vientomarsol is lovely, but so far, I have not been able to spend more than an hour or two in it. I think of you and bless you every time I enter the cottage."

"My sweets 'business', though very humble, is continuing, I now have a standing order for eight trays a week, true the trays are miniature ones, still, Rome was not built in a day. I enjoy making the sweets, though one must have complete peace of mind during the process, something quite difficult when my poor little mother is not well. She becomes so weak and frail after each bout, my heart just aches when I look at her and then I have no energy to do anything. I'm afraid I'm very tired and weary which must account for my depression and pessimism. Better not dwell on this theme.

I'm most sorry for your *Shea Shea*. Pets become members of one's family, and when they go one grieves and feels sorrow for them. Especially when they are constant companions and show so much trust and affection."

"I have just been given a most pleasant surprise. The Government of Venezuela has invited six of my senior Spanish students for a one-week stay in Caracas. Their passages will be paid and all their expenses taken care of by the Venezuelan Chamber of Commerce. It is a wonderful chance for them to improve their

Spanish, so with the Ministry of Education's blessing, three of my boys and three girls are getting ready to make the trip. It seems that Venezuela wants to establish cultural relations and exchange of students with the West Indies. Therefore, they have invited six students from Antigua, Montserrat and St. Kitts to start this project. My only worry is that the youngsters will be going on their own. Of course, their ages range between 17 and 19 years, still I would have been happier if they had an older person accompanying them. Still, since it has all been arranged by the Governments of both countries I suppose there is nothing to worry about.

I am now sure that my enemies at Conaree are crabs. Last week two more periwinkles had been gnawed right through, so I sprinkled some sevin all around each remaining plant. That was four days ago. The plants have survived but I have been picking up defunct crabs all around them, every day.

My little old ladies are both as well as they can be, life has become beautifully relaxed thanks to you. May your days be always happy, they should if our prayers for you are answered."

"I sometimes think that I have been dreaming and will wake up and find that nothing is real - yet your letters certainly confirm that everything really exists. It is all so wonderful that I am still not used to the idea and will never be able to express my thanks. Mr. Beckett, the manager of the Royal Bank of Canada has returned and this morning told me that he has received the communication from Hong Kong and that he will advise me when he receives the one from New York. There is all the time in the world for I am hoping that my present contract will be extended until June, so that I shall not need anything until then and not even then as I hope to obtain a part-time job and embark on my candy business. I am very proud of my progress in this field, people are actually asking for my sweets. Unfortunately, I cannot increase the output at present, house-work, school full time and over time, and my little old ladies take up every one of my waking minutes, so there are none left over, I can make just four batches a week.

You have acquired a new goddaughter, a very serious, intelligent and good girl whose school fees you have already paid last term. She is now in the sixth form having passed all her 'O' level subjects with excellent marks. Her name is Michelle. As usual she comes from a broken home and lacks not only food and clothing but kindness and affection as well. She replaces Arnold Thompson who has been successful in getting a teaching post in the village of Cayon, seven miles from Basseterre. Thank you for them.

I am having a little trouble with my eyes so have decided rather to write than type, hope you will make out the scrawl."

"This has been, so far, the most trying, tiring and frustrating term that I have ever been through. The Ministry says that no teachers are available, they have invested some of our ex-sixth-formers as full-fledged teachers and have placed some of the actual sixth-form students as part-time teachers. They are still school-children, immature, unprepared and quite unable to take charge of such responsible positions. Even with their help we are still short and the new Headmaster has not been able to draw up a proper time-table, has made out the time-table for Monday, Tuesday and Wednesday but has not been able to conclude it, therefore, when Thursday comes, we are to consider it as Monday. Friday becomes Tuesday and Monday of the following week is Wednesday after which Tuesday becomes Monday and we all get hopelessly mixed up. Add to this that almost every teacher is to be in two or three different classes at the same time and you will have some idea of the bedlam that we are in. For instance, I'm to teach Spanish in the third form at the same time as French in the fourth and also the sixth. Since we have three buildings and since each of the forms is in a different one, how am I to attend to them all simultaneously? One teacher was to be in four different places during one period, therefore decided to go to none and remained in the staff room. And you can imagine what kind of discipline we have when the children are left all day without supervision! Also, there are still not enough chairs or desks, therefore the pupils wander all around the building each one lugging his chair behind him or carrying it on his head - picturesque perhaps but certainly noisy and disorderly. On top of it all, whatever classes there are, they constantly get interrupted because the Minister wants to speak to the school, or because it's Health week and we get nurses coming to lecture the children, or because there is a film to be shown, etc. Two more teachers have left the school for further study and will be away for three years, they have been granted Government scholarships, that is, the Government, knowing the shortage, makes it even worse. Well, at least two of our old members of staff, who are now on leave, will be returning for the second term, that will help.

My little old ladies, with the Lord's help, are as well as can be, and in spite of everything we are contented and happy, thanks to you.

I think I have won the war - no dead crabs for the last three days and my plants are doing well, even the Lady-of-the-night has started to bloom, in spite of having had half its leaves eaten up by my enemies, crabs, grasshoppers and even lizards."

"This is to bring you my greetings for the New Year and my very best wishes for your health and happiness, I wish you every possible good thing in this world.

I am writing to you *la mort dans l'âme*, as the French say; I am so terribly distressed. This has been the bleakest and saddest Christmas ever; a week before school ended my aunt was taken ill, she had a pain in her leg and this was due to blockage of the lymphatic channels and was followed by thrombosis of the vein. She is a little better now, but has to be kept in bed all the time and cannot move. A week ago my poor little mother was taken ill too, first it was some infection -started off like food poisoning which was ruled out since we keep track of everything she eats, but it was so virulent that after four days there was hardly anything left of her, absolutely dehydrated, just skin and bones. She was in a comatose condition for a day and a night, then she rallied, but to-day, although the doctor has controlled the infection and that disease has been mastered, her heart is now in danger of failing. I have not the heart to write any more, please forgive me for the sad note that spoils the happy holiday spirit, but I just had to tell you my sorrow, there is nobody to share it with me here. Excuse me if I can't write for some time, all my moments are devoted to my little beloved ones, and there is all the work at home."

1973

"Mother is holding her own, but her recovery is desperately slow, she is extremely weak and in spite of injections, tablets and pills her appetite remains very poor, we all try to coax her to eat, I rush off to get anything she fancies for the doctor says that it is most important for her to replace all she has lost during that terrible fortnight of her illness. Her will is back and her mind functions perfectly but her body is so emaciated and wasted that she can hardly walk and of course she wants to resume her old way of life, cooking, working in her garden and playing the piano. I know that it is essential for her to feel that she still leads a useful life, and if she is prevented from doing anything at all and she imagines that she is just a useless burden then this retards her recovery more. We have to take this psychological factor into account but it just wrings my heart to see her trying to creep about, her arms and legs so pitifully thin and shaky. She tires very easily and quickly and becomes irritable and cross, scolding us all, but I don't mind that, the great thing is that she is still with us, all the rest doesn't matter.

School is in full operation but I'm not alone in counting the days till end of term, the other teachers are as disappointed and frustrated. On top of it all I feel tired and weary, I don't dare sit down during a test in class when all is quiet, I'm afraid of falling asleep if I do. However, I'm again able to visit my *Vientomarsol*, now that both my little old ladies are getting better. The first time I came up there after three weeks of neglect I encountered a wild set of weeds everywhere, sheep managed to get in under the barbed wire and ate up some of my plants, but I'm gradually putting everything to rights again. Thanks again. May the good Lord bless you and keep you."

"I am so happy that you like the pictures of *Vientomarsol* and am delighted that you approve of the project for an extra room at *Chalet La Serena*. I can now go ahead with it since I have your blessing. I consider this addition a sort of investment, it would greatly increase the value of the house and contribute to the comfort of my little old ladies. Now, there are just two bedrooms in the house, one downstairs for them the other upstairs for myself. I am going to make a rough sketch of the ground floor, with the proposed building so that you would see what I have in mind. The room will communicate with the present bedroom but it will also have its own entrance into the garden, so that it can be quite independent. It will have its own shower - which will be placed under the water tank that I have installed several years ago, a toilet, and a tiny niche where I am planning to put a minute sink and hot-plate, to have everything handy in case of need. As soon as I get all the figures from the builder I shall write to you in detail, for since I'm going to use the interest - a part of it I mean - of that enormous fortune that you have placed for me, I'd like you to know exactly what is happening.

There is something I would like to mention, but do not quite know how to go about it. You see, I have very gratefully accepted the use of this huge amount of money that you have placed in my name and we shall take full value of the interest, but would very much like to keep the capital quite intact and have it sent to you if and when I leave this world. How do we arrange this? If I go before my little old ladies, I would of course beg you to give them the use of the interest, during their life-time, after that, the funds should go back to you. How is this to be done? Please give me your advice."

"I do not know how to put into words my gratitude for your wonderful deep understanding of my problem. I am forever haunted by the thought that if anything were to happen to me, my poor little old ladies would be left quite helpless - they are capable of looking after themselves at home but they have no idea of worldly or financial matters and would have no aid or protection from anybody. Logically I should survive them, but there are so many hazards nowadays that one never knows what may happen.

I have written to Mr. Slade but have not been able to furnish all the particulars to the ultimate destination of all assets. Quite rightly he wants to draw up a definite will, although I feel this is not just, since whatever I possess is yours and you, not I, should dispose of the whole matter.

However, this being your wish, I shall write to him again but not just yet, this business requires thought and concentration and for the time being I'm afraid I'm in no state for either. I can't tell you how terribly tired I am, so utterly exhausted that I just can't do anything properly. This school year has cost us more than we could afford and all responsible members of staff who have been mercilessly overworked are on the verge of collapse. I know I am, for coupled with the stress at school due to the tremendous amount of work and the uncongenial atmosphere, I have the continuous strain at home. Had it not been for your magnificent and generous action of relieving me of all financial worries, I'm sure I would have succumbed long ago. Therefore, morning, day and night you are always in my thoughts and I constantly pray for your health and happiness, that's all I can do.

I am now in Nevis where I came to examine the Cambridge G.C.E candidates in modern languages. There are quite many but, having had to overnight here, I'm through now and have a few moments to write to you. I'll mail this letter in St. Kitts as the Nevis Post Office is often worse than ours."

"I was just getting ready to write to you when I received your letter, for I wanted to communicate that the first dividends of your shares, due on June 1st. have just arrived. The Royal Bank of Canada Trust Co., of New York has remitted to the bank in St. Kitts US$2,900.00 which has been deposited into my account as WI$5,437.52. This, joined to other bits and pieces I had, is just what I need to pay the contractor for the new room AND the garage at

Vientomarsol, so now, everything can be completed and paid for. I can't tell you how wonderful it feels to be able to afford those additions, it's luxury. It's a dream come true, and all of it is due to your kindness. The second installment of dividends, due on July 1st, I have asked to be kept in New York and will draw monthly $200 which I am sure added to my part-time job salary will be quite sufficient to keep us going. It still seems incredible to me that next school-year I will not have to spend the whole day in distasteful, noisy, dirty, unpleasant surroundings. I will teach in the mornings only, and will not be obliged to undertake a host of extra-curricular activities as all full-time members on staff are forced to do and which keep us at school, or working for the school till all hours. It is thanks to you that I'll be able to stop working at top speed under continuous stress and strain, which has been relentlessly sapping all my strength and energy. I will be able to remain at home all afternoon, attend to my poor little old crocks, who sorely need looking after, and then, of course, there is my project of cakes and sweets. All this is possible just because of you. Do you wonder that I bless you all the time? Just one more month to go, school breaks up on July 13th, after which I shall be free! It sounds too good to be true. I must sound terribly selfish to you, but you cannot imagine how utterly tired out I am, and this prospect of being able to work less yet have my poor little old ones living in comfort gives me courage to finish this school year."

"I am very happy that you have had a restful holiday. Motoring in Scotland must have been delightful, the country should be lovely at this time of year - though I feel a bit chilly even in summer - and driving on your own, without having to depend on travel buses or planes is most relaxing. As for Paris, it is always full of interest and charm. However, it is good to know that you are back safely. With so much unrest, accidents and airpiracy, I'm glad that you have reached home without mishap.

During your absence, I received a letter from Mr. Slade which I answered as well as I could. I still feel that I have no right to bequeath your assets to my relatives and charities - to my little old ladies, if they survive me, yes, but for the others, I feel as if I were giving away something that doesn't belong to me. Still, if you say so, I comply with your wish and as soon as school is over will try and sort things out.

We have just started our internal exams with accompanying invigilation, corrections, assessments, etc. I'm absolutely exhausted, drained of all energy, like a squeezed-out rag just unfit for anything. I know that I need a rest with a complete change of surroundings. A sea journey, on a quiet, slow, cargo ship would bring me back to my normal state in no time as it always does, but I'm afraid it can't be done at present. As my contract ends I'm entitled to a one-way passage to Chile, or the equivalent of it if I wish to go elsewhere, and this could easily give me several weeks aboard a freighter, but I can't leave my poor little old crocks, who are so dependent on me, so frail and helpless and in such constant need of care and attention! No salaried person could give them the thousand and one little services that only love and affection could foresee and provide. Besides, there is the ever-present fear of loneliness. They felt completely lost and abandoned when I went to Nevis for a day and a night. Had my sister come to stay with us as she had planned, I could have risked going away for a fortnight, as it is, I don't dare. Besides, we too, are going through a crisis. Our Government and the only air-line that connects with the world at large have had some trouble between them, the result being that the air-line has stopped its flights to and from St. Kitts indefinitely, so we are cut off from everywhere. I don't even know how this letter is getting to you.

We are looking forward to a very welcome event. My good old Jane Ying is planning to visit us. She is now in Hong Kong for weeks and after that, on July 22nd, is to come to St. Kitts. We hear that the Government and the airline will patch up their differences and that there will be no trouble about getting here.

The room is finished and looks lovely, but alas! The garage at *Vientomarsol* is still in the realm of things to be. There is no cement on the island. Not a single bag of the stuff and nobody knows when the next shipment is to arrive. All building life has come to a complete stand still. Such a pity! I was looking forward to spending a few weeks at Conaree when school ends, in the summer, but am reluctant to expose the car to the sea blast for hours at a stretch. The 'crab' war is still on and I pick up a few 'casualties' every day - there's a long row of corpses along the veranda, so that the others would be scared and go away. In spite of all the pests the plants are growing - it's most rewarding to see my hibiscus, bougainvillea and lady-of-the-night produce new blossoms every day."

"St. Kitts is back on the map, we are receiving mail at last - only there is so much accumulated that it will take days and days until it's all sorted out. Planes come in and out and visitors arrive, of which Jane Ying was one, she reached here yesterday evening. We are now looking forward to a pleasant fortnight together. So many plans, so much we want to do, and will probably end up by just sitting and catching up on all news and events since seeing each other five years ago.

School ended on Friday, I do not have to attend any more meetings, having handed all my work in, but of course have not had the time to get the house into shape for Jane's visit. Well, never mind, we are such old friends that she'll not mind a bit of dust.

Cement has arrived and the workmen have started on the garage, I have great hopes that in a week's time we'll be able to spend most of our days and nights at *Vientomarsol*, now I just go up to water the plants, but as soon as the workmen finish the job and the place is neat and tidy again we'll be able to enjoy the sea and the sun and Jane will get all the rest and peace that she needs after the hectic life of the States. What a dreadful place to live in! That's the last place on earth I'd choose to spend my life in.

I have received a letter from the Government, they are asking me to continue teaching part-time, mornings only and are offering me a 'take home' salary of about £63 a month. Thanks to your kindness, with the monthly income of $200 from the second batch of shares that you have so generously given to us, we shall be able to live in full comfort. The interest on the first batch of shares I have used to build the new room, the store-room and the garage with apron in *Vientomarsol.* You cannot imagine how happy we are and how grateful, without your help we could never have survived. May the good Lord reward you for your magnanimity."

"Time has flown. Jane Ying has gone away again after a little over a fortnight's visit. We had a very good time to-gether and I think she has really had the rest she craved. The way of life in the States seems to be a perpetual strain with eternal hurrying and rushing about. Existence seems to be sheer stress. No wonder Jane has contracted ulcers! However, she has had no discomfort from them here, had all the foods she wanted and slept for hours on end, leading a leisurely, relaxed life. Probably her ulcers are due to nervous tension more than anything else. We paid short visits to Nevis and Anguilla, just going one morning, overnighting and returning the next day as I was afraid of leaving my little old ladies for longer periods. The doctor was on the alert during the trips having promised to be at the house in five minutes if called. Fortunately, there was no need and all was well. My worry was Jane herself, of all things she is allergic to cats and I have three of my own, without mentioning the eight strays who come in regularly every evening for their supper. Luckily nothing happened, she didn't even sneeze once although just the presence of a cat in the room was supposed to bring on an attack of asthma; and one of mine, a longhaired, fluffy one had to be dislodged from Jane's bed every day. We were all very sorry when she left, and to take my mind off sadness I have plunged into my long-delayed housecleaning, turning everything upside down and restoring law and order.

The garage at *Vientomarsol* is finished at last and now I can keep the car sheltered, but the turning space is so limited that it is with great caution that I turn about. Having such strange eye-sight owing to which I can't appreciate distances, it takes lots and lots of concentration, but I'll get used to it.

There is something I would like to ask you concerning a poor student of mine, a sort of 'part-time' godson of yours. I don't know if you remember him, his name is Robert Swanston and he was one of my outstanding pupils. As usual, no father or mother, or any relatives at all. We were fortunate in getting the St. Kitts Sugar Factory to give him a job and he eventually went on to the University of the West Indies in Barbados. He did all sorts of odd jobs, coached students in French and Spanish, played in a band and worked as a carpenter and painter. All this during the academic year, and yesterday he had received the results of his first year B.A. examination, successful in all subjects. I think this is wonderful, but of course he is terribly tired, overworked and undernourished. May I give him a monthly allowance out of your Help-The-Needy-Students-Fund? I have almost $3,000 (West Indian) in that account and Swanston really needs and deserves help. Please say yes."

"What a good memory you have to remember Robert Swanston! I am so happy that you say I may help him. He certainly deserves it. I know what a tremendous effort it must have been for him to work and study at the same time, and study so successfully too. With no family to encourage him, no word of praise or consolation when needed, it is a wonder that he has kept himself away from all pitfalls; drug-addiction has become so common in all Universities and this invariably leads to law-breaking and crime, and yet he has managed to avoid all those temptations and has emerged victorious. No mean feat.

Now I would like to share some good news with you. Our 'A' level G.C.E. Cambridge results have just arrived and you can imagine how happy I am. All eight of my students have passed in my two papers, every one of them getting the highest possible mark. This is my last 'graduation' form and they have really placed a *broche de oro* to my teaching - a Spanish expression to say that something has been concluded in the best possible manner."

"You have acquired a new god-daughter. I hope you don't mind. Her name is Cynthia Weeks. She has obtained excellent marks in all her subjects, English included, and should indeed go on to do her 'A' levels. However, she belongs to a very poor family, or rather has only distant relatives. Her mother died when the ferry-boat, the *Christena*, sank four years ago, the father died before that, and she lives with an aunt. Because of her ability Cynthia was granted a scholarship to continue her studies in the sixth form. This scholarship consists of school fees and books, but the aunt did not want her to return to school as there would be the expense of buying the uniform. Therefore, she wanted Cynthia to become a pupilteacher but because she has only 'O' levels, her pay would be insignificant, but it would go to the aunt. If she becomes a pupil-teacher with 'A' levels, this means far better pay in two years' time. I think I have convinced the aunt that it was to her advantage to have Cynthia stay in school for the sixth form and you have very kindly purchased her uniform. So Cynthia goes back to school-tomorrow. She is only 16 years old."

"Term has started on Monday and I have begun my part-time work. It is quite different from my previous position and I think it can be very interesting if I can do things according to my plan and get the necessary cooperation from the people concerned. The Education Department wants me to guide and give help to young teachers of Modern Languages as they have no experience, nor training and very little idea how to go about the teaching of French and Spanish. I have started visiting all the High Schools as from Monday - and having seen three of them I have discovered that no school has a syllabus or method. There are no books, neither for pupils nor for teachers' reference, therefore of course not a single G.C.E. candidate passed in Modern Languages from those schools. My task will be to organize the whole business, work out a syllabus, common to all schools, teach the young members of staff how to go about imparting the necessary knowledge, work with each one training them how to plan their lessons, teach, give work to the pupils, check it, etc. This activity involves traveling all around the island's schools, five here and two in Nevis. Some of the teachers are old students of mine, and it will be easy to work with them, but others do not look upon me with friendly eyes. Well, I hope there are no difficulties and that this year will be interesting and fruitful. I am working mornings only - except when I'm to go to Nevis, which means flying early in the morning and returning late evening, but this will be only once a fortnight. The rest of the time I'll be more at home, looking after my little old ladies.

The news from Chile[21] is so terrible, it makes us dreadfully anxious."

"I have now completed my visits to all the five high schools in St. Kitts and to the two in Nevis and have made some appalling discoveries. Not one establishment has a syllabus for Modern Languages, many have antiquated text-books that teach nothing but verbs and do not awaken or stimulate the student's interest to learn to speak and practise [sic] the language, many teachers are not interested at all in achieving results, they do not want to work themselves, prepare classes or mark homework, very few are qualified or experienced and only my old students who speak both French and Spanish are trying to teach their pupils to do so also and to enjoy learning to speak foreign languages. Some look upon me as a sort of enemy and resent my presence, but I'm hoping that with a great deal of diplomacy and patience I'll be able to turn their attitude to a more cooperative one. My first job was to get a working syllabus, common to all the High Schools, so for the last week I have been very busy composing a detailed programme, year by year, of what is to be taught, how it is to be taught, incorporating advice, suggestions, teaching hints for inexperienced teachers, in short, writing a sort of syllabus plus a teacher-training course, all rolled into one. I have finished it now, have cut the stencils, the Ministry has run off about a hundred copies of this 'treatise', this morning I have stapled them into booklets and to-morrow will start on my rounds accompanied by the Chief Inspector of Schools to distribute them. I am confident that if all teachers work with me, we shall achieve

---

[21] Salvador Allende was overthrown in a Coup d'état on September 11, 1973.

great success. Of course, it's only in theory that I work part-time only. The writing of this syllabus, typing it, etc., has kept me busy all day and part of the night as well, but I enjoyed those last ten days, it's organizing, creating and I love that. You say you hope my pay is commensurate with the work I am doing. I leave you to judge - my take-home pay is about £65 a month, so you see, if it were not for your great generosity, I don't know what we would have done. Cost of living rising every day, people have barely enough money for necessities, and cakes and sweets are something that very many do without, so my business is not booming so far. Do you wonder that we bless you every day for your kindness and constantly pray for your health and happiness?"

"Your letter of Oct. 23rd was most welcome though you hardly ever give news of yourself. I hope you are well and not working too hard - but knowing you, I'm sure you are. Cynthia is very happy back at school and Swanston writes that he is studying hard, they are both extremely grateful to you for your help and are trying to live up to your kindness.

My work keeps me busy all the time, but the going is very slow, it demands perseverance, patience, tact but also firmness, the proverbial hand of steel in a velvet glove - but so far, the results are not spectacular. Perhaps I'll have to shed the gloves or just use thin nylon. Sometimes I wonder why those teachers have taken up this profession, so many of them show no interest in either classes or children, do you know that after two months of term and seeing the pupils every day some of the teachers don't even know their names or faces! How can there be any contact, confidence or wish to do well when the child knows that his teacher doesn't care two pence about him, whether he's there or not, whether he studies or just wastes his time. And some of those teachers don't even know what to teach or how to teach it. One of them quite candidly told me that although she's to teach French, she herself can't speak it at all! As for preparation, lesson planning, corrections, those simply do not exist, that is why the lessons are so boring and tedious, and that of course brings up discipline problems, when a child is busy and interested it doesn't even occur to him to be naughty, rude or indifferent. Sorry, now I am boring you.

We have had better news from Chile, my sister writes that things are getting back to normal, that she has actually seen some sugar and meat for the first time in months, could buy a loaf of bread without having to queue for it from 6 a.m, and has even acquired some tooth paste! However, the unrest continues, she says that just before she started the letter there was machine gun firing in their block, it continued for quite a long time, it seems that the soldiers were hunting down some guerillas and finally killed four of them. Well, I do not consider this is returning to normal, but it makes one wonder what things were like when they were not looked upon as normal."

"Thank God for the Prince of Wales! To-day being his birthday we have a public holiday and I have been able to do the hundred and one odd-jobs around the house that I can never find the time to complete otherwise. I'm even able to answer at once your letter of 5th Nov. just received, for which I thank you. It was nice to know that you have actually taken a day off to go into the country and relax - although a day is so little! I hope you will make many more such visits. It is fascinating to watch progress in gardens and farms, even with just the one scant half-hour I can spend working in *Vientomarsol*, I can see results. My flowers are doing very well, even though I do have to erect screens to protect them from the sea-blast, and they of course detract from the appearance. I'm waiting for the Christmas holidays when I hope to paint my fence, the new spans, and then I'll take a few pictures of the garden to send to you.

Thank you for your kind comments about my work. I'm certainly trying to do my best, and even if the results are still not spectacular, at least all of the Modern Language teachers grab their books and start teaching when I appear on the premises. However, there is progress, even if things are slow. In some cases, I really don't know how teachers can manage. Do you know that in one school there are three classes of 38 children each going on simultaneously in the same room? I have seen that yesterday and am certainly going to tell our educational authorities that it's quite impossible to expect the children to learn in such conditions. They must at least put up partitions to divide the room into smaller ones so that the pupil's attention doesn't wander. Besides, the noise is terrible as quite often a teacher is supposed to take two different forms at the same time and this means that one class is left on its own. You can imagine what happens in that room when of the 3 groups of 38 only one has a teacher and the other two can do what they like. It is simply lack of organization and unwillingness to modify time-tables.

At home things are all quiet on the 'health front'. On the 11th of November Mother reached her 89th birthday. We wanted to celebrate it and have a fiesta, but she became quite cross and said there was no occasion to rejoice. Still, she relented somewhat later and accepted the special cake I made for her - not with 89 candles. My aunt was 86 last month, so as you see, I have two very venerable old ladies in my care."

"I am indeed sorry to hear that burglars broke into your home at *Vientomarsol*. It is very fortunate that you were not there when they called and that Mrs. Bynoe did not meet with them, otherwise they might have been tough with her. I am glad that nothing was stolen.

Have you got electricity at the house and what is your voltage? It strikes me that it may be possible to install some sort of alarm device which would ring a bell in Mrs. Bynoe's home should thieves try to break in through your windows or door. This would allow her to phone up the police. Here in Hong Kong we are also pestered by petty thefts. Indeed, I witnessed one on my way home last night.

The Festival of Hong Kong has just taken place. We have had a week of festivities which reacted very favourably with the Chinese population. Now starts a period of austerity with oil rationing. It means that we not only will have difficulties in cutting electricity consumption, but we anticipate restrictions on the use of motorcars. I believe it is the Government's intention to try and keep the industries going, though in some cases where basic requirements are oil, we will have difficulties. I do hope you are all well. With every good wish to you and the old ladies."

1974

"It is quite some time since I have had news from you. I hope you are well and able to cope with the present disquieting situation. I can well imagine how the world-wide fuel shortage must be affecting Hong Kong as there are so many industries there that require incalculable quantities of fuel. The losses are probably staggering. You are constantly in our thoughts and we pray that you may be protected from all harm and anxiety.

As everywhere else, life in St. Kitts is becoming difficult, some products are scarce, others have disappeared completely and prices rise from day to day. However, we are trying our best to keep smiling and be cheerful. Term has started this morning and there will be enough work to keep me busy. I hope my efforts will help those boys and girls who depend on me to see them through their exams.

Petrol has appeared again - at an increased price - but it is available, and this means that I can 'recharge my batteries' at *Vientomarsol*. Half an hour spent in the peace and beauty of Conaree gives me strength for the next twenty-four. My little old ladies are both well, so I have a great deal to be thankful for. Half way across the world there are grateful people who wish you the best of everything."

"Thank you for sending the article about the experimental farm. What a marvelous enterprise, and how like you to help so many people. I can well imagine how grateful they must be to you. There is no better way to help people than to enable them to create and produce crops and animals. I have always been fascinated watching things grow - even on the tiny scale as we have here: a bed of tomatoes, Chinese cabbage which grows very well here, and Mother's latest pride - a square patch of the sweetest corn we've ever tasted. Even at *Vientomarsol* I have managed to coax some spinach to grow, not the spinach that we knew elsewhere, this is a sort of climbing vine but the leaves taste like the genuine plant. Of course, your farmers are Chinese, and besides being patient and industrious they have always lived by agriculture, they love and understand earth and farming. In my opinion, there is nothing more important and rewarding than being able to produce food from the land.

Our Government is making a half-hearted attempt to encourage farming, but the people do not understand that their salvation, their very life depends on what they will be able to produce from the land. Our sugar crop decreases every year and nothing is being done to supplement or replace it. There is great talk of the 'tourist industry', but that again, depends on agriculture - a tourist will visit the few monuments and places of interest once during their visit, but he has to be fed three times a day - and all food is imported to St. Kitts, hardly anything is grown locally, and yet, as my little old ladies have proved, anything can grow on this island. I do not know why, perhaps it's the heritage of slavery, but people look down on those who work with their hands, they consider it degrading whereas to me it seems one of the more noble activities.

I have been very busy all week; A Parliamentary Delegation of Deputies from France paid us a visit and I gathered all my old students to-gether at my home and we entertained them. The boys and girls really did their best, Michelle Ward recited a poem by Theophile Gautier and James Connor (do you remember him? He was one of your early god-children) rendered beautifully *Le Lac* by Lamartine. His performance was truly excellent and the Deputies - one of them from Paris and another a delegate at the United Nations - were so touched by the children's knowledge of the language that they made me a present of three scholarships for a six-week course in Guadeloupe to three of the students and have promised us books, and films. I am now trying to organize a wider French and Spanish club, since I'm now supervising all of the seven High Schools in the State in the teaching of Modern Languages. I've come into contact with all the French and Spanish teachers, who are almost all of them my old students, but who, since they have no chance to practice the languages, are beginning to forget them. My difficulty is to find a place where they could all meet. My house is too small and besides my little old ladies would be upset with the noise and bustle. I have a half-promise of a room at the old hospital, now used by the Teacher Training College. At present it is full of archives, books and broken apparatus and if we can find where to remove all that we can paint the place and brighten it up for use as a meeting place. It looks out on to the cemetery, which the youngsters don't like, but it's better than the old morgue which had also been offered to me for the club premises. No amount of paint could make that look cheerful, with its cement slabs, so we declined."

"Since writing to you last we've had one calamity following another. First of all, Mother starting teasing *Cher Ami*, the dog, while he was gnawing away at a bone - even a child knows you've got to leave a dog alone in such circumstances. I warned her, but of course, as soon as I was out of the room she started again, result he snapped at her, and as her skin is tissue-paper thin there was a deep gash on her hand, right to the bone. I took her to the hospital phoning the doctor beforehand, fortunately he came right away and she had to have three stitches and an antitetanus injection. Luckily no complications have set in. Then, when after all that excitement I went to *Vientomarsol*, I found that some sheep had managed to pass under the barbed wire and had eaten up all my plants - hibiscus, bougainvillea and my little almond tree, besides doing away with the spinach and some coconuts. I have palings on two sides, a beautiful thickmesh fence but the fourth side had only barbed wire, and that has become slack and rusty. I had started replacing it span by span with wooden palings - the only material except concrete that the sea blast doesn't destroy quickly - but there were 18 spans left to put up. Now Mr. Bynoe has kindly lent me one of his farm boys and he's making me a fence of coconut branches, it becomes rather ugly and straggly after a while but at least it'll keep the sheep out for a few months.

Finally, my aunt forgot to turn off the water in the garden again and the washing machine started to leak while I was out, so that when I returned there was a flood, both within and without. Never a dull moment! Well, everything is under control now, but of course I never know what my little old ladies are going to do next. I have to spend more and more time with them. Only a member of the family will put up with their whims and tantrums, no hired help would survive more than 24 hours and when I did get a nurse during one of Mother's occasional illnesses, she sent her packing in a matter of hours. She is also indomitable and independent, will accept only my help and services, therefore I have to be in perpetual attendance. But I am so happy to have her, whom I love so much, that no matter the tantrums, she's with us, the Lord is kind and lets me have her still.

My work is very interesting, but, although it's supposed to be just a part-time job, it's taking up not only the morning but a good deal more time. This is a very selfish letter - all about myself. I hope you are well, we always pray for your health and happiness."

"I certainly need some friendly words as I am feeling terribly frustrated, indignant and angry. Since the Modern Language Club has come into being I cannot go to *Vientomarsol* on Friday afternoons when we have the meetings. I drove to Conaree yesterday, Saturday, to find that again the house has been broken into. The whole place has been ransacked, the burglars smashed the new door and probably spent the evening in the hut as I found the curtains drawn to prevent being noticed. The Bynoes had gone out that evening to a party and returned after midnight so the miscreants worked undisturbed. Evidently, they were looking for money or valuables - as if any person in their right mind would keep these in a beach hut - of course they didn't find anything worth taking and left just carrying off my little clip-on reading lamp. Worst of all I now feel helpless and insecure, whatever means I devise to protect the property seem ineffectual and I don't know what else to do. On Saturday I couldn't get hold of any workmen or materials, so I simply boarded the place up using planks left over from the last span of the fence. Mr. Bynoe came along to help when I was half-way through and finished the job so thoroughly that I couldn't get in this afternoon. To-morrow the contractor is coming, he advises making a new door again, but this time of solid wood, not the plywood that the doors in St. Kitts are usually made of. I want to get an iron bar to fit across the door, but the main thing in that case is a padlock that could not be smashed or sawed through, it seems they have them in Barbados and in St. Martin, none in St. Kitts.

To-morrow I'm going to the Technical College - a Canadian establishment - and will try to get some sort of siren installed which will go off if locks or door are tampered with. The Bynoes would hear it then and get help, and even if they didn't hear it I'm sure the sudden noise would drive the burglars away. Such sirens are not available here, but I have been told that they exist in St. Martin. I'll try and find out if that is so and then will make a one-day trip to buy one. I wish I could have the door electrified not to hurt seriously but to give a good shock so that thieves would leave the house alone; unfortunately, this is against the law and can't be done. Yet, since the police cannot help - do you know that the policeman who came when I called them, arrived with a portable radio and all the while listening to the cricket commentators relaying the match in which he was far more interested than in finding out where the burglars had gone and what they had taken. Therefore, since the law does not do anything to protect the property, it seems most unfair not to be able to do anything oneself. Can you think of some means to safeguard my poor little house?
Sorry to have taken up so much of your time with my tale of woe.

Thank you for your kind offer of help to the student teacher. He is one of my old students from the school and his economic situation is far from brilliant, I am most grateful to you and if needed will certainly help him. His name is Ronnie Powell and a long time ago you have already helped him."

"Welcome home! It is so good to know that you have returned safely, even though you did have that alarming mechanical trouble with the plane. I hope you have had a pleasant holiday and a restful one. Please do not let your office activities engulf you and destroy all the benefits derived from your enjoyable trip. All three countries, England, Spain and France have so much charm, so many delightful spots and such interesting places that memories of the journey will surely help tide you over the return to daily work. Only spare yourself and do not use all your energy at once!

This is our 'long vacation', but I'm afraid I have not had a holiday yet, and it seems that I shall not have time to rest this summer. I have been very busy arranging student exchange of children between Guadeloupe and St. Kitts, looking after a camp - in full swing now - of twenty Rangers from the French islands and French Guyana, attending meetings and translating for the Venezuelan trade mission whose members have spent the last week here and it seems that the matter of the factory, training etc. is almost settled, and next week I have to take charge of the College of Preceptors exam in Modern Language. After this the Induction Course for new teachers is starting and this means going back to regular work already. Still, I hope to get a few days and nights at *Vientomarsol*. Mother has not been well again so we have gone through a very gloomy period. She is better now, but every little illness leaves a deep mark on her and she is so extremely frail that my heart hurts when I look at her."

"I have had some very serious talks with the Minister of Education who, after promising in May that the Ministry would pay for a student's university study, now, in September a fortnight before the boy is ready to leave, calmly announced that the Ministry had no money to pay for him. I have called on several ministers in turn and ended up seeing the Premier[22]. Having given them all a piece of my mind and having told them a few home truths, the matter is now settled and the money for the first term has now been found. The second term is to be paid in January and the third in March. The Premier assured me that the funds will be available.

---

22 Robert Llewellyn Bradshaw (1919-1978), first Premier of St. Kitts-Nevis.

So this matter has been definitely settled.

We have had several hurricane alarms, but, mercifully, they have passed us by. What terror the survivors in Honduras must have endured and their ordeal is not over yet. Besides, even if they are saved at last, how many families have lost their dear ones and they will return to a dreary prospect, homeless and ruined.

The dry spell has at last been broken and after several days of torrential rains - the tail-end of the Honduras hurricane[23] - the hills are all green again, but alas, the weeds in the garden have covered everything. However, my Mother is waging battle on them and has started several boxes of seedlings. I'm very happy about that as it gives her an interest and makes her feel useful and contented. She is feeling as well as can be expected."

"I have sent Ronnie Powell off to Guadeloupe on Monday Sept. 30th, and expect to get news from him soon, I hope, as mails between the French West Indies and St. Kitts seem to take longer than between Hong Kong and our island. I have paid his passage which is still worth £23, but his equipment cost far more than I expected. Fortunately, he has the indispensable football gear. He was ecstatically happy to be going to the course. So far our 'honorable' ministers have given the funds to pay for his first term, I only hope they will not go back on their word when it will be time to pay for the second and third terms. Before leaving Ronnie brought me a letter for you that I am enclosing.

I should have answered your letters earlier but this last week has been so terribly exhausting that I just hadn't the strength to write. We experienced the most violent earthquake that I have ever lived through - the Chilean ones seemed quite tame compared to this. It lasted three whole minutes - in Chile it was always a matter of seconds - everything fell off the tables and shelves. I expected the house to collapse at every moment. It happened a little after 5 a.m.

---

[23] Hurricane Fifi, September 1974, later named Orlene, killed at least 8,000 people in 9 Caribbean nations.

and I was already up so could go downstairs and try and get my poor little old crocks out, but Mother is so frail and weak that it was very difficult to take her out to the garden, away from the threat of crumbling walls. Mother had barely recovered from the earthquake when another blow hit her: her favourite, beautiful pet cat, Siamese and half Persian, became ill and in spite of all our efforts could not be saved.

Our Minister of Education has decided to reform our whole system of education and has come up with the most impractical, not to say harebrained suggestions. I only hope the other members of the Ministry will make him see reason, if not, he will wreck everything. As it is there are no teachers available, and to make his scheme work at least four times as many teachers are necessary. Even in England and the States there are not enough teachers and his plans are far more ambitious than those of any large country. It is all very well to have ideas and ideals, yet one has to be practical too and realize that changes in education have to be made gradually and consistently.

Still another month to go before the hurricane menace is over, but at least we have rain now, so there is no shortage of water and all the countryside is beautifully green."

"It is so good to know that you are back again safely. What is Nepal like? What language do they speak there? And what kind of climate do they have?

My poor mother has not been very well for the last three weeks - her right foot swells very badly and towards evening it is about three times its size and hurts very much. It is some sort of circulatory trouble and the doctor says that it is serious for there is the ever-present threat of gangrene and I do not want to think of what would happen then. Of course all this makes me very depressed and this casts a pall over the whole household.

The radio is forever giving news of typhoons and cyclones in your part of the world. I hope the reports are exaggerated."

1975

"I do sincerely hope that your mother will be much better. I can well imagine your anxiety and sincerely hope you will try not to overdo things and take as much rest as possible.

I found Nepal most interesting. The people are honest and very poor. We have started a number of projects there - in all about thirty and during my recent visit, I approved of three schemes which will help no less than 20,000 people - two are to bring water to their areas and one is a village clinic.

I have recently returned from Manila where I went for the groundbreaking ceremony of our new Peninsula Hotel, which when built, will I hope prove a great success. Unfortunately, due to the recession there is much unemployment there. In Honk Kong we are also feeling it, but people here seem more optimistic than in other countries. Good wishes to you and the 'old ladies' for a healthy, happy and prosperous 1975."

"Your letter of Jan. 10th came just as I was leaving for Nevis on my monthly 'inspection visit' to the two high schools on the island. In one, two of the young teachers are my old students and the third has also been a pupil of mine, they are all intelligent capable girls with 'A' levels in French and Spanish and are doing a good job. In the other school the outlook is very dim as the two young teachers there know very little themselves, do not want to teach, have no interest to learn and have undertaken this work only because they could find nothing else to do. They are very reluctant to accept advice or suggestions, and it's a pity as many children are keen students but do not get competent teachers and soon lose interest. I love Nevis, and although I have to work very hard, trying to squeeze a week's worth of work into two days, I feel quite rested because of a good night's uninterrupted sleep, something I can never get at home.

How interesting to hear about your projects in Nepal - 20,000 people served - why, that's more than many an entire Caribbean island and how grateful all of them must be to you. You say they are very poor but honest. It must be a great satisfaction to you to be able to help people worthy to receive aid. Here the inhabitants take it all as their due and in many cases seem to think that they are doing the donor a favour when they take what is being given - and grumble instead of saying 'thank you'. Your 'godchildren' are an exception."

"I am answering right away hoping that this note reaches you in time to wish you *Bon Voyage* and a most enjoyable stay in the South of France. I have most pleasant memories of the Côte d'Azur. While I was studying in France, during the summer holidays, I'd take a job for the first month tutoring some rich lazy child and during the second month, on the proceeds, would rest and relax in some part of France. In this manner, I made several visits along that coast, but I also enjoyed the region of the Loire, Tours and the Châteaux. I hope your stay there will be just as pleasant as you wish it to be.

I am sorry to say that again I'm going through a very worrying time. Yesterday I returned home in the middle of the morning as I was on my way from one school to another and found that my Mother had had a rather bad accident. She wanted to turn off the hose in the garden as my aunt had forgotten all about it, but on her way to the tap she stumbled and lost her balance. As she fell she struck her shoulder and her whole side on a stone ledge and since her leg had been giving her trouble for the last six months, she could not get up by herself. She remained lying there, in a pool of water for almost half an hour. She called and called but as my aunt is deaf she didn't hear her. Fortunately the neighbors came and helped her - carried her into the house and that was when I arrived.

Unfortunately, Mother's doctor is now in Jamaica undergoing an operation, but the medic substituting for him came at once. Luckily there are no bones broken, but she is in considerable pain and of course cannot move, sit up or stand. I cannot tell you how many times I have thanked you mentally for all your help to us for it has enabled me to get all the medicines, injections and medical attention required. I tried to get her a bed in the hospital where she would have constant care from the nurses, but there is not a single bed available and she will not allow a private nurse to care for her at home. At the Ministry they have been very understanding and I have been granted two days' leave to remain with her at home. I look after her as well as I can, but not being a trained nurse I'm afraid I'm not very competent. Our fears now are only of a complication from the long soaking, but so far - 24 hours later - her temperature is still normal which it would not have been had she contracted pneumonia. It is so difficult to get somebody to stay with my little old ladies when I'm out of the house, they are so independent that they do not want to hear of my getting some sort of daily help. However, when we get the long summer holiday, I'm going to try training a maid. The trouble is nobody wants to do housework, and those that offer their services usually do so with the hope of stealing and never stay for a worthwhile period. If only my little old crocks were more careful and not try to be so active at their age, we could manage. Anyhow I cannot tell you how relieved I am that this whole business has turned out this way and that Mother has not been fatally hurt. She did get an awful shock, but after the injections the doctor gave her she rallied very favourably. Sorry to have worried you with my troubles, I know I'm very selfish."

"School has ended a month ago but I have been very busy and there is still a very great deal of work to be done, these past weeks I had to attend to the camps, the student exchange with innumerable arrangements and working out of details. I had to arrange to transport 78 children between Guadeloupe and St. Kitts, and since there are no ships between the islands and all planes were booked up because of the carnival in Antigua, I finally chartered four planes - twin otters of Air Guadeloupe - and everything was solved. It came out much cheaper too, each child had to pay $96 for the round trip instead of the ordinary fare of $113.80, so everybody was happy. All the youngsters enjoyed their stay here and are now hosting Kittitian counterparts in their homes. The campers went off by French warship, a transport/landing craft combined, with space for 150 soldiers, 50 tanks and 30 lorries, but because it is a landing craft, it rides only 6 ft. deep. I accompanied the boys and girls to Guadeloupe on it and came back the very next day by plane as I could not leave my poor little old crocks for a longer period.

I'm afraid my news about my mother and aunt is not good. Three weeks ago mother had a very severe heart attack and since then requires constant supervision, which she does not want to accept, she still wants to move about too much, gets very cross, it takes all the patience in the world, diplomacy and strategy to make her obey doctor's orders, and although I try my very best, I usually end up by losing my temper. My aunt's condition is not too bright either, her leg heals very slowly, the doctor and nurse have been to put on new dressings and bandages. The number of pills, tablets, capsules, syrups and mixtures looks like a chemist's shop. When mother had the heart attack we had to have the doctor in morning, noon and night - literally, for I went to fetch him in the middle of the night. He has his telephone disconnected as his own wife is very ill, so the only way to get him is to go to his home, in the country. I cannot tell you what anguish I went through - and now that the acute danger is over, I have time to think and again thank you constantly for your generosity, the cost of all treatments, medicines and attention is such that I could never have managed. Thanks to you I do not have to worry at all. I wonder whether you realize how much you have done for us and the peace that you have given me."

"How right you are when you say that people no longer seem to have the will to do things well. When I went to Nevis, as I was going to be away for two days I decided to have my car patched up as the fenders are full of holes due to rust and rot, and wanted it to get a coat of anti-rust paint. Remember I asked you if you knew of a specially good one? My mechanic who is wonderful with engines and motors does not do body repairs, so I had to take the car to another garage. Well, when I returned the patches were finished but he said there was not enough time to paint the car underneath, he would do it later. I drove off and was soon aware of a very strong smell of petrol. I could not go back then, nor the next day, and the smell was getting stronger. I crept under the car but could find no leaks and phoned my mechanic that I'd bring the car to him in the afternoon, I had to be at the Junior High School that morning. When I arrived there, I needed some books that I usually keep on the back seat. I opened the rear door - and almost fainted away. The floor was full of petrol, there was a deep pool and some books were actually floating in it. Can you imagine what would have happened if somebody had thrown a match into it by accident! I phoned my mechanic to come right away as I was afraid to drive the car. He discovered that when they were putting on the patches on the back they had pulled out the hose of the petrol tank and had not replaced it properly, so the petrol simply leaked into the back part of the car, and as I hardly ever have any passengers in the back seat I hadn't noticed it. And when I went to the office to inform them of what had happened, the man in charge just shrugged his shoulders and said, well, nothing happened, did it?

We have had two scares of hurricanes, *Eloise* which was very wicked, and *Gladys*, which was supposed to hit the island but turned away just a few hours before doing so. We consider ourselves very lucky, we only had some heavy rains and high winds. The waves at Conaree were covered with foam but the ocean looked magnificent. I am trying to convince my friend Jane Ying to buy the property next to my *Vientomarsol* at Conaree. It is a beautiful plot of land, 73 ft. of ocean frontage and 240 ft. in length, and has a house on it. The house is not in a very good state but can be easily repaired. I consider the price extremely reasonable, they are asking W.I.$18,000 that is somewhere between U.S.$8,500 and $9,000. I hope she acquires it, it would be very pleasant to have such a neighbour and she would make a good investment as cottages along Conaree beach are rented out to Tourists at U.S.$100 a week in season and $60 in the off-season. There is enough land to build at least two more houses on the plot, if she wanted to do so."

"I must apologize for not answering sooner - I am not feeling very bright and have not been able to do my letters at night as is my custom because of very bad headaches. They usually start during the night, at the base of the skull and then spread along the neck to the shoulders and are so severe that I cannot sleep and end up by taking a few 'pain-killer' tablets, which usually carry me through the morning but leave me extremely tired. I think this is due to nervous stress. Mother has not been very well and that of course is a constant worry. Also, we have a great deal of trouble in the school situation. After waiting for a new French teacher from Canada ever since September, one finally arrived on Nov. 4th but yesterday, Nov. 7th She announced that she does not like the island - she was stationed in Nevis - cannot stand the children and has decided to go back to Canada immediately. She was in charge of the 'O' level French in Nevis and this means that those children have had no lessons for the term and are doomed to failure in June. There is no chance of getting another French teacher from abroad so late in the year, so I shall probably have to bring Cynthia Weeks from the Gingerlands High School into Charlestown and give her this class. It is a great responsibility for so young a girl, but I'm afraid that is the only solution. I shall go over to Nevis on Tuesday, that is if Mother is well enough for me to leave, and will work for a day or two with Cynthia to explain exactly what it is she has to do.

What strange weather we are having this year! You say there was yet another typhoon in Hong Kong, and we have had such torrential rains that cars have been washed away into the sea, roads blocked with mounds of sand and debris and floods all over the island. Even my bedroom was inundated, the roof started to leak and the floor was covered with water in no time, I can just imagine what would have happened had a hurricane hit us. Fortunately, the rains have stopped and I've asked the contractor to send somebody to fix the roof as quickly as possible.

The repairs at the beach house are almost finished, the carpenters are working in the kitchen and putting in shelves, the painters are coming next and my contractor has promised to have everything ready for Dec. 1st. The cottage promises to be very attractive, I already have a prospective tenant for three weeks in January, a young couple from London, friends of the Permanent Secretary in the Ministry of Education.

Our Premier has dissolved the House of Assembly and has made it known that General Elections are to be help on Dec. 1st. This is a 'surprise' move, although we could all guess it was coming: roads are being repaired, gifts of free food issued to workers and pensioners, many promises of all kinds made. I do not foresee much change in the present composition of the Government."

"It's most kind of you to tell me of the Sinutab tablets, I'll ask our local chemist if he has them. As the headaches usually start during the nights, so much the better if they make me drowsy, at least I'll get a sound sleep and by morning drowsiness will be over and I can drive safely. I'm ready to take any medicine to get relief.

The repairs of the cottage - I'm calling it *Coral Reef* - are finished. The burglar bars, or as mother calls them, Spanish grills, have been put in today, only the painting is left and then I can bring in all the furniture which is ready and waiting. I hope to pay off the debt, or at least the greater part of it, in June, when the interest on your shares comes in, as for the contractor, he is willing to take some gold coins that I've picked up years ago, when in Chile, in payment for the repairs. Unfortunately, in St. Kitts the banks do not know how to deal with gold coins, they will probably have to be sent to England, which seems so complicated, the coins are not collector's items as they are not old, the contractor is getting them by weight, but as I say, the banks here don't even know what an ounce of gold should cost. I had no idea it was so difficult to get rid of gold! Not that I have great quantities of it, but it should be sufficient to pay for the repairs."

"Thank you for your beautiful Christmas card, it is lovely and brings back so many happy memories of Hong Kong, I'm framing it and hanging it up on a wall in my bedroom to cheer me up, when needed. How strange to have below zero temperature in Hong Kong and icicles everywhere. It must have been a fairy-like decoration, but of course, as you say, it has probably done a great deal of damage to the plants, they are not used to frost in that part of the world. Talking of plants - I actually managed to produce a real pumpkin on my land, or rather, sand at Conaree. How it escaped the sea blast and the crabs is a miracle, the vine climbed up on the fence, that's why the crabs didn't get it, and as it hid in a thorn-bush and a tangle of its own leaves, the sea-blast didn't affect it and the thieving little boys didn't spot it. We cooked it and it made very good eating.

The cottage was hardly finished inside when some Canadians here on a week's visit asked to rent it. Therefore I now have my first tenants, just for a week, true, but I hope they bring me luck and that I can start paying my debts with the rent. The painter is still working on the outside of the house, but they don't mind it and are delighted with the place. They promised to advertise it for me when they get home and plan to come back to it next year. I'm enclosing a little leaflet advertising it. This year it was too late to include an advertisement in the Tourist Brochure on St. Kitts, so I had these leaflets printed and they promised at the tourist bureau to clip those leaflets to the existing booklets for this season. Do wish me luck."

I do not know what a Topping Out Ceremony may be, I am sure it must have been very impressive and I wish you every success with the new Manila Peninsula Hotel."

1976

"I am glad to hear that the Canadians whom you had at *Coral Reef* enjoyed their stay and wish you the very best in succeeding to rent it to the Americans and to other people. Your investment seems to have been well worthwhile. The repairs to this building have undoubtedly prevented an eyesore and will make your home more valuable. I hope the planting of your garden will be a great success.

I think you are right in not giving up your French and Spanish lessons. If you were to stop them it is the same as retirement and unless one is kept busy, one cannot be happy.

I enclose a Demand Draft for US$2,000 - to be used as you think best for our 'god-children'.

We have had a disastrous fire at the farm, the biggest hill fire ever known in Hong Kong. The whole of the mountain, (Tai Mo Shan) went up in flames and with it a part of the farm. Luckily, we had just completed our fire breaks at the farm the day before the incident, and this helped us to a certain extent. With every good wish to you and the 'old ladies'."

"It's with a heavy breast that I'm sending you this note. My sorrow is so deep and sharp that I cannot write much. My aunt has passed away quite suddenly. She died on Tuesday early morning, we buried her yesterday. She had a cerebral thrombosis and although I had the doctor within half an hour when it happened on Monday there was nothing he could do. She lingered for twelve hours but although conscious almost to the end, fortunately and mercifully there was no pain.

I cannot write more, please excuse me as there is now my poor little old mother who needs all my attention. It has been such a shock, I'm afraid I cannot think coherently, I know you'll forgive me."

"I am indeed sorry to hear of the passing of your aunt and on behalf of all the members of the Kadoorie family, I hasten to send you and your mother our deepest sympathy and condolences."

Mrs. Katzen tending the graves of her mother and aunt.

"Thank you so much for your kind letter of comfort. Death is so final and irrevocable; I suppose time will blunt this feeling of loss. I am extremely worried about my poor mother, her physical condition is already not good, and with this added deep emotional loss her frailness is increasing. I fear the future. She misses her companion and is so often alone. Our Easter break is starting in two days, and then I'll be able to stay with her constantly.

Forgive me for not writing more. Thanks again for your note, you cannot imagine how much I need sympathy and kindness at present to cope with all that I have to do. Your letter brought both."

"It seems that misfortunes never come singly and here am I in bed with an injured hip. At first the doctors thought that the bone had been broken completely, but fortunately the X-rays show that it is only cracked. Still the pain is very great and worst of all I have to stay in bed, no bandage or plaster cast is possible. I had to remain in hospital for almost two days until all the X-rays were taken, developed and discussed by the doctors. You can imagine in what state my poor mother was. I had asked one of our teachers to move into our home and look after mother. She did it right away and most willingly but - as I have written to you before - only one member of the family can look after her. Now that I'm back she's a little better but the situation is very difficult, although all my friends have rallied and come to my assistance - they do the shopping, feed the chickens, dogs and cats and run all the errands. The servant comes for half a day and today, with the doctor's permission, I tried moving a little on crutches, but it is most arduous and progress is so slow! It was such a stupid accident too. I had taken Desirée to the vet and when she came out I said to her, 'We are going home'. On hearing 'home' she streaked off at about 100 miles an hour and as I had her leash rolled around my arm she pulled and knocked me off my feet and dragged me out to the street until I managed to unwind the leash; but by that time I had struck my side against a stone ledge by the gate. She weighs 90 lbs, she's an Alsatian, while I weigh 100 and her strength is extraordinary."

"This is just a short note to welcome you home. I hope you have had a good and restful holiday in Europe. Which country did you visit this time? There is so much to do and see, so much to be appreciated in that old continent that you must have had a pleasant vacation. Still, on the other hand, there is so much unrest, and especially so much air-piracy that I am always happy when you are safely back in Hong Kong.

St. Kitts is still muddling along, inflation is rampant, unemployment growing, essential commodities disappear and whatever can be bought costs about three times as much as it did two years ago. However, compared to other islands, we have more peace, less crime and violence and it is still possible to work here. Of course, without your generous help, we would not have been able to survive, thanks to you, we can live quite comfortably, we pray for you and thank you mentally every day. I have just paid off half of my debt on the Conaree property, and if all goes well, should be able to pay all during the next tourist season. I have just had a honey-mooning couple spending a week at *Coral Reef* and another family is planning to occupy the place next week. This being the off-season, the rates are cheaper, but everything is welcome since I'm using this rent money to pay my contractor who is very patient and is kindly waiting and accepting whatever whenever I can give him.

My little beloved Mother is well for her age and state, she is weak and frail, but still full of plans, although I have to bring them to life now, and although I'm very willing to do so, it's the time I lack. Still, I have been doing some gardening for her: she sits there and gives orders, and I carry them out: making up the beds, plant the seedlings, water them, add fertilizer, etc., and surprisingly all the plants seem to thrive in spite of the onslaught by caterpillars, ants and grasshoppers, not to mention my ministrations.

School work has been very difficult. For the last three weeks I have been composing, typing and cutting the stencils for the promotion exams in French and Spanish for every form in the seven high schools of St. Kitts and Nevis. My eyes are on the point of giving out, but I have almost finished the task."

"It's so good to know that you are safely back home - although it seems that no sooner do you come back than you set out again! Of course Manila, to you, is just a stone's throw away from Hong Kong, still, even a short air journey nowadays may present its hazards. Our prayers will accompany you, mine I'm afraid are not much good, but Mother's always get good response. I'm very happy that your trip to Europe was so pleasant and that you have enjoyed it, in spite of the heat and the drought. Something seems to be very wrong with the climate at present. This is supposed to be our rainy season, but apart from a brief shower last week we have had no rain for more than a month. Everything is parched and covered with dust.

We are supposed to be on holiday, but there is more school work than ever. Our education policy is beginning to bear its fruits and standards have dropped appallingly - as I warned the minister that they would - that it is becoming obvious to him that less and less is being learnt and that fewer and fewer students will ever reach the G.C.E. level. We have now been told to produce a new syllabus to suit this programme, which is to start in September, and since the first examination according to this new curriculum is to be held in June 1977 or even May, we are all working very hard to have everything ready when school opens. This is terribly hard on my eyes. We have no eye specialist on the island, and the doctor who visits St. Kitts from time to time and who is supposed to be an occulist is in fact a simple optician who brings along his wares and tries to get people to buy new spectacles from him.

Mother has been keeping more or less well, nothing serious but a host of nagging little aches and pains that make her rather miserable. I'm doing my best to cheer her but unfortunately I cannot devote my whole day to care for her. Before, my Aunt used to keep her company, talk and read to her, now she is all alone when I'm out. Her sight is quite dim and her hearing is impaired, therefore she cannot read, write, sew or listen to the radio. I understand her plight and try to do all I can. It is rather difficult at present for I am exceedingly tired and was looking forward to a few days of rest, but as I have already mentioned, we are all back at work and cannot relax. Fortunately, thanks to you, I have no financial worries. With the interest of your generous investment I have been able to pay off three quarters of my debt for *Coral Reef* and I'm hoping that the last quarter will be paid off during the tourist season. After that I can make things easier. I have kept back a good portion of the interest to supplement my salary.

You can imagine what our situation would have been without your assistance, my monthly take home pay of £93 is just sufficient to pay Mother's doctor and medicines, water, gas, telephones and electricity bills and the part time servant who comes in the mornings as I cannot leave Mother all alone in the house. All the rest comes from you. Lord bless you for your kindness."

"I hope you have already gone and come back from Manila before this dreadful earthquake and tidal wave struck the island of Mindanao yesterday. So many perished, it must have been horrible. One of the reasons why I left Chile was this constant fear of earthquakes, you can never know when one will strike, and when it does happen, nobody knows how it will end. I trust you will not have to visit Philippines again soon. We have very little news of the earthquake in China that seems to have been a great disaster too.

Two islands away, there is also a natural calamity, the volcano in Guadeloupe has exploded and 70,000 persons have been evacuated from the vicinity of the volcano. They have all been taken to the opposite side of the island, which so far has not been affected, but conditions there are terrible. Fortunately, when the volcano first showed signs of unusual activity in July, I cancelled my student exchange programme, thirty-eight of our French students were to go to Guadeloupe for 17 days and after that they were to return accompanied by as many youngsters from Guadeloupe for a similar stay here. How much worry would have been caused! I am extremely happy that those trips did not take place, the responsibility would have been nerve-racking. It seems that the whole of the volcano may be blown up in the next eruption - that is what the team of observers has said.

The situation in Guadeloupe may affect Michelle Ward and Cynthia Weeks. If you remember, they were to go to that island in September for a year's study on scholarship granted by the French Government. However, in this present state of affairs I am not at all sure whether it is advisable for them to go if by September things do not return to normal. Thank you for suggesting helping them, I have a large sum of money in the fund, and if needed, will give them some from you, but do not send anymore as there is a good reserve at present, almost E.C. $4,000.

We have already started work at the Teacher Training College, the induction course for new teachers. I think I did not explain things clearly enough: the fruits of the new education policy are not good at all. Since the Minister has decreed that every 12-year old child is to be admitted to High School, regardless of his mental ability or academic achievement, the classes are full of children some of whom cannot read, write or even make themselves understood. In these circumstances it is almost impossible to teach. All teachers who could do so, have therefore left the island, and we are left with a host of inexperienced and unwilling people who have turned to teaching because they could not find other jobs. The induction course is to train - in TWO weeks - a group of youngsters, just fresh from the 5th and 6th forms to become teachers in September when the new school year begins. How can they teach after just ten days of abstract lectures? Of course standards are bound to fall."

"It is good to know that you are not contemplating another long trip in the near future - there seems to be a plane hijacked every other day. However, with the weather being what it is, and your getting 33-34 inches of rain in two days, it seems to be unsafe even to stay put. Did the farmers suffer much? The fields must have been flooded, and what about the livestock? I do hope the weather will settle now and will remain clement for some time to come. We have had several extremely heavy showers following in the wakes of hurricanes *Emmy* and *Frances*, but no ill effects. Except a losing battle with the weeds. They are waist-high again. It was only last week when I was admiring my efforts and the garden looked so neat. Now it's a jungle.

Schools are opening on Monday. We have been working for several weeks already but it seems that all we have done will have to be scrapped as the Minister of Education has had another set of bright ideas and is going to change the education policy of the State. As far as I can see he wants a 'social' system, based on what Guyana and Cuba are doing. I'm afraid it's going to worsen everything still further. There is just talk, talk and talk, no action taken at all. For instance, we are supposed to begin teaching French according to the audio-visual method. The French Government very generously has made me a present of the whole unit: books, tapes and film-strips. That was due in June. I asked the Minister whether we could start an experimental class. He agreed. Then I told him that we would need a tape-recorder and a projector. He said he'd order them at once. Well, it's September, school starts next week and those instruments have not been bought, nor have they been ordered. That, in spite of reminders and letters from me. This is a typical attitude of the

Ministry - all enthusiasm during the talking stage, but as soon as it is time to do something, then everything is dropped and forgotten. Without a tape-recorder and a projector the method cannot be used and the Minister knows that. Thanks to your great generosity I'm hoping that this is the last year that I'm going to work. I hope to pay off all my debts and loans and contractor's work, so that after June 1977 I plan to devote all my time to my mother. I would have done so this year, but I have to train my successor, or rather successors, for there is nobody available to supervise the two languages, French and Spanish. I shall therefore have to train two persons, one for each language.

I have managed to acquire, through my niece in Boston who teaches at Harvard University, several cassettes of short stories in Russian and Mother enjoys listening to them. I am so happy to have obtained them, as now, from Monday, she will have to spend a great deal of time alone, and those cassettes will prove most useful. Her eye-sight is very dim, although in spite of that, when she is feeling cheerful, she still plays the piano. Unfortunately this happens more and more seldom.

I'm afraid Cynthia and Michelle will not be able to go to Guadeloupe this year because of the unsettled state of the volcano. Both are very sorry that they cannot take up this scholarship. They will continue teaching and I hope that next year the scholarship will still be theirs."

"Many thanks for telling me about chlordane, I hope the chemist here has some for the ants have become a real problem, they destroy everything, seeds, young plants, roots and fruits. There is so much talk about agriculture in the West Indies and the need to grow more vegetables but our agricultural department sadly lacks trained staff, their only answer to everything is 'sprinkle some sulphate of ammonia and give it a chance!' I do hope I'm able to get some chlordane.

The Cogans have returned to St. Kitts, they are still full of enthusiasm about the lovely time you have given them last year when they were in Hong Kong. Thank you so very much, it was so kind and thoughtful of you. They are very sorry that they were unable to see you during their stay. I do not know how long Mr. Cogan will work here now, the Government is nationalizing the sugar industry and is taking over the sugary factory - in which case I do not imagine many foreigners will be kept on, the transfer is to be effected quite soon it seems.

There are many changes in St. Kitts and I'm afraid that things are not getting any better. Inflation is still increasing, there is a scarcity of essential supplies and what can be had is so terribly expensive that working people just can't make ends meet. If it were not for you and your wonderful generosity, Mother and I would never have been able to survive. You cannot imagine how grateful I am to you, without your help my poor little Mother would lack everything. One of the consequences of this dreadful rise in the cost of living is a marked increase in crime, houses are being broken into not only at night but in broad daylight. Every single member of Staff in the Teacher Training College has had a burglary so far. I'm the only exception, I put this down to the reputation enjoyed by my dogs. They give such a show of ferocity - barking, snarling, growling and hurling themselves at the gate whenever anybody comes near, that the whole neighborhood is scared of them - and yet, I know them to be such cowards that if anybody just raises a stick they'll turn tail and slink away!

Drugs have also made their appearance, and again, because of unemployment among young people, the situation is becoming most serious. Some time ago the Government was preaching that sugar meant slavery, and this idea has become so firmly implanted in young people's heads that they all believe working with their hands, in the fields, tilling the land, is degrading and reminiscent of 'massa' and oppressed slaves. Now, in spite of cajoling and trying to convince young people that the only salvation lies in working the earth, they will not listen, they do not realize that farming and agriculture in general is their only chance of survival.

Last week we actually started our audio-visual class in French. After waiting for a whole month for Public Works to put in the necessary electric wiring, I gave up and to-gether with my young teachers we started doing things ourselves. We managed the wires, plugs, etc., and obtained a projector on loan until the new one arrives. None of us had ever operated one and there were no instructions and the people who lent it to us didn't know how to use it either. However, by trial and error we managed to get it going - without blowing one fuse - and synchronized the film-strip with the tape on my ancient tape-recorder and the course is in full swing. Enjoyed by all, pupils and young teachers alike.

On the whole, with this course going on well, I'm quite happy, my only worry, and a very distressing one, is my Mother's health. I'm most concerned about her as she is very weak. On top of it all she has now contracted bronchitis and this means more discomfort. I try my best to cheer her, but my heart is heavy."

"Thank you for your letter of 25th October. I am indeed sorry to hear that your mother had bronchitis and do sincerely hope she is now perfectly recovered. I know how difficult it is to look after elderly people and wish you every success.

You mentioned inflation is increasing. I am afraid it is the same everywhere and the crime rate has gone up all over the world. Hong Kong, being a port, is now prone to drug trafficking and we suffer from the same marked increase in crime of all sorts. Fortunately, people here are hard workers and farming comes natural to them. However, many have gone to Europe where they have taken jobs with the result that agriculture is becoming less frequent as the people are turning to fish farming which requires less labour than vegetable farming.

Bravo on having your audio-visual class going. You have certainly become a good electrician.

I leave for Manila tomorrow and will be returning to Hong Kong via Singapore on a Concorde. It will be my first experience on this plane which is extremely fast. I hear that it has rather narrow seats and passages and is not as comfortable as other planes. However, I shall judge for myself."

1977

"All sorting and posting of mails in St. Kitts stopped on Dec. 24th and has started again just yesterday. Since Christmas was on a Saturday, Boxing day was a holiday on Monday instead of Sunday, and the rest of the week was taken up by Carnival Festivities. Why Carnival should be held at Christmas time, I have no idea, but the whole island goes mad with street dancing, starting at 6 a.m. which is called 'pyjama jamming', when crowds prance in the wake of several steel bands and going on through the whole week with costume parades, calypso king competitions, queen shows and pantomimes and plays in the streets and squares. All traffic stops and Government and business places close. Even the bakeries are shut. Yesterday, after a whole week's revelry employees, still bleary-eyed and sleepy, people have begun to turn out to work. This year's festivities were marred by a great fire when 'Carnival City' was burned to the ground. It seems that one of the candidates for the Calypso King crown was dissatisfied with the judges' decision, so at 3 a.m. they set fire to the whole building, the stage was burned up, but the greatest loss were the instruments of two large bands - estimated at $50,000. The electrical installations, stage, decorations and furniture were lost to the value of $100,000. The whole thing is so daft, after all, who suffered? Not the judges - if their decision was really unjust - but people who had nothing to do with their choice.

We have just had some news for Michelle Ward. She is to go to the island of St. Lucia where there is a Venezuelan Consulate to sit the scholarship examination on Jan 12th. If she succeeds - of which I have no doubt - she will get a four-month scholarship at the University of Caracas, after which, she may get a further bursary if they consider her worth it. Our Government is paying her passage to and from St. Lucia, but will not give her any money for other expenses, she has to spend two nights there, so I hope you will not mind my giving her some funds to stay at some respectable guest house or hotel. If she gets the scholarship then she will go to Venezuela in March, at that time the Venezuelan Government takes over all her expenses, travelling, tuition, board and lodging and even gives her some spending money for everyday personal needs. I do hope she is successful, it means so much to her, with no family to speak of to help, advise and encourage her.

Thank you for your advice about tomatoes and eggplant. I am planning to plant cabbages and lettuce in their place once the 'crops' are in! So far there are only flowers, no fruit as yet. We have too many lizards and I believe they bite the flowers off. I have a couple of kittens that chase and catch the lizards but I'm afraid they don't do much good to the plants when they jump on them.

Mother's health, thank the Lord, is as good as can be expected. If only she would admit that she is not as young as she was and not try to do too much, everything would be perfect. As it is, she starts on all sorts of projects and then has to give up and that frustrates her and affects her very much emotionally, which in turn brings anxiety and heart trouble. However, since I spend more time with her - alas, until the end of this week only - she does not feel so lonely and is happier."

"I am very happy that you approve my helping Michelle Ward. She really deserves to be helped and I hope she gets the scholarship to Venezuela, even though it is only for four months. But then, if she responds well, which I'm sure she will, she may get another one from the Venezuelan Government for a longer period. You see, the University of the West Indies charges such fantastic prices that private individuals of lower and middle class standing cannot hope to enter. The St. Kitts Government gives several scholarships a year to the University, but these bursaries are usually allocated to friends and relatives of government employees, and when politics play such a great part in those awards, a poor girl with no 'high' connections has absolutely no hope to receive one of those grants. The

Venezuelan scholarship as well as several French ones that we have received through the French Consul General are awarded only to those who really are capable of making good use of them, that is, on merit alone. Even when one of my students gets a 'foreign' scholarship, he or she still has to sign a bond and is obliged to work for a certain number of years for the St. Kitts Government.

I have also paid the Cambridge 'O' level examination fee for a student in the Cayon High School; those Cambridge fees have gone up very much, and this child, Philip Lake, an orphan, dependent on an older brother, could not scrape up enough funds to enter. As he is one of the very few brilliant students we now have, you very kindly paid the $95 he needed. I am enclosing a thank you note from him.

What a sight your 80 tons of oranges on the trees must be! I can imagine the hum of the bees around the orange blossoms. On the tiniest scale compared to large gardens, I find my efforts are yielding good results. The tomatoes especially, some of the plants have more than a dozen large tomatoes and still blooming and promising more. I'm very proud of them. The rest of the vegetables are doing well, too. Also, as my rose bushes are getting very old I have tried to produce new plants from cuttings and to my amazement - never having tried such experiments in my life before - I actually have six of them taking."

"I am planning to go to Europe towards the end of May and am coming back in July, possibly via the United States. A friend, Captain Torrible[24], will be travelling with me.

It is a long time since I visited Bermuda and I have never visited the West Indies. If we were to come for a short while, are there any reasonably comfortable hotels that you could recommend on these islands? We would each require a room and a bath attached. Of course, this is very tentative and may never take place, but I would

---

[24] Graham Robert Torrible, OBE was born in 1904 and joined The China Navigation Company as a deck officer in 1925. He served on the China Coast and Yangtze River during the 1920s and 1930s and was interned at Bangkok during the Second World War.

like to know more about your part of the world. I leave for Nepal this weekend."

"What a wonderful piece of news! I'm keeping my fingers crossed and hoping and praying that you will not change your mind, that nothing untoward happens and that you will really come to this part of the world even if it is for the briefest of visits. I cannot tell you how happy this idea of yours makes me, as for my mother, she is delighted and is already talking of your visit.

Which of the West Indian islands are you interested in? Each one has its own charm, all are beautiful and every one of them is worth seeing. There are quite comfortable hotels in almost all of them, I'm enclosing a brochure of the accommodations in St. Kitts, Nevis and Anguilla - St. Kitts is colourful and picturesque with every possible shade and hue of green in its mountains, fields and woods, Anguilla has the most wonderful beaches and Nevis has the best hotels. St. Kitts is famous for the fortress of Brimstone Hill, which is really worth seeing, Nevis boasts Lord Nelson's souvenirs and makes much of its being the birthplace of Alexander Hamilton, while Anguilla is supposed to have the most friendly and polite inhabitants - although beaches apart, there is nothing much to see there. Antigua is flat and dry, but its beaches are of dazzling white sands, but not as lush and dark green as Grenada and St. Lucia, which also have gold and silver sand beaches. Dominica is wild, mountainous and rugged, St. Vincent peaceful and quiet, Montserrat has a hot-water lake and picturesque, winding roads. Jamaica, Trinidad and Barbados have many beautiful spots but are more sophisticated. Whichever islands you visit, I'm sure you will enjoy. Just tell me beforehand and as I have been to almost all those islands, I shall be delighted to make all the necessary reservations. However, please put St. Kitts as your first stop in the Caribbean.

I am enclosing two brochures, one of Antigua, the other St. Kitts-Nevis-Anguilla. The one in St. Kitts that is comfortable and where you are well looked after is The Ocean Terrace Inn. As soon as you decide what other islands you want to visit I shall send you their hotel lists. Please come."

"I have just found out that the Antigua Carnival starts on July 22nd and ends on August 2nd. During this period the inhabitants go quite mad and there are so many visitors that all hotels are full and the planes - although there are many extra ones and charters - have no room, unless one books well in advance. Even if you are not interested in the carnival itself, we shall still have to book in advance as all planes pass through Antigua - unless you come from the States, then you get to St. Kitts by Prinair via San Juan and out of St. Kitts either by Prinair or Winair to St. Martin where you can get an Air France jet to Guadeloupe, thus by-passing Antigua altogether. In any case, whenever you have a more or less definite idea of your dates, please let me know and I shall start working on the reservations.

At present, your prospective visit to St. Kitts is the only bright spot on my horizon, I hope and pray that you will not change your mind and thus shatter my day dreams. You see, I am going through a most distressing time - my poor little beloved Mother is very ill. When I wrote to you last she was already unwell, then she had a stroke and even the doctor thought it was the end. However, with her amazing vitality she rallied, is slowly improving and I thank the good Lord for his mercy in letting her stay with me a while longer. Her mind remained lucid all the time, her speech is gradually returning and although sometimes thick and slurred it is quite understandable. She is beginning to move her left arm but cannot use it yet as her fingers will not obey. Her left leg, unfortunately is quite useless. I'm getting the loan of a wheel chair to see if she can use it. The first week was dreadful, but now we are all adapting to a new mode of life and I have everything under control again. What I really need is to get a member of the family down as Mother will not accept a nurse and it is rather difficult for me to look after her night and day. My sister is in Chile and cannot come, but I'm trying to get a distant cousin, (about twenty times removed) she lives in New York and I hope she agrees to come.

Do not be afraid that the atmosphere here will be sad and gloomy. We are all keeping cheerful and bright so your visit here will be pleasant and happy. We are looking forward to it."

"First of all, may I say how sorry I am to hear that your mother is not any better, and sincerely hope that she will improve in time. I think you did wisely in getting a member of your family to stay and look after her. Provided she has the right temperament it is the best thing you could have done under the circumstances.

Regarding my trip, we are not quite certain of our bookings until the agent confirms them. On Monday 13th June, we intend to fly from Miami, via San Juan to St. Kitts and plan to remain in St. Kitts on 14th and 15th June, leaving on the 16th of June for Fort-de-France and from there on to Paris on the same day if it is at all possible. I shall let you know as soon as I am able to obtain something definite. Meanwhile we have suggested to our agent to book two rooms with bath for us at the Ocean Terrace Inn. Therefore there will be no need for you to worry about this on your end.

Carnival day at Antigua should not affect us in any way. Please excuse this very short note as I am in a rush to catch the post."

"I had no idea that you were planning to go to Paris through Fort-deFrance, and I am therefore very happy that I sent you a brochure of Martinique and Guadeloupe a few days ago. You must have received it by now, and if you cannot go on to France on the same day, June 16th, as you arrive in Martinique, at least you will know something about the place and can plan your activities there.

As you will be arriving in St. Kitts in June instead of July, schools will be in session and you'll be able to see for yourself how some of your godchildren are getting on. However, you have very few here now as almost all of them are growing up and are either at universities or have left the island for better jobs. Michelle Ward will still be in Venezuela and Cynthia Weeks in Barbados, I'm sorry about that for I was very keen on your meeting them. The others get casual, temporary help. It is certainly no trouble but great pleasure to have booked rooms and tickets for you, but since your travel agent is doing that, I shall not insist, however, I'm going to call at the Ocean Terrace Inn to specify good rooms with a view - they are now building an annex, and although very comfortable, the rooms will not face the sea. It's a pity you can spare just two days, if you had some time extra you could visit Nevis which has many beautiful parts to see. We get rain in June, but I hope the weather-man will be kind and not send us downpours on 14th and 15th June.

I am happy to report good progress in Mother's condition. Unfortunately I have been unable to get that distant relative of hers to come, and since there was no one else I have been 'on duty', 24 hours a day sometimes getting just two or three hours sleep per night. After a month and a half of this lack of sleep I find myself so weary and worn out that I have very little energy left and seem to walk about like a somnambulist, falling asleep on my feet at most unlikely times. May is the hardest month for me as I have all the Cambridge examinations in French and Spanish to administer not only in St. Kitts but in Nevis and Montserrat as well. The doctor says that Mother is now out of all danger and in excellent condition and can be left if I get a suitable person to assist her. A 'suitable' person is the snag, for although I can get a nurse here and somebody to sleep in, Mother cannot understand them, and not being able to communicate frustrates her and makes her nervous and despondent. However, my niece in Boston has promised to send a Russian-speaking lady for the month of May. Thanks to your generosity I have been able to pay all the doctor's and nurse's bills and will be able to afford paying the girl my niece is sending down. I wonder whether you realize the magnitude of your help to us? A whole life-time should be spent thanking you and praying for your health, happiness and general welfare - and the only thing I am doing is just saying a trite 'thank you'. Will I ever have a chance to do something for you?

I'm counting the days till June 13th. Please don't change your mind!"

"Thank you for the new dates of your proposed arrival in St. Kitts. No matter when you arrive, my mother and I will be delighted to welcome you. I am now working overtime on the understanding that when you are with us I can have the entire two days absolutely free to take you around and spend all the time with you - that is if you'll wish me to accompany you.

It is most kind of you to allow Michelle Ward to have the U.S.$100. I received a letter from her some time ago saying that the course she is attending is most interesting and that she is making good progress - but there has been an unexpected delay in paying the scholarship-holders their allowances, so that having spent the little they had with them, they were in a difficult position not having enough to pay even for their food. However, owing to the St. Kitts foreign currency regulations, I could send her only U.S.$92.02. As the mail between St. Kitts and the rest of the world moves at a snail's pace, I was obliged to send the money by cable, I hope you do not mind as Michelle's situation was desperate, not having any friends in Caracas.

My mother is getting her energy again and is making good progress trying to move about with her metal walking aid; we had a worrying setback last week when she had a heart spasm, but it was over very quickly and the doctor says she is none the worse for it. I am happy about that as the G.C.E. Cambridge exams are starting to-morrow and I must have peace of mind to do my examiner's job properly, something very difficult to do if I have to worry about my beloved little old lady all the time. So I'm keeping my fingers crossed and hoping she will continue to be as well as she is now."

Seven months later, on January 30, 1978 Madame Katzen's mother passed away at the age of 94, a painful blow coming two years after she lost her aunt. Her little old ladies were a great part of her life and now they were both gone. She had done everything in her power to take care of them, shepherding them to safety across the globe from Siberia to China to Chile to St. Kitts. All along the way constantly ministering to their needs, calming their fears, nursing them back to health from their many illnesses. To ensure their safety and wellbeing, she had indeed made a great deal of personal and professional sacrifice. Although it was extremely painful to have lost the two most important people in her life, she was comforted by the thought that she had done right by them. Uprooted from the cradle of their heritage and traditions, as best she could she helped them to live 'normal' lives in the midst of alien cultures halfway around the globe. They were now resting in peace side by side less than a mile away from her home in Springfield cemetery.

Like her mother and aunt, Madame would spend the rest of her life in St. Kitts. She never did receive a pension from the government. But thanks to the largess of Horace Kadoorie there was no longer need to worry about life after retirement. In her remaining years, she continued working as the official foreign language interpreter for the government, feeding feral dogs and cats and running her guest cottage at Conaree.

Her *Coral Reef* guests, who by and large hailed from North America and Europe, enjoyed the rustic charm of her Conaree beach no-frills cottage on a stretch of undeveloped, weather-beaten ocean property on the Windward side of the island. Secluded and off the beaten path, they enjoyed the briny mist and the music of the roaring surf crashing against the reef. *Vientomarsol,* her cottage on this windy sun-bleached stretch of sand, became a place of solace for Madam Katzen. She would come here often to walk her dogs and commune with the wind, the sea and the sun.

Over the course of time she would befriend Bob and Ken, a Boston couple who frequented *Coral Reef.* Annual visitors to her cottage, she took them into her confidence, regaling them with stories of a time when she lived a life of relative luxury in a home with servants and lots of silver and gold artifacts. When she was no longer able to drive her little green car because of her failing sight, they could be seen driving her around town on her errands to the vet, the bank, the post office, the supermarket, taking her and her dogs to Conaree beach at 6:30 am for their daily walks, wherever she needed to go. They marveled at the number of people who knew her. On the street she would be greeted with respect and reverence, mostly in French and or Spanish, by a great many people from all social status; the prime minister, cabinet members of the government, bank tellers, lawyers, teachers, doctors, beggars on the street corner, one with no teeth and one leg. It seems that everyone in Basseterre knew Madame Katzen.

Bob and Ken both fell madly in love with her. Each consecutive year since their first stay at the cottage, they would spend longer and longer stretches of time at *Coral Reef* voluntarily investing a great deal of time and money helping her to do needed repairs in order to keep the cottage in good condition. They would become part of her extended 'family'. Subsequently, Madame refused to accept payment for their use of the cottage. The last time they departed the island, the day they said their last goodbyes (they were certain that they would never see each other again) Madame was now almost ninety years old, frail and bent face down almost ninety degrees to the ground. She endowed them with some of her most treasured items - a Russian samovar (one of the few artifacts the family was able to take with them when they fled Russia), a beautiful ornately engraved Chinese mahjong set and a Chinese wicker vase that Horace Kadoorie gave to her filled with orchids just before she fled Shanghai in 1939. Very much an observer of Chinese traditions, at their farewell she combed her hair with a Chinese wooden comb and presented it to them for good luck.

Now in her late eighties, losing her sight, unable to drive, living alone at *Chalet La Serena* with her cats and dogs, Madame Katzen was surrounded by a whole community of extended 'family' members. Apart from her immediate neighbors who checked in on her daily, there was also a host of former students who made frequent visits to chat with her and to make certain that she was ok.

In 2001 a group of her former students and the late former Governor Sir Probyn Innis surprised her, showing up at *Chalet La Serena* on her 90th birthday with a bouquet of flowers. It was a wonderful surprise that touched her dearly, a fun evening filled with French and Spanish songs, old standards sung at her home in the 1960s and 70s during language club.

A few months later Madame fell and injured her hip.

After a brief period at The Grange Health Care Facility, one of her former students, Ronnie Powell, accompanied her from St. Kitts to Puerto Rico where he turned her over to her son Fyodor. Mother and son then flew to Miami for the connecting flight back to Chile. The medical treatment she could get in Chile far surpassed what she could receive in St.
Kitts.

Eighty-nine years old, traveling from St. Kitts to Puerto Rico to Miami to Santiago was no picnic, a journey that took her the better part of eighteen hours. With a broken hip, Madame predictably was at her irascible best. Fyodor did all he could to mitigate her pain during the long journey.
After the inflight dinner Madame asked a flight attendant for a glass of Cinzano.

"Sorry Ma'am, we do not have Cinzano but we do have Baileys," replied the attendant. Madam turned to Fyodor and asked.

"What's Baileys?" to which Fyodor replied,

"It's Irish whiskey with milk."

"No, I don't like it," responded Madame dismissively. Despite her protestations Fyodor ordered one anyway. Curious, Madame asked for a taste.

"Ooooh, it's very good," said Madame. Two more glasses went down the hatch in quick succession and before you can say Jack Robinson, she was fast asleep. She slept the rest of the way to Comodoro Arturo Merino Benítez International Airport in Santiago.

Dr. Alfonso Diaz Fernandez, one of her first students who attended her school in La Serena from 1947-1950, performed hip surgery.

Anxious to get back home, Madame was back in St. Kitts in less than two months after surgery. Her dogs were beside themselves with glee to see her, leaping, barking and wagging themselves silly with unabashed happiness. Her cats, determined not to indulge in such silly exhibitions of affection for a mistress who 'abandoned' them for such a long time, greeted her with a few perfunctory meows and quietly left the room.

Madame's many friends and neighbors and countless former students would rally around her, making a point to check in on her regularly, helping her with tasks she could no longer do. In spite of such overwhelming support however, one morning in May 2002 a neighbor checked in to see her and found her dead, collapsed on the kitchen floor, seemingly in the act of feeding her dogs who were lying protectively next to her.

◊◊

Afterword

I started this project eager to learn more about this extraordinary teacher who landed on the tiny British Caribbean island of St. Kitts and proceeded to singlehandedly transform the lives of a generation of youngsters. My desire to learn more about this *femme extraordinaire* led me on a fantastic journey the world over to discover, among other things, that she had already impacted the lives of countless others in China and Chile before arriving in St. Kitts in 1961.

My journey of discovery enabled me to get a fairly good picture of this great woman, this animal lover with an indomitable spirit and an unequalled talent for teaching modern languages.

Deciphering the puzzle of Madame Katzen, understanding the essence of this complicated woman for the ages - the whys and wherefores of her improbable journey from Siberia to St. Kitts, was quite thrilling. Without question, her fifty years of dedication to the education of children in China, Chile and the Caribbean has secured her a permanent place in the Pantheon of great teachers.

As I tell stories about this extraordinary teacher, a question frequently posed to me is, "What ever happened to her husband?" It seems that he was really only part of her life for roughly five years - from 1934 to 1939. After he accompanied Madame Katzen and his three sons to the Americas, he simply disappeared. No family member I spoke to could account for his whereabouts after 1939. According to immigration documents, he returned to Shanghai after the war and subsequently migrated to Australia in 1951 where he remarried and had another family. He died in 1992 and is buried in a cemetery in Queensland Australia.

Though they appear to be few, Madame is not without her detractors. There are those who feel that she was somewhat of an elitist, in the sense that if she had her druthers she would have taught only the brightest students. There are even those who suggest that

Madame preferred to teach boys. Some go even further, intimating that she simply hated girls. My conclusion, having interviewed many of her former female students, is that Madame Katzen did not hate girls. This perception of Madame arose around the time when the Girls High School merged with the all-boys Grammar School. Before the merger, she taught exclusively in the all-boys Grammar School.

One of her first female students from this era shared the following story.

At the end of my first class with Mrs. Katzen (a small class consisting only of eight girls), Madame marched me down to the headmaster's office and requested a transfer for me to another class because, according to her, I did not belong in her Spanish class. I think she was concerned that, unlike the other girls in the class who had been taught by her before, this was my first time with her and she was unsure whether or not I would be able to measure up to her standards. The headmaster told her that he was sorry, but he could not, or would not comply with her request. Madame would have to keep me for the rest of the year. It was a year in which I was persona non-grata in Madame's class. However, despite the fact that she did not grade any work I submitted, I was determined to show her that I was capable. At the end of the year I received a distinction in Spanish on the G.C.E. exam. No, I don't think Mrs. Katzen hated girls. I think she was primarily concerned with maintaining a reputation of having a high percentage of success on the G.C.E exams.

As one of '*Mrs. Katzen's boys*', a moniker given to a great many of her former students in St. Kitts, we have an untold number of anecdotes about our experiences with Madame. To this day it is still a thrill to run into old schoolmates and reminisce about the good times we had studying languages with her. Through it all, one thing was always abundantly clear. Her commitment to making certain that her students achieved academic success was as unwavering as her concern for our individual wellbeing was genuine.

I will forever remember an incident from a memorable trip to Martinique aboard the French minesweeper *Arcturus* in 1967. Lodged at the navy barracks at Fort Saint Louis, the activity for the day was a sailing cruise to an uninhabited island off the South-East coast of Martinique. It was a beautiful day for sailing with a scattering of cirrus clouds above and a breeze steady and stiff enough to get us to the island. We were sixteen youngsters and three French sailors on an open sailboat with a large mainsail and no outboard motor. After a pleasant and uneventful sail, we dropped anchor seventy feet off the shore of our destination, *Îlet de Toiroux*, and enjoyed a lunch consisting of baguettes, cheese and fruit.

There was also red wine, which was consumed mostly by the sailors.

In the late afternoon, we weighed anchor and headed back to Fort Saint Louis. Progress was slow as the sailors, tipsy from consuming too much wine, tried their best to catch the wind which was now dying as the sun sank slowly behind the horizon in magical hues of gold, red and orange. As the sky darkened, we drifted further and further away from the direction of the homeport. It wasn't long before it became evident that we were in danger of being lost at sea. With an uncooperative wind, no outboard motor and no marine radio aboard, our only chance was the hope that Madame and our hosts, the navy officials at Fort Saint Louis, would send out a search party to rescue us, having realized that it was past the time of our scheduled return.

A search party was indeed sent out to rescue us. When we returned to port Madame was standing on the dock waiting to greet us. With moist eyes, she hugged every single one of us as we stepped from the boat. Visibly shaken, she must have died a thousand deaths at the prospect of a disastrous end to our sea adventure. Always the consummate professional, never a touchy-feely person, it was the first and only time I ever saw a publicly display of affection from Madame.

Despite the thrill of the hunt, spending as much time as I did researching the life of Madame Katzen did not come without a price. Knowing very little about her, it was indeed exciting to learn about the life of this amazing teacher who impacted the lives of so many of us. Nobody ever forgets a good teacher and we (the long list of boys ostensibly referred to as *Mrs. Katzen's Boys*) consider ourselves fortunate and privileged for having been beneficiaries of her tutelage.

After completing my research, however, I was suddenly afflicted with a kind of malaise, a kind of melancholy if you will, the source of which took me quite a while to identify. I would eventually attribute it to the fact that the excitement of traveling to three continents (South America, Europe, Asia) researching Madame's epic journey had ended. Indeed, I was having so much fun I did not want the research to end. As it turned out, there was an even greater reason for my sadness.

Thanks to my research I had gotten to know this larger-than-life teacher quite well. In fact, too well. In my eagerness to know this teacher nonpareil, much to my chagrin I managed somehow to completely demystify this teacher extraordinaire, this paradigm of foreign language instruction. Now that my one-dimensional schoolboy image of her was quite fully developed, I could see that she was more than just a great teacher. I could see that she was also a humanitarian and animal-lover who had her fair share of idiosyncrasies, frailties and insecurities. For a while my psyche struggled with the idea that Madame was just an ordinary woman, perhaps because I did not want her to be ordinary. After these last few years spent posthumously reading her thoughts, listening to her voice, now, when I think of her I see an ordinary woman who lived an extraordinary life. An extraordinary life doing extraordinary things in spite of, or perhaps because of, her life of relative hardship, a life of displacement caused by revolutions, wars and earthquakes. My pedagogic idol, someone I tried to emulate, she was not supposed to have feet of clay like the rest of us.

The good news? With the passage of time, having now attained a much more nuanced view of the essence of this great lady, she has ascended to an even higher pedestal in the Pantheon of great teachers than I would have thought possible.

◊◊

ABOUT THE AUTHOR

Born on the Caribbean island of Nevis, Ira Simmonds received a BA in French from St. Francis College, Brooklyn, New York, and M.A. and M.Ed. degrees from Teachers College, Columbia University, NYC. After a ten-year stint as House Manager at Alice Tully Hall, Lincoln Center for the Performing Arts, he spent the next twenty-five years in New York City Public Schools as a teacher, Assistant Principal and Acting Principal. He currently works as an educational consultant.